NADINE

SABRENA MONTORA ROBINSON

Quill Pen

Publishing, LLC

Quill Pen Publishing LLC
5075 Morganton Road, Suite 10C-1565
Fayetteville, NC 28314

www.quillpenpublishingllc.com

Printed in the United States of America

Acknowledgements

Writing this book has been an emotional yet healing experience. There were many who supported me through this process and deserve to be acknowledged and thanked.

To those who kept me grounded, encouraged me to keep writing, supported my concepts and kept me inspired:

To my mother Patricia, who through her love and support, and encouragement gave me the confidence to write this book.

To my brother Owen who became my writer's confidante and allowed me to bounce my ideas off him. Who hand painted the artwork of my book cover.

To my sister, Carlin for her support in helping to ignite *Nadine* by sharing stories of our cousin's journey in an abusive relationship. And thanks to the surviving children for their support as well.

To my sons, Coy and Darrett, many hugs and kisses for the support and encouragement you have shown me over the seasons. It is nice to get a little back.

To both my aunt Veronica, my cousin Nicholas, and my uncle Darrett who have always been my biggest fans – inspiring my work and cheering me on even when I felt like this process was too much. My uncle fell asleep in death before the publishing of this book. But I know he would be proud of me.

I must thank my editor, Barbara Lawing, and my publisher, Debra Funderburk. I love these two ladies. They have kept me grounded and taught me a lot.

A big thanks to Vanessa S for her keen interest and ideas, and for allowing me to write late at night in her home.

Much love and gratitude to all my family and friends for their support.

Dedication

This book is dedicated to my beautiful cousin, Veronica Elizabeth Graves Williams, who was brutally taking away from us by the hands of her abusive husband.

We (her family and children) miss her sweet smile, her tender spirit, and her unique humor. She will always dwell in our hearts.

December 13, 1979 – November 20, 2008

See you in paradise.

This story is also dedicated to the many victims and survivors of domestic violence.

Domestic violence is pervasive in every community regardless of age, socio-economic status, sexual orientation, gender, race, religion, or nationality. Victims of domestic violence face a number of personal and societal obstacles when attempting to leave their abuser or reach out for help. Some may even face death.

Nadine's story is inspired by real events. A story that many women may relate to. It is a story that needs to be told.

The National Domestic Violence Hotline 1-800-799-7233 (SAFE)

Contents

ONE

The Beginning

At Fort Campbell, the Non-Commissioned Officers Club was the happening spot during the sixties. One evening, Nadine and her sister Claudette met Claudette's friend there. The flashing lights, loud music, and fog at the foot of the dance floor peaked their excitement.

"Do I look alright?" Maggie shouted. She tucked a loose strand of hair from her ponytail underneath the rubber band that held it all together.

Nadine patted her own shoulder-length curly dark hair and said, "You look fine. I'm the nervous one. This is my first time here."

"We come here all the time," Claudette said. "You'll be fine, Sis. Most of these dudes are harmless. They just want a good time. And the women here are all show and no go." Claudette and Maggie laughed.

Nadine scrunched her brow. "What does that mean?"

"It means they have nothing going on but their looks. They're just looking to snag a soldier. You know, someone they think will take care of them and show them the world," said Claudette.

Through the crowd of people, they managed to find their way to a table and sat down to order drinks. Laughter and chatter mixed with the music and filled the club. Glancing around, Claudette noticed a tall dark-skinned man staring in their direction. He was leaning against the bar with a drink in his hand. She noted his clean-shaven face and short texturized haircut, his button-down brown shirt with a long collar, and matching geometric pants.

He took one last sip of his drink, put the glass down, and strolled towards them. Claudette smiled. "Don't look now."

Nadine looked up as the man approached the table and was instantly smitten by his deep mahogany eyes. His smile was more than she could take.

"Ladies." His voice was like satin.

She turned her eyes toward Claudette to avoid looking at him.

He was obviously a lady's man—a man who could woo any girl he wanted. At the moment, his sights were set on Nadine. This was understandable. She was beautiful. Nadine had big amber eyes graced with thick long lashes, and her 5'4" frame was small and slender yet sturdily built, with curves in all the right places.

His eyes fell upon her smooth warm autumn skin as she nervously crossed her legs. "My name is Charles. May I join you, ladies?"

"Sure," Claudette said.

Charles pulled a chair over from another table and placed it right beside Nadine. She looked at him and smiled, then looked away and pushed her soft ebony curls behind her ears.

He said, "So, where're the men?"

"You tell me," Claudette answered.

"I see plenty in here. And I see three beautiful women sitting over here alone."

Claudette giggled. "We're not alone. You're here."

He chuckled and glanced at Nadine. "So I am."

He bought their second round of drinks and they sat together for a while—talking, laughing, swaying to the music. A few people stopped by the table to speak to Claudette or Charles. Nadine sensed he seemed interested in her—but did not understand why. She thought Claudette was much prettier than her. Claudette was more free-spirited and adventurous, and she wore the latest styles.

Eventually he asked Nadine to dance, and for the rest of the evening they were inseparable.

When it was time to leave, he walked the trio to their car. Nadine stood in front of him, looking up at his handsome face. He took her hands in his and said softly, "I could take you home."

Before Nadine could answer Claudette said, "No, we came together—we leave together. Dig?"

"Yeah, I dig." He and Nadine kept their eyes locked on each other. "What about tomorrow? Can I take you out to dinner?"

Nadine turned and looked at Claudette for reassurance. Claudette shrugged her shoulders.

Nadine said, "That will be fine."

From then on, they couldn't see enough of each other. Charles was very protective, sometimes overly protective, defying any other man who wanted a chance with Nadine. He was swift to strike out with words, even swifter with his fists. His charm was excessive, not just towards Nadine, but Claudette too. He bombarded them with gifts.

Claudette cautioned Nadine that Charles was getting too serious too soon. She felt he was beginning to control Nadine, even down to how she dressed, but Nadine did not see it that way. She took Charles's behavior as his way of expressing love.

They had dated for six months when they found out they were going to be parents.

Nadine was scared about breaking the news to her parents. From the start her father, Sam, had been against her dating Charles. He had too often seen soldiers pursue young girls and move on, leaving them pregnant and alone. He did not want that to happen to his daughter, nor did he want her to drop out of college.

But Charles had been Nadine's first lover, and she was addicted to him. She first told her sister about the baby.

Claudette exploded. "That's what birth control and condoms are for, Nadine! You enjoy your womanhood—but you don't get knocked up!"

The sisters were four years apart. Claudette's personality was opposite to Nadine – independent and free with an outspoken tongue, while Nadine was more of a homemaker – strong, but timid.

They came from a family of old-fashioned values in southwest Kentucky and had grown up surrounded by beautiful farmland and rolling hills, with several lakes for fishing and winding trails for horseback riding. Their mother, Martha, instilled in her girls strong domestic skills, including gardening, cooking, and keeping house. In those days, these skills were important since most black women made their living cooking and cleaning for white folks.

Though Nadine and Claudette were opposites in personality and interests, they were close. Maybe their differences made them that way.

Despite her disappointment, Claudette stood by Nadine while the news was told to their parents. Sam remained silent, refusing to look at Nadine.

Nadine lowered herself to her knees beside his chair. "Will you look at me, Daddy?"

"No," he muttered. His lips tightened and he got up and left the room.

Martha sighed. "Well, I knew something was wrong with you. Nadine, I knew if you kept running around with that man this was gonna happen. This is just the kindda thing your daddy was afraid of. So now what you gonna do? What about school?!"

Nadine cried out, "We're gonna get married!" She added, "And I'll finish school, Mama. I will—I promise."

Martha set her hands on her hips. "Nadine don't bother to make promises you know you can't keep. You're going to be a mother and a wife. Where you gonna have time for school?"

Claudette stepped forward. "You love him, Nadine? Cause being pregnant ain't no reason to get married."

"More than anything! And he loves me too."

Later in the week, Charles was invited to dinner with Nadine, Claudette, and their parents. He wasn't sure of the reception he would receive but decided to take flowers for Martha and a bottle of the most prestigious red wine made in France in the early sixties.

Nadine watched for him from the living room window.

When he pulled up in front of the house he sat in the car. He closed his eyes and took in a deep breath – slowly releasing it. Normally, he was not a nervous man, but Nadine was pregnant, and he had to face her parents.

Nadine opened the door and called out to him. "Well, ain't you comin' in?"

He got out of the car and walked up to the door with one hand in his pocket—not knowing what to do with them. As soon as the greetings were over, they sat down to eat.

Sam frowned as he passed around the mashed potatoes. "Young man, that's my baby girl. And I don't mind saying you don't have my blessing to marry my daughter." No one rushed to say anything.

Sam peered over his glasses, his gaze still on Charles. "But Nadine says she loves you, and the baby is gonna need both of you—so you do right by my daughter *and* my grandchild—you hear?"

"Yes sir, I intend too. I'm gonna take real good care of them both."

Martha put a smile on her face. "Well now. If you've said your peace, Sam, how 'bout you saying grace so God can bless this food and we can eat?"

When it was Nadine's turn to meet Charles's parents, she was just as nervous. They lived in Clarksville where they owned a small bakery, selling everyday pastries and filling orders for special occasions. They made good money and could afford to live in a nice neighborhood where a lot of well-to-do blacks lived. Phyllis, who was actually Charles's stepmother, was one of those uppity black women who thought owning a business and being well known in Clarksville made her better than most. She was known to carry her head high and snub other blacks who did not seem as privileged.

She had an hourglass figure underneath her A-line dresses and took pride in her dyed and neatly styled hair and perfectly polished nails. She religiously wore wrist-length lace gloves, so the polished nails showed through.

As Charles related the news about the baby, Phyllis looked Nadine up and down. She then said to her son, "And you want to get married?"

Charles nodded. "Yes, ma'am."

"Well, I'm sure I speak for your father when I say we'll pay for a small wedding." She rolled her eyes in Nadine's direction and said, "I know your people can't afford one."

Nadine sat twiddling her fingers in her lap, as she often did when she was nervous, and managed to say, "They do alright."

"Oomph! Anyway, I'm not so sure this pregnancy wasn't intentional," Phyllis proclaimed, looking from Charles to Nadine.

Nadine smiled and put her hand on her belly. "No, ma'am. Although this baby was conceived in love."

"Uh, huh. Well, be that as it may, Charles is not ready for a family. You'll see I'm right about it."

Charles kept his head down and uttered not a word.

Phyllis planned an outdoor wedding in their backyard which included the best food, wine, and decorations. As Nadine stepped out toward Charles in a sleeveless satin tea-length dress graced with tulle lace and embellished with beads and sequins, no one cared about the decorations or the food. All eyes were on her.

Charles stood proudly tall in a single-breasted suit with a light blue satin hanky peeping from the single breast pocket, and a small white carnation pinned to his lapel. It was an unsullied celebration. Nadine wished to bottle it in frozen time, so nothing beyond this day could spoil what she and Charles were feeling.

A few weeks later, time forced their honeymoon to an end.

Charles was to be sent to Vietnam. He said he felt it best for Nadine to stay with her parents, because the duties of motherhood plus going to school would be too difficult for her.

During his military service they kept in touch as often as possible, sending letters and pictures. After the baby came, Nadine decided on part-time classes so she could take a job at the church's daycare center and save some money.

She wanted to surprise Charles with a place of their own. She made curtains and matching bed attire for their room and bright flowery curtains for Carolyn's room. Over the crib she suspended a bright yellow dream catcher to sway in the air and catch her child's dreams.

Nadine was intent on teaching her child about her Native American and African American roots. At night, as she rocked Carolyn to sleep, she told about the close-knit community where she had grown up and shared the stories her grandmother had told.

"Ye ho waah created the earth with amazing animals and people like the Cherokee who took care of the land and made it grow. The land grew and grew with trees as tall as the sky and mountains as powerful as Ye ho waah himself. And oh, how the rivers and streams flowed wild and free. All had its place in the world, just like you and me."

She followed a story with a tender kiss to Carolyn's forehead.

Nadine's father, Sam, was the child of a little Cherokee Indian woman. It was she who passed on to her granddaughters the skills of her native ancestors. The granddaughters called her Agilisi, *my grandmother* in the Cherokee language.

Native Americans, blacks, and whites lived in the Kentucky community, as did some of the servicemen stationed at Fort Campbell. The opportunity to meet traveling people from different places with diverse backgrounds made the town interesting.

Four months passed without a word from Charles. Nadine began to worry. Finally, a letter arrived from Vietnam, but it was not from Charles. It was from the military officials stating that some soldiers would be coming home injured. Charles was one of them.

A couple of weeks later, he was returned to the base. He took a taxi to Nadine's parents' house—hoping to surprise her. The taxi passed by crowds of people in hippie garb with signs in their hands protesting the war. It wasn't much of a welcome for returning soldiers.

Her father drove Charles to his home. He got out of the car and let his glance run over the house and smiled slightly as he limped towards the porch. His smile grew bigger at the sight of Nadine excitedly flinging open the front door and running to him with open arms. She almost knocked him down. He embraced her tightly as he struggled to keep his balance.

"Welcome home, Charles," she whispered. "Did I hurt you?"

"No, I just got this bad leg now—thanks to the damn war!"

"Well, come on in and tell me all about it. Carolyn's waiting. I'll fix you something to eat."

Sam smiled with satisfaction and tipped his hat before getting back in the car. Charles nodded his gratitude. Nadine waved. "Thank you, Daddy!"

As soon as they entered the house, Nadine introduced Charles to his child. Finally, they were a family.

Nadine busied herself around the kitchen in a poor boy sweater and hipster jeans as Charles watched her from the kitchen table where he held Carolyn on his lap. He realized how he had missed Nadine's contagious smile, and the way she had of sweeping her hair behind her ear.

For a while, they couldn't keep their hands off each other. They did not go out much – not just because they were making up for lost time, but also because protesters still roamed certain areas of town, speaking out against the war. They yelled rude things to the returning soldiers—things like *baby killer and murderer.*

Claudette was finally able to reach Nadine on the phone. "You need to come up for air, little sister," Claudette said. They laughed.

"Hey, I love my man and I'm glad he's home. I've welcomed him over and over again."

"I bet you have, you little tramp." Again, they laughed. "Poor Carolyn must feel like a third wheel. I'm coming over to get my niece for the weekend."

"Carolyn's fine, girl. You know how it is out there. It's crazy. A man puts his life on the line for the sake of his country and this is how they treat him."

"Well, you know me. I'm with the crowd."

Charles had served his time. Jobs were hard to find for returning soldiers.

Nadine watched him day after day attempting to drown his experiences of the war and his treatment by some in the community with a bottle of Vodka. The more he drank, the more distant and short-tempered he became.

One night he sat in the living room watching TV while Nadine washed the dinner dishes. He yelled, "Nadine! Nadine!"

She appeared in the living room wiping her hands on a dishtowel. "Yes, Charles. Where's the fire?"

"Gimme another drink."

"Haven't you had enough?"

"I say when I've had enough." His eyes were locked to the TV as he stretched out his arm with the glass in his hand for her to take. "Why don't you just do what I tell you?" She took the glass.

Later that night, Charles woke up in a cold sweat from recurring nightmares of the war, afraid to return to sleep.

Nadine sat up. "Do you want to talk about it?"

"You wouldn't understand."

He threw the blanket back and got up. After putting on some clothes, he took money from her purse.

"What are you doing?"

"I'll be back," he mumbled. He left the house, making his usual trip to the bar. He would come home drunk and wake her up repeating the same war stories, yet when sober he never told the stories.

One day Nadine met Claudette for lunch to talk about Charles's behavior. She started with a sigh then said, "Charles has changed."

"How so?"

She shrugged her shoulders. "He's cold. He's here in body, yet he's still far away. We're like strangers now, just existing together. Even when we make love, I don't feel loved anymore. I'm just someone there—for him to get off on. Then he rolls over and falls to sleep. He wakes up later from crazy nightmares he won't talk about. He's been leaving me in the middle of the night, taking money from my purse and coming back drunk and crazy."

"Taking money from your purse? Hide your purse, Nadine."

"Oh, it wouldn't do any good. He would just…" She paused, looking away wearily.

"Just what? Does he hit you?"

"No—just so angry all the time. He scares me."

"Well, Nadine, what kind of life is that? You know you don't have to live that way."

Nadine sipped her coffee. "What do you mean? I can't leave him. He needs me. The war changed him, Claudette. I can't just leave. He really does need me!"

"It doesn't seem like it. And if you're scared of him, you don't need him. What you're describing will only get worse—and if he's not beating on you now, he will."

"No, Charles loves me. He tells me so all the time. It'll get better. You'll see. He's just going through some things."

"And taking you with him."

"It's hard for a man nowadays. No job to support his family. You know how proud black men are. But I'm working as much as I can at the daycare. But it's not always enough. He doesn't even want me to work."

"So, how long do you think you can continue to support your household and his drinking habit?"

Nadine reached for her fork and stabbed at her food. She said not a word.

"Nadine, you're my little sister. I love you—and I just don't want to see you hurt or suffering in any way."

Charles got a job at Mr. Miller's garage, but every day after work he stopped at the ABC store or a bar. It was not long after he took the job Nadine hit him with the news of a second pregnancy.

"I can't even get my first paycheck before you come around talking about having another baby!"

"Well, it's not as if I got pregnant on my own," she smirked.

Charles snatched a glass from the kitchen table and threw it against the wall. Her smirky smile vanished.

"You better do something about getting pregnant, Nadine! I'm not gonna be spending all my money on a house full of babies! And I don't want you working! I mean it! Now clean this mess up!" He stormed out the door, letting it slam behind him.

She quit her job at the daycare and some months later gave birth to William. Carolyn, now three years old, called him Brother.

Now that she wasn't working, Charles expected Nadine to keep an immaculate house, keep herself and the children immaculate too, and have supper on the table when he arrived home.

At some future point, the director of the daycare where Nadine had been employed called and asked for Nadine's help. It was from that point on Nadine's life with Charles went from a mere battle to plain-out war.

The daycare director begged for her help. "Please, Nadine, just this once."

"I'll have to ask Charles and get back with you."

When Charles was sitting in front of the TV in the living room drinking a beer, she came and stood quietly just behind him. He felt her presence and took a gulp of his beer.

"What is it, Nadine?"

"Um, well, the daycare could use some help and I was wondering…"

"No!" He continued to stare at the TV.

She didn't easily give up. "But, Charles, we could use the extra money and I'd be home before supper. It'll only be a week and the children can come with me." She walked around where she could see his face.

"Nadine, your place is here!" He clenched his jaws so tight she could hear his teeth clash. He slammed the beer can down on the end table, stood up and stepped close to her, pointing his finger in her face. He growled, "I don't want to hear any more about you working."

"But what harm…" His hand across her face ceased her words.

"Don't you ever talk back to me, woman! I said no!"

Her eyes grew large in disbelief as she clutched her cheek. She cried, "Are you crazy?" She even raised her hand to return the aggression, but he grabbed her wrist and shoved her slender frame to the floor.

Carolyn, sitting on the couch, held her breath for a moment. She waited till her father left the room, then climbed down from the couch to sit on the floor beside Nadine.

"Mama, are you okay? Mama, are you crying? Don't cry."

The child placed her head on Nadine's lap. Nadine smiled through the tears dripping off her chin as she stroked her little girl's hair. She said softly, "I'm fine, Carolyn. Mommy's okay. I'm okay."

Carolyn looked up with an innocent gaze. "Why did he hit you?"

"He was just mad, that's all. He didn't mean nothing by it." Nadine wiped her cheek, pressing her lips together. Some seconds passed before she said, "I'm fine."

After that first time, hitting Nadine apparently became easier for Charles. And therefore, more frequent. Any attempt to defend herself only made him angrier. She was no match for him.

TWO

An Ugly Turn

Charles leaned over the bathroom sink to look at his reflection in the mirror as he trimmed his whiskered face. He had not shaved in over a week.

Nadine rolled over in bed, opening her eyes to the empty pillow beside her. She could hear water running in the bathroom. She went in and wrapped her arms around his waist and rested her head against his back.

"Happy anniversary," she said. She smiled at him in the mirror. "I'm going to fix you a nice big breakfast."

"Don't bother. I have to go out."

"You're going out? Today is our fourth anniversary. I thought we would spend the day together. I can even get my parents or Claudette to watch the children."

Charles rinsed off the razor and put it on the shelf over the sink. He turned around. "I have a couple of errands to run. I'll be back."

He moved past her into the bedroom and began getting dressed. Nadine walked down the hall to the kitchen. While preparing breakfast for herself and the kids, she heard the front door open and close. At the sound of the car engine, she wiped her hands on her apron and went into the living room to look out. As Charles drove away, she sighed.

Hours later, Charles returned to find Nadine sitting in the living room with a shoebox full of letters. Her eyes were filled with tears as she held one of the letters in her hands.

He stood in the doorway with a giftwrapped box in his hand. "What are you doing?

The blink of her eyes set free her tears. She wiped at them with her sleeve. "I – I was just—" She paused – her eyes focused on the box in his hand.

She smiled. "You remembered. Is that for me?" She put the letter in her hand on the couch and stood up.

"I asked you what you were doing? And where are my kids?"

She stopped smiling. "The kids are down for a nap. I was sitting here reading the letters you sent to me when you were in Vietnam. We were in love. You said some sweet things to me then." He closed the door behind him and ordered, "Throw them away."

She frowned. "Why?"

"Because they came from a bad place."

"They came from your heart—didn't they?"

"They came from the war—and anything from the war, I hate!" He crossed to the couch and placed the box on his lap. "Sit down."

Nadine obeyed. He handed her the box. She smiled. "Thank you. May I open it?"

Charles rolled his eyes and sighed. "Of course."

She opened the box to find a pair of dangling crystal and faux pearl earrings. She gasped. Her face lit up like the sun. "They're beautiful. Oh, Charles, they're so beautiful!"

Though he had a satisfied look, he did not actually smile—never did.

Nadine reached over and kissed him on the cheek. She held the earrings up to her ears, never taking her eyes off Charles. She waited to see his reaction.

"Yeah, they're nice."

She hopped up and ran to the bedroom, saying as she went, "I have something for you too!" She returned with a slender gift box. "Open it."

He frowned. "Where'd you get this?" It was an Elgin wristwatch with a brown leather band.

"Don't you like it?'

"You have no job. How could you afford this?"

Nadine's eyes fell away from him. Her brows knitted together in thought. "I don't understand—it's a gift, Charles! An anniversary gift. Do you not like it?"

"I asked you where you got the money from to buy it. You don't work."

His words were firm. The air suddenly thickened. Nadine sat on the couch beside him. She cleared her throat, seeking the courage to look at him. She said, "I borrowed the money from Claudette."

To thin the air, she took his hand and smiled gently. "Please, put it on."

He did. Yet Nadine did not understand why he was more concerned about how she bought the gift rather than being pleased. It was their anniversary, though, and she was determined to make him happy. She quickly put on her new earrings.

"I'm going to fix us a nice dinner. I have steaks thawing."

"We're going out to eat."

"Really?" Her smile widened. She threw her arms around his neck and pressed her lips against his. "I knew today was going to be a good day," she whispered, kissing him again.

Claudette agreed to babysit. Charles and Nadine had reservations at the Mason House. Rarely did they dress up to go out. Nadine put on her best dress and wore her hair in an up-do style to proudly show off her new earrings.

The hostess greeted them. "Welcome to the Mason House."

They were escorted to their reserved table. The waiter soon approached the table and introduced himself and wrote down their drink orders. "I'll get those drinks right away and give you a few moments to decide on your entrees."

Nadine smiled, looking around. "This sure is a nice place, Charles." She opened the menu. "Mmm, the menu looks good too. I bet you'll want the ribeye. That sounds good, huh?"

"I'm thinking about it," Charles replied with his face behind the menu.

"You didn't say anything about my dress."

He looked over the menu. "You look nice, baby. Real fine."

The waiter returned. "Still deciding?"

"I'm actually thinking about the bone-in pork chops," Nadine replied.

"Oh, those are delicious, ma'am." He leaned over Nadine's shoulder to point out the choices of sides. Charles lowered his menu and watched for a moment. Nadine glanced up at the waiter, brushing her hair away from her face. She noticed the glare in Charles's eyes as he watched them with clenched jaws. He closed the menu and slammed it on the table.

Nadine flinched. The waiter turned his gaze toward Charles. She said, "I'll have pilaf rice and mixed veggies with it."

The waiter stepped to Charles's side of the table and took his order. After he left the table, Nadine was aware of a thick air about them, the same thick air as earlier back at the house. Charles narrowed his eyes and stared hard at her. She glanced around at the crowd, trying to avoid eye contact with him.

His stare felt like the flame of a candle burning a hole into her thoughts. Her thoughts were of what he must be thinking, though she already knew.

He opened his mouth and confirmed her thoughts. He spoke through his teeth. "What was all that flirting about? I swear, I can't take you anywhere!"

Nadine continued to avoid eye contact. Then came the slam of his fist pounding the table.

She begged, "Please, let's not make a scene. People will start to stare."

"I don't give a damn about these people!"

"He was just helping me decide what to order."

"Well, maybe he can help you find a way home—huh?"

"Please, you're getting upset for nothing. It's our anniversary, baby. Can't we just enjoy it?"

"Yeah, you enjoy it, 'cause it'll be a long time before I take you anywhere else—I can tell you that."

Nadine sat silently, fiddling with the cloth napkin in her lap.

The waiter returned with the food and served Charles first. "Now, I hope you enjoy this. It's certainly one of my favorites." He winked at Nadine, placing the food in front of her.

"Say man, just serve the food and move on!"

"Charles," Nadine frowned, shaking her head.

"My apologies, sir. Can I get you anything else?"

Charles raised his brow. "No."

"Well then, please enjoy."

Nadine picked up her knife and fork and began cutting into her chops. The sound of the chatter in the restaurant and the clatter of flatware was loud, sufficiently loud for her to ignore Charles's continued murmuring about her flirting with the waiter. She was tired of being accused and forever having to defend herself against his imagined infidelity. She ate in silence.

Charles refused to leave a tip, but while he was in the bathroom Nadine managed to slip the hostess five dollars to give to the waiter.

They picked up the kids and headed home. Nadine put the children to bed while Charles sat in front of the television in the living room sipping his usual Vodka. He eventually came to the bedroom and stood in the doorway, watching Nadine as she sat on the bed gliding lotion across her skin. He walked to the bed and bent down over her. He whispered, "Mmm, you smell good, baby."

She wrinkled her nose at the stench of the alcohol on his breath. "You've been drinking."

"I've been celebrating." He sat on the bed beside her and touched her shoulder. She curved her shoulder away from him. "So, what? You don't want me to touch you now? Maybe you'd rather that punk waiter."

"You sound ridiculous. The waiter has nothing to do with anything."

He grabbed her arm. "I'm ridiculous? I saw you."

"You saw what you wanted to see. Now, please let go of me."

He let go and stood up. He unfastened his pants and got undressed. Nadine slipped her nightgown on and slid underneath the blanket. She let out a sigh of relief after Charles went into the bathroom. She lay in the bed, afraid to fall asleep. She could never sleep until he was, anticipating what would come next.

He came out of the bathroom, climbed into bed and cuddled up behind her. He began groping at her breast, kissing the back of her neck.

"You've been drinking, Charles," she mumbled. "It's not the same when you're drinking. Just go to sleep."

"I don't want to go to sleep! I want to make love to my wife! You hear me?"

She threw the blanket back to get up, but he pulled her towards him. "The whole neighborhood can hear you, Charles."

He climbed on top of her, his weight pressing her face into the pillow. She allowed him to have his way, for she had grown used to his drunken sex. He concerned himself with his needs, not hers.

Her needs suffered. Intimacy was no longer fulfilling and romantic for her. It was a necessary burden.

The next morning, she sat at the kitchen table staring out the window. She sipped on a cup of hot tea as she daydreamed into the rain outside. With a distant rumble of thunder in the background, she lost herself in thought. After a while she smiled slightly. When Charles was good to her, he gave her pleasant memories. Such as Christmas in the mountains.

One of his customers from the garage lent him his cabin in the Tennessee mountains. Charles drove up a day earlier to set up a tree and leave gifts. At four o'clock on Christmas Eve morning, he woke Nadine and the children.

"What are we doing?" Nadine asked.

"It's a surprise. Pack some things for you and the kids for a couple of days."

Nadine couldn't think of a time when Charles had awakened them before daybreak and him sober. Where were they going? She quickly gathered some things in a suitcase.

It was a peaceful drive to the cabin, listening to holiday music on the radio. Once Nadine saw where they were going, she became ecstatic and reached over to massage the back of Charles's neck as he drove.

They pulled up at the cabin. He smiled and said, "This is it! Let's unload."

"Oh, Charles, this is nice. So nice!"

The kids couldn't wait to trudge in the blanket of snow. Nadine joined them while Charles started a fire in the fireplace. With the fire crackling behind him, Charles watched his wife and children from the window. He soon stepped out on the porch.

"Come on, big daddy," Nadine called. She rolled a handful of snow into a ball and threw it his way, hitting him in the middle of his chest.

It was times like this when she could actually get away with smacking him with something without retaliation. Charles leaped off the porch and scooped up a wad of snow.

"So, that's how you wanna play?" He grinned. He aimed a large snowball at her. She turned to run but the snowball caught up with her before she could get out of the way. The force caused her to stumble and fall, giggling as she went down.

The kids laughed along with her. "Get up, Mommy!" Carolyn shouted.

"Oh, no," Nadine laughed, trying to get up.

The three of them pelted her with snowballs. She said playfully, "I'm gonna get you guys!"

The snow brought the kid out in both Charles and her. Eventually all four of them had lain on the soft ground – piled on each other and covered with snow. They laughed so hard their smiles were frozen from the icy air. Charles stood up and extended his hand to help them up. Nadine smiled at him. Her nose and cheeks were reddened from the cold.

"Let's get inside," he said. He picked the kids up and she followed behind. They stripped off their wet clothes in front of the fire, and Charles gathered some blankets while Nadine went into the kitchen to make hot cocoa.

That day had been perfect. As were the next three days. Charles managed to control his drinking and abusive behavior. It was times like these that gave her hope.

The family's fun at the cabin was short-lived. Charles was soon back to the drinking which made their home a living hell. Nadine finally broke down and confided in a friend at church. Jean encouraged her to leave Charles. Jean's husband had gone to jail for a few years after he pistol-whipped her on their front lawn.

"For better or for worst," Nadine answered quietly. "Those were our vows."

"Or till death do you part, Nadine." Jean set her hands on her hips. "Those were your vows too. The thing about that part is, men have been known to kill their wives. So goes the 'death do you part.' It's not worth it, girl—don't stay there long, Nadine. Get out now. I was one of the lucky ones."

But she could not leave him. She felt deep in – like she had been swallowed up by the marriage. All she knew how to do was try and make the best of it.

On Sundays after church, she and Charles often had dinner with his parents. A few times Nadine attempted to talk with Phyllis about Charles when he wasn't around. Phyllis was well aware of her son's heavy drinking and abusive behavior, but all she did was make excuses for him.

"Men are under a lot of stress nowadays, Nadine," Phyllis said. "You have to be a strong enough woman to hang in there and keep your family together. Never say what you can't take—because we can handle more than we think."

"But, um—well, some days—I'm afraid for my life."

"Oh, that's just plain foolishness. Charles may be a bully, but you shouldn't fear for your life. Besides, if you really feared for your life...well, you know the rest."

Yes, Nadine knew the rest. LEAVE.

She understood Phyllis was not encouraging her to leave—she wouldn't do that. No, Charles's mother would never support the idea of her taking the kids and forsaking Charles. Phyllis was just trying to say life couldn't be all bad.

Later in the day they gathered around a spread of food and joined hands while Joe said a prayer, then passed around the dishes hand to hand. Nadine scooped some peas onto Charles's plate.

"That's enough," he said.

"Oh, you usually have a little more."

"I said enough, didn't I?" He snapped. There was a moment of silence in the room as Nadine placed the bowl of peas on the table.

"Well, pass the peas to me," Phyllis snickered. "Matter of fact, I forgot the butter." She got up and went to the kitchen. When she returned, she did most of the talking, attempting to engage Charles and Nadine in conversation, but Nadine had been embarrassed and Charles had been drinking so neither of them were up for much conversation.

After dinner, Phyllis invited Nadine to her bedroom to look through some old clothes. The children sat in the living room watching TV with Charles and Joe.

"Oh, Nadine, I have the cutest dress," Phyllis giggled, pulling clothes out of a box from the closet. "Yes, here's the dress. Isn't it cute?" She held it up. "I can't wear half these clothes since I gained weight, but you probably can—you being so thin and all. You need to take better care of yourself. Eat a good meal once in awhile. Here, try this on."

"I eat," Nadine said as she took the dress and draped it over her arm.

"No, try it on now. I want to see how it fits."

"I'm sure it'll be fine."

"Nadine, try it on. Come on now."

Nadine hesitated for a moment with a worried frown on her face.

"Ok," Phyllis said. "Is it me? I mean, we're both female, but I'll just turn around if you want." She turned her back to Nadine, waiting for her to put the dress on. "Do you have it on yet?"

"Yeah, just needs to be zipped up."

Phyllis spun around. "Oh, let me." Her eyes soon grew big and her mouth widened at the sight of the many bluish hues and faint yellowish discolorations on Nadine's back. Phyllis moved slowly towards her and slid one side of the dress off her shoulder and gasped. She put a hand over her mouth.

"Dear God, Nadine! Dear God! What happened to you?"

Nadine quickly pulled the dress back up to cover her shoulder and spun around. Her face was warm and flushed. "Nothing! It's…it's nothing."

"That doesn't look like nothing. Now don't lie to me, child. What happened to you?"

Nadine stood in silence and looked away. Finally, she managed to mumble a name. "Charles."

"Charles what? Did this? My Charles did this to you?" Nadine's

eyes filled with tears. She nodded yes.

"Why? Why would he do this to you?" Phyllis demanded.

Nadine's forehead crinkled. "What do you mean?"

"I mean what did you do to make my son do something like this?"

Again, Nadine's voice was no more than a whisper. "Nothing, that's just it—nothing." She caught her breath and continued. "You know he has a temper. I told you before how he can be. I don't have to do anything wrong, but I can't seem to do anything right. I take care of him, the children and the house. I even quit working – 'cause he insisted I stay home!"

Phyllis shook her head. "I don't understand. Only a monster would do this, and Charles is no monster. Oh, Nadine, Nadine. I've been in Charles's life since he was ten. And I love him as if I gave birth to him myself. We're close, you know? I do know he has a temper at times. But my advice to you is to do whatever it takes to make him happy. It's what wives do. We keep our men happy."

"Well, I guess I don't know how. I don't know what he wants from me."

Phyllis's gaze was unblinking. "Then you need to figure it out."

"Will you talk to him? He listens to you," Nadine pleaded.

Nadine jumped at the knock on the door. Charles's voice. "Nadine, we're ready to go."

Phyllis opened the door. "So soon?"

"Yes, ma'am! Gotta work in the morning."

"Of course, you do. Well, we're finished here anyway. We were just trying on some old clothes of mine. I think Nadine is going to like this dress."

Nadine put a smile on her face. "Yes, it's nice. Thank you."

He said, "I'll be waiting outside."

Phyllis stepped out of the room just ahead of Charles. "Nadine, I'm going to fix you guys some food to take home. You might get hungry later."

Charles followed Phyllis into the kitchen to get the food. "Son, I want to talk to you before you leave. How are you and Nadine getting along?"

"We're fine, Mom. Why? What did she say?"

"It's not what she said, it's what I saw."

"Saw?" Charles raised his eyebrow.

"I saw the bruises, son."

"She showed you some bruises?"

"Well, she didn't mean for me to see them. So, what's going on? Huh?"

"Mom, I don't want to talk about it."

"Okay, now look. I understand couples have their troubles, misunderstandings, disagreements—whatever you want to call it these days. And I know things can get out of hand. But you've got to watch how you put your hands on that girl."

"She just does things to get on my nerves sometimes. She always has something to say back. You don't talk back to Dad. She doesn't have the same respect for me. I'm a man, Mom. Ain't a man supposed to have control in his own house?"

"Charles, your dad and I are different. You gotta find your own way with your marriage. Hitting her is not the way. I don't want no trouble."

"Yeah, and ain't gonna be none."

The ride home started quietly. Then Charles broke the silence. "So, what were you and my mom talking about?"

"Nothing really. We were just going through some old clothes."

Charles grabbed Nadine's hand and began squeezing it tight. She whimpered, closing her eyes with her lips pressed together as she tried to loosen his grip.

"If you think you can say anything or even show my mom anything that's gonna make her turn against me, you're dead wrong," he said with clenched teeth.

Once he let go, Nadine placed her hand between her legs as tears rolled down her cheeks. William had fallen asleep, but Carolyn knew something was wrong from the look on Charles's face.

"What's wrong, Daddy?"

"Nothing, baby girl. You just sit back and be quiet."

They arrived home and Nadine helped the children in the house and put them to bed. She flopped across the bed, face down, and soon was startled by Charles's hands round her ankles. He snatched her towards the floor, dragging her off the bed. Her attempts to clutch the sheets and mattress did not save her fall.

"What are you doing?" she cried.

"Get the hell out of my bed! Go sleep somewhere else!" he demanded as he threw her a pillow.

Nadine grabbed the pillow and got to her feet, confused and crying. "What did I do?"

He said not a word. She sighed heavily and went downstairs to sleep on the couch.

Their children often heard her crying as she lay alone and thought no one could hear her pain. She never knew how many times her young children lay helplessly listening to what was happening in another room in the house. The children dared not share any of these details with their mother, and certainly not with their father.

The ladies at church formed a quilting club which met twice a week. They took turns hosting in their homes and Nadine was invited to join. Charles saw it as a bunch of old hens getting together to gossip about everyone's business, but he agreed to allow her to join after she promised it wouldn't interfere with their home life.

During the day when Charles was at work, Nadine started taking in alterations to earn a bit of extra money. She hated the chore of asking him for money. He always gave her just enough to get what she needed, nothing over. She made a little sachet pillow with a slit in the back to hide her money in and kept it in the back of a dresser drawer. She used some of the money to buy extra snacks when it was her turn to host the quilting club.

Charles was right to think the ladies sat around talking about everything and everybody.

Carol was threading her needle. "Well, if you ask me," she said, "I think she should leave him. I mean, if he's not working, he can't take care of his family. That poor girl works round the clock to take care of him and those children."

Janice thought otherwise. "I was always raised to believe if he's not cheating on you, or going upside your head, you better stay."

Carol came back with, "You know people are always stickin' their noses in other folk's business, telling them to stay with a man. But they're not the ones who have to put up with his crap, you know what I mean?"

Helen chimed in. "I'll tell you the truth. I don't know what the worst is—a man who would cheat on you or beat on you. I don't think I could stay with either."

"Oh, did you know, staying is what landed Christine in the hospital not long ago?" As Carol said this a few in the room gasped. She continued. "When a man puts his hands on you once, he'll do it again and again if you let him. Now, Daniel tried that stuff with me one day—and ladies, I'm here to tell ya, I let him have it."

Helen grinned. "What did you do?"

"I landed a vase right over the top of his head."

Everyone except Nadine laughed. She kept her eyes on her needle – never looked up.

"Yep, seven stitches later, he never touched me again. Sometimes you gotta let 'em know they don't always have the upper hand."

Carol noticed that while everyone else laughed, one remained quiet. "Nadine, are you alright? Girl, you haven't said two words on the subject—or on anything else for that matter."

"I'm fine."

"What makes women stay with a man who beats them?" Janice asked.

"Some say love," Helen said. "But I say that's foolishness."

"Crazy!" Carol said. "There's not that much love in the world."

Janice agreed. "But some say they stay for the kids, or they don't think they can make it on their own."

Helen leaned forward to begin stitching a new row. "Well, some women are afraid of leaving. You do know some men have the nerve to try and kill you if you leave them?" She rolled her eyes and added, "I mean, the God-forsaken nerve!"

Nadine got to her feet. She seemed to be in a hurry. All eyes were on her. She asked, "Would anyone like more coffee?"

Helen looked up from her work. "Oh, yes, honey. Thank you. I could sure use some."

Janice put down her needle. "I'll go help her."

Janice followed Nadine into the kitchen and found her standing at the sink as though in a daze. "Are you ok?"

Nadine sucked in her breath and let it out slowly. She said softly. "You know, no one knows what a woman has to go through in her own house. Some women don't know how to leave. So people shouldn't talk like that."

"Oh, don't pay Carol no mind. She was just talking too much as usual – don't let her get to you."

"No, she's right. Why would anyone stay and take such abuse from their man? Some women aren't as lucky as her. You know? Fighting back sometimes makes things worse." Her hands trembled.

"Nadine, what are you saying? Does Charles hit you?" Nadine

glanced at her.

Janice put the cups down and dried her hands. "Oh, Nadine, I didn't know. None of us knew. It must have been very awkward listening to us carry on. I'm sorry."

Nadine's words came in a whisper. "Please, don't tell anyone. It's embarrassing, you know?"

"I promise I won't say a thing. But, you know, I am a nurse at the health department. We help abused women all the time. In fact, we have a support group which meets there every Thursday morning. Won't you think about coming?"

"Oh, I can't do that! If Charles knew I was…no, I can't. Besides, how's some meeting gonna help me?"

"Nadine, you are not the only woman in this situation. Lots of women come even though they do fear their husbands finding out. They come anyway because they need support in getting out. The reason why they can have their meeting there is because it's safe."

"No place is safe! I can't even be safe in my own home. God forgive me but—sometimes I feel like the only way out is death… but then I think about my children."

Carol called from the living room. "You two need some help in there?"

Janice spoke a few last quiet words. "For the sake of you and your children, Nadine, please think about it."

She shook her head. "No, I can't even think about it."

That Saturday, Charles invited his buddies over. He had built a small hangout area off the shed. They were drinking, listening to music, talking and playing cards. The more they drank, the louder they got and the harder the cards came down on the table. The laughter was loud, the trash talks even louder.

The children were playing nearby. Charles called to Carolyn, told her to go tell Nadine to bring them more snacks.

Nadine's sister and her mother were also visiting. Martha walked over to look out the kitchen window. "Hey, isn't that Maxine's boy out there? Um, Harold or something."

Claudette joined her. "Oh, yeah, that's him. You know he can't keep a job, cause he's always drunk."

Nadine said, "Will y'all come away from that window?"

She put chips and pretzels with dip on a tray and a few sandwiches cut in fours. Claudette got the pitcher of tea and said, "I don't know why you made tea. This ain't hardly what they want."

Nadine sighed. "Well, maybe someone will want some."

They walked outside to the sound of BB King blasting from the shed. The men became distracted, watching the two of them walk closer. One commented, "Woo wee, Charles, how in the world did you manage to marry into a family with such fine women?" "Say man, are you diggin' on my wife?"

"Nah, just paying the fine ladies a compliment, especially your sister-in-law. Hey sweet thang, what's your sign?" Claudette rolled her eyes and planted the pitcher of tea firmly on the table.

"Now, don't be like that," he slurred. "Come on, baby, don't be like that." He followed Claudette to the door. She whipped around with her hands on her hips and said, "Look, turkey!"

Charles interrupted. "Ok, ok, y'all can go on now. We trying to play cards here. Come on man. It's your turn. Won't you dig yourself?"

"Drunken jive turkey!" Claudette yelled.

"Oh Claudette, be nice," Nadine said, taking her hand.

"Girl, please. They're just a bunch of horny drunks, including your husband."

"I can't believe you."

"What? I'm not wrong. I just call them like I see them."

Martha was at the table peeling an apple. "What are y'all fussing about now?"

"Nothing, Mama," Claudette answered. "Just Charles's old drunk friends hitting on somebody."

"Well, men are gonna be men, Claudette." Martha turned to Nadine. "Nadine, we're gonna have to go soon. Can't stay away from your daddy too long. He gets to missing me." She winked.

"Sure, Mama." Nadine gave her a hug.

Claudette said, "Come on—give me a hug too! Don't let that crazy man come in between us. You're still my little sister."

Once they had gone, Nadine called the children in for supper. Afterwards, she bathed and dressed them for bed. She could still hear the loud music and laughter from the shed as she sat in the living room crocheting in front of the TV. By the time the men left, Nadine had taken a shower and was standing in front of the bathroom mirror brushing her hair.

Charles hobbled in. "Kids asleep?" he asked.

"Yes, for a while now."

He stood in the doorway of the bathroom. "You think a lot of yourself, don't you?"

She continued brushing her hair – watching him from the corner of her eye. He walked up behind her and leaned over her shoulder. "You and your big mouth sister are two little conceited hussies, always thinking you're the cat's meow, head all big, strutting around in front of my friends." His words slurred as he glared at her through the mirror.

The strokes of her brush slowed down as she anticipated what was coming. He ran his fingers through her hair. "You're definitely fine, though. I'll give it to you," he whispered in her ear. "Wonder how'd you feel if something happened to this pretty little face or all that fine hair? Huh?"

Nadine cleared her throat. "Excuse me."

He followed her in the bedroom and kept taunting her. Her attempt to leave the room only resulted in him pinning her to the bed and forcing himself on her. When he was done, he collapsed on top of her, sweating and breathing hard like a crazed bull.

"It would have been better for you if you would have cooperated. Maybe you would have even enjoyed it."

She remained still and he soon passed out. She then slowly moved from underneath him, rolling his drunken body over on his back, and went to the bathroom to clean herself up. She crept past the bed and out down the stairs. The sound of his snoring faded in the distance as she made it down to the living room where she spent the night on the couch.

The next morning, Charles opened his eyes to William standing at the bedside.

"Where is Mama?" his little voice whined.

Lying on his stomach, Charles lifted his head and looked around the room. "I don't know, son." He sat up, rubbing his head. Noticing the time, he grabbed his robe. "Come on, William. Let's go find her."

After looking in Carolyn's room, they headed downstairs. Carolyn got up and followed them. They found Nadine asleep on the couch.

"Nadine! You plan on sleeping all day?" Her eyes opened wide as if someone had just raised the blinds. She immediately sat straight up, alarmed by the sound of Charles's voice.

"Why are you sleeping on the couch?" Carolyn asked.

"Um, well, I had a bad dream—and didn't want to wake your daddy."

"What was it about?"

"Nothing. Nothing really. Are you guys hungry?"

"You don't have time to cook breakfast," Charles said. "We'll be late for church. They can eat cereal."

"And what will you eat?"

"Toast and coffee."

Nadine prepared a pot of coffee and poured a cup for Charles and placed it on the table. Before she could bring back the sugar, he stood up and reached over her for it. Their hands touched the dish simultaneously. She snatched back.

Charles frowned. "What's your problem? I got cooties now?"

She took the butter and apple jelly from the refrigerator and put it on the table.

"Would you like anything else?"

"No."

When they set out for church Charles didn't take the usual route. Nadine asked, "Where are we going?"

"Going to a different church today." He kept his gaze straight ahead with no expression.

"Why? What's wrong with our church?"

"It's time for a change."

Upon their arrival they were greeted by several members – no one they knew. After the service was over, the pastor shook Charles's hand. "Good to see you and your family here today. I hope to see you come back again soon."

Charles smiled. "Most definitely, sir."

On the ride home Nadine silently gazed out of the car window.

He looked at Carolyn in the rear-view mirror. "So, baby girl, did you like our new church?"

"Yes…but what's wrong with our old one? You don't like it anymore?"

"Well, I thought we should make some new friends. We're going there from now on." He glanced over at Nadine. She still made no response.

THREE

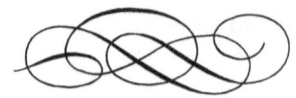

The Separation

Most people believe alcohol abuse causes a person to be violent. Nadine was not different in her belief. Charles's drinking justified in her mind his abuse. It did not make the abuse right, but it gave him an excuse. The day came when that belief was shattered.

Nadine stepped into the shower with him, hoping to spend an intimate night together without drunken sex. He asked, "What are you doing?"

She smiled. "I'm taking a shower with my man."

"Well, I'm just about done. Wash my back." He handed her the washcloth.

She began rubbing the cloth over his back and gently kissed his skin.

"Are you done?" he asked, looking over his shoulder. He stepped out of the shower, leaving her alone.

She said, "Yeah, I guess I am."

When she entered their room, Charles was laying on his back in bed with his eyes closed. She slid in next to him and rested her head on his chest, longing for his response, but he remained motionless.

"Charles, are you sleep?" she whispered. He didn't answer. She looked up at him and again rested her head on his chest. He finally moved his arm from his forehead and pushed her away. "What are you doing, Nadine?"

He rolled over – putting his back to her. She said, "I thought we could be together tonight."

"I'm not in the mood for you tonight. Isn't that what you tell me?"

She put her arm around his waist and buried her face against him.

"I'm trying to sleep. I wish you would stop pawing over me like some whore." He pulled the blanket up under his chin.

Nadine sat up in bed and pulled her knees up to her chest. She wrapped her arms around her legs and rested her chin on her knees. Before she realized it, her thoughts sprang from her lips. "Any other night you would be forcing yourself on me like some drunken soldier, reeking of alcohol."

He swiftly turned over and frowned. "What did you say?"

She almost stopped breathing when she realized she had said her thoughts out loud. "Nothing," she answered in a barely audible voice.

"See, that's what I'm talking about. Your mouth. Always complaining about something. What is it now, Nadine? Huh? If you're being mistreated here, get out! Why you still here?" He rolled back over.

She shook her head and said with a sigh, "My husband must have died in the war, 'cause I don't know who you are anymore." She got up and gathered some clothes to put on. He turned to look her way. "What are you doing?" "I'm leaving," she said as she put on her bra.

He sat up. "Nadine, you better quit playing with me and get your stupid behind back in this bed. I done told you I was tired. I'm not in the mood for this or you."

She continued to get dressed. She knew the risk of taking a stand, but she had had enough of this life.

He jumped up and snatched the shirt out of her hand. "Now see? You gonna make me hurt you tonight—cause you're pissing me off!"

She flinched and froze at the rise in his voice. He threw her shirt on the floor and turned back toward the bed. He paused. Then directed his look her way. "No, you know what? If you want to leave, leave. Get the hell out! I'm sick of you anyway. You do nothing for me. You're a sorry excuse for a woman and a wife. Just don't think you're leaving with my kids, you understand?" "I can't leave without them," she said softly.

"Oh, you can leave without them—and you will!"

She bent down to pick up her shirt. From the corner of her eye, she could see Charles stepping towards her. She didn't have time to react to a sudden blow of his foot that forced her against the bedroom door. He clutched her arm, slung her away from the door just enough to open it and shoved her out into the hall.

She fell against the wall, hitting her head and shoulder.

He yelled, "You sure you wanna leave?"

Before she could get up strong blows came from his foot. Stomping and kicking her against the wall. "Leave, Nadine! Get up! Get up and leave! Get up, I say!"

But she was unable to get up. He grabbed her left hand and pulled off her wedding ring.

"You won't be needing this anymore—since you're leaving."

He stepped back inside the bedroom and put the ring on the dresser, then opened the drawers and began throwing her clothes out in the hallway.

With all this commotion, Carolyn was now awake. She peeped out of her bedroom and saw her mother on the floor in the hallway. She could hear her father's ranting, but she couldn't see him. She could not see him snatching clothes off the hangers in the closet, but the fact was evident with clothes and shoes sailing through the air. She hastily closed her door and jumped in bed, pulling the blanket over her head—trying to drown out the sound of what was happening.

Nadine had dragged herself off the floor, was on her feet and scurrying about as best she could, picking up her things and begging Charles to stop, but by this time he was so worked up with rage all pleas fell on deaf ears. Nadine was also aware her daughter had seen or at least heard her humiliation.

She cried, "Please, Charles, I don't want to leave. I'm sorry!"

"Nah, it's too late now. I told you. You see what you made me do? I told you I didn't want you! I told you to leave me alone!"

Funny he would say that, considering there were so many nights when he wouldn't leave her alone. Countless nights he staggered in from the local bar after everyone had gone to bed, reeking of booze and pressing his drunken body up against hers. The nights he came to bed sober were few and far in between. What she wanted was just one normal night with him.

Charles limped forward and grabbed a handful of her hair. He pressed his forehead against hers. "You made me do this, Nadine. This is your fault. It's always your fault, see? Nobody knows what you do to me."

She begged softly. "Please."

"I'm gonna help you leave." He led her down the hall by her hair. She tried to loosen his grip, pleaded with him to stop.

Carolyn could no longer remain in her room. She stood outside and yelled down the hall. "Stop it, Daddy! Stop hurting Mama!"

"Get back to bed before I whip you! Your mama has to learn a lesson tonight."

William came and stood beside his sister, rubbing his eyes. When he saw his mother was crying, he began crying. His mother was being yanked across the floor by her hair. His big sister stepped forward, took him by the hand and led him into her room. They huddled together, each one trying to comfort the other. They had learned at an early age to comfort each other and stay out of Charles's way when he was on a rampage.

When they reached the living room, Charles let Nadine go long enough to open the front door. He snatched her small frame up by her arm and attempted to push her out. Screaming and kicking, she braced her hands and feet against the doorway to keep from going.

"No no!" he said. "You wanted to leave. So, leave! Go! Get out of my house!"

The harder she fought to stay the more determined he was to shove her out the door. She fell on her knees and wrapped her arms around his legs. He tried to shake her, then finally reached down and pried her hands off and pulled her out on the porch. Then he stepped back inside and locked the door.

"No, please!" She stood up on her knees, beating on the door.

After a few moments, Nadine pulled herself up on her feet and staggered next door. As she knocked on the door she moaned, "Please help me."

After what seemed hours, the door opened. A woman stood staring at Nadine. Nadine knew what she must look like standing there with a torn bra, scattered hair, beaten and bruised.

The woman shrieked, "Oh, my God! What in the world happened?"

"Please, Sadie, can I use your phone?" Nadine uttered these words through swelling lips.

"No," came the answer. "I don't know what happened—but I can't get involved."

"But our children play together. Won't you please help me?" The door slowly closed.

Nadine made her way across the street to another house. After a bit Ruth opened the door and gasped at the sight of Nadine's injuries.

"Please, I need to use the phone."

"Jesus Christ! What happened to you?"

"Charles and I had a fight. I just need to use the phone."

"A fight? I bet he don't look like you. Look, my husband is working tonight and it's just me and my daughter."

"Please, I promise no trouble. I just want to use the phone."

"Do you want me to call the police?"

"No. No, I want to call my sister."

Ruth hesitated then stepped back and let Nadine come inside.

Shortly thereafter Nadine was saying in a quivering voice, "Hello, Claudette—please come get me."

"What? Where are you?"

"I'm at Ruth's house. I'll tell you more when you get here. She lives across the street."

"Did that nigga hurt you?"

"I'll tell you when you get here. Please hurry."

"I'm on my way."

Ruth helped Nadine to the bathroom to clean up some of her cuts. "What kind of man would do this?" Nadine didn't answer.

"We would hear things from over your way, but we didn't think it was our place to get involved."

Nadine whispered, "Nobody likes to get involved. It's probably best."

"Well, I got involved once and the young lady cursed me out. She said I had no right to call the police. But he was beating the mess out of her in a parking lot that night. I don't understand some women. No offense."

"Has your husband ever hit you?"

"Hell no! Look girl, I've got a Saturday night special hidden in our room. If he ever tried, I'd put a bullet in him so fast! I have a daughter to think about. You know, we have our ups and downs like anyone else. But he's good to me."

"Yeah, Charles used to be good to me. For the most part anyway. Sometimes I blame it on the war."

"Well, the war did change a lot of people, but it's no excuse for beating your wife. After all, what did you have to do with it?"

When the knock on the door came Ruth went to answer it and said, "She's in the bathroom."

Claudette hurried that way and gazed in dismay. Nadine started wailing uncontrollably at the sight of her sister.

"Oh, my God, Nadine! Oh, my God!" Claudette cried. "What did he do to you? That bastard! I'll kill him! Did you call the police?"

Ruth butted in. "I tried to get her to do it, but she wouldn't."

"What?! Well, I'm calling them, 'cause this is not the first time." Her voice dropped in pitch. "You gotta do something about it, Nadine."

"I can't. Please don't call. He has the kids, and it would only make things worse. It was my fault."

"Your fault? Are you kidding me?"

"I pushed him to it. I wanted to be with him, but he didn't want me. He didn't want me."

Once again, Nadine began sobbing uncontrollably.

When the weeping subsided a bit Claudette said, "Nadine, I've seen how controlling he is. I've heard how he talks to you. This is not the first time he's assaulted you—and now you're saying he beat you like this because he didn't want you? What is he? Your pimp?"

Nadine moaned, "You don't understand."

"No, I don't—and I want you to stop making excuses for that nigga."

Claudette tried to help Nadine get up, but Nadine could hardly move.

"I'm calling an ambulance."

"No, no—I can walk." With one woman on each side of Nadine, they managed to help her to the car.

"We're going to the hospital. I don't want to hear nothing else about it."

Nadine lay in the backseat with a throbbing head and much discomfort in her chest and stomach where she had been kicked. Black and blue hues covered her arms and the side of her face. When they arrived, Claudette got a wheelchair and rolled Nadine into the emergency room. After going through registration, Nadine was triaged by the nurse.

"So, what happened?" the nurse asked.

Nadine sat in the wheelchair with her head down in shame, too embarrassed to answer.

"Look! My sister is married to a maniac—he did this to her."

"Is it true, Mrs. Hunter?"

Nadine slowly nodded, still too embarrassed to look up.

"Ok. Well, lets get her into a cubicle so she can be properly examined."

Claudette followed and helped Nadine undress – careful not to hurt her. She shook her head when she spotted the older faded bruises on her sister's body.

The curtain was pulled back. The man who entered said, "Mrs. Hunter, I'm Dr. Myers. I understand you've been assaulted."

Claudette blurted, "Yes, by her husband!"

"And you are?"

"I'm her sister."

"Mrs. Hunter, why don't you lie down so we can have a look at your injuries. Your sister can stay with you if you'd like."

Dr. Myers noticed the yellowish discolorations and the tenderness of her skin; traces of fingerprints embedded in her upper arms. Nadine winced as Dr. Myers touched the yellowish discolorations and tenderness of her skin. He noted traces of fingerprints on her upper arms and a bruise over her swollen cheekbone.

He said, "Mrs. Hunter, this isn't the first time, is it?"

Nadine squeezed her eyes shut and turned her head aside. She wanted to crumple into a ball and roll under the examination table. Her face grimaced with pain when Dr. Myers pressed on her stomach.

He sighed heavily, sounding exasperated. He dropped his gloves in the trash can and as he turned to leave, he said, "We'll need to get some x-rays."

Seconds later Claudette spoke through clenched teeth. "He's an animal, Nadine—I just want to kill him!"

A couple of hours later when he had the x-ray results the doctor returned to say, "Mrs. Hunter, you've got two cracked ribs and multiple contusions everywhere. Now, I can't make you press charges, but I am under obligation to report domestic abuse."

Claudette piped up. "Yes, do what you need to do, doctor."

Nadine said, "Claudette?"

"Nadine, you can't let him get away with this. He's been doing it too long and getting away with it – and you know it."

"I'll be back," the doctor said as he exited. Soon thereafter he returned with the police, who asked Nadine multiple questions. But she was afraid to answer.

Finally, one of the officers said, "Okay, we can't make you talk, Mrs. Hunter. Maybe you need a little time to think about it."

Nadine nodded her head, while Claudette exclaimed, "Nadine! What's there to think about?!"

The other officer said, "We'll need to speak with your husband, Mrs. Hunter."

Nadine's eyes grew wide. She looked like she was trying to sink into the sheets.

Claudette motioned with her head after she made eye contact with one of the officers. The three of them stepped beyond the curtain and moved down the hall.

"My sister is scared—and with good reason. This man is a narcissistic monster. She won't ever press charges! He has her programmed. She thinks this is her fault."

The taller of the two pulled a card from his chest pocket. "I understand. If your sister decides she wants to talk, call me. Meanwhile, we'll go see what Mr. Hunter has to say."

When the officers pulled into the driveway Charles spotted them from the living room window. He stepped out onto the porch. The first thing he asked was why were they there, though he already knew. He just didn't want to believe it.

Charles said, "I never wanted to hurt my wife. I just lost it. It can happen, you know? You guys married? You ever argue with your wife?"

"Yes, I have," the taller of the two said. "But I've never beat her. And it doesn't look as if this was the first time for you, so looks like you have a problem with your fist, Mr. Hunter. Personally, I hate wife beaters."

Charles's lips tightened as his eyes narrowed. "What are you gonna do about it?"

"Well, unless she presses charges, there's nothing we can do about it," the other officer said.

"Then get the hell off my porch."

Officer Lowry stood as tall as Charles with his thumbs hooked in the belt loops of his pants. Men like Charles always tested him. He wished he could take off his badge and teach this sucker a lesson. Instead, he bid him a good day and left.

About the same time Nadine's parents, Martha and Sam, arrived at the hospital. Sam stormed, "I'm gonna get my pistol and put a hole in that nigga!"

Nadine mumbled, "Daddy, it won't make things better."

"Now, look, Nadine—that nigga has got to pay. We can't let him get away with it."

Claudette folded her arms across her chest. "That's what I said."

Martha put her hands up. "No! Now the best thing for Nadine to do is let the authorities handle it properly. That's all there is to it, Nadine. And you better stop all this nonsense about not telling us stuff. This is not something you keep a secret."

"You don't know how Charles can be when he's angry."

Claudette rolled her eyes. "Oh, please. I'm looking at how he gets."

Nadine put her hands to her forehead and said, "I can't talk about this right now. My head is pounding. Have either of you checked on the kids?"

"No," Martha said. "But I will."

Claudette stood with her arms crossed and heaved a big sigh. "I don't understand why you're protecting him! You know he's only gonna do it again and again. He may even kill you next time." She turned and walked out.

Martha rested her face on Nadine's forehead and spoke softly, "I know you love him, baby—but he don't love you. No man does this to someone he loves." She kissed her daughter on the forehead, told her to get some rest, and turned to leave.

Out in the hallway Sam said, "You can drop me off at home, Martha."

"What? You're not going with me?"

"I can't go cause I'm gonna want to jump on that S-O-B and kill him. Take someone else with you."

Martha picked up a friend from church and they made their way to the house – only to find no one there. Soon after the police left Charles left with the children, headed for Clarksville. Martha too decided to head for Clarksville, for she knew he had nowhere else to take the children.

When she arrived, she swung the car in the driveway and stormed up on the porch with her friend following behind. Martha pounded on the door and waited for an answer.

Phyllis appeared, speaking as if everything was normal. "Martha. How are you?"

"Yeah, yeah, whatever. I'm looking for my grandbabies."

"Well, you don't have to be so rude about it. They're here. Charles brought them over quite early this morning because Nadine is sick.

Martha glowered. "He the one sick!"

"Now what does that mean? Don't go insulting my boy."

"Yeah, boy is right—because if he was any kind of a man, he wouldn't be beating on my daughter."

Phyllis's mouth fell open as if she was hearing this for the first time. The kids ran from the kitchen and she stepped back to allow their guests into the house.

"Grandma!" Carolyn was evidently happy to see Martha. And William wrapped his little arms around her leg.

She bent down and hugged them both. "How are my babies?"

"Fine," Carolyn answered. "Where is Mama?"

"You'll see her soon."

Phyllis turned to the boy. "Did you finish your snack?" William shook his head.

"Well, go on back and finish. I need to talk to Grandma. Okay?" She gave her guests a look that meant she would be right back and followed the children to make sure they returned to the table. She was back shortly and sat down on the couch. She said in a low voice, "So where is Nadine?

Martha's eyes grew big. "You mean Charles just dropped off the kids without saying a word?"

"Well, like I said he told me Nadine was sick. So, what's wrong with her?"

It was obvious Phyllis was clueless. Apparently, Charles told her nothing about what happened—and probably had even forbidden the children to do so.

"The only thing wrong with my daughter is she's married to your sorry son. I don't believe he didn't tell you Nadine is in the hospital, compliments of his fists and his feet."

"What? No, no—not my Charles!"

"Yes, your precious Charles. He tried to beat the hell out of my child. She's in the hospital—all bruised up and got cracked ribs."

"Why?"

"Why? As if there's ever a good reason. How the hell should I know? You claim you so close to Charles—so reckon you the one should know."

"I know nothing of the sort."

"The kids know."

"They haven't said a word. Charles said she was sick, and I left it at that."

Martha rolled her eyes toward the ceiling. "Yes, you would."

"Look, I don't know what happened—but what do you want?"

Martha crossed her arms over her chest. "To see your son behind bars—or dead, one or the other. Makes me no never mind which."

"Oh, the hell you say! Neither will ever happen."

"Oh? You think he's beyond going to jail? Or that my husband is not out looking for him right now to put a bullet in him?"

Phyllis stood up, pointing at the door. "I think you need to go! And I think y'all are just plain crazy! Just crazy! I knew he shouldn't have married that girl."

Grandma Martha swiftly hopped up from the chair and stepped forward. Her friend sprang forward and came between them before Martha could get close enough to hit Phyllis.

"You see what I mean?" Phyllis yelled. "Crazy! That's what you are. I need to talk to Charles and find out for myself what happened."

"Well, you just do that. And while you talking to him, we'll be talking to the police." Martha stomped past Phyllis and into the kitchen. "You babies want to go home with me?"

William said, "I want Mama."

"Me too." Carolyn said. "Daddy hurt Mama—and pushed her out the door!"

Martha said, "Well, she's gonna be okay, and meanwhile you can go home with me."

"Is Mama there?" Carolyn asked.

"No, baby—but Aunt Claudette is taking good care of her. You'll see her when she feels better."

Martha turned to Phyllis. "I'm taking them."

"No, you're not, because Charles brought them to me."

"That's because he was too afraid to bring them to me. He's a coward. A punk, as the young folks say. Besides, you gonna stop me?" Her eyebrows raised.

Sam got in his truck and headed for the garage, looking for Charles. He couldn't stand hanging around the house knowing Nadine was in the hospital and Charles was somewhere running free.

His boss reported, "Naw, he ain't here. Said his wife is sick so he couldn't come in today. I s'pect he'll be in the next day or two." Next, Sam drove by the house, but Charles wasn't there either.

At that same time, Charles was calling Janice in hopes she could go talk to Nadine. When Janice didn't answer, he left a message on the answer machine. He returned to Clarksville, where he just missed Martha and the kids.

Phyllis confronted him. "Why didn't you tell us that girl is in the hospital?"

Joe lit up a pipe. "Now I want to know. What's going on?"

"We had a fight."

Joe blew a puff of smoke. "A fight that put her in the hospital?"

Phyllis's voice was shrill. "Your daddy and I want to know exactly what happened—so we can help you, son!"

"Help me? What do you mean help me? I don't need no help!"

Phyllis came back with, "You put that girl in the hospital and her family's talking jail time. Now let's be reasonable here!"

"Nah, nah, she wouldn't do that."

"And you're sure, huh?" Joe asked.

"Look, I know Nadine. And she knows she does stuff to get me upset, so, yeah, she wouldn't do it."

"But, son, you took things too far this time. We have to think of the possibility she would—because you don't know what her family is telling her. We need a lawyer."

"Nah, nah—ain't gonna need no lawyer." Charles got to his feet and stuck his hands in his pockets. "I gotta talk to her, that's all. I gotta find out where her head is. You're right, her family could be telling her anything."

Phyllis shook her head. "How you gonna talk to her, son? You can't go near her."

"I'm her husband."

"The same husband who put her in the hospital?"

He answered, "Alright, you talk to her then."

"Me?"

"Yeah, she respects you. See, that's why I moved her from that church, 'cause too many people were in our business."

"Charles, I don't know what I can say. I mean, her mama is crazy."

Joe chimed in. "Phyllis, all you'll do is go up there and get your feelings hurt."

"I said she was crazy—but I'm not afraid of her. Besides, what's a few hurt feelings if it'll keep Charles from jail? I'll go."

Charles paced back and forth – slowly on his war injured leg from shrapnel. He muttered, "She's not gonna take me away from my kids." He stopped pacing and faced Phyllis. "You should have never let her have my kids."

"I didn't want to create a scene in front of them. She was all ready to fight and talking about killing you."

"Yeah, yeah, it's just talk." He headed for the door. "I have to go get my kids."

"No, wait a minute! I'm going to the hospital, son. You stay here with your daddy. You'll just make things worse—probably get arrested or sump'n."

Charles did agree to stay and finally sat down.

Janice walked into the hospital room and surprised Claudette who was sitting in a chair and flipping through a magazine.

"Janice, what are you doing here?"

"Well, I spoke to your mom earlier, then Charles called wanting to know if I'd spoken with you."

Claudette tossed the magazine on the floor. "What?! The nerve of that low-down dog!

"It's okay, Claudette," Nadine said.

"Your mom told me he beat you up pretty bad. I'd say she was right."

Nadine sighed. "Who else knows?"

"I don't think anyone. I haven't talked to anyone else."

"Thank you, Janice," Claudette said. "He's such a Punk!"

Nadine sighed again. "Janice, I'd appreciate it if you wouldn't tell anyone. This is so embarrassing."

Claudette inserted, "Why are you embarrassed? He's the one should be embarrassed!"

Janice paused a bit before saying, "Nadine, remember when I told you about the group that meets at the health department? Would you now consider going? They still meet on Thursday mornings."

"I - I can't do that."

"At this point, you have nothing to lose. I'll be glad to go with you if you'd like. Please think about it. Ok? Well, I hate to be brief, but I've got to get home. I'll be in touch. Claudette, would you walk me to the elevators?"

As they approached the elevators Janice turned to face Claudette. "Thanks for walking me down. Look, I just wanted to tell you that I am very concerned about your sister. The group is a great resource for victims of domestic abuse. Women stay for different reasons—the children, threats from their husband if they leave, or just not knowing how to leave—and sick as it may sound, for love."

"Yes, it does sound sick. But my sister has a place to go. She's already out. She just needs to stay out."

"Claudette, believe it or not, Nadine is not out. This very day that man could talk her into coming back."

"After he beat the hell out of her? I don't see how."

"It's true. And she would go—because so much is invested. It's like being brainwashed or something. The one thing you must not do is get angry or upset with her, because it will only push her that much closer to him. I know none of this makes sense." She shook her head and sighed. "It doesn't make sense to me, but that's the way it works."

"You're right. None of this makes sense. My sister was raised to be a strong woman, not to let some punk beat on her. You know, when she was dating him, I used to cover for her so they could see each other and now I regret it."

"You couldn't have controlled this, so don't feel guilty. Listen, I've got to go, but maybe coming to the group will open her eyes."
"Okay, I'll try to encourage her."

Janice stepped on the elevator saying, "Call me if you need me."

Claudette returned to the room and found Nadine watching TV. She shifted her gaze and said, "You were talking about me, weren't you?"

"We're just concerned, that's all. I'm gonna call Ma and see if she wants to come back up before it gets late."

Once Claudette left the room, Nadine closed her eyes and pressed her head against the pillow, listening to the TV. She didn't hear Phyllis creep in.

Phyllis whispered, "Nadine."

With this she opened her eyes, which grew wider as they focused on this visitor.

"How are you, darling?" A grin covered Phyllis's face. "Well, I simply had no idea you were here, that is until your mom stopped by for the children."

Claudette heard her voice as she neared the door and quietly stepped in behind Phyllis.

Nadine cleared her throat and said in a not so friendly tone, "What are you doing here?"

"I came to see you, darling. I heard about what happened—and well, I just feel so bad about it. I really do. But Charles is sorry. He didn't mean it. Sometimes people can get so angry they do things before they realize it."

She perched on the edge of the chair next to the bed. "Oh, Nadine, sending Charles to jail isn't the answer. I mean, who would take care of you all? You don't really want to do that, do you?"

Claudette clapped her hands slowly. "Unbelievable performance! And I do mean—unbelievable!"

Phyllis spun around so fast she almost fell off the chair. "Oh, uh, Claudette."

"What a performance, Phyllis. To think you actually care about my sister. Not! All you care about is your beloved Charles not going to jail! Unbelievable! Well, I say, get your stuck-up crazy behind out of here!"

Phyllis got to her feet. "Look little girl, I'm not afraid of you."

Nadine struggled to sit up, moaning, "Please don't fight."

Phyllis turned her way and said, "I didn't come to fight, Nadine. I came out of concern for you and the children."

Claudette shook her head vehemently. "You're a liar! You've never been concerned about my sister. You don't even like her."

"Oh, now, that's not so." Phyllis said, then turned again towards Nadine. "As I was saying—"

"Get out. That's all I'm saying." Claudette took two steps towards her. "And I mean right now before I have to make you leave."

"Now, you look here missy, there's a security guard just a few feet down the hall."

"Good, 'cause you may need him to get me off you!" Claudette raised her fist.

"Claudette!" Nadine begged. "Please calm down."

"It's okay, Nadine. I'm leaving. I told Charles this family was crazy."

"Yeah, we crazy! You want to see how crazy?" Claudette drew back her fist as if she was going to deck Phyllis as she moved past her.

Phyllis, if she was afraid, obviously did not want Claudette to know it. She held her nose up so high she almost bumped into the nurse who entered the room saying, "Is everything all right in here?"

"No," Claudette answered. "She needs to leave." Her eyes pointed at Phyllis.

Right on cue the nurse said, "Well, then...I'll have to ask you to leave, ma'am."

Phyllis took her opportunity to speak to Nadine one last time. "Nadine, you better think about your children and whether or not you really want their father to go to jail. I'll go now."

The nurse followed her out the door, and Claudette folded her arms across her chest while tapping her foot. "Nadine, I just need five minutes, just five minutes to beat the hell out of her! I really don't need that long!"

Nadine sunk down in the bed and pulled the blanket over her head.

FOUR

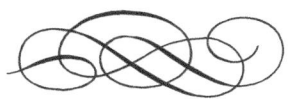

Wooing Her Back

Two days after Nadine's release from the hospital, her family was still insisting she do something about Charles.

Claudette asked, "What are you afraid of, Nadine?"

She answered, "Making things worse, and the affect all of this may have on the children."

"Nadine, you're not really thinking about the children. Otherwise, you would go to court."

"That's not true—I'm always thinking about my children. You have no right to judge me." She began sobbing. "You think this is so easy?"

Their father stepped between them. "Okay, baby girl. We're not trying to upset you. We just want to protect you."

Claudette chimed in, "Yeah, don't be getting pissed with me. I just don't want anything else to happen to you."

Nadine tried to speak forcefully. "Nothing else is gonna happen."

"Oh, my God! Wake up, Nadine! So many women are dead today because they thought the same thing! Please, Nadine."

~❖~

The sisters had gone together to the police station to take out papers on Charles for assault. They approached the front desk and stood in front of an oversized man wearing a uniform. He had a short black afro and untrimmed sideburns, and a small noticeable scar just above his left bushy brow. "What can I do for you ladies?" he asked.

"We're here to see Officer Lowry," Claudette said.

"He's off today. What can I do for you?"

"My sister wishes to file charges against her husband for assault."

He stared down at Nadine over the rim of his glasses. "Is this true?"

Nadine moistened her bottom lip with the tip of her tongue. "Yes."

"Are you sure? Cause you don't seem sure."

"What's there to be sure about?" Claudette asked. "Look at her face?"

He glanced at the bruises and the cuts to Nadine's face. She turned her head with embarrassment.

"Look, man," Claudette interjected. "Can we fill out the paperwork or what?"

Without another word the officer went over to a file cabinet and pulled out a few forms, strolled back to the desk, opened the drawer and pulled out a pen. His disposition said he did not care if they signed or not.

He firmly placed the forms and pen on the desktop and said, "You know, things like this used to be a family matter. Now it's a crime."

"As it should be," Claudette said. "Is this the paperwork?"

"Yes, ma'am. And you can sit over there." He pointed to a couple of chairs in the waiting area. "When you're done, bring them back to me and I'll send you down to the magistrate."

The next day, Officer Lowry was more than happy to be the one to serve Charles with the arrest warrant and bring him in. Charles looked dazed – as if he was caught in disbelief. He took the warrant from Officer Lowry and glanced over the words.

"My wife did this?"

"Yes sir," Officer Lowry answered as he removed the handcuffs from his belt. "I'll need you to turn around and put your hands behind your back. Officer Davis will read you your rights."

Charles was driven down to the police station and processed. He used his one call to call Phyllis and Joe, who came right away and bailed him out. During the entire ride home, Phyllis blabbered on and on about knowing this would happen and how crazy Nadine and her family were. Charles sat in the backseat trying to ignore her. He was already mad. He didn't need Phyllis to edge him on further. They dropped him off at the house and left for Clarksville.

The court date was scheduled a few weeks out. Charles was convinced if he could talk with Nadine, they wouldn't have to go to court, and he could get her back. He drove by her parents' home almost daily in hopes of seeing her outside alone.

Nadine had not left the house without someone by her side since the news of Charles's release. She knew he was furious, so did not want to take any chances of running into him alone.

One morning her parents drove out to the nursing home to visit Agilisi. Nadine slept in. When she woke up, she took her mother's car down to the BBQ shack, just down the street. She didn't notice Charles trailing behind. He eased his car slowly around, not wanting to be noticed, and parked where he could watch her go inside. He waited a few minutes before following her inside.

She was standing at the counter gazing at the floor, waiting for her order. She took in a deep breath and looked up. Her purse, which she had been clutching under her arm, fell to the floor when she spotted Charles walking in. It was as if her heartbeat suddenly appeared, throbbing so loud she could barely think. For a moment, she even forgot to breathe.

"Hey, baby." His cheek raised. "We need to talk. Come on, have a cup of coffee with your man." He bent down and picked up her purse.

She was unable to move or speak. He snapped his fingers twice in her face to get a response. She blinked and turned away.

"Are you coming?" He stepped over to a booth and sat down.

She followed and slid into the booth opposite to his. "Charles, we have court tomorrow."

He said, "I want to apologize."

She looked away, watching for her food. Her eyes darted around the café as she tried not to make eye contact. She didn't want his apologies anymore. She wanted peace. She wanted to feel safe in her own home. She wanted to be a normal family. She wanted him to stop drinking. But she was sure he wasn't there to talk about what she wanted.

"Baby, I said I was sorry. Now, it ain't easy for a man to do that. I want you and the kids home so we can be a family again. It just ain't right for us to be separated like this."

"I gotta get outta here." She saw the man at the counter motion to her. She jumped up, grabbed her bag and ran out the door. Her hand trembled as she attempted to insert the key in the car door. Charles caught up to her and placed his hand against the top of the car door, holding it shut.

"Where you running off to? We ain't finished."

"I gotta go home. Please, let me go home."

"Home? You ain't been home in weeks."

Through the car window she spotted a small paring knife on the passenger seat. Her mother must have left it there. It might be she could get to it if she had to.

When she wouldn't turn around and face him, he moved his hand from the door and stepped back. "Okay, I see how it is." He laughed. "So, you afraid of me now?"

Nadine remained quiet. She had tightly closed her eyes. Her body jerked as she caught the sound of his hand hitting the top of the car. Her mind was suddenly replaying the last night at the house.

"Please, Charles, I can't do this anymore."

"Okay, okay—I'll leave you alone. But not for long. I want my family back!" He slapped the top of the car again. "You hear me, Nadine? I want my family back! You not gonna get away with taking my kids either!" And with that he walked away.

She moved so fast she almost stumbled trying to get in the car. Once behind the wheel, she could not steady her hand enough to start the ignition.

Again, for many days she did not leave the house, not even to go to court. The judge had no other choice but to drop the charges when she didn't show up.

Claudette finally convinced her she would be safe if she accompanied her to her job. She had several houses to clean and could use some help, and Nadine could certainly use the money.

When they reached the job, Nadine smiled for the first time in a long while. "Woo, girl," she said, "these white folks sure live in some fancy houses."

"Yep, for some fancy dollars too."

"How do you learn about these people?"

"Mainly word of mouth. People like my work, so they refer me."

"Well, this house is bad." She lay down across the bed and closed her eyes. "Mmm, satin sheets."

"Girl, you don't know what these folks been doing on them sheets!"

"Oh, you're right." Nadine bolted up and they both laughed.

Claudette added, "Besides, satin sheets ain't no big deal."

"Well, they sure feel good. You ever think about what it would be like to live in a house like this, Claudette? Lots of money, and people waiting on you hand and foot. Never lifting a finger for nothing. Must be nice. I bet these women…" She paused.

"What?"

"Nothing, just thinking."

"Oh, I know what you were thinking. All the money in the world don't keep women from getting whacked upside the head by their man."

Nadine wandered over to the window. "Wow! They got a pool in the back? What do these people do?"

"Oh, the husband is vice president at a bank, so the wife doesn't really have to do anything, but she writes for a women's newsletter."

"That's nice. She makes her own money."

"Nadine, you can work with me anytime. You're a good housekeeper, too. I make enough money to share."

"No, I think I still want to teach."

"Then do it. Hey, let's have a party, Nadine."

Nadine turned around. "What?"

"Yeah, let's have a few people over. Eat, dance—socialize. We'll have it at our parents' house."

Nadine chuckled. "Okay, but where did the idea come from?"

"It'll lift you up."

Martha and Sam were all for a party and eager to pitch in. There hadn't been much laughter in the house lately. Even the children were excited. Nadine's daughter, Carolyn, made rainbow-colored flowers out of tissue paper and put them in Dixie cups to decorate the living room.

It had been a long time since Nadine wore make up. Charles never liked it.

Claudette asked, "How are you wearing your hair, Nadine?"

"What's wrong with my hair?"

"Everything. You always wear it in a ponytail, or a bun—like some old woman."

"That's the way—"

"Charles liked it? He always did want you to look plain. Here, let me try something." She let down Nadine's hair and formed two twisted braids to the front, then pulled the ends together in a clip at the back. She then graced the back of Nadine's hair with dangling curls.

"What do you think?"

"It's cute."

"See? And I got the perfect outfit for you too."

"It's just family and some old friends."

"Yeah but look at what you're wearing."

"What's wrong with what I'm wearing?" She was dressed in an old Indian Hippie Maxi dress and some flat sandals.

"Well, for starters, you got on an old dress." She held up a halter top. "Now, here's something cute to wear."

"No, absolutely not. It shows too much skin."

"You've got a nice figure. Why are you hiding it?"

"I'm not hiding."

Claudette went through her entire wardrobe before finding an outfit Nadine would wear. A pant set in an earthy shade. The pullover top buttoned down to mid-chest and had long flared sleeves, and the matching pants had flared legs and a midriff waist. The outfit conformed to Nadine's shape as if it had been custom made for her.

Claudette selected a mini dress with flared sleeves and boots. Right before the guests were due to arrive, she put on the music. Soon after, they were all dancing and enjoying the sounds of Motown hits, KC and the Sunshine Band, and Earth Wind and Fire.

The party turned out a big success. For Nadine, it was an act of freedom—a chance to be herself without any oppression, if only for a day. How she had missed times like these with her family, especially with Claudette.

The sisters were so close. And Charles knew it.

Claudette was the one person he feared for Nadine to be around. He knew if anyone could get her to leave him, she would be the one. Charles aimed to make sure his wife was not influenced by her family.

Every other day, the florist delivered flowers to the house. And the mailman delivered cards and gifts.

Martha grumbled, "What does he think this is? A funeral parlor?" She set her hands on her hips and sighed. "Listen, Nadine. Don't fall for this jive. If you return to him, the flowers and love letters will stop."

Claudette added, "Amen! And the beatings? They'll pick up right where they left off."

Martha said, "Someone called here the other day and hung up when I answered. I know it was him. Probably thought you were gonna answer."

"What?" Nadine stretched her brows then lowered them in confusion. "Why didn't you tell me?"

"Why? He called my house."

Sometime thereafter Nadine received a letter from Charles asking her to have dinner with him. Eventually, she agreed to meet him. She planned to keep the meeting a secret, but Martha overheard her on the phone and asked, "So, you're going to meet him, huh?"

Nadine was at the table. She put her head down on her arms.

Martha pulled out a chair and sat down. "Please, Nadine. Please don't go back. You'll only be hurting yourself and these children."

"Ma, I need to be home in my own house. The kids need to be with their father."

Martha shook her head. "Now that sounds like Charles."

"Well, he does promise things will be different this time. He says he's going to AA meetings."

"So he says."

"I know you don't understand or agree. But we've been here long enough."

Martha leaned over and put her arm around Nadine. "Long enough for what, baby? This is home too—and it's safe." She sighed. "Lord knows, I wish I had all the answers."

Nadine leaned over and rested her head on her mother's shoulder.

Martha said, "Hey, you know what? How 'bout we go for ice cream?"

While in the store, Nadine heard a voice in the distance calling her name. It was her old school mate, Candace—the only white girl who closely befriended Nadine during desegregation. They used to hang out with each other all the time until Candace left for college.

They ran towards each other with open arms, screaming the whole way. "Nadine, oh my God, you still look the same. Beautiful – as always."

"Oh, you too. You remember my mom, don't you?"

"Yes. Mrs. Pearson, so nice to see you again."

"You too, Candace. Nadine, I'm going over to the next aisle. Meet me at the register."

Candace's smile was big. "So, what have you been up too?"

"Not much. What about you?"

"I lived in Atlanta for a while with my aunt while I went to school. My goal was to become a lawyer, you know – but I ended up being a paralegal. I like it though."

"That's great, Candy. I do remember you wanting to be a lawyer so you could fight *for equal rights.*" They both laughed. Nadine added, "So where are you staying now?"

"In Lakefront."

"Lakefront? Wow. You must be making good money."

"I do okay for myself. So, did you become a teacher?"

"No, I was going to school, but I got pregnant and married. I don't know if I'll ever get a chance to go back."

"Well, don't give up. So, married with children? Anyone I know?"

"No. He was in the military. He got out when he returned from Vietnam."

"Sounds like we have a lot to catch up on. Here's my card. Call me so we can get together."

"Okay. So nice seeing you, girl!"

"You too. Let's catch up soon."

They hugged goodbye and Nadine headed off to meet her mother. She was glad Candy had cut the interaction short. The last thing she wanted was to tell her friend any details about her life.

Later, Nadine took the kids to the Pizza House where Charles was waiting for them in the parking lot. The kids ran to hug him.

Charles chuckled and picked up William. "Hey, what's going on? I got something for you guys." He took a bag from the front seat of his car.

He reached for Nadine's hand and said, "Come on, let's go inside."

She hesitated but took his hand. They settled in a booth and a waitress came to take their drink orders. Then Charles reached inside the bag and pulled out a red truck and handed it to William who smiled big and said, "Look what I got!"

Charles said, "Huh—you like it?! Whadaya say?"

"Thank you, Daddy."

Charles winked. "Now, let's see what's in the bag for Carolyn. Hmmm, I don't think I have anything for you."

"Yes, you do, Daddy." She propped herself up on her knees and stretched across the table and said, "Okay, let me see the bag."

"Why? You don't believe me?"

"No."

"Okay, close your eyes and hold out your hands." He reached into the bag, pulled out something and put it in her hands. "Alright, open them."

It was a book of paper dolls. "I knew you had something for me! Look, Mama!"

"Oh, it's nice."

"Now, what did you bring Mama?" Carolyn asked.

"What did I bring Mama? Nothing."

"Yes, you did."

He turned the bag upside down. "Look, the bag's empty. But, let's see what's in my pocket." Nadine was watching carefully, and he was soon reaching for her hand and saying, "I do have something for you." He slipped a ring on her finger.

Her eyes stretched wide as her lips slowly parted. Charles kissed her hand.

She smiled. "It's my wedding ring. Thank you."

Not long after the waitress took their order, she brought to the table a large pepperoni pizza fresh from the oven. Charles put two slices on Nadine's plate.

She said, "That's enough."

"You could stand to eat more. You're all skin and bones. I don't like that."

"I eat."

"Oh, yeah? Well eat this." He put another slice on her plate.

Nadine didn't argue. She said, "So I thought you had something important to talk about."

"Yeah. Do you remember Nate and his girlfriend? Harriet? I think they're married now."

"Sure."

"Well, I ran into old Nate several days ago, right? He's driving trucks now for this warehouse over in Clarksville. They live there now, too. So, the warehouse is hiring and it's good money."

"You want to drive trucks?"

"It's good money. I'm ready to get away from all the grease and mess at the garage. Besides, we need a change."

"We?"

"Don't start, Nadine. We're family, so where I go, you and my kids go. If I get this job, I'll be on the road a lot. Eventually, I'm gonna want to be closer to the warehouse." "In Clarksville?" She frowned.

"Yeah. Mom will be glad to help you with the kids."

Nadine looked away. Living near his mom was the last thing she wanted.

As they were leaving, Charles walked them to the car. Now Nadine had more to think about than just returning to Charles. She had to think about leaving Kentucky and living near Charles's parents.

Soon after, that time rolled around for the Pow Wow at the Trail of Tears. Each year Nadine's father, Sam, took the whole family to the event. There was horseback riding and many other activities. Usually, Charles wouldn't go with them.

This time, on this date, Charles showed up to take Nadine and the kids somewhere for ice cream. It was upsetting to her family to see them go, but they could not keep her from going. At the small ice cream parlor downtown, he played with the kids and made jokes with Nadine. She hadn't laughed like this with him in a long time.

As they headed to the car Charles playfully wobbled against Nadine and said, "You enjoyed yourself today, didn't you?" He smiled.

"Yes, I did."

A brief memory crossed her mind, of when they first started dating. There used to be lots of playful moments.

The children were skipping and playing on their way to the car. Charles said, "You know, Nadine, you can't keep denying me my family. They're my kids too."

"I know." She looked down at the ground and rubbed her foot back and forth in the dirt. Charles was standing close in front of her. He lifted her chin and gave her a couple of pecks on the lips which almost led to an intimate kiss, but she pulled away. He whispered, "Come home, Nadine." Then he pulled her closer. "You know you want to."

If she looked in his eyes, the tears she was holding back would fall, so she kept her gaze down and said, "I've got to go."

He stepped back. "Okay—okay! Well, I'll call you."

The next day, Nadine anticipated his call. By nightfall, she still hadn't heard from him. When morning came around again, she left the kids with her mom while she drove out to the garage. Charles had taken the entire week off. She used the payphone on the side of the garage to call Phyllis.

"Oh, he's been studying hard for his CDLs. Passed the test today," Phyllis said.

"Wonder why he didn't call to tell me the news?"

"Maybe 'cause you haven't been much of a wife lately."

Nadine sighed heavily and hung up, mumbling, "How I hate that woman!"

On the other end of the line Phyllis said, "Hello?" She slammed the receiver down and said under her breath, "Crazy girl!"

By Thursday, Nadine still hadn't heard from Charles. She lay in bed thinking about the battered woman's group and decided to get dressed and go.

Janice spotted her and cried out, "Nadine, you came!"

"I wanted to see what the group was about."

"Oh, I'm so glad. Give me a moment and I'll walk you down."

The meeting room was on the other side of the nurse's station towards the end of the hall. As they proceeded, Nadine said, "Janice, umm, well I want you to know I'm thinking about going back."

Janice stopped. "To your husband?" Nadine nodded yes and Janice added, "Why would you do that?"

"I still love him. The kids need him. I think he needs them!"

"I don't know what to say. But I think you don't know what you need."

They stepped inside the room and found Tracy, the group's leader. Janice introduced Nadine, then left.

"It's nice to meet you, Nadine. Come, let me introduce you to some others."

Nadine followed Tracy over to the refreshment table where the women were congregated. Tracy introduced her to each individual. Nadine then busied herself fixing a cup of coffee. She grabbed a donut and quietly took a chair beside a woman she had not met. The woman was dressed in a long sleeve shirt, a long skirt, and a floppy wide-brim hat that hid her face.

"Hi, I'm Nadine."

"Denise," the woman said without looking up.

Nadine tilted her head, trying to see Denise's face. "Are you okay?"

"I'll be fine."

"Is this your first time here?" Denise nodded yes and Nadine added, "Me too."

The meeting was about to begin. There were fourteen women seated in a circle.

Wanda introduced herself first. "I've been married fifteen years and I have a twelve-year-old daughter. I'm here because..." She cleared her throat. "Um, because...because I can't seem to do anything right. He criticizes everything I do. He constantly calls me names, makes fat jokes—and embarrasses and humiliates me in public. It's hard to lose weight, you know?"

Tracy, the group leader, asked, "Has he ever hit you?"

She whispered, "Many times." She pulled in a deep breath. "I'm not a fighter, you know? But I've called the police a few times. They never do much. By the time they get there, he's calm. They always ask me if I have somewhere to go or if I want to press charges."

Tracy asked, "Have you ever pressed charges?"

"No."

One of the women exclaimed, "Then why call the police?!"

"It makes him stop hurting me at the time. He seems to respect the police."

The woman who had been sitting beside Nadine with her head down spoke. "The police never helped me." She lifted her head and revealed her face. Her left eye was bruised and her cheek red and swollen. The right side of her lip was swollen with dried blood scabbed over in the corner of her mouth. Gasps and other reactions came from everyone.

Tracy squatted in front of her. "When did this happen?"

"Last night."

Tracy took the woman's hands. The woman's tears and words sparked emotions in everyone, including Nadine. A man wearing a name tag that read Frank walked over with a Kleenex. Denise looked up at him and frowned.

"It's okay," Tracy assured her. "Frank is a member of our group."

Another voice asked, "A member?"

"Yes. Men can be victims too. Physical abuse is not the only type of abuse, although men aren't beyond it either." She spoke again to Denise, asking if she had called the police.

"Yes, but I left before they got there." "What

happened?" another asked.

"I had a headache, so I took a little medicine and laid down. My husband called but I didn't hear the phone ring. I fell asleep. I woke up when I heard him come in. Before I could say anything, even 'Hi,' he had me by my neck and started punching me in my face. I kept saying 'What did I do wrong?' but he wouldn't answer me. He just kept pounding me and throwing me up against the wall."

She started coughing to clear her throat. Another member brought her something to drink. After taking a sip, she continued. "He said the next time he called, I damn well had better answer the phone. When he left the room, I crawled over to the phone and called the police, but they asked too many questions—I didn't have time to answer. I heard him coming and hung up. He demanded to know who I was calling. I managed to get away and run out the backdoor. I ran into a cemetery and hid." Tears were running down her cheeks. "I slept there all night, 'cause I had no place to go."

Tracy pulled a chair close to Denise and put her arm around her. "It's okay. We're here for you. Do you need to see a doctor?" "No, I don't think so. But I might be pregnant and if I am, I won't keep it. I don't even have a place for me to go, let alone a baby."

"We'll find you some place. There are shelters for battered women," Tracy said.

"No!" Denise snapped. "I ain't gonna stay in no shelter like some homeless person on the street. No, I can't do it."

Another voice in the circle said, "But you can sleep in a cemetery?"

Tracy asked, "What about family?"

"What little family I have—they're in Texas. I can't go back there, 'cause he would find me. Besides, my mom has five other children to take care of. She ain't gonna want to take care of a grown woman and a baby."

"When was the last time you talked to your mom?" Tracy asked.

"Four years ago. When I left home. I was seventeen and I quit school to run away. Every time I looked; my mom was pregnant. I couldn't take staying there helping her raise all those babies. I ran off with my husband."

Now Frank spoke up. "So, you do have somewhere to go. It has to be better than staying with him. I don't understand."

An indignant voice chimed in. "I don't understand why you're here. What man let's a woman beat up on him?"

"Now, see that's where you're wrong. I could ask what woman lets a man beat her. I love my wife and I don't want to leave her because I feel sorry for her. She's an addict and doesn't respond to my help. We have two kids. I try to keep them from seeing their mom strung out, but it's hard. She hits, throws things, yells, screams, calls us names. I endure a lot of verbal abuse from her. She tells me I mistreat her 'cause I won't give her money to go buy sanitary napkins and things she needs, but I can't, because she won't go buy them. So I have to buy them for her. It's crazy!"

Another voice. "Why not take the kids and leave?"

"I've thought about it, but I can't. So, I go to NA meetings. And I come here to learn how to deal with her. I pray for her every night. I really do love my wife," he said, hanging his head.

Nadine spoke in a quiet voice. "Love is a trap. It's powerful. People don't understand how you can love someone who hurts you. I don't even understand it myself. After awhile, you just feel powerless. You feel like you're under some sort of spell."

Tracy moved closer to Nadine. "Why are you here, Nadine? What do you want to do?"

"I don't know. I've been with my parents for a little while, but, I really want to go home."

She glanced around at the faces of the others. They all had perplexed expressions on their faces. She got to her feet, said "Excuse me," and left the room.

Tracy followed. "Wait!" she called. "Please, don't go. We're here for you too, Nadine. Everyone in that room understands—without judgment—what you're going through."

Nadine turned and moaned, "Did you see the look on their faces?!"

Tracy took her by the arm and pulled her aside. "Nadine, you have no reason to be ashamed. Each and every person here is going through or has gone through some form of abuse—including me."

"You?"

"Yes, me. My ex-husband almost killed me six years ago. He shot me twice."

Nadine put her hand over her mouth. "Oh, my God."

"Yeah, I didn't think I was gonna live. I have been volunteering my time to this group for three years. This group has helped victims gain confidence, independence, self-esteem and protection. We have made a contribution in helping victims get out of their violent situations. Women like Denise come to me every week."

"I feel so bad for her."

"Do you think you're any different?"

Nadine moved over to a window and wrapped her arms around herself, rubbing her shoulders. She said, "He still loves me. Sometimes he can be a good man. Those are the times I try to hang on to. But when he starts drinking…"

"Nadine, alcohol is no excuse. Abusive men who drink are just as likely to be abusive when they're sober. Substance abuse is just used as an excuse. If you're honest with yourself, you will admit he's been violent towards you when he was sober."

Nadine knew she was right. "Thank you, Tracy, but I really need to go. I left my son with my mom."

"Ok but let me just say this. Almost all the time when a woman leaves and goes back, the stakes are higher. And when you finally decide to leave, I mean *really decide to leave*, it could be too late. I lost a very close friend that way. He stalked her and killed her. So, believe me, it's best to stay out while you're out."

"Charles is not a killer. I don't know why people keep saying that to me."

"Nadine, you've been talking to him, right? And you're still in town. He doesn't feel like he's really lost you yet—but if you ever leave and make no contact with him whatsoever, he'll find you. And he will kill you."

"That's a terrible thing to say."

"I'm sorry to be so candid, but this I know."

Nadine cried all the way home. She was relieved to see no one was there when she arrived. She cupped her hands over the bathroom sink and doused her face with cold water, and quickly dried her face and hands when she heard someone at the front door.

"What are you doing here?"

"Is that how you greet your mother-in-law?"

"I'm sorry. Of course not. Come in."

"That's better. Anyone else here?" Phyllis peeped around before entering.

"No. Why?"

"I have something for you." She appeared to inspect the loveseat for its cleanliness before she sat down.

Nadine took a seat on the couch across from her and asked, "Ok, what is it?"

"You know you're awfully rude—not to mention, you hung up on me the other day. Anyway, Charles asked me to bring you this." She reached in her purse and pulled out an envelope, placed it on the coffee table and slid it towards Nadine.

"What is this?"

"Money. Seeing as how you're not working and staying here with your family – you probably need it."

"Why didn't he give it to me himself?"

"He's been working. Nadine, it's not right for a man to be separated from his family. So, why don't you and the children just go home? How long are you gonna keep this up?"

Nadine looked at her vaguely, shaking her head. "What about his drinking?"

"Oh, he stopped drinking, Nadine. Didn't he tell you? He stopped. He's been going to AA. Look, marriage is about the ups and downs. You know, for better or for worse?"

"Why does it always seem to be for worse?"

"No marriage is perfect, not even mine."

"Really?"

Phyllis sensed Nadine's sarcasm. "Don't be cute. We've been together for twenty years. Yes, we have ups and downs, but we're still together. That's the point. Besides, you can't run home every time something goes wrong, little girl."

Nadine closed her eyes and tightened her lips. "So…do you think it's okay if he beats me?"

"Whatever the problem is, you can't very well work on it separated, now can you? Charles is no saint, but he's a hardworking man and a good provider. You've spent some time with him lately. Don't you know he's changed? Personally, I feel he deserves the best. Maybe you're not the best."

"You know, I always knew you never liked me."

"Look, you claim to be a Christian. The Bible says God hates a divorce?"

"Please, don't do that to me. Don't try to lay guilt on me, quoting the Bible to me like I'm the bad guy here. You're the hypocrite! I'm a good wife!"

Phyllis squinted her eyes. "You lower your voice when you speak to me."

Nadine glanced beyond Phyllis, out the window behind her. Martha was home and wouldn't be too happy about finding Phyllis in her house. The door swung open.

"You! I thought that was your raggedy car in my yard." Martha helped William in and closed the door behind her. He ran over and gave Phyllis a hug as she picked him up.

"How's my big boy?" She ignored Martha.

"Nadine, why is this woman in my house?"

"She came to bring me some money from Charles."

"I've got grocery bags in the car, Nadine. And this witch is not welcome here. You got some nerve!"

Phyllis put William down and quietly stood up. "Well, I best be on my way. Give Carolyn a kiss for me, will you?" She walked around Martha and out the door.

Martha stomped out behind her, and Nadine came out to help carry in the bags. When Phyllis's car disappeared around the curve she said between her teeth, "So, what did the hussy really want? You know I can't stand her and her uppity attitude."

"She just brought me some money."

"How much?"

"I don't know. I never opened the envelope."

"Guilt money is all it is. You should have given it back."

When they were in the kitchen Nadine said, "Mama, I'm still thinking of going back. Charles has been trying."

Martha took the vegetables from the bag and placed them in the sink. "What did she say to you?"

"It's nothing she said."

Martha washed off the cucumbers and began slicing them. She stopped and slammed her fist on the counter, startling Nadine. "Darn it, Nadine, what is going on with you?"

"I don't know what you mean." Her voice sounded childlike.

Her mother's eyes blazed. "You think things are going to be better?"

"Deep down he's a good man, Mama. I just want things to be normal again."

"A life with Charles will never be normal, Nadine. It ain't never gonna be normal for a man to treat his wife this way. You're a beautiful woman, a good mother and wife. He doesn't deserve you—and I didn't raise you to be nobody's punching bag!"

"I have to give my marriage another chance."

"Says who? His evil mammy?"

"Wouldn't you give Daddy another chance?"

"If he put me in the hospital? Hell no! Your daddy has talked his share of junk to me, but not put his hands on me. I don't know where you get this stuff, Nadine. You didn't get it from us. You should be more like your sister. If it wasn't for you and those kids, your dad would have been put Charles out of his misery."

Nadine didn't say a word. She cut a hotdog into small pieces for William and watched him eat. When he was finished, Martha got a napkin and wiped his hands. "You know, like any parent, I don't want to see you hurt. That's why I say these things."

Nadine took William by the hand and went to her room. She opened the envelope. It contained two hundred dollars and a note.

"Nadine,

Find a babysitter and get yourself something pretty to wear. We're going out on the town Saturday. Meet me at the Chandelier at seven. We have a lot to celebrate.

Love you,

Charles."

On Saturday, Nadine prepared for her date with Charles. She got ready at Claudette's house. Claudette did Nadine's hair and make-up.

"You look so beautiful, Nadine. I hope he sees what a jewel you are tonight."

"Thank you for helping me."

"Just like in the beginning. Nadine, if anything should happen to you, I would feel responsible."

"Nothing is gonna happen. I'll be fine."

"You call me if you need to. You call the police if you need to."

"We'll be in a public place."

"Oh, that don't mean nothing."

"I'll be fine. I don't want to be late."

Nadine stepped inside the restaurant, taking a glimpse around for Charles. A voice said, "You must be Mrs. Hunter."

She swirled around. "Excuse me?"

"Mrs. Hunter, right?"

"Yes, how did you know?"

"Your husband described you perfectly. You are stunning."

She wore a long black evening gown with one shoulder showing – the other side a flower-applique strap. The gown draped her figure and flowed asymmetrically just above the top of her strappy sandals.

The same voice said, "Please, let me show you to your table where your husband is waiting."

Nadine took in a deep breath as she gracefully followed the host through the restaurant. Charles stood up when he saw her. To

Nadine's eyes he looked handsome standing there in a navy blue suit with a fleur-de-lis red tie. He pulled out a chair for her.

She murmured, "Thank you."

He sat across from her and ordered the best wine. She spread the cloth napkin in her lap. She looked up and caught his dark eyes fixed on her. "Is something wrong?"

"No. You look great tonight, baby."

"Thank you. You do too. So, what's the big news?"

"Hold on, now. First, how are the kids?"

"They're doing fine. Keeping me busy as usual." She opened the menu.

"You're about to be a little busier, baby." He paused while the waiter poured the wine, then took their orders. "So, I got the job at the warehouse. And I have to drive out of town occasionally. The money would be better than at the garage." He took a sip of wine. "But, the best part of my news, baby, is this house. I know you're gonna love it. It belonged to Nate's mother, who had a stroke. She's in a nursing home now, but, well, Nate agreed to rent the house to me!" He smiled big.

Nadine smiled slightly and took a sip of the wine.

"It's a two-story yellow farmhouse with three bedrooms, two and a half bathrooms, and a large kitchen you're gonna love."

Nadine politely listened, not wanting to interrupt his excitement.

"Two and a half acres surrounded by a wooden fence, and a barn in the backyard. I'm telling you, baby, this is the perfect place to raise the kids."

His voice blended in with the background noise. She zoned out, thinking of how miserable she would be living in Clarksville— near

Phyllis, who would probably be popping over every chance she got.

"So, I thought we could go see it next weekend, then I can let Nate know what you think—and we can go from there. Are you listening to me?"

"Yes, yes, of course. Umm, how soon are you trying to move?"

"Soon, baby. Real soon. I don't plan on driving back and forth to Clarksville every day."

When the food arrived, Nadine began eating but Charles did not. He watched her for a moment. She heard him take in a deep breath while she stuffed her face.

He picked up his knife and fork and said, "So, what's going on in that pretty little head of yours, Nadine? You haven't said two words about what I've been saying."

"I - I really don't know what to say. I mean, well—it's a lot to think about."

"Think about? What's there to think about? I've already thought it out."

Nadine took another sip of the wine. Over the rim of her glass she glanced at Charles, then put another bite of food in her mouth. She chewed for a bit then said, "We're not even together." "Oh, that's about to change," he said as he picked up his wine glass. He turned it up and emptied it.

"I thought you quit drinking."

"It's just wine."

Nadine felt a quiver inside and tried to control the tremor of her hand while bringing the fork to her mouth. Had he really quit drinking?

When they left the restaurant, they took a drive down to the lake in Charles's car. Nadine slid over and moved into his embrace.

"A nice home, nice family life—and whatever you desire, baby. Yeah, things are gonna be different for us now. I just want y'all to have the best, you know?"

She forced a smile. "It all sounds real good, Charles."

He could see the somber look on her face. He kissed her on the top of her head and whispered, "I want my family back. You hear me?"

Nadine slowly nodded her head. She did want to believe things were going to be different.

Claudette was waiting up and the kids were sleeping. "I was worried sick about you, Nadine. What happened?"

Nadine took off her sweater and shoes, plopped on the couch and told her everything.

"You can't move to Clarksville, Nadine. Please tell me you said no."

"I can't Claudette," she sighed.

"Oh my God, Nadine."

"He's my husband and the children's father. I just miss being in my own home. I just feel so displaced."

"How? You're with family. People who love you. You grew up in this family. We share the same blood. How can you possibly feel displaced?"

"I can't explain it. I just know I still love him, and I have to do whatever I have to do to make my marriage work."

"Well, it won't work."

"You don't know that."

"Yes, I do. And deep inside you know it too. Did he threaten you? Your family? Did he threaten to take the kids? Did he make a lot of promises?"

"No, no, none of that. Charles is not gonna just let me walk out of his life and with the kids so easily."

"Trust me, nothing is gonna be different. It won't last, Nadine. Shortly after you go back, you'll be nursing your wounds again."

"Stop it!"

"Come on, Nadine. You deserve better."

Nadine curled up in a fetal position on the couch. She didn't want to talk about it anymore. She closed her eyes and didn't say anything else. Claudette watched her for a moment. The thought of Nadine returning to Charles created a sick feeling deep in her stomach. Claudette got up from the chair and stomped off to her room, not knowing what more she could say.

FIVE

Going Back

Today was the day. Charles would be picking up Nadine and the kids, and after the church carnival they would go see the house.

"I've got to hurry down to the craft store and get some more colors," Nadine said.

"Well, take a look at this first." Claudette reached in a bag and pulled out a blue and white one-piece bathing suit. "What do you think?"

"Nice. What's the occasion?"

"I'm gonna work with Henry at the dunkin' booth."

Nadine giggled. "Are you serious? You're really gonna get dunked in the water?"

Claudette rolled her eyes. "Yes, I am. I've got to be crazy, right?"

"No, I think it's great!"

Carolyn chimed in. "Well, I think it's funny, Aunt Claudette. And I can't wait to dunk you!"

Claudette tapped the top of her nose. "I bet you can't."

Right after breakfast they all went their way. Martha and Sam headed straight to the church to set up their table for the pies

Martha baked. The year before she sold out, so this year she baked fifteen more.

The church grounds soon began to get crowded. Many attendees were trying their luck at winning prizes at various booths. The smell of many kinds of food in the air from the concession stands was enough to make everyone hungry. William and Carolyn stood patiently in line for a funnel cake. Nearby, there was cotton candy. The lights, the music, and the screams of people on the rides were all exciting and merry.

Sam cleaned William's sticky hands and took him over to the dunking booth. He put the ball in his grandson's hand and showed him how to make his Aunt Claudette fall in the water. Across from the table where her mother was selling pies, Nadine was enjoying all the little children who wanted their faces painted. It reminded her of when she worked at the church daycare.

Some hours later Martha had sold all her pies and Nadine was looking at her watch and scanning the grounds for Carolyn and William. There they were! Her dad had them on a ride. As soon as they got off, she insisted, "The kids and I need to leave—we're meeting Charles!"

Her dad said, "Yeah, yeah, I heard. I'm not happy, but you gonna do what you gonna do anyway."

She took the kids by their hands and headed for her mother and sister. Their looks of disapproval were stinging to her, but deep in her heart she felt like she would never know if Charles had really changed unless she went back to him.

When they pulled up at the house, Charles was waiting in the car. That was just as well for Nadine, for she had not been in the house since he dragged her out and was not sure she was ready to go back in.

The ride to Clarksville was somewhat quiet. Charles told the kids about the house they were going to see. Nadine had already heard most of it and would have preferred listening to music on the radio. They rode a good while before Charles turned down a long dirt driveway lined with tall Bradford pear trees. Up ahead stood a yellow two-story house with a wraparound porch.

The wooden fence around the yard needed a paint job and a few repairs. Nadine also noticed that some shrubs in the yard needed trimming and the flowerbeds were unkempt. It appeared obvious that no one had maintained the grounds for some time.

As they climbed out of the car Nate waved from the front porch and called, "Hey, come on in." Nadine noticed a woman stood behind him.

The children immediately raced to a tire swing suspended from a rope on a big oak. Nadine yelled, "Carolyn, William, no! You'll get hurt."

Charles said, "Now, Nadine, let the kids play."

Nate chuckled. "That old tire's been there a long time—I guess it's still safe. My daddy first put it there when I was a boy."

Charles and Nadine exchanged handshakes with Nate and Harriet on the porch. Nadine glanced around. "Wow!" she said. "This is a big house!" As they turned to enter, Nadine called the children to come along.

In the small foyer was the stairway at left with a closet behind it and a half bath to the right. The kitchen was large and country style—lots of cabinets and counter space wrapping the walls and the stove on an island in the middle. Nadine smiled as she looked into the backyard through the windows over the sink.

The laundry room was handy, just off the kitchen, with a washer and dryer and a pantry. The dining room was graced by a bay window, and both the living room and den had a fireplace.

Nate's wife Harriet was following along too. She said to Nadine, "So, what do you think so far?"

"It's beautiful."

The men observed this interchange and Nate trumpeted, "Well, let's go upstairs!"

Again, Nadine was much impressed: a master bedroom with walk-in closet and bathroom, and two other bedrooms. The bathroom at the end of the hall had a tile floor and tile halfway up the walls.

Back downstairs, they passed through the screened back porch where there were rocking chairs and began a tour of the backyard. Nadine smiled at the sight of a garden space and a clothesline. These were things she had grown up with.

Charles noticed her smile and reached over and took her hand. "I knew you would like it, baby."

Nate was saying, "Now right over here, we used to have a couple of horses. When my dad was alive, there were other animals too. Yeah, my daddy loved to farm!"

A storage room in the barn held tools and Nate told Charles he was welcome to use whatever he needed. The men soon agreed Charles would do some of the repairs needed in exchange for rent for the first three months.

Charles appeared as happy as Nadine had ever seen him. He met her eyes and said, "So…whadaya think, baby? You like it?" "Yes, I do."

"Well, alright!" Nate reached out to shake Charles's hand. "Follow us on over to our house and we'll get some signatures on paper. Harriet fixed food for y'all."

Nadine automatically crooned, "Oh, Harriet, you shouldn't have gone to that trouble."

"No, no – no trouble, girl. I'm used to whipping something up right quick." Both women laughed.

In the following two weeks, Nadine and Charles spent a lot of time preparing for the big move. He took her shopping for the house and surprised her as he said, "You can buy anything you like, baby."

She grinned. "Anything?"

"Hey, as long as we're a family again, anything you want."

Nadine hadn't heard those words in years. That was the man she married—the man she so desperately wanted to get back.

She agreed to go back to the other house to help with packing. He had not kept it as clean as she would have liked, and she did muse how it seemed rather strange that he always insisted she keep it spotless. There were dishes in the sink, dirty clothes on the bathroom floor, and newspapers scattered about alongside full ashtrays in the living room.

"Sorry," he said. "Didn't have time to clean up."

She forced a slight smile and without a word began picking up the newspapers and dumping the ashtrays. She couldn't help remembering how *not having time* had always been an excuse that did not go over well with him. With two kids, there had been days when she really did not have time to keep the house spic and span. Some days she could barely get dinner on the table in time, but it all was behind her now—or so she was determined to believe. Charles was a different man now.

Claudette came over and helped Nadine with packing and cleaning. If they left the house in good shape, the deposit would be returned. "Nadine, I remember when you first moved in this house."

"Yep. Charles was in Vietnam. It was just me and Carolyn then."

"Are you sure you want to move?"

"Oh, Claudette, we've been over this before. You know I'm trying to work out my marriage."

"I know, I know. I just believe in the saying a leopard never changes his spots. But I guess sometimes you have to see things for yourself."

"You know the worst part about this move to me right now? Living close to his mama."

"Yes! You should have turned away and let me snatch that bun off the top of her head at the hospital."

"It's her real hair, Claudette."

"So?!"

They laughed and Claudette said, "Don't be afraid to stand up to that old bat, Nadine." "I won't."

Once the move was finished, Nadine began right away making curtains and matching bed attire for all the bedrooms. She took her time, focusing on one room at a time. For the first few months in the house, everything seemed like it should. Seemed normal.

While Charles was busy working, she stayed busy fixing up the place to meet his approval. Occasionally he traveled out of town, making deliveries as far as Georgia. When he was away, Phyllis would come over to help despite the fact that Nadine did not need nor want her help – not even a visit from her.

"Nadine, this house is beautiful. I hope you appreciate what my son has done for you and these children. He's been working hard, you know?"

"Yes, I'm well aware." Nadine was up on the ladder putting a nail in the wall. When Phyllis turned away, Nadine held the hammer back as if she was about to hit Phyllis right on the top of her head. Phyllis turned and caught sight of the motion. Nadine pulled back and smirked. "Would you pass me the picture on the chair, please?"

Phyllis frowned. She seemed to be wondering if Nadine had something else in mind besides hitting the nail with that hammer. "I think I'm gonna go, Nadine. I've been here long enough."

Nadine whispered under her breath. "Thank God!"

"What was that?"

"Thank you. I appreciate your help."

"Well, no need to come down off the ladder. I'll see myself out."

Nadine listened to the door close behind her mother-in-law and realized just how much she hated being so far from her folks— especially from Claudette.

On his road trips Charles gradually began drinking again. He hadn't been to an AA meeting in months. He had gone a bit, while trying to convince Nadine to come back. Even then he had parked his truck in the parking lot of what was known as Hole in the Wall, a small joint where he could drink and converse without being noticed.

At one of his pit stops, a large-breasted woman wearing a long wig, red mini-dress and platform heels settled on a seat beside him at the bar. She turned his way and said, "Light me up."

Charles looked up from his drinking. She fluttered her fake eyelashes and held up a slim Kool between her fingers. Her nails were coated in red polish. She was not the most attractive woman in the face, but Charles did like what the dress was doing to her body.

"Sure." He pulled a lighter from his pocket. When he was ready to leave, she wrote her number on the back of a napkin. "It's been real, man. Next time you're looking for some conversation, call me." Charles stuffed the napkin in his pocket.

Some days later, Nadine was washing clothes and found it. She said not a word but put it in her apron pocket. All day she wondered who this woman was. She did not know anyone named Cheryl. She thought about how to confront Charles. Or if she even should. Things were going so well. She didn't want to rock the boat.

That night, after the children were settled in their beds, she got in the shower. Charles came in to use the toilet. He glanced down on the floor where Nadine had stepped out of her clothes and noticed the corner of the napkin peeking out of her apron. He reached down and picked it up.

"Are you still in here, Charles?" she asked from behind the curtain.

He put the napkin in his pocket. "Yeah, I'm going to the barn."

By then Charles had made the barn into a clubhouse for him and his friends—with a pool table, stereo, and a locked refrigerator full of beer and liquor. This was his way of hiding his drinking from Nadine. After several drinks, he returned to the house and got ready for bed. He propped a pillow up behind his back, stretched out his legs and crossed them at the ankles. Nadine was in bed too, watching the news.

He held up the napkin. "Where did you get this?"

She turned towards him and froze. When she could speak, she muttered, "I was washing clothes and found it in your pocket."

"What were you gonna do with it?"

"Nothing."

"Why would you keep it?"

She stared at him in silence as the tone of his voice almost stopped her heart. Her chest felt tight and her palms sweaty. Her tongue thickened. She couldn't speak.

"What were you gonna do with it, Nadine?"

She managed to push one word through her lips. "Nothing."

He sat straight up, glaring at her. "Don't lie to me!"

"I was—I was thinking of asking you about it, that's all. But I changed my mind."

"That's all? What makes you think I know her? Maybe I borrowed this from someone."

"Charles, you're on the road often. I don't know what goes on out there."

"So, you assume I'm screwing around? Is that it?"

"I didn't say that."

"But you were thinking it—weren't you? Well, I ain't gonna lie, she was definitely a fox. She might even be better in bed than you, I don't know yet." He slid closer to Nadine. "You don't check me. Do you understand? I pay all the bills. I'm the reason why you live in this nice house. You don't contribute nothing around here—so don't you ever question what I do, you hear?"

She promised Claudette she would be strong and not allow Charles to bully her. She would do so even if it meant making him angrier. She would take it.

"I'm your wife, Charles." She swallowed hard. "I'm not your child. If you're seeing someone else, I have a right to know."

He gripped her arm. "You don't have any rights, not in this house! I say what rights you have! I make the rules! You understand?"

Nadine snatched her arm away. "I'm not your child."

He leaped off the bed and over to the chair where he'd left his pants and began pulling his belt from the loops.

Nadine stood up. "What are you doing?"

"You said you're not my child, right? You think I treat you like a child? You wanna see what it's like to be treated like a child?" He wrapped the belt twice about his hand. Nadine jumped across the bed and ran for the door—but he got there first. She ran into the bathroom.

He forced his way in before she could lock the door. "You can run, but you can't get away." "Please," she cried.

He raised the belt in the air and brought it down across her bare shoulder. She tried to shield the lashes with her hands, letting out a soft whimper with each lash, trying not to scream for fear of waking the children. But Charles was not letting up. She tried unsuccessfully to grab the belt. His swings were swift and hard.

She backed away, wedging between the toilet and tub. With him in front of her she had nowhere to go, so she squatted there, tucking her chin against her chest and pressing her forehead into her knees. She covered her head with her arms. Lost in her pain, she blocked out his ranting and cussing.

Finally, he did stop. He threw the belt on the floor and knelt in front of her. "See what it's like to be treated like a child? So, don't you ever, ever question my business again! And if you think about taking my kids and leaving again, you better think twice— because there is nowhere you can go I won't find you. I will even go through your old man to get to you next time. You hear? I will kill you." He grabbed her arm. "Now get up!"

When he left, Nadine dragged herself over to the sink, turned on the faucet and began splashing water on her face to wash away the tears, but they kept coming. The voices of everyone who told her he would kill her spun around in her head. And his too: *I will kill you, I will kill you, I will kill you.*

She looked in the mirror and shook her head at the belt whelps on her shoulders, arms and hands. Her gown was bloody. Turning her shoulder forward, she got a good look at the belt marks—and knew there were more under her gown.

Charles appeared in the doorway. "You need to come to bed."

His eyes followed her as she walked past him. He got a good look at the injuries he'd inflicted on her. She lay on the bed and pulled the covers up to her waist, her back to him. He came with peroxide and cotton balls. She flinched, closing her eyes tightly at his touch.

He whispered, "I'm not gonna hurt you." Very gently, he cleansed her wounds.

Nadine waited to hear an apology, but he never apologized. Maybe this was his way of doing so. He promised he would never hurt her again. He said he was a changed man.

Afterwards, he turned off the lamp and spooned close to her with his arm around her waist. Tears silently damped her pillow. She could never bear the embarrassment and shame of telling anyone about what had happened here tonight. She did not want to hear, *I told you so*. Besides, she felt like tonight was her fault.

That napkin should have been thrown away.

SIX

I Will Kill You

Summertime in the country was so tranquil. Charles and Nadine enjoyed a new and refreshing feeling with the atmosphere of their new home. This time the honeymoon phase seemed to last longer. Together they worked on repairs in the house and outdoors. Nadine enjoyed working in the yard. She planted flowers and grew vegetables.

On this particular day, she proudly made a salad using the vegetables from her garden. Charles cooked steaks on the grill. When Nadine removed the potatoes from the oven, she went over to help her daughter set the table.

Soon thereafter Charles was exclaiming through a mouthful of food, "Mmm! This is good, baby. You grew this?"

Her smile almost covered her face. "Yes, I did."

"Well, you kids eat up. Show your mama how much you appreciate the hard work of her hands."

Nadine included cucumbers, green peppers, tomatoes, squash, and onions in the salad. Charles watched William pick the onions out.

"Young man, you better not leave the table until you've eaten everything."

The boy whined, "But I don't like onions, Daddy."

Charles jabbed his fork into a piece of meat. "You heard what I said. Leave this table without cleaning your plate if you want to and I will tear your hide."

Nadine never interfered when Charles disciplined the children. She was raised, as Charles was, to respect the father's role as head of the family. She cleared the table and started washing dishes. William sat alone, staring down at the onions on his plate as if his hard look would make them disappear.

A few minutes later Charles returned to the kitchen. "You still sitting there? Guess you'll be there all night. I tell you what," he said as he took off his belt, "you got thirty more minutes. If you haven't eaten those onions by then, I'm whipping your butt."

Nadine kept washing dishes. After Charles walked out, she turned to her son and begged him. "Please, William. Eat the onions, baby, for Mama." But he wouldn't do it.

After Nadine left the kitchen Carolyn tiptoed in, making sure not to be seen. She reached across the table and put the onions in her mouth. Her brother observed her with his mouth slightly parted and his little eyes stretched as wide as they would stretch.

Carolyn said, "Shhh…I'm trying to keep you from getting a whipping. Don't tell anyone, you hear?"

He nodded his head and she scooted out of the kitchen without being noticed. William did not move. He looked down at the empty plate. When time was up, Charles returned once again. "See, it wasn't so bad, now was it?"

"No sir."

Charles patted him on the head. "Okay, you can get ready for bed."

Nadine helped William get bathed and dressed for bed. She peeped in Carolyn's room and smiled. "Good night, angel."

"Mama."

"Yes, baby?"

"Can I tell you something? It's a secret. You can't even tell Daddy. Promise?"

Nadine sat on the edge of the bed. "I promise.

"I ate Brother's onions."

"You did?"

"Yes, 'cause I didn't want him to get a whipping."

Nadine stroked the child's hair and kissed her cheek. "You're a good big sister, Carolyn."

And from then on, the fact remained a secret between the three.

The summer was going by fast. It came time again for the annual celebration of the Native American Pow Wow. Claudette invited Nadine and the kids to stay Friday night with her so they could all go together. Nadine walked into the den and calmly sat down. Charles was in the recliner watching television.

Without looking up he asked, "What's on your mind, Nadine?"

"Why do you ask?"

"'Cause I know you."

"Well, the Pow Wow is this weekend and…well, Claudette wants us to spend Friday night with her, so we can all go together. Can we go?"

"What time will you be back?"

"I'm not sure."

He looked directly at her. "You better be back before late Saturday. I mean it."

She smiled. "Of course."

Nadine's favorites at the Pow Wow were the crafts, especially the handmade jewelry. And the food. It felt good to get away from Clarksville and spend time with her own family. She had braided her hair in two braids, one on each side. Claudette took a lot of pictures.

As the day went on Nadine kept looking at her watch. Finally Claudette said, "Nadine, stop. We don't get to spend much time with you and the kids as it is – and I hate what he's doing to you."

She answered, "I just want to keep the peace."

When she and the children got back, they found Phyllis and Joe there. Charles looked up and said, "You were cutting it close, Nadine."

"It's not that late. Just eight o'clock."

Phyllis picked up William and said to the children, "Did you have a good time, babies?"

Nadine smiled big. "Oh, they had a great time!"

Phyllis said, "I wanted the kids to spend the night with me." She faced the boy in her arms and added, "I can make you some yummy pancakes in the morning with chocolate chips. Your daddy used to love that. What do you say—huh?"

Nadine said, "Well, it's time for me to give them a bath and get them ready for bed."

"Oh, please, I can bathe them at my house—and tomorrow I can take them to church. Carolyn, would you like to stay with Nana tonight? I got a great movie we can watch. And you can show me all the pretty little things you got at the Pow Wow."

"Ok, Nana."

"Then it's settled. Let's go get your things together. You too, William."

Nadine knew if she said anything else, the peace would be over between herself and her husband. Phyllis was going to win anyway—she always did when it came down to something like this.

Joe said, "So, Nadine, you guys had a good time, huh?"

"Yes, we did."

"I haven't been to one of those things in years. Ain't no Indian in my family though, so guess I don't have no cause in going. But taking the kids is a good thing—teaches them about their culture, right?"

Nadine wanted to say, *Shut up!* Instead, she forced a smile. "Yeah, it's good."

Joe rambled on. "They good people. Indians, that is. I don't have anything against them. I've had some try and cheat me though, but I'm too slick for them." His laugh blared throughout the house.

Then he said, "So, Nadine, listen to this. A driver, who was obviously drunk, was heading the wrong way down a one-way street. A cop pulled him over." Here Joe deepened his voice. *"Didn't you see the arrow, Mister?* The driver looked at him all confused and said, *An arrow? I never saw the Indians."*

Joe threw his head back and cackled and slapped his knee. His son laughed with him.

Joe was always cracking some corny joke about Native Americans in Nadine's presence, but she found no humor in them, no more than she felt he would find humor in listening to a white man crack Negro jokes.

She said, "Well, if you'll excuse me, I'm going upstairs to see if I can help with the kids."

Before long they had told the children goodbye. Nadine stepped back into the den and settled on the couch. Charles sat next to her and put his arm around her shoulder. "Let's go upstairs."

She picked up the remote. "I thought I'd sit here and watch a little TV first."

"That's why I don't like for you to go nowhere or be around your sister. Every time you go around your family, you come back with an attitude."

"I don't have an attitude, Charles. And you've been drinking."

He stood up and snatched the remote from her hand and threw it on the floor.

She gasped. "Why don't you just leave me alone?"

"Oh, I'm gonna leave you alone." He grabbed her by her shoulders and pulled her off the couch, took hold of her wrists and began leading her down the hall.

She resisted. "Stop it! What are you doing? Where are we going?"

Despite her resistance Charles kept pulling – dragging her along. "I'm putting you somewhere where you can be alone." He opened the closet door under the stairway.

She was crying, "No! No!" They struggled as Charles attempted to push her in the closet, and at last he succeeded. He closed the door and locked it with the key that hung on the outside. He yelled, "You wanted to be left alone, so you can stay down here and be alone!"

"No, please, no! Please! It's not what I meant." Nadine knocked and kicked on the door, begging to get out. Charles, winded from the struggle, settled on the floor with his back against the door.

He called out, "I know you been thinking about leaving me, Nadine. But I'm not gonna let you."

"No, Charles, I haven't—I promise. Please let me out. I'll go upstairs with you, ok?"

"Naw, you stay right here."

"Please." Her voice was calm. She was kneeling just inside the door. She could hear his breathing.

Charles stood up. He lingered for a moment before heading away. Nadine heard him climbing the stairs and banged on the door and begged. "Please come back and let me out! Charles! Please, Charles!"

Finally, she just sat on the floor and cried. Charles was soon upstairs and passed out across the bed.

The next day he awoke and stared at the ceiling, but soon headed down the stairs. Nadine heard his footsteps and roused herself from her curled position on the floor. She came to her feet and waited.

He opened the closet door and said, "Come on. We're going to church."

She slowly moved out of the closet and followed him upstairs, like a child. She got in the shower and let the water run over her. She soon slid down in the corner, weeping. The water kept running till it ran cold.

Charles had showered in the hallway bathroom and gone downstairs to prepare breakfast. A bit later he went back up the stairs and knocked on the bathroom door and entered. "Nadine, what are you doing?" He pulled back the shower curtain. "Why in the hell are you sitting in cold water?" "I don't know," she whispered.

"Come on. I've got breakfast waiting." He turned off the water, grabbed a towel and reached down to help her up and out of the tub. He dried her off, took her by the hand and led her into the bedroom. "What are you wearing?" "I can get it."

"Baby, you're standing around like you don't know what to do. Do I need to get you dressed too?"

"No, I can do it."

"Okay, hurry—before the eggs get too cold."

She dressed and went downstairs—as he had told her to do. He had fixed coffee, cheese eggs and toast. "It's not much," he said, "but it's breakfast. Sit down, Nadine…I have to tell you everything this morning."

He spread some jelly on toast for her and poured her coffee. After breakfast, Nadine lay down on the couch until time to leave for church. It sure felt a lot better than sleeping on the floor in the closet.

Their ride to church was quiet. Nadine didn't have much to say. She had been forced to spend the night in a closet. And she didn't like her mother-in-law's church, but Charles insisted they attend. For Nadine, that church didn't have the family warmth the church she grew up in did. It seemed a bit snooty, everyone there as hypocritical as Phyllis.

They sat on the pew next to Charles's parents and Carolyn and William. After the service the children rode with their grandparents, and Charles and Nadine followed—to dine at Phyllis's table.

The days continued to go by and with every day Nadine felt she was moving farther and farther from her own family. Her trips to Hopkinsville became fewer and fewer because of Charles's obsessive notion she would leave again.

If she went to Hopkinsville during the times he was away with his work, she had to lie and swear the children to secrecy. It didn't seem fair to put them through it. Claudette, wanting to avoid conflict, made most of her visits to see Nadine when Charles wasn't around. Claudette despised the way he treated her sister—and was not afraid to speak up about it.

On one of her visits, they drove into town to a beauty salon and afterwards took the children for pizza. While they waited for the pizza Claudette said, "I feel like we're always sneaking around to see each other, like lovers in the dark—but we're sisters, for Christ's sake. Nadine, you gotta stand up for yourself!"

"I do stand up, only to get knocked down. If it keeps the peace, I just keep my mouth shut.

"Well, that's gotta be hard."

"Of course it is. Last time I told him to leave me alone..."—here she lowered her voice, "he locked me in the closet."

Her sister's eyes went wide. "Wait a minute. He did what?"

Nadine sighed. "Locked me in the closet."

"You're kidding, right?"

"I wish I were." Eventually, she told Claudette everything.

Charles came home early. No one was home. He called Phyllis, but she hadn't seen Nadine or the kids all day. He grabbed a couple of beers and waited in front of the TV.

"Oh, no," Nadine whispered to herself at the sight of Charles's car in the yard. "Kids, your daddy is home. Please, Carolyn, take William to your room and play until I tell you to come out. Ok?" The child nodded.

Nadine entered the house hesitantly and watched Carolyn and William do as they were told. Charles spoke up immediately, his tone icy. "Where in the hell have you been, Nadine?"

"I went to get my hair done and took the kids out for lunch."

He jumped up from the recliner to take a closer look at her. "Yeah—and you know I don't like makeup!" He grabbed her lips, smearing her lipstick across her face. She turned her head away as he said, "Let me find out you're cheating..."

She jerked her head back and faced him. "Are you kidding me? This from a man who had another woman's number in his pocket!?"

Immediately his hands were around her neck and he slung her to the couch. "Nigga, I will kill you! Don't you ever talk to me like that! You hear me?!"

Gasping for air, Nadine tried to pry his fingers from her neck. He maintained his grip with one hand while reaching in his back pocket. He pulled out a knife.

Tears rolled down Nadine's cheeks as she struggled.

Carolyn did not stay in her room. She decided she had to come out to see what was going on. At the sight of her father holding a knife to her mother's face, she began screaming and raced over to help. William followed. The children pummeled him with all the strength of their little fists.

Carolyn screamed, "Stop it, Daddy! Stop it!"

William begged, "Get off my mama!"

Charles let go of Nadine and stood up, his hands in the air, still holding the knife. He was so surprised at the children coming to Nadine's rescue that he backed away without a word and eased the knife back in his pocket. He watched them make a fuss over their mother as she lay on her side coughing and gagging.

Carolyn tried to make her sit up. "Come on, Mama. Sit up."

Charles scoffed. "Leave her alone! She's okay!" He turned away and soon was back with a cup of water. He sat on the couch beside his wife and offered the drink to her while the children stood watching.

He muttered, "I'm sorry," and kissed Nadine's cheek. To the children he said, "See, she's gonna be okay."

Carolyn took a seat on the other side of her mother and put her arm around her waist.

"Mama, are you okay?"

Charles's voice hardened. "Go on back to your rooms now."

They went, but slowly, looking back. Instead of going to their rooms, they settled at the top of the stairs so they could hear their parents.

"One day, Nadine—you're gonna really piss me off."

She sputtered, "I just wanted to look nice for you."

Immediately Charles left, headed for the barn. He remained there for hours—drinking beer, playing solitaire, listening to music.

The next few weeks saw them back to normal again, at least what was normal for them. Nadine tried, consciously, as best she could, not to encourage Charles's paranoid behavior—but no matter how hard she tried, sooner or later, whatever she did, she set him off.

One day she and the children were playing a board game in the den while Charles was upstairs sleeping. She said, "How about some ice cream?"

"Yea!" The voices rang in harmony.

"Ok. Go get your shoes. I'll put this stuff away. Oh, and don't wake your daddy."

Carolyn soon slipped back down the stairs and she and Nadine walked outside to wait for William. Charles heard his son starting down the stairs and yelled, "Hey boy, where you running to?"

"Outside."

William was just getting his seatbelt on when Charles came running and yelling, ordering them all to get out of the car. Nadine locked the doors.

He banged on the driver side window. "Nadine, get out the car!"

"No, we're just going for ice cream! Why are you so upset?"

"Open the damn door! Get out!"

"No, not until you calm down and tell me why you're upset. We're just going for ice cream."

He stepped back from the car, giving himself enough room to kick the window. The children started screaming. Nadine shoved the key in the ignition, her hand trembling as she fumbled about. She thought she would be able to protect them by driving off, but before she could put the car in gear, the window shattered. She screamed, shielding her face. Charles ordered the children out of the car and reached in the window to unlock the driver's door. The children got out and ran to the porch.

He snatched the keys from the ignition and dragged Nadine out of the car. Her knees hit the ground as she stumbled to stand up. He began dragging her across the ground towards the back of the house. When she was finally able to stand, blood began running down her legs from her scrapped up knees.

With a tight grip on the back of her neck, Charles walked Nadine around to the barn. Inside, he locked the doors behind them and shoved her to the floor, then reached behind the refrigerator and pulled out a shoebox. From the box he pulled a small caliber gun.

"Oh, God, no!" Nadine leaped up, heading for the door, but he pointed the gun at her. "Move away from the door, Nadine. I swear, I'll kill ya."

"Please, Charles. Please think about the children. I didn't do anything wrong."

"You were trying to leave with my kids, Nadine."

"No, no—I swear! We were going for ice cream. Ask the children."

"Yeah, you could have told them to say anything. You thought I was asleep, huh? I was trained to sleep with one eye open. Nothing gets past me."

She struggled to make her voice sound calm. "Please put the gun away."

"I told you I would kill you if you ever left with my kids, didn't I? Didn't I?!" He put the gun to her head. She closed her eyes tight. "Or maybe you'd rather see me kill myself." He put the gun to his head. "Cause I'm not gonna live without you and I'm not gonna let you live without me, Nadine. My mom will take care of the kids."

She whispered, "Please put the gun down—I'm begging you."

Nadine had taught Carolyn to call the police if anything ever happened to her. Carolyn looked out the back door but did not see her parents. She pulled a chair up to the phone on the kitchen wall and dialed. "My daddy pulled my mama in the barn. I think he's hurting her. Please send the police. My brother and I are scared."

The dispatcher was a woman. She asked for the address. "Are there any other adults around? Maybe a neighbor?"

"No, ma'am, but I can call Nana. She'll come." Carolyn hung up before the dispatcher could say another word and called Phyllis. "Nana! Please come! Daddy's hurting Mama! He took her in the barn. You better come quick. I called the police."

"What?"

"Come now, Nana! Hurry!"

Phyllis sighed. "Oh, alright, I'm on my way."

William stood on the couch, looking out the window, waiting.

115

Charles had sat down on the barn floor and pulled Nadine down with him. "Why do you keep testing me, Nadine? It's like you want me to do something crazy."

"I don't mean to."

"I love you, Nadine. I don't want to kill you. I really don't. But you make me do things I don't want to do."

She remained quiet. She did not want to make the mistake of saying something to aggravate him.

"You see, when I was in Vietnam, I seen some terrible things. I even did some terrible things to people. I did." He cocked the gun and put it against Nadine's head.

Her sniffles turned to loud crying. She moaned, "What about the kids? They will be devastated."

He kissed her on the side of her head. "Did you think about the kids when you were trying to separate them from their daddy?"

"I wasn't trying to leave. You have to believe me. What will you tell my family?"

"Your family? I don't even like your family, especially your precious sister. I can't stand her. She's a bad influence. I could shoot her too, just like those Gooks over in 'Nam."

"Charles, we need to check on the children."

"They're okay. This is between you and me. See, you tried to be slick. Going out for some ice cream. You must think I'm stupid. I been watching you, watching your every move. Even when I'm not around, I know what you're doing. I even know what you're thinking." He tapped the gun against her head. "You and your sister plotting for you to leave. But you know what, Nadine? The only way to leave me is when you're dead. So, if you want to leave, I can make it happen. It's as easy as this."

He pressed the barrel harder against her head. She closed her eyes as tight as she could.

He pulled the trigger. She heard the click and felt a jolt, but she was still alive. There was no bullet. Once she realized it, she opened her eyes and let out a horrified wail that echoed throughout the barn and could be heard by the children in the house.

A faint, dizzy spell came over her. Her heart felt as if it had stopped. She began speaking hysterically. "Oh, God! Oh, God! Why? Why are you doing this to me? Why? What have I done to you? What have I done?!"

"Shut up! You shut up! You're not dead yet."

Soon the police arrived, a male and female officer. Phyllis rushed down the driveway and hopped out of her car and hurried into the house ahead of the officers. The children were huddled together on the couch. They had heard Nadine's scream.

"Are you alright?" Phyllis demanded. "Where is your daddy?"

Carolyn said, "In the barn with Mama—she's been screaming."

The officers stepped to the door. The male officer asked, "Where are they?"

Phyllis hurried out saying, "I'll show you."

The same officer stopped her. "Ma'am, you need to stay here with the children. We don't yet know how serious this is."

Phyllis returned to the house where she stood watching from the kitchen window as the officers approached the barn and knocked on the door. "Mr. and Mrs. Hunter, this is Officer Stevens. Are you in there?"

Charles turned toward the door – his eyes wide. He put the gun in the box and tucked it back behind the refrigerator. Nadine made no move. He reached down, grabbed her by the hand and pulled her to her feet as he whispered, "Come on."

The knock at the door sounded again. Charles called, "Yeah, we're coming! He grabbed a towel and wiped Nadine's face and her knees.

"Mr. and Mrs. Hunter, we just want to know if everything is alright. Open the door—open it slowly, please."

Charles did as instructed and stood in the doorway with Nadine by his side. Her dress hid the scrapes on her knees, but it was obvious she had been crying. Phyllis came and stood just behind the officers.

Charles said, "We're fine. Why are you here?"

"Your daughter called us," the female officer said. "She said you were hurting your wife. You want to tell us what's going on?"

"There's nothing going on. Children exaggerate. As you can see, we're fine."

Phyllis stepped forward. "Are you sure, son? Nadine, are you okay?" "Please stand back, ma'am," the female officer said.

"Mrs. Hunter, are you alright?" Officer Stevens asked.

"My son wouldn't hurt her. I'm sure there was just some misunderstanding. Right, Charles?"

"Ma'am, let us ask the questions. What happened to the car window?"

Charles did not answer. Nadine kept her head down.

"Look, Mr. Hunter, it's not just the car window. Your daughter called for a reason. These kids were obviously scared. And from the looks of your wife, something is wrong here. Now, you want to tell us what?"

"There is nothing to tell. We're fine—aren't we, baby?" He turned to Nadine. She did not look up or utter a word.

The female officer said, "I need to hear it from Mrs. Hunter."

Officer Stevens waved his fingers. "Why don't you come with me, Mr. Hunter?"

"For what?"

"Well, you look like you might need to speak with me alone."

"No, I don't. And if I'm not under arrest, you can leave."

"I do need your cooperation."

"Go on, Charles," his mother urged. "I'm sure you don't have anything to hide."

Charles took a deep breath and reluctantly followed the officer. Once the two men were out of sight the female officer stepped closer to Nadine. "Mrs. Hunter, my name is Officer Bryant—but you can call me Nancy. I'm in the domestic violence unit. Your daughter called because she thought you might need some help. Can you tell me what happened here?"

Nadine focused her eyes on the dirt beneath her feet. She couldn't move and couldn't force any words from her mouth. She could only think of how Charles put the gun to her head and easily pulled the trigger.

"I can't help you if you don't talk to me."

Phyllis said, "Well, it's obvious she doesn't need help.... I mean, nothing happened." The officer frowned at her.

Carolyn was peeping from the front door. She watched her daddy stand by the car with the policeman. She could not hear what Charles was saying.

"I got angry. So what? It's my car—and it's insured. Besides, I'm a mechanic. I can fix it if I want to."

"Mr. Hunter, did you assault your wife this evening?"

"Man, you must be crazy. I told you everything is okay here. Why don't y'all just leave us alone? Get the hell on."

"Any time we get a call, Mr. Hunter, we have to respond. Now you may not want to tell us the truth—and your wife may be too afraid to. But sooner or later, we'll be back."

Officer Stevens gave Charles one last opportunity to answer his questions, but Charles continued to insist the children had exaggerated and there was nothing to be concerned about. They returned to the backyard.

Officer Stevens headed for Officer Bryant and pulled her aside. "How's it going back here?"

She lowered her voice. "Well, Mrs. Hunter doesn't have anything to say. Too afraid to speak." She sighed then and strode over to Nadine and placed a card in her hand and closed her fingers over it. Nadine finally looked up at her.

Officer Bryant spoke softly and confidentially. "Mrs. Hunter, call me if you need to, or when you're ready to talk, 'cause I don't believe for one moment you're safe here. We have a new unit that helps women like you every day – women who are afraid to speak up against their husband."

As soon as the officers disappeared around the house, Charles headed towards the back door. He turned to look back at Nadine. "You coming?"

She followed, moving very slowly. She found the children at the table. Charles and Phyllis had slipped into the living room—then a knock at the door and a voice as Charles's dad came in. "Hey, what's going on here?"

Mother and son reappeared, and Phyllis said, "Come sit down, honey. I'm not sure myself. But the police just left."

"Yeah, I saw them."

Charles paced a bit before speaking. "She tried to leave with my kids. So, yeah, I lost my temper and kicked the car window in. Then I took her to the barn to talk to her in private. Carolyn called the damn police."

Phyllis sighed. "Well, with you kicking the window in and everything, Charles, I guess she was scared."

Nadine was leaning against the inside doorway to the kitchen. Phyllis said, "Where were you really going, Nadine?"

Nadine looked over but did not speak, only shook her head.

"Well, I can't imagine you were trying to leave with the kids. I mean—why would you do that?"

Looking over at Phyllis, Nadine said, "He put...." She cleared her throat. "He put a gun to my head and pulled the trigger! He put a gun to my head! How dare you ask me anything?! You need to be asking him why he put a gun to my head and pulled the trigger!" Her hands went to her face, wiping her tears.

Charles's voice, raised to a high pitch, "Look, I—I was upset! It wasn't even loaded! I just wanted her to listen to me."

Joe's eyes went wide. "So, you put a gun to her head?"

Nadine stomped her foot. "And pulled the trigger—he pulled the trigger!"

Phyllis frowned. "Okay, okay—but, well, you're here! You're alive!" She heaved a long sigh. "What is going on between the two of you?"

Charles clenched his fists. "It's her, Mom!"

Nadine gasped. "Me?"

"She don't respect me or appreciate what a nigga tries to do for his family. It's not easy working in that warehouse and being on the road trying to make sure they have what they need. And then she gonna try to leave me?" Charles began pacing again.

Nadine shook her head. "It's not true—I already told you. We were going for ice cream. He's so paranoid! Thinking I'm leaving—and then wanting to kill me!"

Phyllis murmured, "Oh, it's not all that bad."

"He put a gun to my head—and pulled the trigger! You have no idea what I go through here!"

Charles snapped, "You lower your voice to my mother!"

Nadine nodded her head. "Right. Because I can't raise my voice, but you can raise yours." She blew out air. "It's a nightmare here. The kids feel it too. Ask them. I'm a prisoner here—in my own house. He don't even want me to see *my* family. And I have no friends here. I have nobody."

Phyllis shrieked, "Oh, stop it, Nadine! I've heard enough whining. You have two beautiful children; you have a wonderful home—you don't go without anything!"

"I go without love."

"What does that mean?" Joe asked.

"It don't mean nothing. She just talking crazy like she always do," Charles said.

"No, I'm not crazy. But you're making me crazy. You're driving me out of my mind. I don't know how much more I can take."

Charles jumped in with, "See what I mean?"

Phyllis said, "Well, maybe y'all can talk to the pastor about your marriage. He's a good counselor. Nadine, you really should try every avenue before you walk out and take those kids away from their father."

"I wasn't trying to leave! What is wrong with you people?" She wiped her eyes. "You know what? You talk to a pastor." She pointed around at each one in the room. "You ask him if it's right for a man to beat on his wife. I don't need no pastor to give me the answer to that. And I'm not gonna let you gang up on me like I'm the bad guy." She brushed past Charles and stomped up the stairs.

Charles yelled, "Get back here!"

Joe said, "Oh, let her go."

SEVEN

There Has To Be A Way Out

For the next few weeks, Charles was barely home. He spent a lot of time on the road. For the first time, Nadine did not miss him, and it scared her.

One afternoon she sat on the front porch sipping on a cup of tea while watching the children play. In her mind, not missing him meant she was ready for a change. But, in her heart, she still loved this man. When Charles was in Vietnam, she had longed for him and anticipated the day of his return, so they could be a family again.

Although she still loved him, she secretly looked forward to him leaving. The short time they spent together in between his runs felt distant. She went through the motions, but she was tired. Most of all, she was tired of Phyllis popping in when Charles was gone.

The next moment Nadine was moaning, "Oh, my God, here she comes!"

Phyllis stepped out of the car crooning, "Hey, my babies. Come give Nana a hug." They ran to her and she took a bag out of the car and headed for the porch saying, "I bought dinner."

"The kids and I were going to have something simple."

"Oh, nonsense. They're growing kids—they need a good hot meal. Come on in, Nadine. Let's wash the kids up so they can eat."

Nadine closed her eyes, pressed her lips together and said to herself, *I hate this woman.* Aloud she said, "Come on—your Nana's brought dinner."

Phyllis was placing containers of food on the table. "Nadine, you set the table and I'll serve. Come on babies, let's wash your hands."

The children were soon back and seated at the table. Nadine sat down and Phyllis served the food and said grace.

Nadine asked, "So, where is Joe?"

"He's gone fishing with the pastor. I wanted to come eat with my babies." Some seconds went by and she added, "Charles called me from the road and said to make sure everything was alright here."

"Why wouldn't it be?"

Phyllis smirked. "Charles is a strong man. I don't know how he ended up with such a weak woman."

"Where is this coming from?"

"Just thinking. Despite what you may think, he loves his family."

"He loves his children. He stopped loving me a long time ago."

"How do you expect to keep a man like Charles when you're always crying and walking around all sad? Complaining about your poor little life?"

"I don't know where this is coming from, but I take a lot from Charles. You don't live with the man that I do."

Phyllis picked up the knife to cut her meat. "No, but he was my son before he was your husband. And I know him."

The more Nadine said in her defense, the worse the conversation became, so she stopped talking. When she finished eating, she excused herself and went back out on the porch.

Phyllis cleaned the kitchen and sent the kids in the den to watch TV. Soon she was stepping off the porch, on her way out. She said, "I've cleaned everything up and the kids are in the den. I hope you have a good night. Charles should be home in a couple of days. Call me if you need anything, Nadine."

Nadine was thinking 'she' would be the last person she'd call on for anything.

Several days later Charles returned home. The children were already in bed and she was sitting in bed reading a novel. He came upstairs, kicked off his boots near the dresser and said, "Hey."

She said hey to him. Before he headed into the bathroom he said, "Reading trash again, huh?"

She folded the tip of the page to mark her spot and put the book in the nightstand drawer, slid down in the bed and pulled the blanket over her shoulder. He soon returned and they lay with their backs to each other. Nadine finally drifted off to sleep—but only when she was sure Charles had slipped off to sleep first.

The next morning, she was out of bed before the sun came up. When the children woke up, they went looking for her and found her on the couch. Their father was still upstairs. They awakened their mother and she said groggily, "Okay, how about some cereal?"

The last time the children had found her on the couch was after he roughed her up because she did not want to have sex. For her, the desire just wasn't there anymore. His drinking turned her off, but it was the thought of him being with another woman on the road that really got to her.

He did not come downstairs till almost noon. He found his family in the den. Right off he demanded, "Hey, y'all—how long were you gonna let me sleep?"

Nadine did not look up from her needlework but said, "I figured you needed it."

He sat beside her on the couch and kissed her shoulder. "How do you feel, baby?" She curled the shoulder away from him. He said, "Ok, well, why don't we take the kids out for lunch today?"

Carolyn and William, with their sharp young voices, cheered, "Yea!"

Charles turned his gaze their way and said, "Give me and Mommy a moment." When they left the room, he took her hand and stood up. "Come on," he said.

She dropped the needlework on the couch. "Where are we going?"

"We're going upstairs."

"Why?"

"Because I don't want to talk where the kids can hear."

He led her upstairs and closed the door. Nadine remained standing. He sat on the bed. "Look, I don't know what your problem is, but when I touch you—you don't move away from me! So, what the hell is that about?"

Nadine folded her arms across her chest. She knew her next words would be dangerous to say but they needed to be said. "I don't want this marriage anymore."

"What!?"

"You're always clearing the slate. Starting over again. Only to end up the same, every time. I'm tired, Charles. This marriage has been the hardest thing I've ever endured in my life."

"Well marriage is hard—it's hard, Nadine."

"It shouldn't be this hard. If two people love each other…." She sighed. "Years of abuse, emotional neglect, this distance between us. I can't do it anymore. Sometimes, you just make me wish I was dead."

"Well die then, Nadine! We'd probably be better off without you anyway, huh? Cause you're not leaving with my kids. Nah, that will never happen!" He got up and shoved her against the bedroom door. "In fact, you're not leaving at all. You must be crazy to stand here and talk to me like that."

She swallowed deep. A gnawing nervousness set up in her stomach. "What are you gonna do? Beat me up like usual? Kill me?" Her eyes filled with tears.

She winced when Charles slammed his hand against the door behind her. "You keep pissing me off and I will! The only reason why I don't do it now is cause the kids are downstairs waiting for us."

He pushed her away from the door and up against the dresser. Then left.

She smiled to herself. It felt good to say what was on her mind, regardless of the consequences. She didn't want to believe he would actually kill her, but she knew he would definitely beat the hell out of her. It was only a matter of time.

By the following Friday, Charles was back on the road and things were once again peaceful. Martha and Claudette visited for the first time in months. They had great fun catching up on the family news over one of Nadine's cakes while enjoying a fresh pot of coffee.

Afterward Nadine put the dishes in the sink and turned on the water. Martha walked over to help.

"It's only a few things, Mama. I got it." She rolled up her sleeves.

"Nadine, what happen to your arm?" Quickly, Nadine pulled her sleeve down.

"Nothing. I bumped it on the dresser in my room."

"You sure that's all it is?"

Claudette stepped forward. "Or is it Charles?"

Nadine picked up a dish from the sink and began wiping it. "It's nothing to make a big deal over."

"Nadine, you don't have to tell me the truth, but I know my child. What I don't know is why you're still here. Did you really think when he brought you to this nice big house and talked you into coming back, things were really going to be different?"

"Yes, Ma. I did."

"Well, are they?"

Nadine hesitated. Claudette answered. "No."

Her mother said, "You can always come home, Nadine.

"I know. I just don't want to burden anyone."

"It's not a burden. The burden will be the day I have to bury my daughter."

Nadine dried her hands and started toward the living room, speaking over her shoulder. "I've been thinking a lot about leaving. And when I do, you may still have to bury your daughter."

Martha turned toward Claudette, who shrugged her shoulders, and they followed Nadine.

129

Martha said, "Nadine, what do you mean?" "He's gonna kill me whether I stay or go. I can't win. If something happens to me, promise you'll take care of my kids. Don't let his evil mammy have them."

Claudette sat close beside her sister. "Don't talk like that, Nadine. We can protect you when you leave here."

"Claudette, do you understand? He will kill me—whether I stay or go! You can't protect me—I can feel the tension brewing in him."

"All you have to do is come home. He can't hurt you there."

"Yes, he can, and he will—as well as anyone else who gets in his way."

Charles returned home from his trip two days earlier than expected. Nadine and the children were in the kitchen with the radio blasting 'Respect' by Aretha Franklin – the three of them dancing and singing and holding to their mixing spoons while making cookies.

Their laughter and the music were so loud Charles could hear it outside. As soon as he showed his face, all three stopped instantly and glanced around at the mess.

"So, this is what goes on when I'm not here?"

They were all frozen, staring at him. Nadine exhaled. "Oh, Charles, you scared the crap out of me."

"You didn't even hear me come in? Turn that music down!"

Nadine hurried to turn it off. Carolyn skipped over and said, "Would you like a cookie, Daddy?"

"No, baby girl. My house is a mess!"

"We can clean it up, Charles. It's nothing to get upset about."

"Nadine, I darn near broke my leg stumbling over the kids' shoes in the living room. There are crayons and books all over the place. You know what? I'm going back out. When I return my house better be clean." He headed out the back door toward the barn.

Nadine sighed. "Okay, let's clean up."

"But what about our cookies?" Carolyn asked.

"We can finish them tomorrow. Please don't give me a hard time."

Together they went through the living room, picking up toys and putting everything in place. Nadine sent the children upstairs to clean while she washed dishes. By the time Charles returned from the barn, the children were in bed and Nadine was sitting in the den folding clothes before the TV.

"The kids gone to bed?"

"Yes."

"What did you cook?"

"We ate hot dogs."

"Hot dogs?"

"We weren't expecting you, Charles."

"So, when I'm not home, you don't cook. You don't clean. You sure as hell don't make sure the kids do what they're supposed to do. So, what do you do when I'm gone, Nadine?"

She kept folding clothes without a word. He came and stood in front of her. She wouldn't look up. He had been drinking.

"I'm talking to you!" He snatched a towel from her hand. "And what the hell are you wearing?"

131

She was wearing a skirt and halter top. She remained silent – putting the folded clothes in the basket.

Charles kicked the basket to the side. "I said—I'm talking to you!"

"Charles, I always take good care of the house and the kids. We were just having fun."

"Fun, huh? Well, this doesn't look like fun." He grabbed her top and ripped it from around her neck.

Nadine crossed her arms over her chest to cover her breasts. "We were fine until you got here. Why can't you just leave me alone?!"

"'Cause I don't like what you're wearing. You don't even have on a bra."

"I don't need one on around the house."

"How do I know you didn't wear this out of the house? My money better not have bought it."

"My sister bought it."

"Figures…cause your sister dresses like a whore and now she's trying to dress my wife. I didn't marry a whore, did I, Nadine? But, if you want to dress like one, I'll treat you like one."

She moved to stand up, but he pushed her down. She slid to the floor. Before she could get up, he straddled her. She struggled to get away.

"You know what? I'm gonna treat you like the whore you're trying to be. This is what happens when you dress like this."

They struggled back and forth over her skirt – him pulling it up and her pulling it down. Nadine clenched her legs tightly together. He pried them apart, forcing himself between them.

"Stop! Please, stop!" she begged as he ripped her panties. She began punching him with everything she had. He wouldn't stop.

He took her wrists and held her arms above her head, pinning them to the floor. He positioned himself on her chest, his knees pinning her shoulders down, leaving only her legs to move freely. Her attempts to kick him were unsuccessful.

He loosened his grip on her wrists to undo his pants and was soon trying to force himself into her mouth, but she kept turning her head side to side – tightening her lips. Each time she refused him he slapped her. He grabbed her by her throat and threatened to choke her to death if she didn't cooperate. Finally, she just gave up the fight.

He grabbed her by her hair and stood up on his knees, still pinning her shoulders, motioning her head up and down to meet every thrust. Nadine felt nauseated, started gagging and attempting to catch her breath. She could taste blood in her mouth from the cut of her lip.

He got off her shoulders, holding her arms down as he slid down in a prone position to penetrate her. Nadine lay motionless, trying not to think about the pain and humiliation of what he was doing or saying to her. She drifted away, lost in her thoughts, as she had learned to do—detaching herself from the experience.

"Tell me you like it," he demanded. "Say it!" he yelled, but she wouldn't. "Yeah, you like it," he whispered before collapsing on her, sweaty and breathing hard.

"You see, Nadine," he whispered. "You get what you deserve—dressing like that." Then he got up and staggered away.

Nadine slowly dragged herself off the floor. Her hands trembled as she looked through the clouds of tears at the laundry basket. She pulled out a gown, towel, and washcloth. She could feel Charles's fluids running down her leg as she shuffled to the bathroom. The stroke of the washcloth across her face couldn't wipe away the many teardrops. It was like wiping beads of sweat from someone's forehead in the dead of summer. The tears just kept coming. She grimaced as she wiped between her legs, looked at herself in the mirror and thought of herself as pathetic. After she put the gown on, she curled up on the couch in the den and cried herself to sleep.

Shortly after that incident Nadine began drinking, thinking it would make her care less about anything. Charles first observed her drinking at a cookout at Nate's house. He watched her take her third drink. "How many drinks is that Nadine?" "Why?" she replied.

Charles squinted and slapped the glass from her hand. "That's why," he said. Everyone stopped what they were doing and stared at them. Nate's wife ran over to clean it up, but Charles said, "No, let her do it."

As she cleaned up the mess Nadine could feel the discomfort in the room. Charles apologized to everyone for her behavior and for the broken glass. He offered to pay for it, but Nate refused.

The ride home was silent. Charles took the kids in the house and locked the door behind him. Nadine sat in the car for about an hour before deciding to face her inevitable punishment.

She found both the front and back door locked. She didn't have her keys, so she timidly knocked.

Charles swung open the door and peered down at her. "Why are you on my porch?"

Nadine kept her head down. "I just wanted to come in."

"In my house? After you embarrassed me in front of my friends?" He smirked. "You must be crazy!"

"I don't have anywhere else to go tonight."

"And that's my problem?"

After standing there for a moment, she turned to walk away. He snatched her toward him and said, "Nadine, get your narrow behind in here." She flinched as if she was expecting to be hit. He looked at her for a moment and began laughing. "I'm not gonna hit you, girl. Nah, because it's what you want me to do. I'm going upstairs, and don't you follow me, cause I don't want you in my bed."

When she was sure he was up in the bedroom, she fell asleep on the couch. He exiled her to the couch for a week, barely speaking to her or acknowledging her presence. He wouldn't eat anything she cooked. Instead, he picked up food and brought it home to eat.

His mother stopped in with some of his favorite foods. "Charles said he's been eating out for a week. Honestly, Nadine. What kind of a wife would allow her husband to eat fast food for a week— when she has a perfectly good kitchen to prepare hot homecooked meals in?"

Nadine didn't bother to explain it was Charles's choice. Instead, while Phyllis busied herself in Nadine's kitchen, she slipped upstairs to the main bathroom. In the tank was hidden a small bottle of vodka. Nadine locked the door and sat on the toilet, turning the bottle up to her mouth. She wiped her mouth with the back of her hand and began fussing in a whisper at the bathroom door as if it were Phyllis, saying all the things she wanted to say to her, but couldn't.

The following week, Claudette visited. She noticed Nadine pouring vodka in her orange juice. "You don't usually drink, Nadine."

"I just feel like having a drink. It's nothing."

Claudette raised an eyebrow. "Are you alright?"

"I got it under control."

It was on the day little William was rushed to the hospital she gradually lost that control. Carolyn had come riding her bike around the back of the house just in time to see William fall from the top of the doghouse. He fell against the two cinder blocks he always stood on to get up there.

Nadine was asleep on the couch. Carolyn came sprinting into the house screaming and began shaking her. "Hurry, Mama! William is hurt!"

Nadine took her time gathering herself together and sat up slowly. When she understood what she was hearing were her son's cries she hurried out the door behind Carolyn. He was holding his right arm and crying so hard she could barely understand him.

She scooped him up from the ground, rushed him to the car and called to Carolyn, "Run in the kitchen and grab my purse. And my keys! Run!"

From the emergency room, Nadine called Charles at the warehouse. In turn he called Phyllis and Joe. They all made their way to the hospital.

"Where the hell were you, Nadine?" Charles demanded.

She answered in a low voice. "Asleep."

Phyllis put her hand on her hip and said, "Oh, that's so neglectful!"

Joe shook his head. "How can you watch the kids while you're asleep?"

A hospital social worker overheard and walked over and asked what happened. After he got the story, he set a hand on Nadine's shoulder and assured her William was okay.

"Mrs. Hunter," he said, "every parent makes a mistake now and again. Why, just last week a lady left her baby in the car while she ran in the store to pay for gas. She came out and realized she had left the keys in the ignition and the door was locked. The mother was devastated, of course—but it did not make her a bad mother. She just made a mistake. So, you fell asleep on the couch."

Nadine sobbed. "I should have been watching him."

The social worker smiled. "Well, luckily, your son will be fine. Just a fractured arm that should heal in no time."

William left the hospital with a cast on his arm. Charles put the children in the car while Nadine trailed behind alone. Phyllis insisted the children go home with her, but Charles refused.

Back at the house Charles noticed a glass on the coffee table, picked it up and put it under his nose. "Nadine! Get in here—now!"

From the tone of his voice, she knew this would not be good. She took careful steps down the stairs. "Yes, Charles?"

"So, you've been drinking? Is this what you be doing while you s'posed to be taking care of my kids? Huh?"

Her eyes widened at the sight of the glass in his hand. She parted her mouth, but no words came out.

"You just gonna stand there looking stupid? Were you drunk?!" No sooner than the words were out of his mouth, the glass came sailing across the room at her. She ducked and the glass shattered against the wall.

"I'm sorry, Charles. I'm so sorry."

"Not yet, you're not."

He gripped her arm and walked her in the kitchen. "So, you wanna drink, huh? Okay, let's drink."

He took a bottle of wine from the cabinet then walked her to the den and slung her to the couch. With his teeth he pulled the cork from the bottle, spit it on the floor, and cupped her chin with one hand, then attempted to pour the wine in her mouth. Nadine pressed her lips tightly together, pushing him away. She tried speaking, but each time she got strangled on the wine.

Charles kept pouring till the bottle was emptied. Wine ran down her face and neck as she coughed. He broke the empty bottle against the coffee table and stuck the jagged edge against her chin. "If you ever drink in my house or around my kids again...I'll kill you. I will cut your damn throat! You hear me?! Now clean up this mess!"

Nadine had already been moving toward the conclusion of no amount of alcohol was going to solve her problem. So instead, she would—going forward—set her mind to thinking. There had to be a way out. And no matter the consequences, escaping Charles's madness was worth taking a chance.

It was while she was in her flowerbeds and vegetable garden, she could reliably depend on feeling serenity. As she tended the plants, she was better able to keep thoughts of Charles out of her head. She also had a secret in the garden.

Years of threats to kill her if she left or took the children away had made her stay and she'd even convinced herself she would live longer if she stayed, but recently it no longer seemed to make sense, so every penny she could earn and save without his knowledge she buried in the garden. Charles would never be the wiser.

EIGHT

Imminent Death

Nadine hurried about the kitchen preparing dinner. Charles would be home soon expecting dinner to be on the table. She sighed heavily at a knock on the door and frowned. "Who in the world?" Wiping her hands on the tail of her apron, she stomped through the house and peeped out the small window of the front door.

It was a well-dressed young black man with a folder in his hand. He smiled as he looked up at her.

She flung the door open. "Are you here to talk about religion or sell me something—because I really don't have time right now, I'm in the middle of cooking dinner."

"Oh, no, ma'am. Um, I apologize for the inconvenience, but my name is James." He shook her hand. "I'm a college student and I'm offering you an opportunity to have any room in the house cleaned with a wonderful vacuum cleaner."

"I can't right now. I'm busy cooking."

"It'll only take a few moments of your time. See, I have to demonstrate our vacuums five times a day to get a bonus at the end of the week, even if you don't buy one. Please help a brotha out—I'm just trying to make it through college, you know?"

"This really is a bad time. My husband will be home soon, and he'll be expecting dinner. Please, come back another day."

"Well, I understand. What day is good?"

"Any day but today. I really need to go." She began closing the door and heard him say, "Ok, Mrs...?"

"Hunter."

"Well, Mrs. Hunter, please take my card. When I'm in this area again, I will definitely stop by a little earlier in the day. I think you'll be pleased with our product. It would cut a lot of time out from your housework."

"Thank you." She took the card, firmly closed the door, dropped the card on the end table and returned to the kitchen. She glanced at the clock. There was no time to waste.

Nadine checked each pot. Everything smelled so good, just like Charles liked it. She greased a pan for the rolls. A pitcher of lemonade and a bowl of banana pudding were waiting in the refrigerator. When the potatoes were done, she put the pot in the sink and turned the cold water on them and let out a loud sigh. "Darn! I forgot to boil the eggs!"

Nadine had just put the eggs on the stove when Charles sped around the house and came in the back door. Before he could utter a word, she said, "Hey, honey, dinner is almost done."

"Why isn't it already done? I worked hard today, Nadine. I'm not in the mood for slacking. Somebody didn't show—which made my work double. Now I come home and I can't even get my dinner on time. I swear, Nadine." He sighed. "Any mail?"

She pulled the rolls from the oven. "It's on the coffee table in the living room."

Charles went in the living room and picked up the mail and noticed the business card and examined it. He called out, "So, what have you been doing today anyway, Nadine?"

"A lot! William had a doctor's appointment. He got shots, so he was cranky. Then I had to bake thirty cupcakes for Carolyn's class and take them up to the school by one o'clock. I went to the grocery store and hurried home to meet the school bus. I helped Carolyn with her homework. I took the clothes in off the line. Before I knew it, it was time to start dinner. My day doesn't slow down for anyone."

Charles stood in the kitchen doorway watching her hurry about. "Oh, really? So who came by today?"

"Who came by? Nobody."

She took the chicken out of the oven and set it on top of the stove, then went over to the sink to pour the water off the potatoes. Outside the window the children were playing.

Charles walked up behind her. "So, nobody came by today."

"No. Why do you keep asking?" She turned around with the pot in her hands and was floored by the powerful jab of his fist across her face. She hit the floor, and so did the pot and potatoes. "Didn't I tell you about lying to me, woman?!"

Nadine propped up on one elbow as she tried to regain herself. He squatted and grabbed her by the hair. She cried, "What did I do?"

He got so close she could smell the alcohol on his breath and feel the spit spewing from his mouth as he yelled in her face. "You're a stinkin liar! That's what! You're a liar and a whore! You see this?" He waved the business card around. "Someone named James has been here."

"I forgot. I just forgot. It wasn't important."

"Yeah. What else have you forgotten? Huh? You had this cat in my house?"

"No, I swear. He never came in."

"How do I know that, Nadine?" he asked as he banged her head against the cabinet. "How the hell do I know? You lied and said nobody came by. Why should I believe you?"

With every word he kept banging her head against the counter. She grabbed his hand, trying to loosen his grip on her hair as she sat up, but he gripped tighter. He threw the card on the floor and grabbed her neck holding her head firmly against the cabinet. His fingers tightened around her neck. "I'll kill you! I will kill you! You hear me? You're a stinkin' liar!"

Nadine dug her nails in his skin, but his grip was unyielding to the point of almost cutting off her air. Then he let her go and stood up. Nadine knew she had to get up and make a run for it despite still trying to catch her breath. This was the same rage which put her in the hospital a few years ago. She had endured much abuse since they reunited, but this was different – and she knew it.

He stood over her and unbuckled his belt. She was trying to get off the floor when an agonizing pain from the belt brought her to her knees. He continued to beat her as if he were beating an animal. In all her agony, she scurried about for something to defend herself with and noticed the knife on the floor she used to cut the potatoes. She had never drawn a weapon on him before, but in her mind, she thought, "*No more.*"

No more would she take this type of beating. No more would she let him break her bones or abuse her to the point of needing medical attention. No more would she not fight back—but she couldn't reach the knife, so she began screaming for the kids. She had never called for them before, but they did not hear her.

Charles never uttered a word, just continued to sling the belt. The only sound from him was one that emphasized the effort and power he was putting behind each thrash. He took her by the collar and dragged her across the floor away from the door so she couldn't be heard, demanding she shut up, but she continued to cry out loudly. Again, she spotted the knife on the floor. She rolled towards it, but before she could grab it Charles stood on his knees behind her and put the belt around her neck.

"I'm not done with you, Nadine. This is only the beginning. You'll think twice before you have another man around my house. If you live."

She tried to put her fingers between the belt and her neck.

"How much effort do you think it would take to snap your neck like a twig? Yeah, where's that punk James now?"

He had not yet noticed the knife. She was determined to reach it. She pulled and fought against his grip, and somehow did manage to touch the knife with her fingertips. It seemed to give her the strength she never thought she had – strength to struggle harder, and finally she reached it. Once she had the knife in her hand, she leaned back against him and desperately swung her hand back to pierce him in his side.

He cried out and let go of the belt, then fell to the floor. On her knees Nadine sat back and put one hand to her throat. Her breath was coming roughly, sharply. With her other hand she still maintained a tight grip on the knife.

"You stabbed me?" Charles's tone revealed his utter disbelief. He staggered to his feet and glared at the blood on his hand. "You stabbed me."

Nadine managed to come to her feet. She leaned against the stove, still catching her breath. The warmth of the stove reminded her the eggs were still boiling. She laid the knife down on the stove and put her hand on the pot handle, anticipating Charles's next move.

Yelling to the top of his voice he said, "You have to be crazy to stab me!"

The moment he launched towards her, Nadine firmly locked her hand down on the pot handle and slung it in his direction. He grabbed his face and went down to the floor as if his feet had been swept from underneath him – screaming in misery from the boiling water and hot eggs that hit his flesh. Nadine dropped the pot and snatched up the knife.

As she stepped over Charles, he reached up and pulled the tail of her dress and she slipped and fell. She still had the knife in her hand.

The effects of the hot water did not stop him from clutching her leg, then reaching for her other leg as she kicked and screamed to get away. She swung the knife and cut his arm, but he didn't stop. He wrestled the knife from her hand.

Her screams were deathly loud now and the children came running into the house to find Charles sitting on her with the knife pointed at her throat.

Carolyn screamed, "Daddy! What are you doing to Mama?"

She could see he was bleeding. He turned and demanded they get out—but William, aged five, ran over to his dad and began hitting him as hard as his little fists could. He was crying, "Stop it, Daddy! Get off my mama!"

Seeing that William was standing up to him at five years old, Charles dropped the knife and took his son by his shoulders. He shook the boy and yelled, "You get out!"

Charles pushed the kids out the door. By the time he returned his attention to Nadine, she had quietly picked up the knife. She backed up against the kitchen wall as Charles walked towards her – holding the knife out of sight behind the skirt of her dress. She swallowed deep and froze as if she were a part of the wall, surmising his next move. She could run, but how far would she get before he overpowered her?

"Yeah, you knew it wasn't over, didn't you? You tried to kill me! But it's not gonna be me who dies here today!"

Nadine's gaze focused on him. She did not utter a word. She faded out in thought. His wicked words sounded to her ears like a lot of babbling. Years of abuse flashed forward in her mind and she knew he would never leave her alone. Her day had gone from running errands, taking care of the children, and cooking dinner— to this horrific ending. All because someone came to the door selling vacuums. She thought – *Ridiculous!*

"Is this my dinner on the floor?!" Charles was kicking the potatoes around. "Huh?! I'm talking to you!"

Nadine snapped out of her daze and flinched as he raised his hand to her. Just before his hand met her face – she did it. She jabbed the knife in his belly. His eyes widened and she pulled back on the knife. As he stumbled back, she stepped forward and stabbed him again. He dropped to the floor, landing on his side.

He groaned, "I knew I should have killed you while I had the chance."

"No! No more, no more, Charles! No more!" And she joined him on the floor, only to stab him again and again.

He mumbled, "Nadine, please."

Carolyn and William came rushing in. This time it was their dad they found lying on the floor in a pool of his own blood.

Carolyn cried, "Mama! Stop it! Please, please, Mama—stop it!"

Nadine threw the knife down and slid away. Her eyes widened and her lips quivered.

She stared at the children, watching them cry over Charles's bloody body. He lay motionless, barely breathing. Her hands shook as she raised them and examined the bloody mess. She crawled over to the children and tried frantically to pull them away from Charles, but it was like pulling a hound away from his tracked scent.

"Carolyn! William! Oh my God! Oh God! What have I done? Please God, make him get up! Please God, please! I didn't mean it! Please!"

Carolyn shrieked, "He's not getting up!"

And the child turned and ran to the phone. She dialed 9-1-1. "Yes, my daddy is hurt! Please send someone to help him!" "Tell me what happened," the dispatcher said.

"My mom stabbed him with the knife. Please hurry! I think he's dying!"

"Ok, sweetheart. Stay on the phone with me. Are you alright? Are you safe?"

"Yes, but my daddy needs help."

"Ok, sweetheart. What's your address?"

After verifying the address, the dispatcher put Carolyn on hold but soon was back to assure her help was on the way. Carolyn remained on the phone until the police arrived. Nadine and William remained helplessly at Charles's side.

Carolyn flung open the door. The police officers began immediately asking questions and moved Nadine and William away from Charles to assess the scene. Paramedics soon arrived through the front door.

Carolyn opened her arms to embrace her little brother. Nadine cried for Charles to get up. The paramedics had to keep reminding her to step back, let them do their job.

The female officer—Officer Bryant—who had previously been out to the house, wrapped her arms around Nadine. She said, "Mrs. Hunter, you have to let go—allow the paramedics to help him."

Officer Bryant walked Nadine into the living room where she reached for a couple of tissues from a box on the end table and handed them over.

The two women settled on the couch. "Mrs. Hunter, you're hurt. The paramedics are going to check you out. Is that alright?"

While Nadine was assessed by the paramedics, the children were questioned in the den. Carolyn was asked to phone someone – a neighbor or relative. She called Charles's mother and as directed, passed the phone to the officer.

"Mrs. Hunter, there has been an incident at your son's home. We have the children here and need for you to come right away."

Phyllis gasped. "Oh, my God! What happened?! Are the children okay? Where is my son?"

"Ma'am, can you be on your way? I can't answer any questions over the phone."

In the living room Nadine still had not yet brought herself to telling Officer Bryant what happened because she could not stop crying. As she wiped her tears, her hands smeared blood across her face.

Officer Bryant tried again. "What happened, Mrs. Hunter?" Other officers were standing close by to hear the story. Officer Bryant handed Nadine another tissue. Another officer asked, "Mrs. Hunter, can you tell us what happened here this evening?"

Nadine's words came slowly. "Where are my children?"

Officer Bryant continued her role of reassuring the one being questioned. "Your children are fine. It's what happened here that we need to know."

"And Charles?" Nadine said.

Officer Bryant asked, "What happened to Charles?"

Through her tears Nadine moaned, "I was only trying to protect myself. I just wanted it to stop. I didn't mean it. I didn't do nothing wrong."

One of the officers said, "Mrs. Hunter, your husband will be taken to the hospital. You will have to be in our custody."

Nadine's face showed her confusion. "Why?"

The man in uniform replied, "You're under arrest, ma'am, for assault on your husband."

"No, no, I can't be!! He's gonna be alright! What will happen to my children?"

Officer Bryant spoke reassuringly. "Your mother-in-law is coming to get the children."

"No! Oh God, no! Please don't let her have my children! Please! I beg you to call my mother—call my sister!"

"Calm down, Mrs. Hunter. Do they live close by?"

"No, they live in Hopkinsville—but they'll come. They will, just call them! Please, she can't have my children."

Charles's parents soon came swinging into the driveway, his father maneuvering the car around emergency vehicles with flashing lights. Charles had already been loaded in the back of the ambulance.

Phyllis demanded, "Where is my son?"

An officer told her, "Your son is in the ambulance. He's critical, ma'am. They have to get moving."

"No! I've got to see him!"

The officer told her she would have to meet him at the hospital, then proceeded to fill the victim's parents in on what was known at that point. Phyllis fell to the ground - crying, kicking, and screaming. Joe tried to grab her feet. The children came running outside and held tightly to their grandparents.

Phyllis asked, "Are you ok?" And they nodded.

She said, "Oh, look at all this blood! Oh, my God! Come on and get washed up." They started toward the house, but the officers intervened – ordered the grandparents to take the children away from the scene.

Joe walked the children to the car. He said, "I'm gonna drop y'all off at the house and then I'm gonna go see bout my boy."

Phyllis scowled. "No! I wanna go!"

"The hospital is no place for these kids. After what they've been through, they need to be cleaned up and tended to. Call someone to watch them and meet me there later."

Phyllis was about to get in the car when she spotted Nadine being taken from the house on a stretcher. She rushed over and yelled, "You wicked witch! What did you do to my baby?"

Before Joe could reach Phyllis, two officers grabbed her and held her down on the ground. Phyllis kept struggling to get up as she yelled at Nadine.

Joe said to the officers, "Please, let her go." They made no move to do so until Nadine was in the ambulance. Phyllis dusted herself off and hurried back to the car where the children were soon telling everything that happened.

Joe dropped them off at the house and right away Phyllis called a cousin to come and stay with the children. By the time Cousin Ella arrived the children's bloody clothes had been trashed and both children were bathed. Ella looked at the clothes in the trash and shook her head in disbelief at what she was hearing. Phyllis left and Ella proceeded to prepare food for the children—chicken noodle soup and bologna sandwiches with Kool-Aid.

Carolyn, as the oldest of the children, would remember all her life what they had for supper that night. When Ella put her to bed, she was at first unable to rest, but before long both exhausted children were sound asleep.

NINE

Behind Bars

The doctors did all they could for Charles but now the ventilator was the only thing keeping him alive. It was up to his parents to decide what to do.

Nadine remained hysterical – could not calm down. On arrival at the hospital she was sedated, and her wounds cleaned, and she was admitted for observation. She was not allowed to see her children or her family. She was in police custody and that was one of the reasons for her frantic behavior.

Two days later Joe and Phyllis made the decision to let Charles go, and with him dead Nadine faced even bigger charges. When she got the news, her screams and wails echoed through the jail cells.

Her family could learn no more than what they saw on the news. The police would not answer their questions, nor would Charles's parents—and Phyllis immediately petitioned for temporary custody of the children, which was granted.

It was not until she appeared in court that Nadine got to see her family. They were present for her arraignment. She was assigned a court-appointed attorney and pleaded not guilty.

In jail, Nadine was in the company of women charged with prostitution, drug offenses and assault. Her grief ran deep – though she did her best to keep to herself.

Her cellmate, Margie, was behind bars for a drug offense. "So, did you really kill your husband?" Nadine did not reply. Margie added, "Well, he probably deserved it."

With that, Nadine sat up on the cot. "You don't know anything about me! Or my husband!"

"I saw the news. You probably did what you had to. It happens. I applaud you."

Nadine lay down again and turned her back on her cellmate. She muttered, "I don't want to hear this."

"You should know the courts don't care nothing about you. The laws don't even protect women as they should. And when you try to defend yourself? Well…that's when you become the bad guy, and the men become the victim."

Nadine muttered, "It was self-defense."

"Ha! There ain't no such thing! They don't never see it that way."

Nadine rolled over and faced Margie. "Please don't talk to me anymore about my business. Like I said, you don't know anything about me."

"Fine then."

Nadine's family could visit now—but one at a time. Martha embraced her daughter and held her tight. "How are you, baby?" Nadine shook her head. "Not good. Have you seen the children?"

"No. That awful witch won't let me see them. I can't do anything until the hearing next week. I'm sorry, Nadine."

"A hearing?"

"Oh, they filed for custody."

"What?! They can't do that!"

"Apparently they can. We'll do what we can, honey. Try not to worry."

Nadine's visits with her parents, Martha and Sam, were especially hard for her. Jail was the last place she wanted her parents to see her. Then Claudette's turn came. Neither of the sisters could contain themselves. They hugged and they cried.

They sat down, holding hands. "We only have a few minutes, Nadine—so tell me everything."

"Claudette, it was an accident. I loved him. You know I did. I would never hurt him on purpose. It was such a busy day and I was late with dinner. Someone came to the door selling vacuums— but I didn't let him in. I didn't! But Charles had had a bad day— and he just took it out on me. He just went crazy for no reason— beat me all over the kitchen. A knife I'd peeled potatoes with was on the floor. It was the only way I could get him to stop beating me! I didn't have any choice! I had to fight back!"

Claudette assured her, "It's okay. We're gonna get through it. I knew he was still beating you."

Nadine stared at her hands in her lap. "He said he would kill me. Said he would have never let me go. That's what he said." "We could have helped you, Nadine."

"No, not this time. He was obsessed with the fear of me leaving. He even put a gun to my head and pulled the trigger."

Claudette clasped her hand over her mouth. "What? Did you call the police?"

"Carolyn did."

"She saw it?"

"No, we were in the barn. The gun was empty, but when he pulled the trigger, I didn't know that. Claudette, he threatened to kill you all if I ever left him again!"

Time was up. Nadine gave her sister another hug. "It's so much stuff you don't know. I'll have to write you. Oh, one more thing, sis. Buried in my garden is a few hundred dollars. I was saving it to leave Charles. Take it as far as you can with the children."

Soon thereafter Nadine was offered a plea, but she refused. The district attorney said, "We're trying to offer you a lesser charge, Mrs. Hunter, so you'll serve less time away from your children."

Her attorney visited and advised, "Take the plea, Nadine. Selfdefense may be hard to prove."

"What?" Nadine frowned. "Hard to prove? I don't understand what you mean. I will not plead to anything. I'm not guilty and a plea says I am. It was self-defense and I have the scars to prove it! I want a trial! I want the jury to hear my story and see I'm no murderer! I'm a victim of abuse!" She got to her feet. "You come back and see me when you have a trial date!" She knocked on the door for the guard.

On the day the trial began Nadine ran her eyes around the courtroom, making eye contact with her parents and Claudette. The children were not present. The trial went on for several days with Nadine revealing some details of painful moments with Charles. One-character witness after another had nothing but positive things to say about Nadine. There was also testimony about the time Nadine was hospitalized after Charles abused her.

Phyllis was called to testify against Nadine. When asked if she ever noticed any abuse she admitted, "I do recall seeing a bruise she told me came from Charles. I don't know where she got it from. But I never witnessed my son abusing her. No."

During the closing arguments the DA stated, "Mrs. Hunter had the opportunity to get out of this marriage, but she chose to return. She could have even escaped Mr. Hunter that day in the kitchen, but she didn't. She picked up a knife and waited for him to approach her again and stabbed him to death. I think it's only fair you find her guilty of first-degree murder."

Nadine's attorney, in her closing arguments, pleaded for manslaughter. "Mrs. Hunter is not a malicious person. She's not a murderer. She didn't just stand around that kitchen contemplating how to kill her husband. No, rather she did try to run, as you heard, but he grabbed her, and she slipped to the floor. After years of abuse, she finally stood up and defended herself. I say you have to return with manslaughter."

The judge gave the jury their instructions and dismissed them to deliberate.

Six long hours later, the eight men and four women returned to the courtroom. They had decided Nadine was guilty of manslaughter, and she was sentenced to fifteen years, with possibility of parole in seven or eight.

"It won't bring our son back!" Phyllis cried. "And it's just not enough punishment for what she did!"

Claudette was the only one to comment to the press. "Domestic violence is a crime and my sister is the real victim."

Nadine was transferred to the Tennessee State Prison for Women. Her cellmate there, Sandy, was serving time for felony larceny. They got along fairly well. Some of the women in the Tennessee prison applauded Nadine for what she did. A few decided to break her in, because she was the new girl, so within the first two months Nadine endured solitary confinement for fighting.

The weekend after she was released to her cell, her sister and mother, Claudette and Martha, came to visit and noticed a faded bruise on her face. Martha said, "Nadine, what in the world happened to you?"

"Some strumpet touched me in the shower. The guards and her little friends thought it was funny until we started fighting." She dropped her head and moaned, "Oh how I hate this place, Ma."

"Baby, we're working at trying to get you an appeal for a notguilty verdict. It just takes time."

"Yeah, too much time. How about my kids? Have you seen them?"

Claudette answered in a very tender voice. "No, sis. They won't let us." She sighed and added, "I did find out from a mutual friend Charles changed his beneficiary to his mother. Did it the time you left him, and never changed it back—so she did get the insurance money. But we had figured that would happen."

"I just pray my kids are doing well."

As they were leaving, Martha and Claudette left Nadine money for the canteen and for using the pay phone. In the next few weeks Nadine heard no word of an appeal, a fact which left her feeling desolate. She feared she would not be getting out any time soon.

Months passed as the family went again and again to court, until finally Claudette was granted permission to see Nadine's children. There was also an order for the children to see a therapist. They had lost both parents at the same time – witnessing the death of one. Their mixed emotions were taking a toll on them, and on Phyllis, who added to the children's difficulty in grieving because every chance she got she spoke against their mother.

Carolyn and William were confused. They did not know if they should still love their mother or hate her.

Phyllis refused to take Carolyn and William to see Claudette or their grandparents, so once again Nadine's family was back and forth to family court to have the judge enforce visitation rights. The first visit was arranged at the therapist's office, a neutral location and environment for both sides of the family. But the sad fact was two years had passed since the children had seen their mother's family.

Martha, Sam, and Claudette sat around a table in the conference room at the therapist's office awaiting the children. Carolyn and William followed behind the therapist, holding hands. As they entered, they stood near the door and glared at the family as if they were strangers.

Martha stood up with open arms. "Well, aren't you gonna give your grandma a hug?"

"Go on," the therapist said. "You can give them a hug." The children moved slowly, and one at a time hugged their relatives.

William noticed the gift-wrapped boxes on the table. "Is that for me?" he asked.

Claudette picked up a box with his name on it and handed it to him. "Open it."

The boy's eyes lit up like lights on Christmas day at the sight of the shiny red remote-control car. His smile stretched from ear to ear. "Thank you!"

"You're more than welcome, baby. And Carolyn, I got something for you too." She handed over a box wrapped in pink and white polka dot paper.

Carolyn tore open the gift and pulled a Barbie doll head from the box. When she looked up, she said, "Don't you think I'm too old for Barbie?"

The therapist detected the sarcasm in the girl's voice and looked over her glasses at her and frowned.

Claudette jumped in. "I remember when you used to want one of those, young lady. And ten is not too old to style hair and make her face up.

Martha spoke softly to her granddaughter. "If you don't want it, honey, I can take it back and exchange it for something you do want."

"No, it's fine."

"Your hair is pretty, Carolyn," Claudette said. "It reminds me of your mother."

"I don't want to look like her! I look like me!"

William stopped playing. He joined the others – all eyes on Carolyn. The therapist stood up. "Well, I think we can end our session here. I'm gonna call your grandmother to pick you two up."

Martha said, "So—that's it?"

"Well, we have to ease this reconciliation in on the children. Obviously, they're still very emotional over their mother."

"Oh, obviously," Martha said. "And even more obvious is Phyllis has taught my grandbabies to hate us."

Phyllis was delighted to hear the visit had been cut short, but Nadine's family did not give up, and gradually the visits moved from the therapist's office to public places like Carolyn's ballet recitals and William's football games. Phyllis busied herself with her own agenda on those occasions, completely avoiding them. Claudette made sure to take pictures of the children to send to their mother.

One day Nadine was stretched out on her bunk gazing up at the pictures taped to the wall in her cell. Her cellmate said, "Hey, those are some good-looking kids!"

"Thanks. I'm missing them so much." Nadine sighed. "I don't care for them to see me here, but I would like to talk to them at least. My mother-in-law won't even allow it."

"Sorry to hear that. I know what you mean, though. I got three boys and I don't want them to see me here either. That's why I tell my mama, 'Don't bring them.' I do keep in touch with them. It ain't nothing for kids to get in trouble nowadays."

"Well, not my kids. They love sports, dance, and music. I pray God bless them to turn out well in my absence."

"I think you're lucky to have someone taking good care of them. You should be happy."

Nadine frowned. "Huh. You have no idea how nasty my motherin-law can be. I'll be happy when my kids are with my family, or me, soon as I get out of here." She reached up and traced their faces with her fingers, longing to touch them.

By the time Carolyn turned eleven, she was very good at ballet. She loved dressing up in her pink leotard and stockings with her ballet shoes, her hair twisted up in a ball and pinned on the top of her head. When she danced, she imagined herself a beautiful prima donna, dancing somewhere far away from her current life.

William lived out his passion too. He played the position of wide receiver on the school's football team and was one of the fastest runners on the team. He managed to master eluding most defenders.

As time went by Claudette was granted overnight visits with the children every other weekend. By then, the children had warmed up to her again. She was the closest person to their mother. One Saturday Carolyn, in the bathroom, screamed out and Claudette went running down the hall. She knocked on the door and opened it and peeped in. "Carolyn, baby, are you alright?"

"No! Don't come in! I don't want you to see this!"

Claudette came in anyway. "See what?"

Carolyn was standing in front of the toilet with her panties around her ankles and blood on her hand. "Oh, Carolyn—it's okay, baby. You just started your period. It's natural." She flashed a big smile. "You're becoming a woman now."

"What do you mean?"

Claudette explained everything and helped her clean up, then left the bathroom to go get a sanitary napkin from her purse, plus a clean pair of panties.

The girl was obviously not happy about this part of coming of age. She groaned, "I can't believe this is going to happen to me every month! If this is what I have to go through to have children—I don't want any!"

Claudette smiled and nodded her head side to side. "You'll get through it – month after month like every other woman. And there will be times when you'll be glad to see it. Now, would you like to go get some ice cream? That's what I do when I'm on my period."

"Brother too?"

"Sure."

William was sitting on the porch swing. He said, "Sissy, are you gonna be okay?"

Claudette reassured him. "She's gonna be fine, William. Your sister is growing up."

The next day when Phyllis came to pick the children up, Claudette told her Carolyn started her period and asked, "Why hadn't you explained to her about the changes she would go through?"

Phyllis frowned. "Nadine should have been the one to do that since she's such a perfect mom. Don't blame me!"

"Ok, never mind. I'm not gonna argue with you. But in the past two years I'm sure you've had plenty of opportunities."

Nadine hated the prison environment, but at this point she did get a lucky break – an assignment to the laundry room. Some of the inmates envied her and spread rumors of favoritism on the part of the guard who managed to get her the assignment. A stir-up ensued and the warden transferred that guard and moved in Officer Daniels. The warden's aim was to avoid upset on the block by preventing prisoners and guards from getting too close.

What Nadine got from the new guard was high-alert uneasiness. Officer Daniels frequently made insinuating comments in her presence and turned hungry gazes her way, so Nadine did her best to avoid him.

Nadine was glad to get to work in the laundry room. The assignment gave her a break from the block—and from undesirables, but her happiness with the job ended when Diamond got assigned to laundry. Diamond was an inmate out to get Nadine, though Nadine had consistently resisted her advances. Nadine's resistance became a bigger aggravation to Diamond because it embarrassed Diamond in front of her friends.

One day when Nadine was turned the other way, Diamond took the opportunity to slide a bag of laundry Nadine was responsible for behind a bin. Thirty minutes before time to return to their cells, she pulled it out, tossed it to Nadine and called out, "Hey, Kitten, you forgot a bag."

"You did it on purpose!"

"Hey, watch your tone. You got thirty minutes to wash, dry and fold, Kitten. Looks like you need to get busy." Diamond laughed. "See ya," she said, and turned to walk out.

Nadine shouted, "My name is not Kitten!"

Diamond looked over her shoulder. "Oh, I know your name, Kitten," she purred, and gave a big laugh and sashayed down the hall.

One of the guards remained with Nadine. She said, "Look, Hunter, you gotta hurry up—'cause I've got to knock off shortly. I can't be late picking up my kids."

Nadine's voice was sharp. "I can't leave until my work is done— you know it."

"Well, I can't stay. You'll just have to explain it to the warden."

"No! She'll take my phone privilege this week. You know Diamond set me up 'cause I won't be her girlfriend. Oh, how I hate that witch!"

A voice called, "I'll stay." Officer Daniels, in the doorway, smiling.

The guard in a hurry to leave said, "Okay, fine—I'm outta here." Nadine avoided eye contact with Daniels as she quickly loaded the washer. He stood watching her. She glanced at him and rolled her eyes. Once she started the washer, she stood near it, watching the cycle.

"So, your girl got a thing for you, huh?"

"She's not my girl."

162

Daniels moved her way. Nadine swallowed as if she was trying to keep the content of her stomach down. Daniels leaned against the washer. He smirked. "So, here we are, alone at last." He reached over to touch her arm.

Nadine stepped back. "Get away from me!"

"Hey, be nice," he said softly. "Be nice to me and I'll be nice to you. Just like your old friend Andrew who got transferred out."

"He never touched me!" Her stern look didn't seem to intimidate him at all.

"Oh, but he wanted to, just like I do." He leaned in and took in a deep whiff of her scent and closed his eyes. "God! You don't smell like any prisoner I've ever met. And you're so beautiful." Nadine folded her arms across her chest and stepped back.

"Do you know how many women would take advantage of this situation right here? Do you know what I could do for you? This could be our little secret."

"Stop talking to me."

It wasn't long before the washer stopped. Nadine spun the rolling basket around toward the washer, shoving her way around Daniels, and began unloading the clothes.

"Here, let me help you." He reached in the washer, brushing his arm against Nadine's breast. She moved back.

"You sure you don't want me to touch you?"

Again, she folded her arms across her chest and backed away from him. "I just want to be left alone."

"Calm down. I'm not hurting you."

"Please, I just want to be left alone." She backed up against a dryer and slid down to the floor into a sitting position. She put her head between her knees and began whimpering. Daniels tried to make her stand up, but his touch only made her scream and cry out.

"I said nobody is trying to hurt you. Calm down." She

kicked at him and continued screaming.

"Get up, Hunter. Calm down!"

Now two other guards were coming down the hall. They couldn't see who was screaming or what was going on until they moved around the washers, where they found Daniels straddled over Nadine trying to control her.

One of the guards yelled, "Hey—what's going on here?"

Daniels said, "She's crazy, man."

Daniels was ordered to let go of Nadine, then one guard grabbed her ankles and the other grabbed her arms. They held her down, crossing her arms over her chest. Daniels left and returned with two more guards. Now some of the inmates were on alert, wondering what was going on.

Nadine's roommate, Sandy, checked her watch and said, "Hey, where is Nadine?"

Another inmate said, "Last I saw she was in the laundry room."

The guards eventually got Nadine to be still, but she continued to cry hysterically and was taken to the infirmary where she was given a shot to sedate her. Warden Smith received a call at home about what happened and a couple of hours later showed up.

Warden Smith found Nadine awake and restrained to the bed. She yelled, "Nurse! Get these restraints off!"

Immediately two nurses removed the restraints. The warden demanded, "Who gave permission for restraints?"

One of the nurses said, "We had no other choice, Warden. She was hysterical."

The other said, "It was a nursing judgment."

The warden stood with both hands on her hips. "Oh, really? Well, you have no authority to make such a judgment. That's my call—and next time I see something like this, you're both fired! Now leave us alone."

The warden turned to Nadine. "Are you alright? What happened here tonight?"

"I was being harassed." Her words were slurred and raspy.

"By who?"

"One of the guards."

"Who?"

"I can't say."

"Then I can't help you."

Nadine feared retaliation because she had seen it happen to others. Warden Smith waited a moment, hoping Nadine would change her mind and speak further, but she did not. "Ok, Nadine, after tonight, you will return to your cell. You will be evaluated by one of our psychiatrists. If it is deemed your behavior tonight was inappropriate, you will perform extra duties. You may even go to lock down. I will be investigating this situation, starting with Daniels. I will not tolerate misbehaving inmates—or guards who get out of line."

The warden turned to leave. Nadine said, "Wait!"

The warden turned back. "Yes?"

"Please help me."

"I cannot help you if you do not talk to me."

Warden Smith waited, hoping Nadine would give her some information she could work with. It was impossible to be present all the time and watch everything and protect everyone, especially when the inmates refused to talk. Those who did talk were deemed troublemakers by the guards, and their grievances ignored or denied. Much of the time, grievances did not even reach the warden.

Nadine felt a point of desperation, so without mentioning names she described her plight. "At night, some women are actually raped in their cells. The things that goes on here under your watch is horrific. The guards humiliate us. We can't even take care of our personal needs when we're on our period without being watched and devoured." She took a breath and heaved a sigh. "Warden Smith, I was abused by my husband. I was beaten and raped. If I have to continue like this, I will kill myself. For me it's like I've gone from one prison to another. In here, people won't let you mind your own business. But all I want is to be left alone."

Warden Smith watched the trembling in Nadine's hands and the tension of her body language. She noted the shakiness of her voice and interrupted her spiel. "Nadine, you had a panic attack. I get it."

"No, you don't! I can't do this. I can't, I can't, I can't!" Nadine wrapped her arms around herself and rocked back and forth.

As a result of this incident and verbal interchange, the warden decided to move Nadine up on the list for psychiatric therapy. There were many inmates on a waiting list because there were many more cases than therapists. Inmates with substance abuse issues were always first for rehabilitation.

Battered women who killed were also on the list for psychiatric evaluation. And now Nadine expressed suicide. The warden did not hesitate to get her some immediate help.

"Come in, Mrs. Hunter—have a seat."

The therapist was a heavyset white woman with dark brown shoulder-length hair and wearing a gray skirt suit with a white shirt and black pumps. She said, "I'm Mrs. Simms."

Nadine waited while Mrs. Simms flipped through her folder. "So…it says here you had an outburst. And were restrained." She peeped at Nadine over her glasses. "Is that right?"

"I was being harassed."

"I see." She removed her glasses. "Mrs. Hunter, I know what goes on in this prison. The majority of the women here are being harassed. I've complained, but nothing can be done about it if the women do not stick together and speak up."

Nadine's reply carried a bit of steam. "Unless you're here in it—you don't really know! You come in here, what, twice a week? And think you can tell me what we gotta do and what we need to do? While you sleep peacefully in your bed, the women here are being violated. I told the warden what happened to me in the laundry room, but I could not tell her all the horrific things that go on here—because I have to live here!"

She sighed and looked down at her hands and added in a quiet voice, "We keep our mouths shut to survive."

"I understand, Nadine. May I call you Nadine?"

"Sure. Whatever."

"So, any chance of you sharing with me what really goes on here?"

Nadine wrapped her arms around herself and nervously rocked back and forth with eyes closed.

"Mrs. Hunter, are you alright?"

Nadine whispered, "He hurt me, he hurt me."

"Who? Who hurt you?"

"I can't go through this again. I can't do it."

"Mrs. Hunter—Nadine—stop and listen to me. What are you talking about? Talk to me."

Nadine jumped and opened her eyes as Mrs. Simms touched her shoulder. "It's alright," the therapist said. "I'm not trying to hurt you."

Nadine moaned, "I've gone from one prison to another."

"I'm sorry. I don't understand."

"Living with my husband, Charles. That was a prison. Now I'm here. Locked up behind these bars. It's like the walls of that house we had, and some of the guards just as cruel. And I'm isolated from my family and my children...I might as well be dead."

"Have you had suicidal thoughts?"

Nadine got to her feet and began pacing. "Some of these women are prostituted out to guards or other inmates in exchange for money, cigarettes, alcohol, drugs or favors. Guards on certain cellblocks are paid to turn their heads from any sexual activity. Sheets are tied to the bars for privacy. Then there are inmates willing to perform sex with each other in front of the guards. You can bet they're highly favored. Being in the general population...." She turned to face Mrs. Simms. "Did you know some of these women would rather be here than on the streets? They don't want to return to society because this has become a way of life—but I don't belong here—you hear me?"

She exhaled. Her voice dropped. "I try hard not to become a part of this madness. I can't live like this! I'm not gonna make it." She sat down again then.

Mrs. Simms said, "Excuse me. I'll be back shortly."

The psychiatrist left the room and called Warden Smith. "Did you find out what's wrong with that Hunter girl?" the warden asked.

"I think Mrs. Hunter is experiencing PTSD. Maybe even thoughts of suicide. I want to treat her – move her up the list."

"Treat her? You were only supposed to evaluate her. Your list is as long as both of my arms put together if not longer and you're only here twice a week. You can't treat her and take from someone else."

"Well, ma'am, I can volunteer my time – two evenings a week on my own time."

"No. It's special treatment. I can't allow it."

"No one would have to know."

"No, absolutely not. I just wanted her evaluated, but she's not the only one here with problems. What makes her so special?" The Warden listened for an answer.

"Well, ma'am, don't be upset if you get a call in the middle of the night where she was found hanging in her cell. Besides, if I can help her, I can help a lot of these women. There are several with PTSD."

"Mrs. Simms, there are women who have been waiting for psychiatric services for months. Some of them can't even get weekly psychotherapy sessions and you're…"

"Please, Warden, she interrupted. "I really want to do this. I have a good feeling about this one."

The first thing Mrs. Simms taught Nadine was practical approaches to coping with stress and anxiety and dealing with anger. Their sessions covered everything she went through with

Charles down to his death. The emotions were more than Nadine could stand at times. Mrs. Simms prescribed her Prozac and a benzodiazepine to help with sleep and anxiety.

A gang called Tribal American Natives or TAN as they called themselves targeted Nadine – wanting her to become a member. Some tried indebting her by doing her unasked favors, including her work in the laundry room. She would almost fight them to keep them from doing her work so as not to owe them anything. At times, the fights cost her privileges or a day or two in the hole. Mrs. Simms encouraged her to stay out of trouble if she didn't want to be labeled a troublemaker. Sometimes the hole wasn't so bad – if it got Nadine away from the others.

Nadine's parents, Martha and Sam came to visit her less and less, but Claudette continued to come.

Nadine rushed to the table at the sight of her. "Claudette, it's been weeks."

"I know and I'm sorry. Things have just been so busy. How's it going?"

"Still hating it here, but you know that. How are my kids?"

"Growing like weeds. They're fine."

"Claudette, they belong with our family. Don't give up."

"Our parents can't fight no more, Nadine."

"Why? Is it money?"

"Yes and..." Claudette looked away.

"What? Tell me."

"Daddy had a stroke."

"Oh, my God. When? Why didn't you tell me?"

"Three months ago. They didn't want me to tell you."

"What about another attorney?"

"We're tapped out, Nadine! Between Daddy's medical bills and the attorney for the kids – well there's nothing left but the house. We have to eat, you know."

Nadine sighed. "I know. I'm so sorry. I just want out of here!"

The pounding of her fist on the table caught the look of one of the guards. Nadine flashed a small smile, then leaned in closer to Claudette. She whispered, "Look, I can't even take a shower or use the toilet without being gawked at. They watch us do everything. It's humiliating to be on your period and some guard is getting his jollies watching you stick a tampon between your legs. The only time I can really express myself without reprimand is during therapy."

Claudette listened to her little sister – feeling sorry for not being able to help her. At the end of their visit, Claudette promised to get back soon.

Nadine was escorted from her cell as usual to meet Mrs. Simms. At the end of the session, Mrs. Simms said, "Nadine, I don't really know how to tell you this, but tonight is our last session."

Nadine raised a brow. "What?"

"It's been three months."

"But, no, I'm not ready. I don't know when I'll be ready."

"Nadine, you knew we only had a short time."

"Yeah, but I was hoping you would see I really needed you and ask for more time."

"I did. The answer was no."

"Ask again, please." Nadine stood up and began pacing around the room.

"It won't do any good. There are others who need me too."

Nadine turned to Mrs. Simms. "Am I cured?"

"Oh, Nadine, this is not a disease like cancer. Do you think I've helped you at all?"

Nadine began her pace again. "I don't know."

"Now look at me. What have you gotten out of this therapy?" "I don't know." Nadine shrugged her shoulders.

"You don't know? Well, if you don't know, then we've wasted three months. Time I could have been helping someone else. Tell me you've gotten something out of this therapy."

Nadine stared at the floor for a moment, then she looked up at Mrs. Simms. "I have," she said.

"Thank you. What?"

Nadine replied, "How to cope better with my feelings of anger and guilt – I guess. And I'm writing in my journal more."

Mrs. Simms sat back and crossed her legs. "Yes, but you haven't brought yourself to writing about Charles's death."

Nadine spun around. "You see, this is why I still need you."

"I understand. But it could take months, maybe even years for you to address everything. We don't have that kind of time."

"It seems like I have the time. I'll be in here for years."

"No word yet on an appeal?"

"No and I don't want another court appointed attorney. I don't even think the first attorney cared. My family is working on finding another one. Money is tight for them, but I keep praying about it. I guess he hears me."

"Well, if you believe he does, then he does."

TEN

Attorney Cole

Carolyn was becoming a beautiful young lady – as beautiful as her mother, and she had a secret crush on a boy named Marcus. One afternoon Marcus and his mother came into the bakery. While his mom placed the order for a cake for his sister's sixteenth birthday, he turned her way. They chatted briefly, but Carolyn was unable to enjoy the moment because her grandmother took every opportunity to turn her disapproving eyes their way.

At school the next day, Marcus invited Carolyn to the party. "I was gonna invite you yesterday, but your grandmother made me nervous."

"Oh, yeah, she makes me nervous too." They laughed. "Besides that, I had some work to do in the back. Is it a surprise party?"

"No, she knows about it. She'll be sixteen, though, so it's a big deal to her. So, what do you say? Can you come?"

"I don't know. I'll have to ask my Nana."

"Ok, let me know. I'd like to hang out with you."

That evening, after their grandparents had gone to bed, Carolyn slipped into William's room. He listened to her happy news, hesitated, and then said, "Do you think *Mama* would let you go?"

"Who cares? How do I know what she'd say? All I know is— Nana said no!"

"So, how far does he live from here?"

"I don't know. Not far, I guess. Why?"

"Just sneak out and go."

"Are you serious, William?"

"Look, when I want to play video games with my friends, I tell them I have football practice—and they believe me!"

"Don't they know better when they drop you off?"

"Nope. They don't always pay attention to everything, Carolyn. I went to play video games and got back to the field before Paw-Paw came to pick me up."

They both laughed. Then Carolyn sighed and said, "I can't do that. I'd get caught for sure."

William shrugged. "If you believe that's what will happen, you will."

Carolyn reached for a pillow and playfully hit him.

Phyllis had met Tabitha, Carolyn's best friend, and Carolyn's mother, at one of the ballet recitals. Tabitha was the only friend Phyllis permitted Carolyn to hang out with. The day of the birthday party, Carolyn spent the day at Tabitha's house. Her grandmother expected her home by five. Tabitha's mom had a few friends over for a cookout. While the adults were outside eating, drinking, and laughing it up, Tabitha helped Carolyn get herself ready for the birthday party which started at 2:00.

The adults were too busy having fun to notice the girls had slipped away. It was only a three-block walk to Marcus's house. He was soon introducing them to his family and fixed plates of food for them. After his sister opened her gifts, Tabitha and Carolyn were careful not to stay long. As soon as Marcus's sister opened her gifts, they made their exit, and as soon as they were out of sight of Marcus's house, they took off running.

They ran the short distance so quickly when they reached their goal Carolyn bent over with her hands on her knees and tried to speak. Her words came in short bursts." Girl, I—Um thought we – thought we weren't gonna make it!"

She stood straight, caught her breath, and laughed and laughed.

Tabitha shot her eyes to the corner of the house. "Looks like my mom's been looking for us." She raised her voice and called, "We'll be right there. Just catching our breath!"

They quickly changed their clothes and soon thereafter climbed into the backseat, and Tabitha's mom started the car. The girls soon bent their heads close, whispering and giggling. They had done it! Slipped away to Marcus's sister's birthday party—and no one the wiser.

Grandmother Phyllis, as usual, was at the door as soon as the car pulled up. As soon as Tabitha and her mom waved goodbye and the car pulled away, Phyllis ordered, "Alright—young lady. Get in here. Dinner is ready and we've been waiting on you!"

"But I'm not hungry. Her mom cooked on the grill."

"I cooked spaghetti, one of your favorites."

"Sounds good Nana, but if it's all the same, I'm going to my room."

"Suit yourself."

Late that evening William came to her room—wanting all the day's details. "Well, Brother," Carolyn said with a grin, "sneaking about was nerve racking! But to spend time with Marcus…well, it was all worth it!"

They raised their palms and slapped each other a high-five and laughed – carefully though as always to hold down the noise. "See? I'm proud of you, sis!"

Claudette purchased a house and began going through Nadine's boxes to condense the content for storage. As she was going through one of the purses, she found Candace's business card and slipped it in her pocket. When she called the office, she was given another number – informed that Candace had taken a job elsewhere. When she dialed that number, she learned Candace was out sick. A few days later, she tried again. This time she was able to reach her and tell her everything.

"Claudette, give me a few days to see what I can do to help her. I think I know an attorney who may take her case."

Claudette wrote a brief letter to Nadine to give her this perhaps happy news. Two weeks later, Nadine was called out for an attorney visit. She entered the designated room and found a welldressed man in a suit bent over some papers. He hadn't noticed her standing there. She cleared her throat. He glanced up but appeared to first look at her shoes. He lifted his eyes slowly, as though measuring her small frame.

The man said nothing. He stared, astounded by the beauty of this inmate.

Nadine was hugely ill at ease. Gruffly she demanded, "Are you here to see Nadine Hunter?"

"Um, yes—yes, please forgive me." He got to his feet and murmured, "I wasn't told how attractive you would be. My name is Linfred Cole. I'm an attorney." They shook hands. He motioned for her to take a seat in the nearby folding chair. And informed her it had been her friend Candace who asked him to review the case."

Nadine murmured softly, "What did you expect me to look like?"

Linfred chuckled. "Well, you might be surprised at how quickly women let themselves go in here. But clearly…you're a natural."

"So, what about my appeal?"

"Um, yeah, well, it can definitely be appealed." He still seemed somewhat distracted. Long seconds passed before he said, "Yes, hmm—so has anyone ever talked to you about Battered Woman Syndrome?"

"No. Never heard of it."

"Okay. So, used to be, Battered Woman Syndrome was not admissible in court as a defense for victims of domestic violence who killed in self-defense. Now, however, the courts do permit experts to at least talk about it on the stand—because it helps the jury to understand the victim's frame of mind at the time."

He shuffled some papers, moved some to the side and said, "So, it looks like they didn't find you guilty just for the act of killing your husband. They appear to have felt at some point you could have escaped him—in other words, his death could have been avoided."

She dropped her head and sighed deeply.

He tapped the tip of his pen against the table. "Let me ask you something." When she raised her eyes he said, "Why did you stay?"

The sound came from her might be called a soft growl. She clenched her hands in her lap. "I'm so sick of that question! He would have killed me! He said so numerous times!... And I believed him. He came back from 'Nam a different person. But so far as I know, the time in the military may have just triggered the real person inside of him." She put her hands to her temples and exclaimed, "I don't know!"

Attorney Cole leaned back in the wooden armchair and crossed his legs. He let some time go by before he asked, "So, he wasn't abusive before?"

"No. Well, he never hit me. He was always a jealous man—possessive, and somewhat domineering. After Vietnam, he became worse, even starting fights if someone dared to even look at me."
"I can see that." He smiled.

Nadine returned a slight smile. "Anyway, he went too far. It was flattering at first because I thought it was a sign of love – you know, like he couldn't imagine me with anyone else because he loved me so much. But when he started hitting me…" She looked away.

"It's okay, Ms. Hunter. I – I think we have a good chance at an appeal before the State Supreme Court."

"Why the Supreme Court?"

"Because the court-appointed attorney has already tried to appeal to the Appellate Court with no success. See, courts tend to be tougher on women who kill—versus men, for some reason. I'm sorry to say it." He leaned forward. "Anyway, I'd like to take your case."

"Can you win?"

He said with confidence, "I always win."

"Always?"

"Trust me."

Nadine slowly shook her head. "I trust no man."

"Well, then, you can start with me." He glanced up at her as he began shoving papers into his briefcase.

She watched him stand and walk to the door. She asked, "How much?"

He turned to face her. "For what?"

"Your services?"

"Oh! It's Pro Bono!"

Nadine got to her feet and folded arms across her chest. "Why?!"

"Because Candace is a good acquaintance of mine. Oh, and because you couldn't afford me otherwise. But more importantly, I want to." He winked, smiled and opened the door.

She called out, "So what do you get out of it?"

"Hopefully—more cases like yours." He strode back and extended his hand. She looked at it and after a bit of hesitation responded with a firm shake. He said, "I must warn you—it's not gonna be easy. First of all, I need to know everything. Everything! Even the things you don't care to talk about. So…are you okay with that?"

"No! Of course not. But if it will get me out of here, I'll tell you everything."

"Good. I'll be back tomorrow."

The next day at the same time, Linfred kept his word. "So," he began. "Let's start from the beginning. Where and how did the two of you meet?"

Nadine answered all his questions—questions that led right up to when Charles returned from Vietnam. At the end of this first session, Nadine took a good look at this man. He stood about six feet tall and was athletically built. His tawny complexion had just the right number of freckles across the bridge of his nose to be attractive. She had not yet fully paid attention, but now she was noting his alluring hazel-eyed gaze and reddish-brown shade of the short wavy hair. It would be later in the day before she realized something odd. That moment of observation was the only instance, since that long-ago night when she met Charles, that she had ever really noticed any other man.

Linfred was so intent on winning the case he spent every opportunity available to him with Nadine. He taped their conversations and also made notes. Their conversations, of course, were often intense. When at last they reached the scene where she stabbed Charles, she closed her eyes and paused – a long pause.

She heard him say, "Take your time, Nadine."

In earlier sessions she had frequently paused to gather her emotions. At this point, she could no longer hold back her tears.

Linfred reached in his pocket. "Here, take my handkerchief."

With what followed, he could not write. He just listened intently.

By the time she finished recanting the events of that long ago day, she was obviously exhausted. She huddled quietly, sniffling, wiping her face. He was glued to his seat, still watching her. He was convinced now – Nadine was not a murderer. She was a victim.

She wiped away tears and noticed the intense look on his face. She felt ashamed and tucked her chin down and wrapped her arms around herself and was soon rocking back and forth with her eyes closed.

"It's alright, Nadine. We can stop here for today."

She opened her eyes and moaned, "I hate my life. I hate what I did to him—and what I allowed him to do to me."

He strode the several steps over in her direction and put his hand on her back as he squatted beside her.

She abruptly got to her feet. "So, we're done?"

He stood. "Yes, yes we are. I guess I'll see you next week."

After this dramatic session Linfred decided to visit Crystal Watts, the appointed attorney who had originally taken Nadine's case and filed for her appeal. The secretary informed Miss Watts of Linfred's request to see her and was soon walking him around to her office.

"Come in, Mr. Cole." The voice belonged to a skinny blonde in a blue skirt-suit who remained seated behind the desk. She motioned for him to take a seat. "What can I do for you?"

He reached over the desk to shake her hand. "A pleasure to meet you. I'm here to talk about one of my clients—one you represented some time ago. Nadine Hunter. You also filed her appeal."

"Yes, I remember. Murdered her husband." She reached for a small case on the desktop and pulled out a cigarette. "Do you mind?"

"Not at all, it's your office."

"Care for one?"

"No, thank you. I don't smoke."

She lit up, took a puff and blew smoke in the air. "So, what about Mrs. Hunter?"

"I think her defense could have been stronger."

"Oh? You have a problem with my representation, Mr. Cole?"
"Actually, I do. That's why I'm going to represent her before the Supreme Court."

She took another puff. "Mr. Cole, I don't *misrepresent*. I presented the facts. I appealed the facts. The court didn't rule in her favor. I did my job."

"I see. Is it just a job?"

She placed the cigarette in an ashtray and went over to a stack of folders on a nearby table. "These are my cases, Mr. Cole. You don't get these many cases from misrepresenting. I'm swamped with court-appointed clients. The courts are full, but you know that. I do my best with everybody."

"I'm not saying you don't. I'm just saying you missed some things. Miss Watts, have you ever heard of Battered Woman Syndrome?"

"Oh, sure, but it's not admissible."

"Actually, that's not the case anymore. In fact, you probably could have used it to argue her appeal."

"I appealed for a lesser sentence or charge, which she didn't get. I mean, after all, she did murder her husband."

"Murdered? So, you thought she was guilty?"

She frowned as she picked up her cigarette and sat down. "I don't know what you mean, Mr. Cole." She took a puff.

"Did you think Mrs. Hunter was a murderer?"

"She did murder her husband. She said it was self-defense. But it doesn't matter what I think. People form their own opinions— you know. Maybe the jury deliberated that things could have gone differently. She didn't have to kill him, or for that matter, to stay in that situation."

"How an attorney feels about the client can affect the defense."

"Mr. Cole, I'm not on trial. And I hardly see where it matters what I felt."

"That's what I figured, especially if you're court appointed." He stood up.

"Excuse me? I resent that. But tell me something, Mr. Cole—how is it that you're able to defend her. She has no money?"

"Pro Bono."

"Because?"

"Because I've spent quite a bit of time getting to know her and I believe she's the victim. Oh, and I despise punks who beat on women. Did you even check hospital records or police reports for any prior abuse? Was a blood test done on the deceased for alcohol levels? Did you interview the neighbor who helped her the night she crawled across the street after being beaten and kicked around by her husband? Did you know that she attended a group meeting for victims of abuse?"

"Who do you think you are? I did my job!" She hammered her fist on the desk.

"You know, officers did make a report the day her husband held a gun to her head. And I bet local liquor stores and local bars would help confirm his heavy drinking and violence. Did you talk to the children?"

"She didn't want the children involved and she dropped those charges from that night she crawled to her neighbor and later went back to him. So, life couldn't have been that bad."

"Well, perhaps she believed him when he said he had stopped drinking and the abuse would stop. I'm sure she wanted her marriage to work and her children to be raised by both parents." "Mr. Cole, we can go back and forth, but as I said—I did my best by her. What makes you any better than I am?"

"Because I believe my client and I'm gonna get her out. I won't stop until I do. Thank you for your time, Miss Watts. I understand clearly why my client is where she is now."

He turned and walked out. She took a drag on her cigarette but quickly mashed it out and ran after him. By the time she caught up, he was going down the stairs on the outside of the building.

She stood just outside the door and shouted, "Cole!" He stopped without turning around. She called out, "What do you want from me?"

Seconds went by. No answer. He then continued to his car.

Miss Watts hurried back inside and ordered, "Pull everything we have on a Nadine Hunter. Have it on my desk immediately."

ELEVEN

The Second Trial

The year's wait for the new trial seemed endless. When at last the date approached Nadine's legal team began preparing her.

Her monster-in-law, Phyllis, protested and refused to give permission for the children to testify in court. As an interim step, Nadine's attorney convinced the judge to agree to a meeting in the chamber with the children.

At the meeting Nadine, her attorneys – Cole, Drake, and Morris, and the grandmother Phyllis were present to hear the psychologist's reports. Phyllis still refused to drop her objection to her grandchildren taking the stand but agreed they could give written statements. The jury would see a copy of their written statements along with any relevant information from the psychologist.

The children, now years older, were instructed not to disclose to anyone—not even their Nana, what they shared with the judge. Simultaneously, Nadine's legal team had her see a psychiatrist so they could present as evidence the professional's psychiatric evaluation.

Finally, at long last, the trial began—a nonjury trial before a judge. Nadine sat quietly at the defense table, but her stomach was in tight knots. First order of business was presentation of hospital records and police reports. The D.A. made a big show of reminding everyone present Charles, Nadine's husband, was not on trial here—nor was he able to be present to defend himself.

At this point Linfred, Nadine's lawyer, interrupted. "Your Honor, the abuse is relevant. We need to present to the court the events which led up to the day of Mr. Hunter's death—as well as the state of mind Mrs. Hunter was in on that day."

First up, the paramedics at the scene were called to testify regarding Nadine's behavior. They reported finding her over Charles's body, crying frantically. One said, "She was trying to get him up—we had to pry her away from him."

Character witnesses also spoke on Nadine's behalf—including Ms. Janice, who again described the things she saw and knew. The surprise witness was Tracy, from the counseling group. No one in the courtroom had been aware Nadine had ever attended such a meeting.

At last, the time came for Nadine to take the stand. The prosecutor asked if she called the police each time she was abused.

"Not every time. I was afraid it would make things worse."

"How would it have made things worse?"

"He would have retaliated afterwards."

"I see. Your husband worked away from home a lot. Did you ever think about leaving while he was on the road?

"Yes, but I was afraid. I didn't really have any place to go with two children."

"You have family."

"He would have come for us."

"So, you never tried."

"Once."

"And what happened?"

Nadine sat quietly for a moment, wringing her hands.

"Mrs. Hunter, after leaving once, did you return to your husband?"

She stared at her hands clenched in her lap and whispered, "Yes."

"I'm sorry, Mrs. Hunter. The court could not hear you. Would you speak up?"

"Yes, I loved him. And I wanted my marriage to work."

"This man—this man who abused you for years in all the horrific ways you've described to this court—you loved him? You were out of the relationship and you returned to a violent man, as you've described—because you loved him?"

"I was never really out. He was the father of my children, and my first love."

"So, would you have the courts to believe on the day Mr. Hunter was stabbed, you loved him?"

"Objection!" called Attorney Drake.

"Let me rephrase the question. How did you feel about your husband on the day he was stabbed?"

"I loved him—but he was out of control that day! He beat me mercilessly and he wasn't gonna stop. He was gonna kill me!"

"How many times did you stab your husband?"

Nadine shrugged her shoulders.

"Once, twice, more?"

She frowned at the prosecutor. "I don't know. I wasn't counting."

The prosecutor walked over to the table and pulled out autopsy pictures of Charles and laid them in front of her. Nadine turned away, tears dropping as she closed her eyes. The judge handed her a tissue.

"According to the autopsy report, Mr. Hunter was stabbed eight times."

Phyllis began sobbing. As emotions in the courtroom increased, the judge determined it was time for a recess. Linfred firmly looked at the prosecutor as she walked by his table. Nadine was asked to step down, but she couldn't. She had to be assisted.

Phyllis complained to the prosecutor about old wounds being reopened – having to relive that day all over again so that Nadine could possibly get out. The prosecutor shook his head side to side and shrugged. "It's our great judicial system."

Nadine regrouped in a small room with her attorneys. Attorney Morris said, "Nadine, I know it's hard, but you have to be strong and get through this. I told you it wasn't going to be easy."

Linfred added, "Yeah, you can't allow her to get to you. Remember that it's her job to keep you locked up."

Nadine sniffled and wiped her eyes. "I don't think I can do this. She put those pictures right in my face."

Linfred spoke reassuringly. "That's because she wants you to feel defeated—but you're not defeated yet."

Attorney Morris said, "Do it for your kids, Nadine."

She closed her eyes, took a deep breath and nodded her head several times. Once back in the courtroom, she again took the stand. This time, she held it together and firmly answered all questions asked of her from both prosecutor and defense. She was able to talk about other events that occurred, including the day

Charles held the gun to her head—and the many other times he threatened her life.

The prosecutor asked her to describe why she had not been able to escape, as she could have many times before.

"I was frozen. He had just tried to strangle me with the belt. I knew he wasn't finished with me. I didn't know which way to run. I remember him launching towards me, but nothing after that."

"Are you saying that you don't remember stabbing your husband?"

"I remember him yelling and cursing. When he launched at me, I raised my hand." Tears began streaming down her face as she continued. "There was just so much blood—so much blood. I didn't mean to kill him. I loved him!" She tried to stifle the tears but could not. She rubbed her hands back and forth on her thighs, her entire body trembling.

After a bit the judge asked, "Mrs. Hunter, will you be able to continue?"

She nodded her head. Attorney Morris began the crossexamination. Her final question was, "Do you regret killing Charles?"

"Yes, I do."

After that the expert witness took the stand. Attorney Morris said, "Would you please state your name and position for the court?"

"Certainly. My name is Sandra Wilson. I'm a psychiatrist specializing in family counseling."

"And does that include domestic violence?"

"Oh, absolutely."

"How long have you been a psychiatrist?"

"Fifteen years."

"Licensed and board accredited?"

"Absolutely."

"Tell us your experience with victims of domestic violence."

"I've worked with victims for at least ten years. I also volunteer at two local shelters. I've done lectures at colleges and high schools. And I have a book out on the market on domestic violence in the home."

"So, one could say that you are an expert in this area."

"I'd like to think so, yes."

"In fact, you're currently working on something interesting. Can you tell us about that?"

"Well, I'm joining a couple of colleagues in writing a book on Battered Wife Syndrome—or BWS. It's very similar to Post Traumatic Stress Disorder and often happens in a cycle. Whether the abuse is physical, sexual, psychological, or emotional, if the relationship is intimate there is a honeymoon phase."

Dr. Wilson then explained the honeymoon phase is a loving phase when the abuse stops for a period of time. "But then the cycle starts again. This is partly the reason why some women stay. They decide the partner is not really bad, because they cling to good moments in memory."

Dr. Wilson explained these and other details about Battered Wife Syndrome and added that most women who kill their partner do so in self-defense. "These women are not vicious or ruthless killers. They act in self-defense—based on their sense of imminent physical danger—or imminent death."

Attorney Morris asked, "Have you had the opportunity of evaluating Mrs. Hunter?"

"Yes."

"Please share with the court your professional opinion as noted in the evaluation."

"The strong bond between her and her husband—that's typical. She exhibited the classic signs and symptoms of the Battered Woman Syndrome. I believe she truly was abused—and she learned to endure the abuse. I also believe she loved her husband selflessly and unconditionally—she was very devoted to him."

"How can a woman remain devoted to a man who abuses her?"

"Well, as I stated, there is a strong bond between a victim and the abuser. Victims have a sense of investment in a relationship they have been in for a while and that strongly impacts their ability to leave—and also affects their ability to recognize the negatives."

"But the whole relationship is negative."

"No. Not for the victim. It's almost as if the victim is brainwashed. The fear of leaving plays a huge role—because some actually lose their lives when they do. Another detail: the abuser does not stop because the victim leaves. The children then may become the victims."

With that, the witness was dismissed, and the court recessed.

When it resumed, the prosecutor began cross-examining Dr. Wilson. "Dr. Wilson, I don't understand. Please elaborate about these emotions or the investment which keeps a victim with the alleged abuser? I don't understand." The prosecutor shrugged her shoulders.

"Well, it's like love versus fear. Sort of like two voices of the mind," Dr. Wilson replied.

The prosecutor grinned and said sarcastically, "And which voice wins?"

"Love."

"Well, now I'm really confused."

"Just because a woman is being abused does not necessarily mean her feelings of love toward her partner have vanished. It may seem elementary to the way many of us think. If we're a victim, we choose to leave. So, we think all victims should just leave, but that's not how it works for some people. For those individuals love is reinforced during the honeymoon phase I mentioned earlier, and the spouse will keep thinking and hoping the abusive spouse is going to change. It becomes a very psychological situation."

The prosecutor stood there, looking at the witness. After a long moment she asked, "Do you think Mrs. Hunter temporarily lost her mind or was insane at the time she killed her husband?"

"Mrs. Hunter is not insane. She went through the typical stages of a battered woman who felt the abuse was not going to stop. She experienced what we all experience when we feel death is imminent—a fight-or-flight reaction. It's an innate sense in a human being. If there was a fire here now, or an intruder with a weapon suddenly turned on us—that same fight or flight reaction would kick in."

The witness paused. The prosecutor did not immediately speak, so she continued. "The defendant disassociated herself mentally from the fact this was her husband, a man she loved—to this was a man who was not going to stop until he killed her. And therefore, she had to act. The only thought in her mind was to find a way to stop his action before he killed her. Reality did not set in until she became aware of her children—and actually stepped back and realized what she was doing. Even now the defendant still suffers from depression, and probably has for a long time. She is prone to paranoia and panic attacks."

The witness continued and described the situation in the laundry room at the prison as a prime example of the victim's state of mind. Every person in the courtroom was paying close attention to every word Dr. Wilson uttered.

The prosecutor argued Charles had no weapon in his hand when he was stabbed. Then Linfred argued a person's body can be a weapon, especially if that person overpowers the other in strength and size.

The arguments concluded. For the rest of the day and part of the following day, the judge deliberated. For Nadine, the wait was excruciatingly difficult, though Linfred assured her their side built a stronger case with stronger evidence and better-received witnesses. He repeated his sense she had nothing to worry about.

It was at this point, to his surprise, Nadine nervously asked him to lead a prayer. He exclaimed, "I haven't prayed in years. I don't even know where to begin."

Nadine extended her hand across the table. As she bowed her head and silently waited for him to begin, he took her hand. He swallowed, lowered his head and searched for words. He asked God's Holy Spirit be in the courtroom to see that justice prevailed. He prayed that God would help Nadine remain calm and allow his own hands to work in her favor. He prayed for her freedom, and that she would get another chance at life with her children.

When he stopped, they both said "Amen" and looked up at each other. She smiled and said, "Thank you. That was good for someone who hasn't prayed in years."

~ ❖ ~

When at last the judge was ready for them to reconvene, Nadine breathed in several long deep breaths. Linfred asked, "Are you okay?"

"Oh, I'll be fine—I'll be fine." Even as she spoke a desperate panic in her voice suggested she did not believe what she said.

Attorney Morris peeped into the room. "What's taking y'all so long? Let's go."

Linfred answered, "She's panicking."

The attorney stepped into the room and closed the door behind her. "Look at me, Nadine. You are going to walk out of here a free woman today!"

"I don't know that."

"Well, I do. Now let's go. Come on."

Nadine and her three attorneys stood and held hands as they listened to the verdict. Nadine kept her head down and eyes closed. As she heard *"Not guilty,"* her knees almost gave way. Then the four of them were hugging each other with joy. Those there in support of Nadine gathered around to express their joy, but simultaneously Phyllis was screaming, "You murderer! You killed my baby! You murderer!"

The bailiff quickly removed the screaming woman from the courtroom. And after that the judge required everyone except Nadine and her attorneys exit.

The judge addressed her directly. She was still wiping tears from her eyes. "Mrs. Hunter, today you are a free woman. I don't usually say things like this, but I was moved by your testimony and by that of the expert witness. I'm sure that after this case I'll see more and more women before me such as yourself. I wish you the best."

Nadine wept now because she was so happy. She and her attorneys thanked the judge. Then Linfred drove his car around to the back entrance while the other two attorneys went out front to face the media.

Nadine felt like she was living some storybook tale as she slipped into Linfred's car. He asked, "You hungry?"

"I'm starved."

He took her to a small restaurant out of town, in Fairview. And to a surprise. Nadine's friends and family members were already there, but she did not know it. He asked her to wait a moment and got out and walked around and opened her door. As they walked in, the crowd got to their feet and started clapping. Nadine forgot how hungry she was as each person received her, hugged her, and congratulated her.

The chant began. "Speech, speech, speech!" Her eyes welled with tears. She wasn't sure she could speak, but she did manage in tone muffled by emotion to say, "Thank you...thank you so much... for all of your love, and your support."

She met the eyes of many, still striving to control her emotions. "I thought this day... was hopeless. But thanks to all of you, I am here."

She turned to her attorneys. "I can never repay you guys for what you've done for me."

They moved to the tables then, and when the food arrived Linfred got to his feet and held his glass of tea in the air. "I just want to say I've never met a stronger person than Nadine." He turned his gaze to her then said, "You are an amazing woman. I'm sure I speak for my colleagues too—when I say to you and all the Pearson family, what a privilege and a pleasure it has been to represent you."

A murmur then, around the room—voices of appreciation and agreement. Other encouraging words continued to be passed around the table as they dined.

At the end of the meal Linfred and his colleagues took their leave. He encouraged Nadine to keep in touch. Little by little the others left, until only Nadine and Claudette remained. Soon thereafter Nadine enjoyed the excitement of seeing Claudette's new house. It was a small house but had three bedrooms and a bath and a half.

Nadine said, "It's adorable, Sis. But why so many rooms?"

"Well, I always knew you would be coming home. And it's plenty of space for the kids too."

Nadine's face turned up a smirk and said bitterly, "Yeah…if I ever see them again."

"You will. You didn't think you would see freedom again—but you're here. Besides, didn't Lin say he would help?"

"Yep, that's what he said."

"You doubt him?"

"After today, no. But nothing is free."

They went out to the storage room and began going through Nadine's things. As she brought some of her things to the room designated for her, she noticed a picture of her daughter and son on the dresser.

Claudette noticed how her sister stood frozen before the photo. She said, "They've gotten so big—and Carolyn is interested in boys."

Nadine ran her fingers across the picture. "She's growing up to be a beautiful young lady. We'll have to watch her. And William is so handsome."

"They'll be around next weekend, maybe. She may not let them come now that you're home."

And the prediction turned true. Phyllis made up her mind about that shortly after leaving the courthouse. She would rather violate visitation rules than to allow the children to see their mother.

Soon thereafter Nadine and Claudette were at the Social Services Department to see what could be done to get the children back. "Are you working, Mrs. Hunter?" the social worker asked.

"Not yet. I just started looking."

"As you know, we will be looking out for the best interest of the children. At this point, I don't know if it is in their best interest to be with you."

"Well, I am their mother."

"Yes, and from what I understand from the Hunters, the children don't want to see you."

"I don't believe it. No one can love them more than me. I took good care of them. I—"

"Mrs. Hunter," the social worker interrupted, "I'm afraid I can't sympathize with you. I'm on the children's side. I would suggest you get a job and an attorney, because it's gonna be a battle to get those kids from their grandparents. You also need your own place, one appropriate for the children. The court needs to see you can provide for them. These children are very emotionally scarred."

Nadine was close to tears. She said, "That woman has taught my children to hate me. But they love me. I just know they do."

TWELVE

The Road Back

After three months of pounding the pavements for a job, Nadine was a bit more than discouraged. She couldn't give up though, so she pushed through her feelings of frustration and continued day after day, until finally she was called to an interview by a cleaners. The manager's final words in the interview were,

"Well, thank you for your time, Mrs. Hunter. I'll give you a call."

"That's what I've been hearing. Please, I'm a hard worker. I really am."

"Mrs. Hunter…um, well, you don't have any experience, and…"

"Then why say you'll call me? See, I've been looking for a job for months and it hasn't been easy. All I need is a chance." The look in Nadine's eyes begged for the job.

The manager pursed her lips and said nothing for a momentt. Finally, she said, "Ok, I'll give you a week. I still need to do a background check, but you can start in the morning. Eight o'clock."

"Oh, thank you—thank you so much!"

For the first time in months, Nadine noticed the freshness of the air and the warm rays of the sun as her stride to the bus stop became a skip. She couldn't wait to get home to tell Claudette her happy news. Yes, she was worried about the background check.

But she would show the manager just how hard she could work, and then the background check wouldn't matter so much.

During her first week of training, she gained favor by catching on quickly. By the second week, Nadine was working on her own at the press and the dry-cleaning machines. She smiled at her work with pride. For the first time in years, she felt a sense of accomplishment. In the third week she got her first paycheck and opened a savings account.

The following Thursday, the manager called her into the office. She said, "Sit down, please."

"Did I do something wrong?"

"No, your work is good. However—I hate to be the bearer of bad news, but…well, we got your background check in today."

Upon hearing those words, Nadine felt as if she had just been punched in the stomach. She knew what was coming next. She pressed her lips together and closed her eyes through the next words from the manager, who unfolded the paper on her desk. "Unfortunately, we're gonna have to let you go. If you would have just told us…"

"You would have what?" Nadine cut in. "Still hired me? I had to be dishonest to get this job because I needed it. Honesty got me nothing."

"I understand. But it's company policy not to hire someone with a criminal background."

"You've already hired me. You see how I work! I'm darn good! Now that should count for something."

"It's out of my hands, Nadine. I don't make the rules, but as the manager, I have to enforce them."

"How am I gonna get my kids back? How am I gonna make it?"

"I'm really sorry. But I would lose my job too if I kept you on with this information in hand."

Nadine got to her feet and yelled, "I won my appeal! And still people treat me like a damn criminal!" She turned then and exited to the back room to grab her purse and jacket.

Her co-worker called after her, "Nadine! Where are you going?" Nadine kept walking. Outside, she stood still for a moment – trying her best not to cry.

The co-worker went running to the manager. "What's wrong with Nadine?"

"I had to let her go."

"What?! Why? She's the best we've had in a while."

"Yes, I know, but she has a criminal record."

"Nadine? Darn!"

A block away from the cleaners Nadine could no longer hold back her tears and broke down crying. Soon thereafter she stopped at a gas station. She wiped her face with the sleeve of her jacket and went inside to buy a pack of cigarettes and a cup of coffee. Outside again, she leaned against the side of the building and lit a cigarette. Her hand trembled as she brought it to her lips. She squatted down, in a daze, unable to think of what to do next. She wanted to fall in the crack of the pavement and disappear amongst the many grains of sand that appeared to be trapped there.

At that instance she seemed to hear someone calling her name. The sound seemed to come from a long distance, but definitely someone was calling her name. She looked around in all directions—and there was Candace.

Nadine stood tall.

Candace said, "Hey. You ok?"

"Um, yeah—yeah, I'm fine. What are you doing around here?"

"I was getting some gas. You sure you're alright? I almost didn't recognize you. Do you need a ride somewhere?"

Nadine's brow wrinkled. She shook her head. "No, I can call my sister."

Candace said, "Let me go pay for my gas. You wait right here, ok? Don't leave."

"Sure."

Nadine hurried over to the pay phone booth to call Claudette but since there was no answer, Nadine figured Claudette had already left the house to pick her up from work. Candace appeared and waited for her to hang up. "My car is right over here."

Nadine looked over at the vehicle. A 1978 Mercedes Benz 450 SL, a two-door blue convertible with leather interior. As she got in the car she said, "This is beautiful."

"Thank you. Look, I called in for Chinese before I left the office. Why not come home with me. I never can eat it all alone."

"Oh…I don't know…Claudette would be worried. I couldn't reach her on the phone."

"Well, come on anyway. You can try calling her again from my house, and you and I will have a chance to catch up. You can tell me about the appeal."

As they pulled into the gated community Nadine sat up straight – her eyes gleaming like a child in a candy store. "Wow, Candy, this place is fab!"

The condo was at the end of a cul-de-sac. Candace said, "I've been here about three years now—and I do love it. It's a great community." She was soon entering the foyer and slipping off her shoes, then said, "Well, come on in."

Nadine removed her shoes too and Candace proceeded to give her a tour—starting with the formal dining room, which she used as an office. Her computer table and desk chair were beautiful, of cherry wood, and the spacious kitchen had a wide bay window and tile floor and granite counter tops. Nadine was much impressed. And envious. She had to hold back tears – taking in a quiet breath so as not to start up with the weeping again.

Candace didn't notice. She was putting the food down and moving them into the living room. It too was lovely, a contemporary style with a cream-colored carpet.

Nadine envied most the French doors leading out to the patio. There was even a fireplace on the deck. And each of the two bedrooms, she soon learned, had their own bathroom. The place did seem perfect, and way beyond anything Nadine could imagine for herself.

She realized after a while, as Candace was laying out the food, just how envious she was—and did her best not to show it. Aloud she said, "This is a bad crib. You must make good money at that law firm."

Candace lifted her head and said, "I do alright. I started off as a secretary. My parents knew this attorney, and when I graduated college, they secured the job for me. It does seem like a fairytale, even to me, because after I'd worked for him for some time—we became romantically involved." Her grin was wide.

Nadine giggled. "Wow! Talk about getting friendly with the boss!"

"Well, it was a secret affair. I couldn't afford to go to law school on my own, so he offered to help me, and we spent so much time together it eventually led to an affair."

"As in—he's married?"

"Yep. And I assure you, Nadine, I do not tell too many people that. He took care of me during law school."

Nadine settled on one of the bar stools and caught her friend's eye. "So, are you still seeing him?"

There was no mistaking the look on Candace's face. Not a happy look by any means. Some seconds passed before she said in a low voice, "No. He died in a car accident. About four years ago." She sighed big and added, "I couldn't finish then. It was too much. But he left me enough money to afford this condo."

"Oh, my goodness."

"Yeah…I went to the funeral…the wife confronted me. She said she always knew about us but didn't want to upset their lives over it. Of course, he left her with a lot more than he left me. She lives in a hilltop mansion with their two kids. I didn't know it until after he died—that he had another insurance policy with me as the beneficiary."

"Did the wife know?"

"I doubt it. The two of us shared a lot that she didn't know about."

"I'm sorry, Candy. I guess you loved him."

"More than anyone I've ever dated." She swiped a lock of hair from her brow and said, "Oh, enough about all of that. Let's talk about getting you another job."

"Well, that's not gonna be easy. I'd just give up—if it wasn't for my kids."

"So, first, tell me…what exactly can you do?"

"Before I married, I was going to college to be a teacher, but as soon as I was a wife, that all changed. I didn't get the chance to finish college. So, what have I done? Let's see. Housework, of course, and a lot of it. And I worked at a daycare. And I can still sew."

"Yeah, I remember now. You were good at sewing. That's great— because I have a cousin, right outside of Hopkinsville, and she has the most elegant little boutique you'd ever want to see. Every year she does a fundraiser for some cause or another, and auctions off beautiful dresses. She also raises money by auctioning her models off as dates."

Nadine's eyes were big.

Candace grinned and said, "She does all that just to make it fun. She figured out that old stiffs will pull money out of their pockets for a beautiful face. It's an annual event, and quite a popular one. I'll give her a call tomorrow—and let you know what she says."

Nadine hesitated – not wanting to fall into a hope too big. She says softly, "That would be great—thank you." She thought of her job hunt thus far – and how each *"we'll call you"* had been like waking up on Christmas morning to no presents underneath the tree. It was disappointing.

After they dined, they move to the living room. Nadine tried again to call Claudette. This time she answers right away. "Girl, I didn't know what happened to you."

"I got fired."

"Yeah, that's what I was told when I went inside looking for you. I'm sorry, little sis—but something will come along."

Nadine explained she was with Candy, and her friend is going to try and work something out with her cousin about a job. Nadine crossed her fingers as she spoke. "Anyway, I'm gonna stay here tonight. I'll see you tomorrow."

The two friends stayed up late… sipping wine, laughing, talking about old times as they browsed old pictures and yearbooks. The fifties and sixties were difficult times because of segregation, Jim Crow laws and Civil Rights movements. Many blacks landed in jail.

The friends spoke of many memories, the fun they had together in high school. They became friends at the time when blacks and whites were not supposed to be friends. They had been like soul sisters with different shades of skin. Back then, Nadine called her friend 'white chocolate.'

"Your sister was so big on the movement back then, Nadine." Candace laughed.

"Yep—she'd support any movement that favored blacks and Native Americans. She hated discrimination, as we all did. You know, as long as the movements were nonviolent, my parents wouldn't say much, but Claudette seemed to have a knack for getting involved in protests that led to trouble."

"Oh—and if I remember correctly—she also took you along with her a time or two."

They both giggled. Nadine said, "I know. Daddy used to say to her, 'Girl, those white people don't care nothing 'bout you. You're gonna end up in jail—and drag your little sister along with you.'" Throwing her arms in the air, she added, "Oh, those were the days!"

Time with Candace almost made Nadine forget about getting fired. Nadine became aware of what a blessing it was to just happen to meet up the way they did. After the day she'd had, this evening was just what she needed.

First thing the next day Candace called her cousin and arranged for Nadine to meet her. Candace had held nothing back – explaining Nadine's entire situation, and the cousin agreed to keep Nadine's situation quiet.

Next thing on the list was to get Nadine spruced up. Candace loaned her a dress, and shoes—but Nadine wore a smaller size shoe. Candace dropped her off at the boutique and headed to the office. Nadine's heart was racing, but she took a deep breath and went inside with apparent confidence. It was as nice as Candace described. Elegantly decorated. And burning candles with scents of vanilla and gardenias set the ambiance.

A receptionist greeted Nadine and told her to wait, that Ann would be out soon. When she showed up Nadine recognized her immediately—though she'd never met Ann. She felt she would have known her anywhere, for looking at her was like looking at an older Candace.

And the cousin smiled big. "Why, you're as lovely as Candy said you were. Come on back."

In the office Nadine explained her own sewing experience, then Ann gave her a tour of the boutique. There were so many beautiful dresses! And some a bit pricey. The popularity of the boutique's many gorgeous designs attracted more than just the local women who covet for holidays, proms and weddings. Almost all the dresses needed some alteration to make them fit perfectly. Ann told Nadine about the huge annual fundraiser – an event pulled off successfully for seven years now. The next one was eight months away, so it was about this time of year Ann hired extra people to form a team specifically for the event.

Nadine felt happiness leaping inside her in all directions, a joy such as she had not known in a long while. She was valued here. She was not an ex-con. She had skills this lovely woman needed.

When Ann had shown her all, Nadine could hardly contain her excitement. As she followed behind Ann back to the office, she paused for a brief moment to silently bring her hands together and jump up and down with a smile as wide as her face. For the first time since her release, she had hope – real hope. And reason to think this might really happen.

"So, what do you think?" Ann asked.

"I think it's great."

"Think you could you be a part of our team?"

"Yes! Absolutely!"

"Well then, let's start on Monday at eight o'clock. The attire is casual, but no t-shirts or jeans. I always award excellence—so if you're as good as Candy says you are, you will be rewarded. I have no reason to care what you did in the past. Or why. I am only concerned about what you do from Monday on."

She paused then, looking into Nadine's eyes for a minute before continuing. "I expect you to be here on time. And be aware you may not always get off at six o'clock. Everything depends on the demand. Store hours are 10:00 to 6:00. Starting you off I do pay more than minimum wage, an amount which will increase—per your merit. You do well by me, I'll do well by you."

As usual, Nadine had to tame her emotions - holding back tears. She says a bit unevenly, "Thank you so much."

"I'll see you Monday morning."

Monday morning, it seemed, was a lifetime away, but when it finally came around Nadine was up early, and just before 8:00 Claudette dropped her off. The receptionist buzzed back to a tall woman named Gina, who came out to escort Nadine to the work area – a huge room full of sewing machines, tables, cutting boards, mirrors, and material and accessories of many varieties.

Nadine felt as if she'd just stepped into a fashion designer's heaven.

Gina said, "It gets pretty busy around here, and I don't mind telling you Ann gets a little out of character when we're crunched for time. If she's under pressure, you're under pressure—so don't take it personal. When dresses come in here, they're already made.

We just do the alterations—though sometimes we redesign the whole dress."

"Really?"

"Oh yeah! So…I hope you're creative."

"Oh, I am."

Gina looked as if she meant to comment on Nadine's confidencestatement, but she didn't. She began a tour of the equipment and machines Nadine would be using. Eventually, she stood and watched as Nadine made a few alterations.

Later in the day, Ann looked up Gina and asked, "How's it going?"

Gina grinned. "Oh, I like her."

"Great!"

As Nadine had thought she would, she quickly caught on and was able to progress forward with little supervision. By the time Friday rolled around, she felt like she'd come to the right place. This was her place. It had just been waiting for her.

By the next week, though Ann didn't actually say so, Nadine understood she had been observed and been granted approval.

On Friday of that second week Candace swung by the boutique just as Ann and Nadine were locking up. She called out, "Hey, you two! Nadine, thought you might need a ride home—Friday can be crazy on the bus."

Nadine hopped in the car. "Are you kidding? Every day on the bus is crazy!"

Ann waved them goodbye and said, "You girls get home safe—and have a great weekend!"

Candace steered the car down the street and glanced over at Nadine. "So, what do you want for dinner? I'm starved."

Nadine answered, "I never have understood how a little person like you can eat so much."

"Girl, you're not big yourself. What you say? Wanna stop at the Gin Club?"

"I've never been. It's a club?"

"Well, it's a country club. My parents are members. They're usually there on Friday nights."

"And I can go?"

"Of course, you can. You're with me."

Nadine's eyes widened as they entered the grounds of the Gin Club. She sat upright, taking it all in. An impeccably groomed landscape, tennis courts, swimming pools, and beautifully carpeted golf courses. Glancing down at her old plaid skirt and plain white buttoned blouse, she exclaimed, "I can't go in there dressed like this!"

Candace pulled the car into a parking space, slid her scarf from around her neck and tied it around the collar of Nadine's blouse. "Here, wear this," she said. "And take your hair down. You look like your granny."

Nadine tried to style her hair with her fingers. Candace pulled from her purse a pair of silver earrings. "Put these on—and try a little lipstick." A minute later she added, "You look fine, Nadine." Nadine smiled her thanks.

The host escorted them to the table where her parents were seated and Candace said, "Mom, Dad—you remember Nadine from high school?"

Candace's mom smiled. "Well, Nadine. How could I forget the only little black girl Candy ever brought home? Please, dear—join us."

Candace was quick to note the discomfort on her friend's face and changed the subject. "So…Nadine is working at Ann's boutique." As she spoke, she smiled at Nadine and winked.

Karen, Candace's mother stuck her fork in her salad. "That's wonderful. How is Ann?"

"Great," Candace replied.

After dinner at the club, Candace took Nadine home. Nadine thanked her, and Candace said, "Oh, no problem."

"No, Candace—I mean thank you for everything. For attorney Cole. For helping me get a job. For just being my friend." Her voice quivered as she tried not to cry.

Candace reached across the seat and gave her a hug. "I will always be your friend, Nadine."

As Candace drove away, Nadine stood and watched, then went inside where she found Claudette sitting on the couch. Immediately Nadine sat down and began telling her sister all about her day.

Claudette said, "Wow, I bet that club has no black members!" Nadine stood up and stretched. "Nope, I didn't see a one. Anyway, this girl is tired. I'm gonna take a shower and put myself to bed."

Claudette stood up to give her sister a hug. They lingered for a bit with the hug.

"Um, Claudette—what are we doing?"

"We're hugging."

"I know—but why?"

Claudette let go of her and started chuckling. "Can't I hug my little sister? I don't have to have a reason. But I love you, and I'm so proud of you, girl. You've come a long way."

"Thanks! I've been trying to put some things behind me, you know—some bad dream sort of things."

The following week, Nadine proved her creativity when a woman and her daughter disagreed on how a dress should be adjusted. Nadine cut off the sleeves. "We can make a long lace sleeve on one side—and I could put a sash around your waist and shorten the hem in the front. What do you think about that?" The daughter answered, "I like it.

"No," the mom said. "Where is Ann?"

Nadine stepped out of the room. She soon returned with Ann, who asked, "What seems to be the trouble?"

"Look at this, Ann. She cut the sleeve. I don't like it." "And

I do like it," the daughter said.

"I don't care. Who's gonna pay for this dress?"

"I'm sorry," Nadine said. "I was just trying to help."

The mom said, "Your help ruined the dress!"

Now Ann, being the boss lady that she was, said with a tone of authority, "Okay, mom. Leave the room."

The woman looked a bit like she had been slapped. She gasped, "What?!"

"Wait in the lobby please."

Nadine apologized and apologized again—even offered to pay for the dress. Ann had begun to examine the dress.

Shortly after, she and Nadine put their ideas together and came up with a plan they thought might satisfy Mom and daughter. Ann told the daughter to put on the dress so she could get a better idea of what Nadine was envisioning.

Minutes later, Ann had no more doubt. She was satisfied with what Nadine wanted to do, and called the mom back in.

Now the mom could see for herself and it was time to pose the question, so Ann asked, "So, what do you think?"

It did appear the mother had some trouble admitting it, for she stuttered a bit at first, but at last managed to say, "Well…actually, now that I look at it good, it does look nice. Actually, really nice. You've practically redesigned the whole dress."

"Hmm, imagine that," Ann said. "You can pick it up next week."

Nadine, trying not to be noticed, let out a big sigh of relief. When the customers were out of earshot, Ann turned to Nadine and said, "Sometimes customers have to actually see what you're doing. You did a good job—and you handled yourself well. Keep up the good work!"

Nadine smiled – a glowing genuine smile. Because she too was proud of herself.

THIRTEEN

Ballet and Fashion

Carolyn was far from the little girl Nadine remembered. She was becoming a beautiful young lady and much excited about her upcoming ballet recital. She saw it as a chance to show her grandmother how the studio work was helping her grow up in the right way.

Phyllis, apparently, did not yet want to see how her granddaughter had outgrown paper dolls and tea sets. Looking ahead to the ballet recital, she had ordered a dress from Ann's boutique—a dress with ruffles and ribbons, as though Carolyn were still a little girl. Carolyn hated the dress her grandmother chose but had no say about it. When the dress was delivered to the boutique, Nadine saw right away it was for her daughter and immediately she began making changes —the kinds of changes a thirteen-yearold would like. Nadine smiled as she worked, recalling the many times those years ago when she made her daughter's dresses. By the time Nadine quit, the dress was no longer anything like the one Phyllis ordered.

When Phyllis brought Carolyn to the boutique to pick up the dress, Nadine stayed out of sight. Carolyn went alone to a dressing room, came out and stood in front of a mirror and twirled about. She said with delight, "It's beautiful!!"

Ann smiled. "I'm glad you like it. Let's see how your grandma feels."

Phyllis was waiting in the lobby. She immediately raised her eyebrows and tightened her mouth and spewed in a hushed murmur, "That's not the dress I ordered!"

"Yes, it is, Nana."

"Well...where are the ruffles? And lace?"

Ann cleared her throat. "Well...I authorized changes, because this seems more suitable for a teenager."

"No! You don't get to say what's appropriate for my child. I do! Go take it off, Carolyn!"

Carolyn folded her arms across her chest. She was hugely aware she was taking a gamble yet spoke anyway. "No, Nana. I won't."

Phyllis sucked her lips in tight. Her eyes went large like golf balls and she raised her hand to Carolyn. "Child—what did you said to me!?"

Ann stepped between the two. Her voice was flat and authoritative. "This place is my business—and you will not make a scene here."

Phyllis dropped her hand and looked from Ann to Carolyn and said, "Go take that dress off—and let's go."

"But Nana...I like this dress. If I can't wear it to the recital after party, then I just won't go to the recital!" The girl drew in a breath, exhaled and added, "And you're not my mother!" She turned then and hurried back to the dressing room.

Phyllis set her hands on her hips and snarled, "I will see to it no one ever shops here again—starting with me."

"That's a tall order you're setting for yourself, Mrs. Hunter. You won't be able to fulfill it. You likely don't know, but I'm very popular here—and my annual fundraiser brings in thousands of dollars for various causes. Now…if you'll calm down, I think we can talk about this."

Nadine had been watching furtively, and now had followed her daughter to the dressing room and was standing outside, listening to Carolyn cry. Her heart ached with each sob and her arms longed to embrace her child. Ann was coming down the hall. "Nadine, what are you doing?"

"That's my baby in there, Ann. And I want so bad to comfort her—but I can't."

"Nadine, go wait in my office." Nadine did as she was told. Ann then knocked on the dressing room door. "Are you alright, dear?"

The answer came with sobs but was very clear. "She never lets me have anything! I hate her!"

"I'm sorry. Will you please come out?"

Carolyn slowly eased the door open and handed over the dress. Ann said, "I'm sorry. I should have asked first before changing the dress."

"No!" the girl cried. "I love it!"

"Yes, but your grandma doesn't—and she's paying." Ann motioned with her hand and said, "Come on." Carolyn did as told and followed Ann out to the lobby. She noticed her grandmother, getting to her feet.

Ann turned back toward the girl and said softly, "You can keep the dress."

Carolyn answered softly. "I can?"

Ann, with the dress still draped over her arm, turned to the grandmother and said, "Mrs. Hunter, I can refund your money if you'd like, and you can still keep the dress." She handed the dress to Carolyn.

"No. Come along, Carolyn."

But Carolyn wouldn't leave the dress.

Ann watched their exit then hurried back to her office and slammed the door behind her. She said, "Whew! That woman is a piece of work!"

Nadine blew out air. "Tell me about it! It was hard for me not to punch her in the face!" She exhaled again. "I'm sorry, Ann."

Ann shrugged her shoulders. "For what, Nadine? You did a beautiful job. And your daughter kept the dress!"

Nadine grinned wide. "Really? Huh!"

When the date for the recital rolled around Nadine longed to join her family there, but Claudette discouraged it. Still, Nadine thought, she could sit discreetly in the back row. She wouldn't run into Phyllis.

Nadine had not come prepared for the boiling over of her emotions. She watched Carolyn's every move. It was obvious her daughter was achieving art with those graceful movements— and doing it on a wide stage with a big audience. It took every fiber in Nadine—at the recital's conclusion—not to join in when the audience rose and gave the dancers a standing ovation. She remained seated – hidden by those standing and clapping.

After the recital, Carolyn and her domineering grandmother, Phyllis, went backstage. Soon thereafter Nadine's mother and sister showed up backstage, waiting to congratulate Carolyn—who was changing into her new dress.

Phyllis caught sight of them and spewed, "You have no right to be back here!"

Just then the pretty young dancer came in sight and her grandmother Martha opened her arms wide to receive her. "Come give me a hug, dear. You were so beautiful out there."

Claudette stood back and watched the embrace, and then presented Carolyn with a bouquet of roses and another hug, then handed her a twenty-dollar bill. "This is from your grandpa. He's sitting out in the auditorium. Since his stroke, he doesn't do a lot of walking." She winked and said, "Buy yourself something pretty!"

Martha said, "I'm going back out there with your daddy, Claudette. I don't like to leave him alone long."

Claudette acknowledged her mother's wishes and watched her leave, then turned and exclaimed, "Carolyn, your dress is beautiful!"

The girl said shyly, "Thank you. Miss Ann did the alterations."

"Miss Ann?"

"Yeah, at the boutique in Hopkinsville."

Phyllis faced Claudette and said in a sour tone, "Well, if you don't mind, we have a party to attend."

Claudette gazed directly at her. "Mrs. Hunter, we really need to talk about visitations, 'cause we haven't had the kids in a while—and we haven't—"

"You listen to me! So long as your murdering sister is there, I'll never let my babies see any of you. Now, excuse me—we have some place to be!"

The girl stood by quietly during this exchange but kept her eyes on Claudette. Way down deep, she much wanted to see her mother—but she couldn't dare say so. She had questions that needed answers—answers her grandmother Phyllis could not give her.

And suddenly then, her eyes focused past Claudette and her face took on a strange look. The girl's expression caused Claudette to turn to see what the girl was seeing. It was Nadine. Standing just outside the door.

Simultaneously, the grandmother noticed. Her eyes stretched wide and her mouth gaped. Slowly she managed to push out words. "Oh—my—God!"

Nadine smiled big at her lovely daughter and said softly, "Hey, baby."

Phyllis took a few steps across the room to put her hand on the girl's shoulder and screech, "Don't they have security here?!"

Nadine was smiling. "I'm not here for a fight, Phyllis. I just wanted to see my baby dance. Carolyn, baby, you were fantastic!" She blew out air and added softly, "You always did like ballet."

Carolyn's eyes were fixed on her mother – she could not move. She did blink and her mouth parted, but she had nothing to say.

Phyllis raised her voice another octave and blurted, "Can't you see this child don't want to see you?! Now if you don't leave, I'm gonna call the cops!"

Nadine's smile disappeared. "Yeah, well at least you're finally admitting you do know how to dial 9-1-1."

"I will. I mean it!"

An intense glare spread across Nadine's face. The look hugely increased Phyllis's discomfort but she managed to hide it. She glared back and held her head high.

For just a brief moment, Nadine's sister Claudette closed her eyes. Eyes open again, she sighed deeply and stepped over and said softly, "Nadine…please. Let's just go."

Phyllis's voice quivered. "You better listen to your sister."

"Humph!" Nadine scoffed. "Where is William?"

Claudette took hold of Nadine's hand. "Let's go, Nadine. William is outside."

Nadine rolled her eyes and turned to leave but stopped suddenly. She smirked at Phyllis over her shoulder. "By the way, Carolyn's dress is beautiful. I did a good job."

Phyllis's brow wrinkled. Obviously, she was puzzled.

"Oh, Nadine," Claudette whispered.

Phyllis said, "I paid for her dress. You had nothing to do with it."

Claudette pulled at her sister's hand, but Nadine refused to move. She laughed out loud and said, "Oh, that's right. You didn't know. I work at the boutique, and I was the one who redesigned the dress."

Phyllis snapped her hands on her hips. "You're a liar!"

Carolyn, still much distraught, looked her mother in the eye and said, "Wait a minute. You re-made my dress?"

"Yes, sweetheart, I did. And it's beautiful on you."

Phyllis continued to shake her head. "I don't believe you."

"It's true."

In a flash, Phyllis grabbed the neck of Carolyn's dress and ripped it. Nadine launched forward. Claudette was right behind her, coming between the two—to keep Nadine from tearing her mother-in-law apart.

Nadine was yelling, "You're wicked! And evil!"

Phyllis backed away. "Keep her away from me! You see, Carolyn?! This is the side of your mother I've been telling you about."

People were gathering in the hallway, trying to see what the commotion was about. Claudette grabbed hold of Nadine's arm and began escorting her out. "Come on, Nadine—let's go!"

As they exited, they met Nadine's father-in-law. He had hold of William's arm and demanded, "What the hell is going on?!" Nadine had come to a stop. "William," she whispered.

How she longed to embrace him! But Claudette had a firm hold on her arm and as Joe pulled William close Claudette ordered, "Let's go, Nadine! This is not the place." She grabbed hold of Nadine's hand and pulled her to the car.

Nadine plopped down on the passenger side and said with a smirk, "That witch will regret tearing my child's dress! You should have let me punch her in the face!"

Claudette chuckled. "I'm usually the one who has to be pulled off someone."

"Look, those are my kids!"

"Oh, no one is disputing that, Nadine. But this was not the place. You want to end up back in jail? You know how crazy she is!"

"Ok—fine, fine."

Claudette said, "Did you see the look on her face when she saw you in the doorway?"

Instantly Nadine's frown disappeared as the two sisters joined in huge laughter.

On Monday, Ann approached Nadine. "I just got off the phone with Mrs. Hunter and she said as long as I'm hiring criminals, she will never shop here again."

"Yeah, I saw her over the weekend. It was not pretty. She hates me. Always did. I just don't like my children in the midst of it all. I'm sorry, Ann."

"Don't worry about it. I know it's not about my business. It's personal, I get it. And I know you're a wonderful seamstress. I like what you do—and I like the person I know so far. You come highly recommended—so you got no problems with me. I just wanted you to know."

"Thank you, Ann."

"By the way, I'm putting you in charge of the fundraiser's fashion show."

"Oh, my God! Really?!"

"Let me warn you, though, things will become busier and a lot crazier the closer we get to the date. Are you up for it?"

"Absolutely!"

"Great—'cause we could really use your creativity. Oh, and this year, I'm doing something new. I've been working on my own designs. Take a look at these. What do you think?"

"Wow! These are great, Ann."

"Yes, I'm excited about it. I've always wanted to take a chance—and now that I've established a successful event, I think it's time to introduce my own line of work. Your work has been inspiring.

So, let's see if some of these old rich dogs—will come out of their pocket for it!"

"Oh, Ann—I'm so excited for you! And it sure means a lot to me." Nadine couldn't remember the last time she received such validation for anything. Not since years ago, when she worked in the church daycare. She certainly never received any compliments or thumbs-up from Charles. She always worked hard, wanting to make sure whatever she did was as perfect as she could make it, which meant she tried not to make mistakes.

Two days before the big event Ann and Nadine began setting up the banquet hall. Ann had designed a dress especially for Nadine to model, and no one had yet seen it. Now Nadine was summoned to a room where a beautiful white sleeveless gown hung on a headless mannequin by the window. The gown had a pleated bodice and a wide black gathered sash that hung over to the front side of the waist. The back hem of the dress dragged the floor. It was a slim-line dress and would fit Nadine's figure perfectly.

"Oh, Ann! This is beautiful."

"You like it?"

"Yes, I do. It's elegant and graceful."

"Try it on."

"Try it on?"

"Yes. I want to see you in it."

After Nadine put the dress on, Ann handed her a pair of black satin high-heeled sandals with ankle straps and a diamond stone on the top. Nadine stood in the mirror looking at herself.

Ann watched her employee. "It's beautiful on you! This is what I want you to wear during the fashion show."

Nadine twirled around. "Me?"

"Yes—and I've already made you an appointment at the salon for your hair and nails."

Nadine turned back to the mirror. She could hardly believe it. She would be modeling an original design by the woman in charge of the whole deal.

When the day of the event arrived, Ann kept Nadine's dress a secret until it was time for her to walk out on the stage. The event was catered and the music live. Ann also wore one of her designs, proudly showing it off as she strolled through the crowd, and then took the stage and told of the foundation the charity supported, then added, "And this year, part of the donations will also go to the SAFE organization—which aids victims of domestic violence."

The fashion show began with a runway of girls modeling redesigned dresses for sale. The audience was excited about Ann's line. The real fun started when the auction began. The winning bidder not only won the dress but a date with the model in it.

Nadine was backstage, admiring herself in the mirror. She was a little nervous, knowing it would soon be time for her to walk out. Her hair was in an up-do with long dangling curls on each side, and her face elegantly made up. Next, she opened a small box from Ann and whispered, "Oh my…these are gorgeous!" She breathed in, feeling like a princess in a fairy tale, and began putting on the black and white open loop diamond necklace and matching earrings.

And not so long after, Ann was introducing Nadine. "And now, for my favorite design and my featured model…"

As Nadine came onstage, those in the audience stood up and began clapping and cheering. Never before had she experienced such a reception. Ann started the bid at a thousand. As bids were being acknowledged, Nadine couldn't believe her ears. Such high dollar amounts!

And then, a man's voice. "Five thousand dollars!"

Everyone became silent, looking around to see where the bid came from. Linfred was standing at the top of the stairs leading to the banquet room. Nadine smiled. She hadn't seen or heard from him since the trial.

Ann flashed a smile. "Well, to that I say, going once—going twice—sold to the tall handsome gentleman on the stairs."

Everyone clapped and clapped, and Linfred began walking toward the stage. At the bottom step he stopped and extended his hand to Nadine. She gracefully made her way down and took his hand, as the crowd continued to cheer.

Claudette, alongside their friend Candace, shouted, "That's my sister!"

Linfred smiled. "You are stunning."

It was hard to talk over the cheering, but Nadine had not missed his words. She answered, "You look good too. I didn't know you were coming."

"I wouldn't have missed it."

"So, you think this dress is worth five thousand dollars?"

He winked. "What dress?"

Candace stepped up and said with a laugh, "Must be the woman in the dress."

FOURTEEN

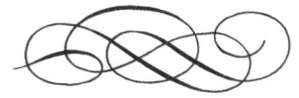

New Beginnings

T he live band started. Linfred turned to Nadine. "Shall we?" He took her hand and put his arm around her waist, pulling her close. He caught the scent of fragrance in her hair and whispered, "You smell lovely!"

She looked up at him and they smiled at each other. He said, "I know it sounds corny, right?"

"No…. I was thinking the same about you."

"Can we get outta here? Just to catch up?" They were soon on their way to Lake Boyd. He spread his jacket on a rock near the water to protect the dress. They sat quiet for a moment, enjoying the cozy night breeze. Nadine turned her gaze to the sky and said softly, "It's so peaceful here."

Seconds later she turned her gaze on him and asked, "What is it like to spend that kind of money all at once?"

He chuckled. "It's just money! And I'd do it again." He took her hand.

Nadine bit her lip and turned her gaze away.

"Am I that terrible to look at?"

She turned back and smiled. "No. Quite the opposite." After a bit she added, "Why did you really come out tonight?"

"Honestly? I heard you were one of the models—and I wanted to see you again. I think of you often, Nadine—but I've been very busy."

"Why?"

"Oh, well, the courts have—"

"No. I mean, why have you been thinking about me?"

"To be honest, Nadine, the first day I saw you I was interested in you."

"When you first saw me, I had on a prison jumper!"

"Oh, that's what you had on? I didn't notice."

He laughed and she joined in the laughter, then he said, "Well, I'm glad I can now express to you how much I really want to get to know you—without it being a conflict of interest."

Nadine's brow wrinkled. In a low voice she said, "Linfred, you don't want all this baggage."

"Please," he said. "Call me Lin. And I'm not afraid, Nadine. I've gone up against the toughest."

"But this is not a courtroom—this is my life! And right now, it's a mess."

"I'm not looking for perfection."

She shook her head side-to-side and sighed. "Right now, I'm dealing with a lot of emotions—that you may not understand, and I may not want to bring into your life. There will always be people judging me. Most people do not see abused women as victims. They just assume those women are weak. And stupid."

"You can move on now, Nadine. You don't have to keep punishing yourself."

She carefully got to her feet. He stood up too and wrapped an arm around her shoulder. They stood facing the lake and remained silent for several minutes.

She said in a low voice, "It's not easy."

He put a hand to her chin and gently turned her head. "Nadine, look at me. You're a strong woman. I could see that in you right away." She began shaking her head, but he continued. "Yes, you are."

She dropped her head. He turned her toward him. Now they were face to face. He took her hands and spoke softly. "Let me make up for what he did to you. *Please*. I feel something here—don't you?"

The light even in the darkness was enough where Nadine could see the sincerity in his face. She gave a slight smile and said, "Yes!"

He leaned forward and kissed her on the forehead, then wrapped his arms around her and held her close. Nadine felt herself sigh inside. His strong embrace felt good. And his masculine scent was intoxicating.

He said suddenly, "Hey, do something crazy with me! Let's jump in the lake!"

"You're kidding, right?"

"No, it can be symbolic! You know, like we're just gonna jump into this thing together—feet first—and see what happens."

"In this dress?"

"I paid for it. Come on." He kicked off his shoes, pulled his tie from around his neck, and loosened his collar. "You ready?"

"No, this is crazy," she said as she carefully placed her jewelry in his jacket pocket.

Lin grabbed her hand. "On the count of three. One…"

"Wait a minute!" She slipped out of her shoes and nodded.

On three, they ran screaming hand-in-hand toward the water—and leaped. Whew! Cold water. But for the first time in years, Nadine felt like a liberated teenager. She playfully splashed about and they soon made their way close, his arms around her waist, hers around his neck. They pressed their foreheads together, and each could feel the other trembling and was not sure whether the trembling was due to cold water or nerves.

Lin whispered, "Come home with me. I want to show you where I live."

She looked in his eyes and spoke softly. "And what else?"

"What do you mean? What else do you want to see?" They both laughed and he said, "I'm a gentleman. I promise I'm not inviting you to my place for a romp. Not yet anyway."

Then he flashed his irresistible smile. And she said, "Uh-huh."

On the two-hour drive they talked nonstop and suddenly he was turning down a curved driveway toward a beautiful brick home. She said, "You've got to be kidding. This is where you live?"

"Yep."

The home sat on three acres of land—and all neatly groomed. Nadine especially liked the lighted fountain out front. He pulled into the garage and they entered through the kitchen where two Weimaraners greeted them. Lin introduced the dogs with her hand on top of his as he petted them, then he gradually moved his hand away so she could interact with them on her own.

"See, guys?" he said. "She's our friend."

"They're beautiful. What are their names?"

228

"This one, with the blue-gray eyes, is Shane. Winston has amber eyes. They were bred just for me—and I think they like you, which is great, because they don't like too many people. I take them with me when I go hunting, and they go with me on my morning run."

"Well, I think they're wonderful. And this is a great home, Lin."

She strolled around the kitchen, admiring the white cabinets with glass doors like windowpanes, and the island with a built-in sink, and a built-in oven and microwave in the wall. All appliances were stainless steel and the floor checkered with black and white tiles. The room was separated from the dining room and living room by tall white pillars and the whole scene decorated with antique-style furniture and looked like something out of a magazine.

Lin explained the portrait above the couch was a painting of himself and his parents when he was five years old, hand-painted from a photo by a family friend in Germany. He said he seldom spent time in the living room. The den was his comfort zone, where he relaxed in his recliner. He also kept his collection of swords from different countries, displayed on a wall. Also on display were the many trophies he won in high school and college sports. He lit the fireplace then proceeded with the tour through the rest of the house, four bedrooms and three bathrooms, which he said his mom had decorated.

Nadine was especially impressed with the walk-in closet in the master bedroom. He kept his suits, dress shirts, casual slacks, and jeans well organized. She grinned. "So, where would your wife hang her stuff?"

"Oh, there's another closet over here. I keep my golf clubs and things in it. I guess if I were married, I'd have to find somewhere else to put this stuff."

"Wow! This bathroom is amazing. Marble countertops and floors?" She ran her hands across the edge of the Jacuzzi tub. The separate shower was enclosed by iced glass with decorative carvings. "What are you doing with this huge house by yourself?"

"Hoping for someone to share it with one day. Come on, let me find you something dry to wear." She followed him out to the bedroom and watched him go through the dresser drawers. He handed her a t-shirt and a pair of sweatpants and said, "Make yourself at home." He added, "I'm sure these are too big, but they're dry."

She thanked him and he left, closing the door behind him. When she was done, she spotted him out back on the patio, lighting the fire pit. She said nothing, just stood watching him through the glass door.

He looked up. "Wow! You look better in my clothes than I do. Come on out. I'll pour you a glass of wine – if it's okay."

"That's fine." She sat down on a lounge chair and said, "Oh, you have a pool. Candy has a nice place too. I guess I was in the wrong field. You know…teaching."

Lin settled beside her. "Nonsense. Teaching is an honorable profession."

"Yeah, but even so, I could never have made enough money to afford anything like this."

He sipped from his glass. "What you see is the result of winning a lot of cases, saving my money, and making some good investments. It's just material stuff, but I enjoy it." He downed another sip.

She grinned. "Well, you should!"

Lin lifted his glass. "Hey! Here's to a new beginning! May we enjoy this journey ahead as we see where it takes us." Nadine giggled and tapped her glass against his.

After a bit he said, "You know, I just made partner. Sure did! And I'm the only black attorney in the office. And I assure you— it wasn't easy!"

"That's great! I suggest we drink to that." She raised her glass, threw her head back and took in several gulps.

Lin smiled. "Am I seeing a different side to you?"

She lowered her glass. "What do you mean?"

"I'm used to seeing this somewhat timid person. Almost shy."

"Well, now you're looking at a new woman." Her laughter echoed in the night air.

"Yep, I see it. And around me—you can be anyone you want to be." He reached for a blanket he had carried out and spread it across their laps.

With the cooling of the night air, the fire pit had them feeling cozy. And the more wine Nadine drank the more she loosened up. She talked about things she hadn't talked about in a long time. The only time she and Charles had ever talked like this was while they were dating. Once the courtship was over, he never had the time or desire to just sit and talk. And she certainly could never have enjoyed a glass of wine with him. He would have spoiled everything by getting drunk and starting a fight.

Lin glanced at his watch. "Do you know it's after three in the morning?"

"No, I didn't realize it was so late."

"Well, relax here for the night. You're home." He put out the fire pit, made sure Nadine felt comfortable in his room, and then proceeded to the room down the hall and crashed. Nadine had fallen asleep almost instantly.

When he got up, he peeped in on Nadine. She was still asleep. He quietly let the dogs out, brought in the newspaper and started breakfast. She awoke to scents of coffee and bacon, pushed aside the blanket, stretched, and murmured softly, "Mmm, he cooks!"

"Good morning, Sunshine. Did you sleep well?"

"I did." She smiled. "You cook?"

He winked. "I dabble a little."

She noted the spread on the table. Grits, toast, eggs with cheese, bacon and coffee. He added a jar of strawberry preserves and said, "Sit down."

"Homemade preserves! You made this too?"

He chuckled. "No, my mom did."

She spread some on her toast and took a bite. "Mmm, so good. Reminds me of how my Aginisi used to do."

"Your what?"

"Not what. Who. My grandmother. It's what we call her. It's Cherokee."

"Got it."

On their way back to Hopkinsville, they discussed the custody hearing. He tried to reassure her. "Don't worry much about it, Nadine. You're with me now."

She thought about it for a moment then turned to him. "What does that mean?"

He glanced over at her and smiled. "It means I'm gonna take care of it. I'll make some phone calls Monday morning. I don't want you to ever have to worry about anything." He reached for her hand.

She said, "Lin, these are my kids. I can't pay anyone, but…"

"I've got this. I know how much you love your kids, Nadine. They *should* be with you." He reached up and pinched her cheek. "Just a little while longer, okay?" She

nodded.

They were soon pulling up in front of Claudette's house and leaning in for a kiss. He said, "I don't want this day to end."

"Me neither. When will I see you again?"

"Soon."

He tapped his lips. She took his face in her hands and pressed her lips against his, then quickly exited the car and walked backwards towards the porch as she waved him goodbye.

FIFTEEN

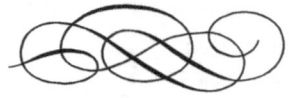

Custody

N early a year had gone by since Nadine gained her freedom. She finally had enough money to get her own place and a used car. After much encouragement from her family, she decided to return to school for fashion design rather than teaching, and in her spare time worked on her portfolio. One day she left the portfolio open on the table in her workspace.

When she returned, she found Ann seated at the table and flipping through the pages. She exclaimed, "What are you doing?!"

Ann looked up at her. "Why haven't I seen some of these designs, Nadine?"

"It's just me doodling on paper—no big deal."

"Are you kidding me? These are remarkable! Why on earth would you ever have thought you wanted to be a teacher—when you have this talent?" She closed the portfolio and gazed up at Nadine. "You have a gift—a hidden talent you should be proudly showing off. I say we do something with this."

"Oh, I don't know. I mean, they're just sketches."

"Sketches that should be made into dresses. There! I made a rhyme."

Nadine chuckled. "Listen, Ann, I've always doodled. It's a way to escape." She paused. "I'm not sure I'm ready to show my work."

Ann sighed. "You're already showing it. You've been showing off what you can do for about a year now." She grabbed a piece of fabric. "Look," she said and placed it by one of Nadine's designs. "And let's do this—and maybe this," she said as she placed lace and ribbon on top of the fabric. "Now, these things could make this design unique. You could even change the collar a little and make it—"

"No!" Nadine said. "I like the collar. But what I don't like is this God-awful ribbon." They both broke into laughter.

"Well, okay…" Ann said. "Let's play with it for a moment." And she proceeded to help Nadine see how to bring her designs to life, and kept playing at it, until Nadine came around to wanting the same.

Often during her day, Nadine tried at different times to picture in her mind what Carolyn and William was doing. Who were their friends? What were their lives like with Phyllis? By now Carolyn would be interested in boys, but Carolyn knew Phyllis wouldn't permit it.

The one person Carolyn opened up to was Claudette. And for the children, their Aunt Claudette served as a breath of fresh air – so unlike their Grandmother Phyllis. Claudette was fun to be around. She kept up with the new music and dances and clothing styles of the eighties. The children missed her.

The day of the custody hearing, Phyllis's attorney, Mrs. Nicholson, argued that any abuse from Charles was irrelevant to the hearing, and therefore Nadine should not be allowed to talk about it. Nadine's attorney argued the abuse was indeed relevant to the case—because it led to Charles's death and to Nadine's imprisonment—which in turn led to the children residing with their paternal grandparents.

Judge Matteson called both attorneys to the bench. "Now, as much as I understand how the abuse plays in this case, the only thing that really matters is Mrs. Hunter's ability to assume care of her children."

Mrs. Nicholson began the examination by questioning Nadine about her mental stability, her breakdown, and the therapy she received in prison. She asked, "Are you still on medication?"

Nadine replied softly. "Yes, I am. But I'm not crazy. I just have anxiety. And sometimes panic attacks, but I haven't had them in a long time."

Mrs. Nicholson turned to the judge. "Your honor, the children are still seeing a therapist. They have their own anxiety. They need to remain with someone who is stable enough to help them cope. Mrs. Hunter's incarceration removed her from their lives, so she hasn't been involved with her children in the last seven or eight years. They don't know her anymore—nor do they want to. They are currently in a stable and loving environment."

Nadine's attorney cut in. "Mrs. Hunter's separation from her children was not by choice. She didn't just abandon them. She lovingly cared for them, protected, and educated them. Your honor, the maternal family wanted to keep contact with the children, but the paternal grandparents refused."

Phyllis blurted, "Your honor, I feel it would be too much for the children to be around Nadine after what happened to their father…your honor."

Nadine's attorney asked, "Mrs. Hunter, what kind of mother was your daughter-in-law?"

For some long seconds Phyllis stared at Nadine. It was obvious from her expression she would rather take a punch to the belly than say anything good about her. She fidgeted with her purse and finally said, "I didn't always like the way they were dressed, but I guess she treated them alright."

"So, you're saying you did not witness Mrs. Hunter abusing or neglecting the children?"

"No, I can't say I have—but these children don't want to be with her. They don't want anything to do with her."

Nadine's attorney faced the judge. "Let me emphasize Mrs. Hunter has adjusted well since her release. She is fully employed. She has a home for her children. She has proven herself stable and more than ready to assume custody of her children, your honor."

Through all this, Nadine continued to look around in hopes of spotting Lin. He had said he'd be here. So where was he? She felt panicky. He was letting her down too! She fought to hold back tears and breathed a sigh of relief when court was adjourned until 9:00 the next morning.

She kept trying his mobile number, to no avail. She would soon learn Lin had indeed been on his way to Clarksville, but a car pulled out in front of him. He hit his brakes hard, causing them to lock up—and the car slid off the road. It bounced over the ditch, came off the ground and landed against a tree on the driver's side. Lin's head hit the steering wheel and he was knocked unconscious.

Someone who lived nearby heard the crash and called 9-1-1. Not knowing what happened to him, Nadine had continued trying his mobile phone and getting no answer. And the next day, still no answer.

The hearing continued. The children's psychiatrist spoke about her sessions with the children. "Personally, I think the children would benefit from a relationship with their mother."

The judge asked, "Has anyone ever asked these children where they want to live?"

Several voices sounded at once. Phyllis said the children did not want to live with Nadine, while the psychiatrist took the stance the children needed to get to know their mother again.

Judge Matteson slammed her gavel. "Alright, alright! You're talking at the same time—and I've had enough. I'll meet with the children in my chamber as soon as you can get them here." She got to her feet and left the room.

A short while after, Phyllis delivered Carolyn and William, and they soon joined Judge Matteson. After introductions, the judge seated herself in a chair between the two children. She looked from one to the other and said, "So, tell me about school." That subject and a few following topics were easy, but eventually Judge Matteson had them talking about the loss of Charles—which was obviously difficult for both children. William was soon sniffling, tears falling in his lap as his head drooped.

His big sister said, "Brother, are you okay? Why are you crying?"

He wiped his face with the back of his hand and whined, "I wish things could go back to how it was."

Judge Matteson handed him a tissue. "And how was it?"

"We lived in a big house in the country...with Mama...and Daddy."

Carolyn said, "Brother, you were too young—you can't remember the way it was."

"I remember!" he yelled. "I remember a lot!"

"Stop yelling at me!"

The judge said softly, "Okay... *now* I want only to hear from William." She gazed directly at the boy and asked, "What do you remember?"

He tried a smile. "We had a tire on a rope hanging from a tree I used to like." He dropped his head again.

Judge Matteson waited. He continued. "I remember being with Mama every day—and seeing her cry when Daddy hurt her."
"How did you feel about your father?"

Carolyn leaned forward, trying to see William's expression, but the judge was seated between them. And the judge was no small lady. She was a smart lady too, so she seated them at an angle where Carolyn could not influence her brother.

He shrugged his shoulders. "I don't remember everything, just him hurting Mama—and I'm angry about it."

"And how do you feel about your mother?"

"I don't know. I don't know how to feel about her. Nana said we should hate her."

Carolyn sprang to her feet. "William!"

Judge Matteson turned a frown her way and Carolyn murmured, "Well, he's not supposed to say that."

Each time Judge Matteson asked William a question his sister thought he should not answer, she interrupted him. Eventually the judge turned to face the girl. "You obviously have something to say. Would you like to share with me how you feel about your mother?"

"No."

William blurted, "She hates her!"

"She didn't ask you!"

"Well, it's the truth—and you know it! Nana said if Mama was so miserable with Daddy, she should have killed herself."

Judge Matteson said, "Okay—I've heard enough already."

An hour later, Carolyn and William were seated on a bench just outside the double courtroom doors. Inside the courtroom Judge Matteson cleared her throat and settled her gaze on Nadine. "Mrs. Hunter, you have some wonderful children, but after speaking with them, I can see why they still need therapy. So, I'm going to order therapy to continue. It occurred to me how much negative influence the paternal grandmother has had on these children, due to her own hurt and bitterness regarding their father's death. I have read and I have considered everything—and I've carefully weighed my decision."

She moved her gaze about the space, looking at all involved. "Don't look so surprised. I've heard all I need to hear in this case." She took in and exhaled a deep breath.

"Mr. and Mrs. Hunter, I am very sorry for the loss of your son, but, instilling your bitterness and anger over his death in your grandchildren is not the way to deal with it—nor does it help the children deal with the loss of their father. They have actually lost both parents because their mother has been absent from their lives for years due to her incarceration. Though the Pearsons have attempted to remain in contact with the children, you have not honored the visitation order. I will not terminate it—the visitation order stays." She paused briefly before adding, "I have neither seen nor heard any evidence, that prior to the father's death the mother was anything but responsible."

Instantly, Phyllis fell to the floor and began crying. Her attorney and the bailiff came to her rescue.

Claudette whispered to Nadine, "She's so dramatic!"

Judge Matteson rapped on the desk with her gavel. "Get her off my floor! We'll recess for fifteen minutes."

As Nadine and Carolyn entered the hallway, they spotted Candace. She had been standing out in the hallway and obviously had been crying.

Nadine hurried over and asked, "What's wrong?"

Candace mumbled, "Is everything over?"

Claudette rolled her eyes. "No! The drama queen is on the floor!"

"What?"

Nadine sighed. "Yeah—before the judge could rule, Phyllis fell to the floor—acting just like the fool she is. We'll be going back in a few minutes." A look of distress crossed her face then and she added, "I haven't heard from Lin. He said he would be here."

Candace began weeping again, but managed to mumble, "Nadine, he isn't coming. He was in an accident!"

Nadine settled on a nearby bench and dropped her face in her hands. She continued to hear Candace, telling the details she'd learned about what happened. Claudette settled beside Nadine and wrapped an arm around her, but soon thereafter they were told to return to the hearing.

Nadine said, as tears ran down her cheeks, "What should I do?!"

Candace said, "Go back in the courtroom, Nadine. I'll try to find out more."

The news Nadine hoped and prayed for did not occur. To everyone's surprise, the judge did not grant custody to anyone. The children were to remain where they were for the time being.

Every weekend they would spend with Nadine. She would pick them up on Friday and return them on Sunday. And she was to be allowed to be involved in any school business and extra activities outside of school.

Judge Matteson added, "It has always been the court's desire to reunite families when possible, so I'll review this case again in six months—to see how well the children are doing with their mother. Then, full custody will be discussed. Having made this decision, I've actually decided the maternal grandparents will no longer need the visitation order. The children can spend time with their grandparents along with their mother."

Phyllis turned in her seat, pointed at Nadine and loudly declared, "You will not get my kids!"

The judge had her gavel in hand and used it. She raised her voice. "Mrs. Hunter, you will be in contempt if you fail to cooperate in any way with what I've decided—and I won't hesitate to throw you in jail! They are not your children. And their mother still has parental rights because the court has yet to find it is not in the children's best interest they be with their mother. As decisions are being made, these children could possibly end up in the foster system. Is it what you want?"

Phyllis brow softened as she shook her head just slightly.

"No, I didn't think so. Court is adjourned." Judge Matteson slammed her gavel and stepped off the bench.

That evening William slipped into Carolyn's room to talk about what had happened. She lay across the bed reading. He said, "What do you think Nana is thinking about?"

Carolyn shrugged her shoulders. "I don't know. I guess about what the judge said. They've both been quiet."

"Well, I'm gonna listen at their door to see if they're saying anything we should know."

"Like what, William?" She put her book down. "You're gonna get in trouble."

Carolyn watched him creep down the hall and stand outside their grandparents' bedroom door. He leaned forward, trying not to touch the door. Phyllis was saying, "So, we can't do anything about her getting the kids on the weekend?"

Joe answered, "Not from what the attorney said."

Phyllis snarled, "I don't like that judge!" Silence for a moment – then she added in a vehement tone, "And I'm gonna fight Nadine tooth and nail—to keep her from getting custody. She will not win!"

Meanwhile, Nadine and Claudette and Candy were at the hospital. When they arrived, they found Lin was in ICU and only family could see him. Nadine said to the nurse, "Is his mother here?"

Lin's mom stepped out of ICU. "Oh, Nadine!" she said, and embraced her tightly.

"I'm so sorry, Mrs. Cole. They told me I couldn't see him because I'm not family."

"Yes, she is family," Mrs. Cole told the nurse. "He needs to see her."

Mrs. Cole remained outside the unit with Candy and Claudette while Nadine went inside, where she stood sobbing at Lin's bedside. Her hand trembled as she stroked the side of his face. Her eyes moved across his body. It was covered with many bandages, and bruises, and one leg was in a cast. She learned firefighters had to cut him out of the car. He lay still – unconscious and unaware of her presence. She soon left him to join the others in the waiting room.

Candy walked over and put her arms around Nadine. "At least he's alive."

"You haven't seen him, Candy. I have to stay until he gets better. It was my fault. He was coming to be with me."

"Nadine, it was not your fault. It was the driver who pulled out in front of him—some fool who wasn't paying attention. You can't *always* carry guilt. Please, Nadine—don't beat yourself up. Lin is not Charles. He will not blame you."

Over the next few days, Nadine and Mrs. Cole took turns sitting by Lin and reading aloud from the books Mrs. Cole brought from home. One of the books was *The Tale of Peter Rabbit* – one of Lin's favorite childhood stories. Lin remained unconscious.

Nadine sat in a chair beside the bed, as usual, and began reading. "But Peter, who was very naughty…"

And then a soft voice was saying, "…ran straight away to Mr. McGregor's garden…" Lin! He had begun to recite the words and now they were saying them at the same time.

Nadine stopped reading, put the book down on her lap and slowly turned—in astonishment—toward this man she loved. Without opening his eyes or moving anything but his lips, Lin added, "…and squeezed under the gate."

Nadine sprang to her feet. The book fell to the floor. "Oh my God!" she said. "Nurse!" She picked up his hand and her emotions overwhelmed her as she felt him squeezing her fingers.

While the nurse assessed him, Nadine went out to get his mother from the family room. They returned to find him responding to the nurse's questions. When he saw his mom, he was able to slowly reach out for her. She strode over and took his hand and kissed him on the forehead. She asked, "How do you feel, honey?"

He replied softly, "I'm not sure yet."

As he turned his gaze to Nadine he smiled. She leaned from the other side of the bed and kissed him on the cheek.

He asked, "Did you win?"

She smiled. "Not exactly. But I do get the kids on weekends. Baby steps, I guess."

"It will be fine. Mom, how are my dogs?"

Mrs. Cole assured him, "Oh, your dad's been taking care of them."

The next day, Nadine went home. Lin was on the road to recovery. Every day she called the hospital to check on his progress and returned when she could to support him during his physical therapy sessions. Time with her children was equally important to her. The weekends were sociable times…eating out, shopping, spending time at the park, visiting Nadine's family, and going to church.

Once Lin was well enough to leave the hospital, he continued outpatient therapy from home. Nadine asked for time off to help him at home.

"Nadine, it's not that I don't think a lot of Lin, but we've been pretty busy." Ann stared at Nadine for a moment, noticing the familiar spark in her eyes. She sighed. "Hey, look, I've been in love before too, so I'll compromise, but only because I know Lin is a good man. Besides, he supports my benefits."

"Who said I'm in love?"

Ann smiled. "It's written on your face. And you wouldn't be doing this if you weren't. So, I want you to take your work with you. I need five dresses completed in the next three weeks. The girls have to be fitted, but I can do it once the dresses come back. How does that sound?"

"Yes, I can handle that."

Nadine packed all she needed to make the dresses and enough clothes for herself for two weeks. She counted on Claudette to pick the children up for the next two weekends.

Once on duty, she soon realized how good it felt to be looking after someone—and not just any someone. Spending time together made their relationship closer than ever. When they weren't spending time together, she worked on the dresses. And so, at last, to her surprise, Nadine felt fulfilled…and at home.

One morning as she prepared breakfast, she heard a loud noise from Lin's room. She rushed down the hallway and found him on the floor. "What happened?" she said as she attempted to help him up.

Obviously frustrated and embarrassed, Lin put his hand up. "No. Wait a minute. Just let me lay here for a moment."

"Well, what happened? Are you alright?"

"I was getting in the wheelchair and forgot to lock the wheels and it rolled out from under me. This damn cast up to my groin is driving me nuts!"

Again, she reached down to help and said softly, "Ok. So, let me try and help you up."

But he shoved her hand away. "No, Nadine! You can't do it!"

"I can try. How are you supposed to get up? Or do you plan on lying there all day?"

"You know what? Can you just go? Please—just leave me alone, let me figure it out! Please!"

"Fine then," she said. In the doorway, she stopped and watched him struggle to get up on his own. And finally, he did pull himself up and onto the bed. His voice was softer as he said, "Can you push the wheelchair over here for me?"

She said, "Oh, may I?"

Noting her sarcasm, Lin chose not to reply. She moved the wheelchair close to the bed and put the brakes on, he got in the chair and followed her down the hall. "I'm sorry, Nadine. I just got frustrated."

"Whatever. I'm leaving as soon as I get my things packed."

"What? Wait a minute. You're leaving? Please, babe—don't go."

"It's time for me to go anyway. Your breakfast is on the table."

He grabbed her hand. "Nadine, please don't go. I really am sorry." She pulled away. He grabbed her hand again. "Nadine, I love you."

She stood very still and shook her head. "No, you don't."

"Yes, Nadine, I really do love you! And I know you love me too."

"I'll tell you what I do know. I know what it feels like when someone hurts your feelings. I was only trying to help."

"I would never hurt you, not on purpose."

She tried to pull away, but he kept a firm grip on her hand. She demanded, "Let go of me!" "You really want to go?"

She didn't answer. He let her hand go and she hurried away and began packing. Mrs. Cole came in the house. She called, "Hello!"

Lin wheeled into the kitchen to greet her. She asked, "Where is Nadine?" He explained what happened and Mrs. Cole turned and left the kitchen. She found Nadine almost finished with getting her things together.

She said, "So, I hear you're leaving?"

Nadine spoke without looking up. "Yes ma'am. It's time for me to go, and Ann is expecting these dresses."

"Is it the only reason?"

"Did you talk to Lin?"

"Yes. I did." Mrs. Cole settled on the edge of the bed and said, "Come here, honey." She waited as Nadine stepped forward and joined her.

Mrs. Cole said, "Listen for a moment. When I was a little girl, over in Germany, there was this couple next door. The husband used to drink something awful. And he would come home and beat on his wife. Sometimes she would come over and talk to my mom, and my mom would say 'Olga, you should just leave that man.' But the wife stayed. And sometime after, there came a day when she was fed up. She couldn't take it anymore. Olga's old man had beat her. Then passed out on the couch – as often happened. But this time Olga poured oil around him, from an old lamp, then lit the wick and threw the lamp on the couch— setting him on fire."

Nadine's face wrinkled in a frown. She muttered, "That's awful!"

"Oh, yes…so what do you think Olga did next? She fled to the cathedral and prayed to God for forgiveness. Her husband died that night, and people thought he just got drunk and knocked the lamp over. She was never charged for his murder."

"Lucky her!"

"Well, years went by. And Olga lived in her own prison." Mrs. Cole paused slightly and looked right into Nadine's eyes, still holding to her hand. "You, my dear, are living in your own prison. You are denying yourself the one thing you deserve the most…. Love. You must not allow yourself to stop loving—because of how that man treated you. And you should not keep another from loving you. Because if you do, your husband wins. Your refusal to love means he is still controlling your life, even from the grave."

Nadine felt chills run along her bones. Lin's frustrated outburst had made her go back in memory to Charles—though Lin was nothing like Charles. And then she understood. She was still afraid to love.

She had these thoughts while staring at her lap. And she felt frozen.

Lin's mother was saying, "Now, I can see you love my son. And I may not know you very well, Nadine—but I do know love when I see it. Please do not allow a little frustration on his part to run you away."

Mrs. Cole got to her feet. She paused to pat Nadine's leg.

Nadine was soon on the road and thinking deeply about Mrs. Cole's story. At one point she had to pull over, for tears had come again as she suddenly understood Charles was still controlling her life. It was a chilling thought!

She thought of all those years of abuse. And the years in prison. It was during those years when she was locked up, she had become stronger and determined to move on with her life. But Mrs. Cole had been right about one thing. She was afraid to love.

The following Sunday, Nadine and Claudette took the kids to see their great-grandma in the nursing home – a frail little Indian woman with a long silver braided ponytail. The children had seen their Cherokee grandma only a couple of times, and those times so long ago they hardly remembered her—or how much Nadine favored her.

At the end of the visit, Aginisi wanted to join hands and say a prayer, and so they did. She also gave the children dream catchers she made during the home's Craft Hour. In years to come the children would remember her because of what she said. "If you hang these over your bed, they will catch your best dreams."

For the young Carolyn, it was the day she learned much about her Cherokee Aginisi, and also the day she secretly felt proud to be Nadine's daughter. The feeling of pride was quickly wiped away when they returned home to Phyllis—who made sure to degrade their heritage, just as their father had done in the past.

Their grandmother shrilled, "I don't want those demonic dream catchers in my house—throw them away!"

Carolyn moaned, "But they're gifts."

Phyllis planted her hands on her hips and said, "Well, I don't care! It's just a bunch of silly superstition. You know, ever since you started hanging out with Nadine, you've gotten quite sassy, young lady. And I'm just not gonna have it. You hear me?!"

Carolyn folded her arms across her chest and looked away—trying not to cry. She and William did as instructed – put the dream catchers in the trash, and when Phyllis had retired to bed, went out and retrieved them. Carolyn hid hers above her bed behind a poster of the Jackson Five. William hung his underneath one of the baseball caps above his bed.

Judge Matteson received regular progress reports over the past three months on Carolyn and William. Their biggest adjustment regarded the weekend visitations with Nadine. They did want to see her, but they were also used to seeing their friends then. When Judge Matteson reviewed their reports, she called a brief meeting with the attorneys.

She said, "I have read the concerns of the children. It is my decision to continue the visitations on the weekends with their mother. After all, it's only eight days a month. There will be no compromise. It is more important for them to reconcile with their mother. They see their friends all week in school. The grandmother can plan some after school activities so the children can spend more time with their friends. Everyone needs to work together."

After the judge's decision, Nadine phoned her ex-mother-in-law to suggest a party for the children and their friends. "We could do it there in Clarksville. I could rent the recreation center."

Phyllis replied, "No."

"No? Why? They don't get to spend any time with their friends on the weekend."

"Well, it was not my decision! You come back—interrupting our lives—and you think I'm gonna go along with you?! Not a chance!"

Nadine muttered, "I don't know how you live with yourself."

Phyllis scoffed, "I live with myself just fine!"

Nadine sighed. "You're so selfish. This is about my children— not you. So I'm gonna have a party for them anyway. You don't have to help. And I don't need your permission to throw my children a party!" With that, she slammed the phone down.

Nadine could see her daughter was beginning to enjoy weekends with her. It had taken some time for Carolyn to open up, but as weeks passed Nadine began to see a difference. And soon after, Carolyn totally surprised her.

Nadine was busy with her work from the dress shop with needle in hand when Carolyn came strolling through the door and made her way forward slowly as she caught her mother's eye. "Do you think you could teach me how to make my own dress for a school dance?"

Nadine was shocked, the precious kind of shock—when you can't believe the good news your ears are delivering. It took a few seconds for her to be able to smile. "Of course," she said, flashing a grin. A few beats later she asked, "Are you sure your Nana will let you go?"

"It's on a Friday. I was hoping you would."

Nadine glanced up from her hemming and said, "I'm not trying to fight with your Nana."

"You don't have to. She doesn't have to know."

Nadine answered, "We'll see."

SIXTEEN

He Is Not Our Daddy

Nadine and Lin had a lot of catching up to do. They decided to meet at the Trail of Tears Park and lunched at a picnic table. This park had always been one of Nadine's favorite places because it felt sacred and peaceful and gave her a sense of closeness to her heritage.

Their time together was splendid and relaxing, in a peaceful setting. She told Lin she wanted him to meet her children. "I just don't want them to think I'm trying to replace their dad."

He said, "No one could replace their dad." He winked and added, "Besides, kids love me."

Later, at her place, she made the introductions and right away Carolyn folded her arms across her chest and said, "So who's he supposed to be?!"

Nadine planted her hands on her hips and said, "Carolyn!?"

The girl had her gaze on Lin, one eyebrow higher than the other. She addressed him in a scathing tone. "Well, I hope you don't think we're gonna call you *Daddy*."

Nadine hurried to say, "I'm so sorry, Lin," then whirled around and faced her daughter. "Young lady, you apologize—right now!"

Lin touched her arm and said, "Nadine, it's ok."

"No, it's not!"

Carolyn spouted, "Apologize *for what?*!"

Nadine heaved a long sigh – seemed to hesitate, then put her hands to her hips again and spoke wearily. "Carolyn, just go on to your room."

Her daughter turned and exited, and her son followed. Nadine fell heavily to the couch and put her fingers to her temples and began massaging. Seconds later she muttered in a weary voice, "Lin…I just don't know how much more of her attitude I can stand." She inhaled and exhaled. "I'm really trying here. And some visits really are fine. But sometimes they're just *attitude-attitude!*"

"Hey, she's a teenager! It will work itself out."

"No, she hates me. Plus, she's spent a lot of time around my mother-in-law—who is evil!"

Lin assured her, "Babe, it will work out. Just give it time."

A bit later, as Nadine prepared dinner, Lin peeped in on the children. "You guys ok?"

They were on the bed, playing checkers. Neither replied. He stepped in and watched for a moment, but still got no reaction. He stood at the end of the bed, looking over William's shoulder, and offered a bit of advice. William didn't seem to mind, but Carolyn glanced up at Lin with a frown each time he uttered a word—until at last she flipped over the checkerboard and pounced to the floor and said, "I quit!"

William began gathering the checkers. "Carolyn—you're such a poor sport!"

Lin said, "I was only trying to help."

She turned to her dresser, snatched up a book and whipped around and spouted, "I didn't ask for your help!" She left the room.

William tilted his head, listening. "Do I hear dogs?" He rushed over to the window then turned back and asked, "Whose dogs?"

"They're mine."

William hurried out of the room and was about to head outside when Nadine called, "Dinner's ready." She smiled at her son and he did follow her to the table. Their plates were soon filled, but Nadine felt little joy because she could see for her son and daughter this was an especially awkward time.

After a few bites, Carolyn asked to be dismissed and went to her room. Nadine sighed heavily and glanced at Lin. William stayed, but never looked up from his plate. She figured that was likely because he was a typical boy with a hearty appetite, but she had learned that he also wanted something. A visit with the dogs.

When all was done and the table had been cleared, Nadine proceeded to her daughter's room and knocked at the closed door. "Carolyn? Are you ok?" She heard no answer but opened the door slightly and then entered. She settled on the edge of the bed and said softly. "Baby, why are you crying?"

Carolyn spoke in the pillow where her face was buried. "That man is not my daddy. My daddy was my daddy."

"You are right. He's not. And he is not trying to replace your daddy."

Carolyn sniffled before she spoke. "Nana said…she said…that killing Daddy was no accident." She turned her face up then and added, "She said you meant to do it!"

Nadine nudged her. "Sit up, child, and look at me. Nana is a huge part of the problem. She wasn't there that night, so she has no idea what happened. She doesn't know *why* I had to defend myself...but she was aware of a lot of things that were going on... and besides, she just didn't care."

She changed her tone. "Sweetie, I've known you since I carried you in my womb. I know you're really hurting right now...but it doesn't mean I have to be punished by my kids... or anyone else... for the rest of my life." She sighed then said tenderly, with tears in her eyes, "And I do love you."

Carolyn sat up and demanded, "Did you love Daddy?"

"Of course, I did, sweetie—but if I hadn't defended myself, he would have killed me. Do you remember the day he kicked the car window out and dragged me to the barn? He held a gun to my head. I assure you; he was not the victim. That was my role, and finally I had to defend myself."

Carolyn sat with her feet dangling above the floor, but kept her gaze down, refusing to look up. After some seconds, Nadine got to her feet and left the room and pulled the door closed.

Carolyn continued to sit in thought. She remembered the barn incident. Yes, she was the one who called the police. She shut her eyes tight and shook her head vigorously, as if trying to say she didn't want to remember.

William burst into her bedroom and cried out, "Sista, the dogs are great!!"

Carolyn's gaze was on the floor. William settled on the bed beside her. "Hey, what's wrong?" She did not speak. He demanded, "Talk to me!"

In slow motion she turned to him. "When you think of Daddy, what do you remember?"

He shrugged. "I don't know. Guess I try not to think about him." He sighed before adding, "Uh…well…he kicked the car window in. And forced me to eat all those onions—but come on Sista, let's see the dogs!" He hopped to his feet. "I don't want to talk about Daddy!"

"And I don't want to see some stupid dogs."

He pulled at her arm. "They're *not* stupid. *Come on.*" Reluctantly, she followed him and when she saw the dogs she immediately softened.

Later, after the children were in bed, Lin and Nadine lounged on the couch. As they talked Nadine opened up more about Charles. "I really did love him, Lin. He was my world."

"Even with all the abuse?"

"Even with the abuse. Strange…but true. No one ever understood it. Sometimes not even me. But, when I was away from him, I longed for him. I mean, when he was good to me, he was good to me."

"And when he wasn't?"

"It was a nightmare. He could be a monster."

Lin pulled her close and she rested her head on his chest as he rubbed her shoulder.

"Many times, I wanted to leave. But my life would have been miserable either way. If he had come home and found we weren't there, he would have stopped at nothing until he found us. His parents had money, and they knew people." She sighed. "And now *she* has my kids."

She paused before continuing. "When you have your heart invested in a relationship, you want so badly for it to work out—

no matter the cost. It's just so hard to understand…how a man so kind and loving one day could be a monster the next day!"

Lin smiled slightly and caressed her face and hair. "I don't know how any man could put a scratch on you. I would be so proud to have you as my wife."

Nadine pulled back and stared at him. "Really?"

"Really."

"Is that a proposal?"

"Would you accept it if it was?"

She laughed. "Wow, look at the time. It's getting late. Um, you staying or…"

"Yeah." He lifted her chin and gently kissed her lips. "I love you, Nadine. I want to be with you." "We can't. My kids are here and…"

"I don't mean sex, although I've thought about that too. I mean I want you in my life."

"I know. I love you too, but I don't think this is a good time for us."

"Then when?"

She stood and shrugged her shoulders. Lin noted the troubled look on her face and the usual fidgeting of her hands when she was nervous. He stood and took hold of her hands. "Nadine, baby, it's okay. There's no pressure. At least we know how we feel about each other." He kissed her on the forehead. Then he whispered, "Let me do something for you. Please…"

"Like what?"

"Come with me." He led her by the hand to her room. He then went in her bathroom, turned the water on and poured in some bubble bath he found under the sink. She stood at the door with a slight smile.

"What are you doing?"

"I just want you to relax."

"And what are you gonna do?"

"You'll see."

While the tub was filling, Nadine shuffled through her dresser drawer for a gown. Lin noticed she didn't have much to choose from. Once she was in the tub, he went looking around the house for a couple of candles. Then he went back to her room and folded her bed linens down and lit the candles, even found a mellow radio station on the clock radio by the nightstand.

Then he went and took a shower in the main bathroom down the hall. He returned in a pair of sweatpants – no shirt or shoes. Nadine was sitting on the bed rubbing lotion on her feet. She glanced up several times, trying not to stare at the chiseled man. As she slid her hands up and down her legs, it became hard to distinguish the moisture in her nervous palms from the feel of the lotion.

He stepped forward and picked up the bottle of lotion and sat on the floor in front of her. Nadine's back straightened as she took in a slow breath.

He first rubbed a few drops of lotion between his hands then took hold of her right foot and began easing the lotion across her skin. He looked up and said in a whisper, "How does it feel?" She sucked in her bottom lip and nodded her head. Charles had never done anything like this for her.

He kissed the top of each foot and lifted her legs onto the bed, then whispered again, offering her a further massage if she would roll over. A lump formed in her throat as he pulled up her gown. She lifted herself up—giving him permission. She tried to relax as she felt his strong warm hands coated with the lotion slipping over her shoulders and neck and down her back. He stopped his thumbs just underneath the waistband of her panties.

She closed her eyes and buried her face in the pillow. And felt a gentle kiss on the small of her back. Chills and goose bumps clothed her body.

"How do you feel, babe?"

She whispered, "Wonderful." She rolled over and pulled her gown down. He sat on the side of the bed and leaned over her. She touched her hands to his face – tracing his features with her fingers as their eyes locked in shared emotions. He parted his lips and touched the tip of her finger with his tongue. She put her finger over his mouth and smiled.

He took her hand in his and held it against his lips. He said softly, "I think I'll let you rest."

When he stood, Nadine grabbed his hand. "Will you stay with me? I mean at least until I fall asleep?"

"You sure?"

She slid over and pulled the blanket back. Lin lay beside her and put his arms around her. She placed her head on his chest and closed her eyes. "I really do want to be with you."

"I'm patient, Nadine. I would never rush you."

The rhythm of Lin's heartbeat put Nadine at ease and she soon fell asleep. She curled up to him as a newborn does to its mother.

Very gently he slid away and made his way quietly to the living room where he settled on the couch for the rest of the night.

In the morning, he awakened to the sound of the television. He opened his eyes to find the children watching cartoons. He stretched his arms in the air. "Good morning! Anyone hungry?"

No one answered. Both Carolyn and William kept gazing at the television.

He sat up and pulled his shirt over his head and said, "Well, I'm going out and bring back breakfast." He went in the bathroom and came out to put on his shoes. "If your mom gets up, tell her I'll be right back."

When he returned, he had three bags and a drink tray with two coffees and two cups of orange juice. The children were still in front of the TV. As he headed for the kitchen he asked, "Did Nadine get up?" When they didn't answer, he turned to face them. "Can I get some help? Please."

Carolyn stood up and sighed heavily. William tagged behind, following her to the kitchen. A few minutes later Nadine came in with a smile. "Hey! Good morning! What's going on?"

"Come on, babe—I got breakfast," Lin said. "Come on, sit down." He pulled out a chair.

"This is nice. When did you have time to go get all of this?"

"While you were sleeping. Did you sleep well?"

"Oh, like a baby. Good morning, William, Carolyn."

The children mumbled a good morning in return without looking at her. William shoved half a pancake in his mouth and muffled out, "Are you gonna be our new dad?"

Carolyn dropped her fork. "No, he's not. He will never be our dad."

"I'm not trying to be, sweetheart."

Carolyn rolled her eyes. "Don't call me sweetheart!" From the corner of her eye, she noted the astonished look on her mother's face. But she didn't care.

"Carolyn, you apologize, right now." "It's

alright, Nadine," Lin said.

Nadine frowned at Carolyn. "No, it's not."

Lin faced Carolyn. "Let me ask you something, Carolyn. Why are you so angry? Do you think what happened to your father was on purpose?"

Carolyn shot a cold glance at Nadine and said, "I don't know—ask her."

Lin spoke calmly. "Have *you* asked her?"

William looked up from his food. "No, she hasn't."

Carolyn rolled her eyes at her brother. "He didn't ask you."

"Well, you weren't saying nothing."

Lin gazed directly at Carolyn. "Is there a reason why you haven't asked your mom what happened?"

"I was there."

Lin pulled a chair up beside Carolyn and sat down. She flinched. He asked, "You loved your daddy, right?"

Carolyn looked in the opposite direction.

Lin said, "That's okay. There is nothing wrong with loving him. But the only person who can tell you what happened is your mom—not your grandparents. They weren't there."

Carolyn shrugged her shoulders. She frowned and looked at Nadine. "I saw her. I saw her stabbing my daddy. Brother saw it too."

William didn't say a word. His gaze was miles away as he listened to Carolyn. Nadine set her cup down and closed her eyes.

Lin cleared his throat. "Carolyn, you saw something else before that. Think about it. What were they doing?" She shrugged.

Lin said, "You don't know?"

"I don't know. I was outside—my brother and me."

"Okay, so, let me ask you this…how do you feel about your mom?"

"Nothing is the same anymore—and I hate her for it."

Nadine excused herself. William left the table too and hurried outside. Lin slipped an arm around Carolyn and immediately she gave way to uncontrollable tears. She dropped her head on the shoulder of this man she hardly knew.

"That's right, sweetheart. Get it all out," Lin said. He picked up a napkin and began wiping her face. Carolyn took it from him and continued to wipe her tears away. Then she sat straight up.

He said, "Carolyn, maybe not today, but I think one day when you're ready, you need to ask your mom what happened before you and William came in the house. You need to know the truth and she's the only one who can tell you. I think once you give her a chance to explain things, you will begin to remember other things as well. It will all come back to you. And then you and your mom can move on."

She blew her nose and said, "Can I go now?"

"Sure. Where are you going?"

"Outside with my brother."

"Sure, sweetheart."

Carolyn found William sitting on the ground doodling in the dirt with a stick. He did not look up at her as he said, "You shouldn't have said all that stuff, Sis."

"Why not? He asked me all those questions."

"He's a lawyer. He's used to asking a lot of questions."

They laughed. And Carolyn found another stick and started doodling. After a bit William said, "You know you hurt her feelings."

"Why do you care?"

"Cause she's still our mom."

SEVENTEEN

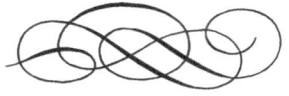

Visitation Is Over

Meanwhile, Lin went to console Nadine. He found her lying across her bed sobbing and settled beside her and rubbed her back. She mumbled into her pillow, "She hates me— she really does hate me! She said it!"

She sat up then and he said, "Nadine, baby…Carolyn is hurting. She cried on my shoulder like Charles had just died."

"Really?"

"Yeah."

"I don't know what to do. The therapist just keeps saying it takes time."

"Well, you have to think about the fact that every time you make a step with them, they go back to their grandparents and get set back two steps. And do remember I'm here for the three of you— in any way I can be. If you want me to, I'll come every weekend."

Nadine reached over and kissed him.

"And what was that for?"

"You're a great man. Sometimes I think I must be dreaming, and I pinch myself. I don't really deserve you." She sank back on the bed with a moan. "Oh, Lin, I've made so many mistakes."

"Who hasn't!" He lay beside her and they stared at the ceiling. "Nadine, you have two beautiful children. They are gifts from God. You deserve to have them back in your life and they need you. How are you gonna heal without each other? You don't really think they hate you?"

Nadine sighed heavily. "I don't know what to think."

He sat up and took her hand. "Come with me." He pulled her over to the mirror and stood behind her. "Look. What do you see, Nadine?"

"What do you mean?"

"Who is that woman in the mirror?"

She shrugged. "I don't know. Just me."

"I see beauty, strength, love—a woman who's afraid to be loved, and a woman I love and adore. You've just got to learn your value."

"You see more than I do."

"You're so deserving of all good things in life. If not, God would have never blessed you with them in the first place. You have to think more of yourself."

Later Lin and Nadine spotted the children sitting on the steps of the back porch and heard William say, "You know Nana is gonna be upset that we didn't go to church today."

Carolyn raised an eyebrow. "So, we won't say anything."

"You know she'll ask."

Nadine said, "We'll go next Sunday."

The children whipped around then but William looked away and mumbled, "That's too late for today."

Carolyn stood. "Can we see Aunt Claudette?"

"Sure," Nadine said. "Ma is probably cooking Sunday dinner anyway."

As Nadine expected, Martha was glad to see them. "You kids turn on the TV, and Lin—you just make yourself at home."

Sam was taking his usual Sunday afternoon nap. And Claudette had not yet arrived. Nadine grabbed an apron from the hook on the wall. "I can help you, Ma."

"So how long has Lin been down?"

"Since yesterday."

"Oh?"

"Yeah, he came down yesterday to meet the kids."

"How did it go?"

"Not well—at least not at first."

She was about to explain when Claudette came through the front door and called out, "Ma, I'm here!"

The children jumped to their feet to greet their beloved aunt with hugs and kisses. Claudette spoke to Lin then made her way to the kitchen where she embraced Martha. "Hi, Ma." She turned then to Nadine for a deep hug and said, "So...no wonder I haven't heard from you, girl."

"Hush up now," Martha said to Claudette. "Nadine was just about to tell me about the conversation Lin had with Carolyn. "Oh. Really?"

Nadine proceeded to tell most of the details. As soon as she stopped Claudette said,

"Well, you know, Nadine—Lin is right." She stuffed a slice of cucumber in her mouth. "You are all he said you are."

Martha sat down at the kitchen table. "Nadine, when you were growing up you never were quite the fighter Claudette was, but you didn't take no junk. I was worried about you though."

Nadine looked the other way. "I guess I was a disappointment."

"Oh no, child! That's not it. But it looked like, somewhere along the way, Charles took your spirit. Like he was breaking a wild stallion, you know? I've seen men break women. Make them move into submission. And many a time it wasn't because they weren't strong, but because he needed to feel in control. Baby, that's why he broke you—but the good news is, the Lord can heal all wounds. I believe it with all my heart. The Lord will help you find you again." She winked. "In fact, I think He's already in the works."

When dinner was over, the family settled in the living room to enjoy music and games, till at last Nadine glanced at her watch and said, "Hey, you guys, time to go! Your nana will soon be at my house."

Sam stuttered through his twisted lips, "Oh, make them come here. The kids are having fun."

Martha chuckled. "Yeah, you got that right. I'll just call and tell them to pick the kids up here. That'll piss ole Phyllis the hell off!"

"Really Ma!"

Claudette giggled. "It does come out every now and again." She winked. "Just stick around. You'll see."

"Well, I'll have to go get their things from the house."

Claudette slipped on her shoes and said, "I'll go with you." As they traveled Nadine was reminded how good it was to be in her sister's company. For as far back as she could remember, she had always been able to confide in Claudette, so now she told her about the bath and the massage.

"And you *didn't have sex?* Woe! Now that's some kind of restraint!"

"Well, he is a gentleman."

"No, I mean you." And they filled the car with laughter.

Nadine's eyes went wide. "Well…it has been awhile."

"A good while! If a man that fine had his hands all over me—you know it would have been on!"

Nadine sighed. "I am ready…but I still want to wait. You know?"

Claudette shook her head side to side. "No! I don't know!"

Upon their return, they found their mother on the floor with Lin and the children, cards in their hands, playing rummy. Martha reported yes, she called Phyllis, who did have a few words to say but did finally agree to the plan. Martha soon joined her daughters in the kitchen and put on a fresh pot of coffee. She said, "Isn't he just great with those kids, Nadine? I think we've got a keeper."

Claudette chimed in with, "That man is your blessing—he's gonna help you get your kids back."

Before Nadine could answer there was a knock at the door and Carolyn got up to answer it. Yes, it was Phyllis. William hopped to his feet and said, "We were playing cards."

"Cards?!"

Lin stood. "How are you?" He reached to shake her hand.

Phyllis gazed at the outstretched hand, took a step back and rolled her eyes. "Aren't you the attorney who got that woman off?"

Carolyn blurted, "He's Mama's boyfriend." The

room went silent.

"Oh, I see. So you're why she's walking free? Children! Get your things and let's get out of this sinful house!"

Martha set her hands on her hips. "Now look here, Phyllis, I'm not gonna allow you to insult anyone in my home."

Phyllis scoffed. "I'm so glad you insisted I come here to pick up the children. Now I've seen for myself what they're exposed to!"

Claudette demanded, "What are you talking about?"

Nadine said, "Well, how do we know what they're exposed to during the week?"

Phyllis ordered the children to the car then pointed at Nadine. "You? You are crazy! In fact, your whole family is crazy! That's why you're not gonna win. The Lord don't like ugly from nobody."

Nadine said, "Hmmph—well I don't see any rays of approval from heaven shining down on you!"

"You're a blaspheming Jezebel!"

Martha yelled, "Oh, go blow it out your backside!"

Lin intervened in an even tone. "Look...this is not good for the children."

Phyllis turned her eyes to Nadine. "Ha! Looks like maybe you best listen to this *boyfriend*."

"And you better get out," Nadine said, her tone cool. "I've had years of you! And can't wait to get my kids away from you. You're a self-righteous witch!"

Phyllis pointed a finger at Nadine. "See! That's why I sent the kids out. This is the side of you they don't know—but Charles knew it—and the courts will too!"

"Charles knew how to put his fist in my face and his foot in my ribs and—"

Phyllis rolled her neck. "Yeah, yeah—because of how you are. You were a shame and a scandal to him—and from the looks of things, you still are."

Nadine stepped forward. "You don't know nothing about me!"

Before Claudette and Lin could stop her Nadine pushed Phyllis against the screen door. Phyllis's mouth dropped open.

Lin took Nadine's arm and said softly, "Come on, babe. She's not worth it."

Tears were streaming down Nadine's face. The witch was still in sight. Nadine, trembling, spoke slowly in a low tone. "All you ever did was stand by and enable Charles in his abuse." She reached to wipe away the tears on her cheeks. "You will reap what you have sown."

"If my son were alive! — he wouldn't allow you to talk to me like this!"

Claudette intervened. "Well, your son is dead."

Phyllis gasped. "My son deserved the best."

Nadine, tapping her chest with her forefinger, cried, "I was the best!"

Now it was Martha's turn. She stared into the witch's eyes and demanded, "Get the hell out of here!"

Phyllis turned to leave but spoke over her shoulder. "Gladly! And Nadine, you will regret this day. All of you will! You're a bunch of heathens!"

Nadine soon had her face buried in Lin's chest, sobbing. When at last she calmed enough to speak she said, "She meant it, you know. She's gonna be influencing the judge—saying I'm not fit to raise my own children!"

He pushed her hair back and said soothingly, "I have confidence it will work out—in your favor."

He followed her to the back-porch swing. At first, they sat in silence, then he reached over and took her hand. She caught his gaze and said, "You promised me you'd help me get my kids back. You promised!"

"And I'm gonna keep that promise. In less than two months, you have a custody hearing. It's gonna work out."

"That witch is as mean as Charles was—and spiteful too! I won't likely see my children again before going to court. I'd bet my life on it."

"Nadine, you've got to trust me. I'm not here to let you down."

"You think you know her? You think you got it all figured out?" She shook her head vehemently. "No!"

"Let the system work for you, Nadine."

"The system stinks. It's all about who you know and how much money you've got. I'd still be behind bars, locked up in that prison cell...if I didn't know Candace and she didn't know you." "You are right, there are times when the system fails, but there are many,

many times when it works. You must trust the court's desire to see families together."

For a moment neither of them spoke, till Lin sighed and asked, "Do you still love him?"

Nadine frowned. "What?"

"Charles. Do you still love him?"

"He was the father of my children." For some seconds, she paused, staring into the distance. "You know, I want to hate him. I want to hate him so bad. But I can't. My children came from a bad situation, a situation I feel guilty about." "I know."

The children kept quiet. They learned there were times when it was best to say nothing. Their grandmother went on and on about their mother. "I knew this visitation thing was a bad idea—I knew it. If it wasn't for jeopardizing the custody of you kids, I wouldn't let you see her again."

William leaned across the backseat and whispered to his sister. "It's all your fault. You shouldn't've said Lin was Mama's boyfriend."

Carolyn rolled her eyes and for the rest of the ride, turned her face to the window.

EIGHTEEN

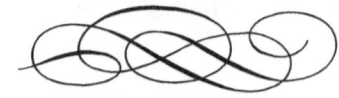

The Breakthrough

Three weeks passed since Nadine and Phyllis's run in. Phyllis remembered what the judge said about her violating visitation and begrudgingly permitted the children to spend weekends with Nadine.

On a Friday, the children wanted to go to a basketball game, Phyllis offered to take them. The children learned she would grant than almost anything to delay their time with Nadine, so though Phyllis didn't like basketball she dropped them off with instructions on where to be when Joe returned to pick them up.

Shortly before the game ended Carolyn spotted David, a boy she'd had a crush on all school year. They stood and talked for a few minutes then wandered outside, away from the crowd. They soon stopped behind a building, staring nervously at each other.

David cleared his throat. "Do you think we could ever go out sometime?"

"No—my nana won't allow it. She thinks I'm too young."

"So, I guess we can only see each other at school, huh?"

"I guess so."

David was fidgety, looking around, rubbing the palms of his hands on his pants. Then he stepped closer. "Carolyn, can I kiss you?"

"What?"

Before she knew it, David's lips were pressed against hers. She backed against the brick wall. Her eyes stretched wide and her heart was pounding. She wasn't sure how she was supposed to feel or what she was supposed to do. Then once more he leaned in and pressed his lips to hers. This time she closed her eyes.

He pulled back and looked at her. She still had her eyes closed as if waiting for more, so he kissed her again, this time opening his mouth a little. She felt the moistness of his tongue and parted her lips. Then she realized what was happening and how quickly she had been caught up in the moment, so she pulled away. The meeting of their tongues felt good—but it felt so good she was sure it was a sin.

He stared into her eyes. "Did I do something wrong?"

Her cheeks flushed. "No, no—but I should go. The game's over, and my Paw Paw—he's probably here by now."

"Okay. But did you like it? I mean, it was your first kiss, right?"

She smiled shyly and whispered, "It was fine…but…but don't tell anybody—I mean it, David!"

"Okay, no problem."

As they went back towards the gym, he took her hand. William spotted them and started running their way. "Where the heck have you been? Nana is waitin'!"

Carolyn let go of David's hand. "Nana? Oh, my God!"

William's lips tightened as he squinted his eyes. "You're in trouble, Carolyn. We were supposed to stay together. Now she'll never drop us off again."

And suddenly, out of nowhere, there was their grandmother. She too had seen Carolyn and David hand in hand and now screeched,

"You got that right!" Phyllis turned then to face David. "Look, little boy! If you know what's good for you, you'll stay away from my granddaughter! You hear me?"

David, stunned, did not answer. Phyllis snatched Carolyn by the arm and yanked her along. When the three of them were in the car Carolyn said, "How could you embarrass me like that?!"

Phyllis whipped her head around. "Oh no you don't! You're in trouble, young lady! And you don't question me!"

The weather was warm, car windows down—so Carolyn figured everybody around had heard what her grandmother said. She wanted to crawl under the seat and shrink, become a little person no one could see. Then she thought of what David must be thinking and peeked around to see if she might spot him.

William, as usual, maintained silence while his grandmother ranted and raged. She was whipping around turns and weaving, hammering down the road, and her eyes darting from him in the rearview mirror and back again to his sister.

"And what were you thinking, Carolyn? Going off somewhere with that boy?! What were you doing?! You better not have been doing what I think you were doing!"

"What?!"

"You heard me."

Carolyn's eyes widened. "You're crazy!" As soon as the words were out, she clapped her hands over her mouth.

Phyllis hurled her fist into Carolyn's chest. "Who do you think you're talking to?"

The car swerved as she continued to swing her fist Carolyn's way. Carolyn was now in tears and William about to burst with his anger.

His body went taut and he heard himself yell, "Stop it, Nana! Stop it! You're gonna kill us!"

Phyllis stopped punching her granddaughter but pointed a finger at her. "Do you see what you have caused? Do you see?! You will not shame this family as your mammy has. I will not allow it!"

Carolyn wiped at her tears. As she turned her gaze to the window, she found she was seeing flashbacks of times like this. She had packed them all away. Refused to remember or think on them. But now her grandmother's words sounded familiar, as though she'd heard them before. And then the memory appeared. She closed her eyes. She was no longer hearing her grandmother's screeching—she was watching a memory. She had been in the backseat. And her daddy grabbed her mama's thigh and gripped hard. She could tell her mama was trying hard not to make a loud cry, yet even at that age, so long ago, she had known her mama did it for the sake of her and her brother.

The memory became even clearer. There was the slap which forced Nadine's head against the car window. And her father's words. *"Do you see what you have caused me to do?!"*

By the time her grandmother was pulling into the driveway, Carolyn's mind had played scenes of quite a few such times during her life with her parents. Now her grandmother was commanding them to go to their rooms and wait for their punishment. So many times, they had heard these same words, but this time Carolyn knew what she had to do. She had to do what her mother had not done—she had to run!

Carolyn grabbed a duffle bag from her closet. It had belonged to Charles. She began filling it with her things. When a knock sounded at her door, she hurried to shove the bag beneath the bed and sat down on the bed. Slowly, the door opened. She held her breath.

At the sight of William, she breathed a sigh of relief, pushed the door closed when he came inside and reached underneath the bed to retrieve the bag. He raised a brow and said, "What are you doing?"

She resumed packing. "I'm getting out of here before she comes in."

"Where are you going?"

"I don't know yet. I just know I have to go—can't take this anymore!"

"Then I'm going with you."

"No, you can't."

"Why not?"

"Because there is no point in both of us getting in trouble for running away."

"Look, Sis. If you think you're gonna leave me here to get all the whippings, you're wrong! I won't stay here without you. You wouldn't stay without me, would you?"

The seriousness in his eyes made Carolyn realize she couldn't leave him. He was her little brother. "Okay," she said. "But get ready quickly. We don't have much time."

William turned his face toward the ceiling and exhaled, "Yes!" He crept back to his room, packed a few things in his book bag and returned to whisper, "Hey! I heard Nana say she might as well come on and deal with us. If we're leaving, we need to go now." She pointed at the window. Outside, William took the lead through the wooded area behind the neighbors' house. They soon arrived—from the back—at a store with a pay phone.

Carolyn said, "No! Not here—we're too close to the house. Who are you gonna call, anyway?"

"Aunt Claudette."

"Really?"

"Well, if we're running away, we need to get far away from here. That's the farthest I can think of where we know someone. And it may be safe there."

"But Nana will find us."

"She won't even think to look there, not at first, anyway."

By the time they came across another pay phone outside a grocery store, it was almost fully dark. They peeked in all directions, making sure no one had seen them arrive. Carolyn dropped in a dime and placed the call.

Soon the operator was saying, "Collect call from Carolyn. Will you accept the charges?"

"Oh, my God, yes—yes, operator!"

"Go ahead, caller."

"Aunt Claudette?"

"Carolyn? What's going on, baby? Are you okay?"

"Yes ma'am—we're fine."

"We?"

"Brother and me. Can you come and get us—please?!"

"Where are you, baby?"

"At a store in Clarksville."

"Where are your grandparents?"

"Aunt Claudette, we ran away. We need for you to come and get us. Please! We're scared!"

"Oh, my God. Yes, of course. What happened?"

"We can explain it to you when you get here!"

"Alright, okay, yes, I'm on my way. What store?"

"A Piggly Wiggly just off the highway. Oh, and Aunt Claudette—don't tell Mama. Don't tell anyone else!"

Claudette, though hesitant, agreed. "Okay, please be somewhere safe until I get there. Don't talk to any strangers. I'm on my way!"

Phyllis, meanwhile, had gone to the children's rooms and found them missing. She called their names, again and again, as she made the rounds looking for them.

"Joe! Where are the kids? Did you see them go out?"

"What do you mean, where are the kids?"

"They aren't in their rooms. They must have gone outside."

"Well, I've been sitting right here all the time and I never saw or heard them leave." He got up and opened the front door and began calling them. No answer, so he headed for their rooms where he searched under beds and in closets.

Behind him Phyllis was tapping her toe. "Okay, Joe…this is not funny! When we find them, they're really gonna get it! And I mean it!!"

"Well, they must have climbed out the window. They can't be far away. Let's drive around the neighborhood."

The more time and distance they spent looking the angrier they became. Joe finally suggested they go back home to see if the kids had showed up, but they found the house empty.

He said, "Phyllis, that's it! If they think this is funny…well, they're going to get the whipping of a lifetime—and you won't have to do it. I will." He sighed. "After today, you'd think they were in enough trouble."

Phyllis had been unusually silent. Now she said, "Joe, maybe we should call the police." After some back and forth they decided first to make some phone calls, but no one they called had seen either child since the game.

The children, meanwhile, kept out of sight behind the store. William frequently glanced at his Spiderman watch. When a police car came by patrolling the area, they ducked behind some trash bins. As the cruiser left Carolyn said, "Brother, do you think Nana and Paw Paw will call the police?"

"It's possible." His eyes were roaming. "Hey, we could hide behind the old building across the street. Let's go before the police come back around." They were soon across the street behind an old restaurant building where they could huddle and watch for their Aunt Claudette, and sure enough, she did at last pull up by the side of the store. They popped up from their hiding place, ready to scurry—but then the police car appeared again, and they dove down again.

The officer lowered his window as he pulled up beside Claudette. "Good evening. Is everything okay, ma'am?"

"Yes, officer. Thanks for asking. I'm just going to use the pay phone."

"Well, the store is closed, and this isn't the best area at night, so make it quick—and be careful."

She flashed a smile. "Thank you, I appreciate it. I won't be long."

As Claudette expected, when she picked up the phone the cop drove off. Then almost immediately the children came jetting across the street. They were calling her name in a loud whisper.

She heaved a sigh of relief, hugged them and ushered them into the car. As she turned onto the highway she said, "Alright you two, what are you doing? Running away?"

They were in the backseat trying to stay out of sight. Carolyn spoke up. "It's a long story."

"Well, I'm listening. All the way here I had scary thoughts but prayed God would protect you two—and let me find you!"

Carolyn then started relating the details of what had transpired. When the girl finally paused, Claudette let a few moments go by before responding. "Well, Carolyn. I hate saying this, but she was right. You weren't together, nor were you where you should have been."

Carolyn sat up and rested her arms on the back of the passenger's seat. "No, Aunt Claudette, you don't understand. *Everything* is a whipping! It doesn't matter whether I'm wrong or I'm right—it's always what *she says it is.* It doesn't matter if it's big or small, the punishment's the same." She sighed and added. "And I just can't take it anymore." She paused just slightly then and added in a lower tone, "And I won't."

William spoke up. "It's true, Aunt Claudette—you gotta believe us!"

"Yes, baby, I believe you. I just don't yet know what to do about it. And I'm afraid that coming to get you…well, it won't likely fare well in court." She blew out air and added, "But it's too late now."

Nineteen

Sanctuary

The ride got quiet as the two passengers, worn out with the drama of the day, fell asleep in the backseat. Claudette pulled up before a house and cut the engine off. "Okay, children. Let's go inside."

They sat up, rubbing their eyes groggily but understanding right away where they were. They glanced at each other with a frown. William shrugged his shoulders. Carolyn opened the door. "Why are we here?"

"Because your mama needs to know what's going on. Besides, I'm not gonna be in this by myself."

Claudette knocked and Nadine was soon peeking out to see who was on the front step. She pulled the door open and exclaimed, "Hey, Sissy—what's going on?"

Claudette said, "I brought you something." Then she stepped aside, exposing the children.

"What in the world?! Come on in this house!"

The runaways were soon warm and enjoying hot cocoa as they told everything. Nadine turned her face to the ceiling and closed her eyes, then pulled in a deep breath and let it out slowly. She looked from one child to the other. "So…you ran away?" Her hands went to her temples and she moaned, "And we're so close to going to court!"

Claudette set her cup on the table and spoke softly. "Nadine, this may end up a good thing. I mean, what the kids are saying is, in that house things are not quite right—so just maybe, the fact they did run away will speak volumes—in your favor!—in the courtroom!"

Nadine shook her head side to side. "Maybe.... But they've got to be out of their minds looking for you two! I would be."

Claudette raised her eyebrows. "So, what are we gonna do?"

"We have to call Phyllis."

Both Carolyn and William jumped from their seats saying, "No! No!" Carolyn begged, "Mama, please don't. She'll come get us! You don't know what that means. Please, *please* don't!"

Nadine looked directly at her daughter and spoke evenly. "Carolyn, sit down. Calm down."

"No!!" her daughter insisted. "Mama, you don't know what that would mean!!" She stepped over to her brother and lifted his shirt. "Look!"

The sisters gasped. On William's lower back were three dark bruises. Carolyn pointed and exclaimed, "*This is because*... because he brought home a C on his report card. We're expected to bring home top grades."

Claudette slapped her hand on the tabletop and jumped to her feet. "Nadine, what do you want to do?! 'Cause I'm ready to hurt someone over my babies!"

"I'm gonna call her."

"Call?"

Again, the children began begging no, but she did. And Phyllis snatched up the phone immediately. "Hello? Carolyn? William?"

"No, Witch. It's neither."

Phyllis went quiet a few seconds before saying in a calm tone, "Who is this?"

"You know who this is. Where are my children?"

Phyllis swallowed deeply. Joe stood by, wondering who was on the other end. Phyllis gulped a breath then said evenly, "Oh, Nadine. What do you mean, where are your children?"

"Just what I asked. Where are they?"

The soft tone in the witch's voice was no more. She flared up with, "Well, first of all, you don't call here this time of night demanding to know something. And secondly, children are usually in bed this time of night."

"Yeah. But mine aren't."

"So, what do you know, Nadine—about the children's whereabouts?"

"I know they're not there with you."

"Where are they?"

"They're safe—and I'm gonna make sure the judge knows what's going on."

Now the voice went shrill. "You kidnapped my children?! Don't play games with me, Nadine. Where are they? I should've known you had something to do with this—I'm calling the police!" Nadine heard Joe in the background. "Hang up, Phyllis! Go ahead and call the police!"

Nadine kept her voice steady. "Yes, you do that. I'm sure they will be *very interested in why my children ran away*. Or maybe they would be more interested in knowing how Will got those bruises on his back.... No, I assure you, you don't want to play games with me."

"I'll be over to get the kids."

"I don't think so. I don't think you want to come to my house tonight, 'cause if you do, I'll mop the floor with you!" And with that, she slammed the phone down.

Carolyn caught her mother's eye. "She's coming, isn't she?"

"No, baby—not tonight anyway. You two go take your baths, then get some rest. We'll figure it out in the morning. Okay?"

As soon as the children left the room Claudette put her hands on her hips and said, "Dang, I was hoping she would come." The sisters laughed big. It felt so good to be on the winning end.

Nadine called Lin, who assured her in the morning he would "get right on it." He added, "Don't worry, Nadine—just get some rest tonight. They're safe with you."

"I know she's scheming up something."

"Trust me, baby. Old Phyllis has stepped in it this time...but hey, your babies are home! They knew where to find sanctuary!"

Nadine grinned and felt tears welling in her eyes. "I guess they did."

Carolyn got up and made her way down the hallway to Nadine's room. She knew Claudette was staying the night, so she tiptoed over to the side of the bed where Nadine lay and whispered, "Mama."

Nadine's eyes sprang open. She sat up. "What's wrong?"

Claudette awakened and switched on the lamp. "It's 2:00 in the morning! Are you alright?!"

"I can't sleep."

"Oh!" Nadine sighed in relief.

"I just want you to know I remembered."

"Remembered what, baby?"

Claudette said, "Come get under the covers." The child was soon settled between the sisters. She started with, "I remembered Daddy…remembered one time when he was hurting you in the car. I can remember some other things too, but I can't put them together. I tried to remember what happened the day he died. Some parts I can see, and some I can't."

Nadine stroked Carolyn's hair and pushed it back. "Carolyn, I'm so-o sorry…but there's something I need you to understand. I really did love your daddy. That day you can't remember much about, he stood over me with a knife. And then you and Will came in, and he put you both back outside. The way he was raging, I knew he was going to kill me. He just kept on beating, wouldn't stop." Her voice broke. "He wouldn't stop, Carolyn."

"I'm sorry, Mama."

"There's no need, baby. You did *nothing* wrong!"

"I know. But that's just it. I didn't do anything."

Nadine wrapped her arms around her daughter. "Sweetheart, there was no way you could have known what was about to happen."

"We were scared!"

Claudette propped herself up on her elbow. "You guys—you have a chance now—to be mother and daughter again, you know?

Make up for lost time."

William appeared in the doorway. "What's going on?"

"Hey, you," Claudette said. "Come join us. What you doing up?" He hopped on the end of the bed. "I couldn't sleep, and Sister wasn't in her bed." Soon they were all snuggled in bed together. What joy, Nadine thought.

Soon thereafter Carolyn began speaking. Her tone immediately told the listeners it was a sad story she would be telling. "I woke up from a bad dream and didn't want to be alone, so I went down the hall and saw grandmother had already left to go to the bakery. So, I climbed in the bed on her side 'cause I didn't wanna be alone. I knew she wouldn't be gone long, just long enough to open the bakery and get the ovens going, and as soon as one of her workers arrived she'd head back. But when she got back, she found me in her bed.

I heard her telling it later, how she stood at the bedroom door watching. I was asleep, and Granddad was asleep."

William jumped in. "Yeah, I spotted Nana when I came out of the bathroom. She stepped in the room and put her purse on the dresser near the door, then backed out. I guess I startled her when I said, "What are you doing, Nana?" And she twirled around with a finger to her mouth and said, "Shhh! We don't want to wake them."

"I said, 'Who is them?' And she said, 'Carolyn and your granddad.' Well, that was a surprise, so I said, 'Why is Carolyn sleeping with Paw Paw?' And she said, 'That's what I want to know'."

In the silence which followed Nadine and Claudette glanced at one another and silently agreed it was past time to put an end to this kind of talk. It was late and they all needed to get some sleep, but the children were on a roll. Carolyn continued. She had been in the bathroom brushing her hair and caught sight in the mirror of her grandmother standing in the doorway. She had a strange look on her face.

"Are you okay, Nana?"

Phyllis continued her silence but took the brush from Carolyn and began gently brushing her hair. "You look so much like your mother." The brushing became sharper and faster. Carolyn was about to ask her to stop when Phyllis demanded, "Carolyn, why were you in my bed?!"

"I had a bad dream…. Nana, you're hurting me!"

"Well, you should have known better than to get in my bed. Joe is a grown man."

Carolyn tried to retrieve the brush, but her grandmother smacked her hands with it. Carolyn spun around and said, "Nana, what are you doing?!"

Phyllis spoke through her teeth as she pointed the brush in her granddaughter's face. "Don't mess with me, little girl. If you think I'm going to let you get comfortable sleeping in my bed— with my husband, then you've got another think coming. You are a young woman with those perky little boobs—and it is not okay! So, I warn you…I had better never catch you in my bed again—you hear me?!"

By then Carolyn was sobbing. She answered, "Yes, ma'am."

Phyllis tossed the brush on the floor and stormed out. Carolyn picked it up and closed the bathroom door. She sat on the side of the tub and sobbed. It was then she thought living with her mother might not be such a bad idea.

William heard his sister's sobs and headed down the hall. He stepped back and stopped by the bathroom door. "Sis? Are you ok?" She didn't answer, so he asked again.

Just then his grandmother opened her bedroom door and demanded, "What are you doing?"

William said, "Sis is crying. Maybe she's sick."

"Oh, she's not sick." His grandmother pushed him aside and began pounding on the bathroom door and yelling, "Carolyn! Carolyn! Open this door—and come on out of there! Stop all this foolishness! Get out of the bathroom now before I break the door down!"

"But, Nana, how do you know she's not sick?"

His grandmother's response to his question was a look so cold William lowered his head. She was still speaking, making her demand in a shrill voice. Finally, she said, "I'm gonna count to three!"

By the time she reached three Carolyn opened the door very slowly. She was wiping her eyes. Phyllis shoved the door wide, and Carolyn stumbled back. "Are you playing with me, girl?"

Carolyn stared at the floor and shook her head. "No, ma'am."

Phyllis planted her hands on her hips. "What were you doing in the bathroom all this time? Huh? You know what? Never mind. You just get your butt in the kitchen and peel those potatoes I'm fixing for your dinner tonight."

Carolyn hesitated, thinking her grandmother would exit the bathroom first, but Phyllis snapped, "Now! Before I smack you. Do you think I won't?!"

Carolyn rolled her eyes then stood straight and went eye to eye with her grandmother. "Yes, ma'am. I do know you will." And then she spun around and exited.

Nadine and Claudette listened in silence. Nadine wasn't sure she could speak but finally managed, "Carolyn, your nana is the one with the issues. I mean, my gosh – to be jealous of her own granddaughter? That's enough proof she's crazy."

Claudette said, "No…what's crazy is, she was punishing Carolyn for reminding her of you, Nadine. She never did think you were good enough to join her family."

"Yeah, I came from a family with little means. And she always did say she thought I got pregnant on purpose to trap her precious son. I was all wrong because I wasn't who she would have picked for him—and on and on and on. Man, I'm so sick of her! I would have liked to like my mother-in-law…but I got her."

"Mama, I didn't mean to upset you."

Nadine took Carolyn's hand. "Oh, it's not you, baby. It's her. It's always her. She had then and still has, issues of her own. But I think, since morning will come around too soon, we should all get some sleep, 'cause we don't know what tomorrow's going to be like."

TWENTY

The Children Return

The telephone rang just after eight o'clock. Nadine jumped up to answer it to Lin's voice. He said, "Hey, babe. I talked to the juvenile attorney. I should get a call back letting me know what time to be at the courthouse. I'll call you back as soon as I know something. The kids okay?"

"Yes, they're fine. Look, I can't let them go back, Lin."

"I know. We'll do what we can. Try not to worry."

Nadine got the kids up while Claudette prepared the children's favorite breakfast of pancakes with lots of syrup and pecans. By the time breakfast was over, Lin called to inform Nadine the judge would see everyone at eleven o'clock at the courthouse.

When they all arrived, the juvenile attorney came around the corner to take the children to speak with Judge Matteson in her chambers. Before walking away, Carolyn turned to Nadine and asked, "Mama, would you promise me something?"

"Anything, baby."

"Promise we won't have to go back. Please."

Nadine opened her mouth, but her words were lost. She didn't know what to say. She managed a smile and said, "I'll do my best."

"No, you have to promise."

"Please," William begged.

"Listen, guys," Lin said. "We don't really have control of what happens in the courtroom. But you can tell the judge where you want to live and why. She'll listen to you."

Without any further thought Nadine blurted out, "I promise. I promise I will do everything I can to make sure you don't have to go back."

The children followed the juvenile attorney to the judge's chambers. Judge Matteson was unable to meet with the families, so another judge was there in her place. Looking over her dark rimmed glasses she waited behind her desk as the children made their way in, then gestured for them to sit down. "My name is Sharon. I want you to feel comfortable, so don't be afraid. I'm a mom with three children not much older than you. So, I understand the two of you ran away. Would you like to tell me why?"

They remained silent. And William was fidgeting in his seat.

Sharon cleared her throat. "Well, I came in today just to talk to you and William. Would you please share with me what's been going on? I want to help."

William glanced up and pleaded. "Please don't send us back."

"Back to where, William?"

Carolyn said, "Back to Nana. We don't want to live with her anymore. That's why we ran away."

"Okay. So, tell me about it."

William looked his sister in the eye then slowly stood and lifted his shirt. Sharon noted the bruises and sucked in her lips. She came around the desk and said, "William, what happened?"

He whispered, "Nana," and began fidgeting again. Carolyn reached over and took his hand.

"So, are you saying your Nana bruised your back?"

William nodded. Sharon squatted in front of him. She lifted his chin. "Look at me, William. Why did it happen?"

Carolyn blurted out, "She wants us to be perfect, but we can't! She ripped the dress I wore at my recital party because our mother made it."

Sharon moved a chair over near the children. "Tell me more," she said. She listened attentively as they told her everything. The judge asked why they had never told these things to anyone before.

William, head down, answered, "We were afraid."

Carolyn did the talking. "We tried to tell the social worker, but Nana said if we told anything the state would take us and put us in a foster home. She said we would be treated worse because those foster parents wouldn't know us and wouldn't care about us, and we would never again see our family."

Sharon crossed her legs. "Well, it doesn't happen quite like that. But tell me—how do you feel about your mom?

Carolyn began with, "Well, Nana said…"

William jumped in. "I don't believe everything Nana says." Carolyn sighed. "Well anyway, for a long time I never really knew how to feel about her, but what I was trying to say is that… that Nana wanted us to feel the same as her. She doesn't like our mother and doesn't want us to like her."

"So, how are your visits going with Nadine?"

William smiled. "They're getting better. We especially love Aunt Claudette. She's always there for us."

Carolyn added, "If we couldn't live with Mama, we'd want to live with Aunt Claudette."

"Okay. But you're sure—both of you are sure—you want to live with your mother?"

"Yes!" they answered simultaneously.

The judge gave an approving smile. "Okay, children, thank you. I want you to know I'm very concerned about these things you've shared with me. They weigh very heavy on my decision. Please, now give me some time, to think about how I'm going to handle this."

Carolyn folded her lips together before asking, "Do we have to go back?"

Judge Sharon smiled. "I need some time to process all of this, Carolyn. I need to think of what's best for the two of you. Okay?"

When everyone involved had assembled in the courtroom, Judge Sharon looked about and sighed heavily. She sighed heavily. "Ok. So, I must begin by saying, I am not happy. The children and I had a long conversation. They made it clear to me the environment they're in is not as stable as it should be."

Phyllis whispered to her attorney. "What?"

The judge continued. "It has come to my attention the children haven't been allowed to properly grieve for their father, nor to miss their mother—which is natural regardless of the circumstances. What amazes me is they have coped as well as they have. Although the Hunters, meaning the parental grandparents, have provided them with their physical needs, it appears those grandparents have been more about their own feelings related to this case, rather than concern for the feelings of their grandchildren. In situations of this kind, the children's feelings should never be disregarded… or shaped by others."

Phyllis was shaking her head.

The judge let her gaze roam then continued. "It is always the intention of the court to see if there is a way the families can be reconciled. I think children should be given that opportunity. Given the circumstances before me, I think it would be especially beneficial for these children to develop their own relationship with their mother. I feel the children should be made to feel loved and safe. However, at this time, today…my hands are somewhat tied. Therefore, I regrettably will have to order the children back to Clarksville with Mr. and Mrs. Hunter."

Gasping and weeping filled the courtroom. Phyllis looked over at Nadine with a slight grin on her face.

Judge Sharon had been watching everyone's reactions. "Let me explain. This is not a *win*. This will only be a temporary stay—based on several relevant aspects. First, this is an unofficial hearing that was put in place because of the immediate concerns about the safety of the children just last night, and the children have confirmed for me those concerns. It is not I don't believe the children. However, for the record, I need more relevant information to make a proper judgment at this time. I was asked to fill in this morning because Judge Matteson could not be here."

The judge proceeded to request reports from both the psychiatrist and the social worker—reports on the progress of the children in the home of their paternal grandparents and the progress of their relationship with their mother and school and recent doctor visits. "Give me a few days to review this information with Judge Matteson and we will meet again next week. It's important to get an immediate home report on the home of their mother."

The juvenile attorney stood. "Um, excuse me, Your Honor, it's my understanding the children ran away because they are being abused in the Hunters' home. And we want to send them back?"

"Yes, counselor. I'm genuinely concerned about the things the children have shared. However, it's important to review *all* the facts. Please allow me to take everything into consideration. This was not an easy decision. But it is about the best interest of the children."

Nadine jumped to her feet and ran out of the courtroom. Claudette ran after her. The children followed. Nadine settled on the bench in the hallway and wept on Claudette's shoulder. She moaned, "The judge, the judge...."

Carolyn stood in front of her and spoke softly. "The judge said we have to go back. You promised."

Nadine looked up, wiping her eyes. "Oh Carolyn, I'm so sorry. I promised I would try."

Phyllis stepped outside the courtroom. As usual her nose was in the air. "Come on, children. Let's go home." She reached for William's hand, but Nadine pounced between them.

Phyllis's mouth dropped open. "Excuse you!" But Nadine wouldn't move. "Well, are you gonna move?"

Nadine's watery brown eyes pierced right into Phyllis, but after some seconds she stepped aside. Phyllis rolled her eyes then took William by the hand and said, "Come along."

Nadine called after Phyllis. "I'll see you next week!"

"You certainly will," Phyllis scoffed without turning around.

"You won't win!" Nadine was weeping harder now, as Phyllis and the children continued down the long hall. Lin took Nadine's hand, and they were soon on their way to her house. He hoped to reassure her as he said, "Nadine, the judge doesn't want to make a decision based solely on what the kids said."

She sniffled, "Then she really didn't believe them. Did you see the look in their little eyes? I promised them they wouldn't have to go back."

"Babe, she doesn't know you anymore than she knows the Hunters. I know this judge. She's fair."

Nadine turned to the window. "No. No judge is fair."

He reached over and took her hand and kissed it. "Babe, listen to me. Just hang in there a few more days. It's gonna work out. I believe that with all my being."

"In the meantime?" she asked.

"Pray. That's what you would tell me."

Phyllis was overly nice to the children, cooking all their favorite foods, taking them to a movie on a school night, and even letting them listen to Run DMC in the house. The children wondered how long this treatment was going to last.

The children waited for the right time, when Phyllis and Joe weren't home, to call Nadine at work. Things had continued, with their grandparents being extra good to them. It was now only a couple of days before the hearing. Nadine was busy fitting a wedding dress for a customer when the receptionist peeped in the room. "Excuse me, Nadine. You have a phone call."

Nadine caught her assistant's eye then turned to the receptionist and said, "Ok, thank you." She excused herself and went to the phone. "Hello. This is Nadine."

Carolyn spoke softly. "Mama."

"Carolyn?! Are you okay?!"

"Yes. Yes, I am…we are. We just wanted to talk to you. I know you're busy."

"It's okay, sweetie. Hold just a moment." Ann was standing nearby going through some mail. Nadine asked her if she could use the phone in her office. "It's my children."

"Oh, certainly. Help yourself."

In the office she closed the door and picked up the phone. "You still there?"

"Yes."

"How are things going? Are you sure you're okay?"

"Yeah, we're okay. She's been overly nice the past few days."

"Figures—that she would be. So, what's going on?"

William stood by Carolyn's side, glancing out the window, on the lookout for their grandparents. Nadine could hear Carolyn's breathing. She clutched the edge of the desk and waited for her daughter to continue.

After a long moment Carolyn said, "Well, I know the final say comes from the judge… but, well, we don't want to live with Nana and Paw Paw anymore. If she says we have to, we'll just run again, but this time we'll go somewhere where we can't be found."

"Oh, no, Carolyn. That's not a good idea. There are just so many stupid rules and things."

Carolyn raised her voice. "But, we told the judge everything!"

"I know honey and she believed you, which means we're gonna win this time. So just take it easy. It's gonna to be fine."

"How do you figure that? When she sent us back?"

"I know, Carolyn. I'm just as upset as you are—but, hey, your Nana knows now that she's under the microscope. It was a real good thing you both did, with what you told her."

William motioned for the phone and Carolyn handed it over. "Mama, we've had enough! We're not gonna stay. When she put me in the closet, it was dark. I cried for you, but you didn't come. I cried for you every night for a long time, but Nana said you were where you should be and you weren't coming for us. She said you would burn in hell for what you did!"

"I'm so sorry, baby. But you know what? I thought about you *all the time*—and I prayed we would be a family again."

Carolyn put her ear to the phone too and heard her mother's talk about praying. She took the phone and said, "I stopped praying a long time ago. I asked God not to let Daddy die and to bring you back—but it didn't happen. I asked God to stop Nana's abuse, but it didn't happen. I asked God the night before court not to let us have to come back here, but we are here."

Nadine let out a soft gasp. "Oh, Carolyn, please don't stop praying. Sometimes God answers us in ways we don't understand. Sometimes He doesn't answer us right away or maybe not at all, but for a good reason. You don't know how many, many prayers I offered up to God as I lay in that prison cell, day after day, thinking of you and William. I wondered what you must be thinking of me—and so wanted to be there for you. But I couldn't. And yes, God took his time answering, but now I'm home. I know you must hate me—at times I hate myself. But every day I regret what I've done and what I've caused you. So please don't stop praying."

Carolyn's face reddened as a single teardrop trickled down her face and then more behind that one threatening to fall. She wiped the tear away, would not allow herself to cry.

"Pray, Carolyn. Pray that we'll be together again—and help each other to heal and mend. Pray that you will finally be safe. I'll pray too."

Carolyn's voice was low and quivering. "I will."

"You promise?"

"Yes, Mama, I promise."

"And William too, okay?"

"Okay. We gotta go. Nana will be home soon."

"I love you guys. I love you so much!"

Carolyn said, "Okay, we gotta go." And put the phone down.

William asked, "What did she say?"

"She loves us."

William nodded his head and smiled.

Ann knocked at her office door and slowly entered. She saw Nadine was sitting behind the desk in a daze. "Are you alright?"

Nadine nodded and sniffled. "Yes, I'm fine. I'm just, uh—just sitting here thinking. That call was from my children."

Ann settled on the edge of the desk. "It's great—they called."

Nadine took in a deep breath and let it out. "Yeah."

"You know, Nadine, not many children actually hate their mothers. Children are more forgiving than most adults. I bet deep inside they not only love you but miss you very much, otherwise they wouldn't have called."

Nadine dried her face with her sleeve. "I know."

301

"So, what did they say?"

"Well...." She sniffled. "I think they just wanted me to know they're ready to come home."

"You see, Nadine, it's going to be alright. I have faith."

Nadine gazed at her boss with tears welling again and answered, "So do I." She wiped the tears. "Thank you, Ann—I mean for everything! I could have never gotten this far—if you hadn't given me a chance."

"No, I'm the one who owes you, because you've brought so much to my business. But I must be honest. If you hadn't come highly recommended by Candy, I would not have hired you. My clientele is too upscale for me to hire ex-cons—but when I saw how talented you are, I knew I'd made the right decision. You're worth your weight in gold and then some." She ended with a big smile on her face and stood up and opened her arms. "Bring it in, girl."

As they stood in the embrace Ann added, "Now the real healing can begin. For the three of you!"

TWENTY-ONE

The Custody Hearing

I n the courtroom Nadine sat just behind the counselor's table. She laced her fingers together in her lap, seeking a façade of calmness as she anticipated the judge's decision. Judge Sharon did not tarry. She opened a folder, smiled and said, "Good morning. I'd like to thank everyone for being here, especially the children. I have given this case a lot of thought…have consulted with all professionals involved, reviewed all the facts, and taken in consideration my conversation with the children. Their input is very important to me because the decision I make today will affect them greatly. It has always been the intention of the court to address reunification of families whenever possible – therefore, it's only fair to assess the possibility of reunifying the children with their mother."

Judge Sharon then directed her eyes to Phyllis. "It is apparent to me the children have been used as pawns to hurt the maternal family or punish their mother."

Phyllis blurted out, "Excuse me, your honor!"

"You are not excused, Mrs. Hunter. I'm talking!"

Phyllis sighed heavily and rolled her eyes toward the ceiling. The judge added, "You may not talk while I'm talking. That goes for everyone in this courtroom.... Now I will continue." She began noting details from all the reports received which influenced her decision. At some point Nadine's thoughts faded off to how Phyllis always seemed to gain the upper hand. Well, Phyllis had money, and influence in the community –which she did not have. And no one else had seen the side of her mother-in-law she experienced those years ago. How could she compete? The Hunters were the biggest contributors in their church, and during the holidays they fed the unfortunate in the community and donated money to many causes.

"Mrs. Hunter." Nadine immediately came back to the present, but no...the judge was speaking to Phyllis, asking about her discipline of the children.

Phyllis cleared her throat. "Yes, I discipline the children when it's needed."

"What type of discipline, Mrs. Hunter?"

"Well, most of the time they're grounded, made to do extra chores... or lose certain privileges."

"Have you ever hit the children?"

"At times – if they need a spanking, yes."

"A spanking. Can you define that?"

Phyllis's eyes darted about the courtroom. She folded her arms across her chest and said, "Well, I would. But I'm not sure what to say, your honor. I mean, a spanking is a spanking. I don't lash them – the way slaves were lashed."

"Well, then let me rephrase. When you *spank* the children, how do you spank them? With your hand? A belt? A switch? Or something else?"

304

"It depends on what they've done. I mean, they are obviously too big for me to be spanking them with my hand." She held up both hands, then dropped them and added, "Look, your honor, children need to be disciplined. I was when I was a child, and I'm sure you were too."

"Mrs. Hunter, have you ever hit these children with a belt?"

All eyes were focused on her, everyone waiting for the answer the children already knew. She blurted, "Yes, yes, yes! I have. I mean – what parent hasn't?!"

"How often?"

"Well, uh… how often? Well, I don't know. Not often, your honor. I mean, they don't need that type of discipline all the time."

"How often, Mrs. Hunter? Once a week? Once a month? And what merits a spanking, as you say, with a belt?"

Phyllis then covered her face with her hands and apparently pretended to cry. Judge Sharon sighed heavily. "Mrs. Hunter, when you are finished, you will still need to answer my question."

Phyllis looked up and spoke as though trying to catch her breath. "Well, your honor… I'm just…just so upset right now – I need a break, your honor. I just need a break!"

"Fine," the judge said with the slam of her gavel. "We'll recess for five minutes to give Mrs. Hunter a chance to get herself together."

Soon thereafter Phyllis could be heard in the hallway saying to her attorney, "I didn't know she was going to ask me those questions. Why am I being interrogated?"

Not many feet away Nadine's family huddled in the hallway. Claudette chuckled and said, "I mean, did you see those phony tears?!"

Nadine scoffed, "I'm not surprised. Oh, how I hope the judge doesn't let that witch get away with abusing my babies."

Back in the courtroom, Phyllis continued to dance around the questions. And then, just as Nadine had hoped, Judge Sharon asked *the* question. "Mrs. Hunter, why should the children be allowed to remain in your custody?

"They're my children. My son would have wanted me to raise them. It's no coincidence I have them. He would have wanted me to be their mother."

"But, Mrs. Hunter, you're not their mother. They have a mother."

Phyllis rolled her eyes in Nadine's direction. "She's no kind of mother. She killed my boy. She doesn't deserve the children."

"Let me ask you something, Mrs. Hunter. What kind of mother was Mrs. Hunter to the children when their father was alive?"

Phyllis shrugged her shoulders. "I don't really remember."

"You don't remember? Were the children clean? Well nourished? To your knowledge, did she ever abuse them?"

"I shouldn't be on trial here, your honor. I'm not the criminal!"

Judge Sharon slowly released a deep sigh. "Mrs. Hunter, we're done. I will now be directing my questions to the children's mother." With that said, she turned her gaze to Nadine. "Would you confirm why the children are living with the Hunters?"

"Because I went to prison for killing my husband." From the corner of her eye Nadine saw Phyllis nodding her head with a smirk on her face.

"How long were you incarcerated?"

"Almost five years."

"And in that time, did you have contact with the children?"

"No, I wasn't allowed – but my family did, and they kept me informed as best they could."

"You weren't allowed?"

"My in-laws wouldn't allow me to have contact with my children."

"How has your relationship been with your children since your release?"

"Uh, well, at first I wasn't able to see them—*they* wouldn't let me. Then I was granted time with my children with the prospect of getting them back."

"What kind of relationship do you have with them now?"

Nadine glanced at her daughter and son and smiled. "It's gradually improving."

"Did the children ever tell you they were abused by their grandmother?"

"Yes, your honor."

"If the children were to live with you again, what type of home would you provide?"

She smiled. "It's not fancy, but it's clean – and they have their own rooms. It's home."

The judge smiled. "One more question, just for the record. When the children ran away, where did they go?"

"They managed to phone my sister, and she picked them up from Clarksville and brought them to me. And once they were with me, they made me promise they would not have to go back." Judge Sharon nodded. "Uh, actually, I do have one other question. What can you give the children that their grandparents cannot?

Nadine lifted her chin high. "Love, your honor. I can give them *genuine* motherly love."

Judge Sharon sat back in her seat. "Okay. Well, I've already heard from the children. I'm ready to rule. I don't feel I need to hear anything more from either side."

The grandparents' attorney got to his feet. "But, your honor, the children have been with their grandparents for years and… "

"Yes, counselor. I'm well aware of where the children have been these past few years. Now, if you don't mind, I'm ready to rule. Carolyn, William… stand up, please. If you had a choice, where would you want to live?"

Their voices came together like a song. "With Mama."

"Thank you. You may be seated." Judge Sharon closed her folder and looked out at her audience. "I want to first express that discipline is good when it is administered properly. It should be administered to instill standards of acceptable behavior at home, school and in our society. There is a line crossed when discipline goes beyond just a swat on the behind and begins to endanger the physical and emotional well-being of children. It then becomes abuse. Now, I've been in family law for many years … and this case goes beyond just the fact the children lost their father at the hands of their mother."

She let her eyes roam again before continuing. Now all her listeners were attentive, waiting. "As I have stated before, it is always the court's intention to reunify families whenever possible. I just can't emphasize it enough. The children's mother's time in prison has no relevance in determining her parenting ability. There is no reason for this court to believe she was a bad mother prior to her imprisonment."

She paused and the courtroom remained quiet, everyone waiting. "Despite the fact the paternal grandparents have provided for the children and have had kinship custody, they do not have parental rights."

A bit of noise came from Phyllis's direction. Apparently, she dropped her purse but immediately grabbed it, and when she leaned back in her seat again, she was holding a handkerchief to her face.

The judge said, "The children still love their mother, and the relationship they have with the maternal aunt has proved to be a healthy one."

Now for the first time Nadine and the children witnessed Phyllis cry. Real tears fell as she sat sniffling and wiping her eyes with the handkerchief. Nadine almost felt sorry for her, but then she thought about all the many times that woman had made her cry— with no remorse, just as Charles had done.

As they continued to listen to the judge's words, Carolyn reached for William's hand. The judge was saying, "Reunification provides an option which means we do not sever family bonds between parents and children forever. As a parent is being integrated back into society, that parent has to prove worthy of reunification. That parent has to progressively show evidence of capability for caring for the children – and providing the children with a safe environment and a healthy relationship." She paused, let her gaze move over those gathered and said, "I find Mrs. Nadine Hunter has shown clear evidence she is capable, and is very much willing – to care for her own children again."

Phyllis could be heard murmuring, "No, no!"

"Therefore," the judge continued, "it is my verdict today … to grant reunification – effective immediately."

About the courtroom some spilled tears of joy, some tears of disappointment. Judge Sharon had to lower her gavel several times to regain attention. "If I may finish…. For the first six months a social worker will continue monthly home visits. And I will receive progress notes on how the children are doing."

Phyllis's attorney sprang to his feet. "Your honor, what about visitation for the paternal grandparents?"

"No. There will be no visitations granted at this time. The children need time to heal and bond – with their mother and her family. They need the nurturing support they've not received in these past few years." She cast her gaze about slowly then said, "We will revisit this case again after one year – unless something pertinent comes up in the meantime." And with that she got to her feet and exited.

Instantly, moving as one, Carolyn and William hurried over to embrace their mother. They were soon exiting together into the hallway. Phyllis and Joe were standing just outside the courtroom doors and Phyllis called to the children. But they did not leave Nadine's side.

Nadine paused and faced Phyllis. "You brought this on yourself – you did this, just like you enabled Charles to do all those rotten things he did to me. In your eyes, he could do no wrong."

"Stop talking to me," Phyllis scoffed. "I didn't put the knife in your hand."

Nadine shook her head. "No, you didn't. And I did not intentionally kill Charles. So, you can go on believing whatever you want, but you will no more be able to plant poison in my kids. And in my heart, I know God has forgiven me." She dropped her voice lower and added, "You are so full of hate for me, Phyllis. But I will pray for you."

Phyllis frowned. "No, I don't need you to pray for me. Pray for yourself." She turned and walked away.

Nadine yelled after her. "I'll be over to get my children's things!"

Phyllis whipped around. "I'll send them! I don't ever want you at my house again."

TWENTY-TWO

The Proposal

When the children returned home from their first day of school in Hopkinsville, they immediately caught the scent of a familiar and welcome smell. Carolyn stuck her head around the opening to the kitchen and inhaled. "Hmmm, gingerbread!"

Nadine smiled. She was pulling from the oven a long pan. "Well," she said, "I thought it would be a nice afternoon snack."

William dropped his book bag on the floor. "Can I help?"

"Wash your hands first. You can put the cookies on a plate."

Carolyn reached in the cabinet. "I'll get the glasses for the milk."

The children eagerly shared the events of school as they enjoyed their warm fresh-baked cookies and cold milk. Nadine also had good news for them. Lin, whom they had not seen since the custody hearing, had invited them all to spend the weekend at his place.

Carolyn turned quick and caught her brother's eye. "We'd better save a couple of these cookies for him."

On Saturday they arrived at his place to find him flinging the front door open so quickly they figured he must have been watching from the window. The children already knew exactly what they wanted to do first – get down on the floor and play with the dogs.

And so, they did. Lin was soon saying he had some good news. "The fair is in town!"

William looked up. "Really? Are we going?"

Lin said, "You bet we are. First, though, my mom wants us to come over for lunch. She's got it prepared already, so everyone to the car."

His parents lived in a beautiful two-story house on an oversize corner lot. It was furnished and decorated with elegant Europeanstyle furniture and décor. Mrs. Cole had the table set with an embroidered tablecloth and doily place mats, and above the table there was a glistening chandelier. It seemed to Carolyn like a huge cluster of dangly diamonds. There was also a framed copy of the famous painting, the Blue Boy. It went well with a fancy candlestick and a silver bowl of dangling grapes on the 'credenza' – as Lin's mother called it.

When they were all settled at the table, they were served by the housekeeper who lived in the mother-in-law suite adjacent to the house. She served a German dish called Fleischkuechle – a dumpling filled with beef, fried cabbage, egg noodles and apple pork chops.

Mrs. Cole suggested dessert be served in the den – apple strudel and hot tea. Nadine glanced around and said, "Mrs. Cole, everything is so beautiful, and the food was delicious."

"Thank you, dear. Most of this stuff came straight from Europe. I grew up in Germany, so I needed a little touch of home. The American style, it's alright – but this is home."

The Coles even shared their love story. Lin's dad started it when he said, "I was stationed in Germany, and she was waiting tables in her family restaurant. I'd been in several times and noticed her. I always made sure the host seated me at one of her tables."

Mrs. Cole laughed. "Yes, he did. I had never been interested in an American man, though in the restaurant I served hundreds of them." She glanced at her husband and winked. "But this one wore me down." They all smiled or chuckled, and then Mrs. Cole caught Nadine's eye and said as though telling a secret, *"Persistence*, Nadine. Persistence has always worked for the Cole men!"

Soon thereafter it was time to head for the fair and Mr. Cole called from the front door, "Have fun at the fair, children. You too, Nadine. And hurry back!"

The rest of the day went much too quickly, with fast rides, cotton candy, ice cream, soda pops, and games and prizes.

Lin showed off his rifle skills and won the biggest panda bear in the booth and gave it to Nadine. She did not notice the curious looks on the two young faces watching her. Now her children were seeing a different side to their mother. Why, there was something free and something adventurous in their mom! They had never seen her like this with their father. Back then she always seemed timid and uncertain, and very careful with what she said and what she did. But now, with Lin, she seemed young and playful.

They were amazed to see her twirl a little cotton candy on her finger and offer it to Lin. After he accepted it, he leaned down to kiss her and whispered something in her ear that made her throw her head back with laughter. The children looked at each other. Maybe Lin *was* the one for their mother—because she was happy with him.

By the time they arrived back at Lin's house they were all too full of food and worn out. The children were told to get their baths. Lin and Nadine went out to the porch and gazed up at the stars.

He stood behind and wrapped his arms around her. She rested her head against his chest and closed her eyes. She murmured softly, "Mmmm…. Thank you for making this a great day for my children. They had a wonderful time."

"It was my pleasure. But you know who I think enjoyed it the most?" He twirled her around. "You!"

She reached up and took his face in her hands. He took one of her hands and kissed her palm. Nadine crooned, "I did have fun."

Lin whispered, "I wish it could be like this forever."

"Would be nice."

They turned at the sound of Carolyn's voice. "Mama—brother and I are off to bed. We just wanted to say goodnight."

Hugs were exchanged, the children went on their way, and soon Lin and Nadine were snuggled up on the couch in the den in front of the tv. He spoke into her ear. "This sure feels nice, Nadine. You…in my arms. And the kids in their beds."

Nadine frowned as she processed what he was saying. And did not respond.

He said softly, "I wish it could be this way forever."

She made no reply. He added, "I want us to be a family. You know – husband, wife, kids. Maybe more kids."

Nadine sat up quickly and turned to him. "You're talking marriage?"

"Why not? You love me."

"I do."

"And I love you. So, what's the problem?"

She sighed. "Lin, I'm just getting my kids back. And still finding my way. I just don't know about marriage right now."

"Nadine, I have been a part – since day one – of you starting your life over. So, what are you afraid of?"

She got to her feet and leaned over and kissed his forehead. "I'm going to take a shower. And then go to bed. We can talk about this later."

"Nadine—"

"Good night."

The next morning Nadine and Carolyn were up early preparing breakfast. Lin and William were at the table. Lin passed the comics section of the Sunday paper to William and said, "I hope you guys enjoyed yourselves this visit."

William said, "I did."

Carolyn smiled. "Me too." She caught her mother's eye. "Mama, wouldn't it be nice to be like this every day?"

"Like what, Carolyn?"

"Like this. Like we're family."

Nadine raised a brow to Lin. He looked over the newspaper as if he knew her eyes were on him, then shrugged his shoulders and went back to reading. Nadine busied herself with placing food on the table and after grace was said they began eating. Lin raised his eyes above his coffee cup, watching as Nadine slowly ate her eggs in silence. He returned the cup to the table and said, "So, Carolyn, this feels like family?"

"Yeah."

Nadine shook her head. "She doesn't need any encouragement."

Lin muffled, "Of course not."

Nadine soon pushed back from the table and said, "I'm going to start packing. You guys finish up."

Lin soon excused himself and followed her. He stood in the doorway as she folded her things and placed them in the suitcase. From the corner of her eye, she saw him but did not acknowledge him.

He sat on the edge of the bed and said, "Running away?"

"From what?"

Lin placed his hand on top of hers. "Oh, I don't know. Maybe... from me...from us."

Nadine pulled her hand free and without a word continued putting her clothes in the suitcase, then closed it and zipped it. Lin reached over and took her hand again. "Talk to me."

She rolled her eyes and said, "About what?"

"About us. Come on."

She sighed heavily then and settled beside him. "You don't really want to be married to me, Lin. I have too much baggage."

"Nadine, you know what your biggest problem is? You. When are you gonna let go and just let someone love you? Let me decide if I can handle your baggage."

Nadine ran her fingers through her hair, brushing it back from her face. "I don't know if I can. How can you really be happy with me if I'm not happy with myself?"

"Because I love you – and I'm happy every time we're together. I can help you work through those demons. That's what love does." "Do me a favor? Take a little more time to think about what you'll be taking on."

Lin shook his head. "I've thought about it for months. I know your pain – and I want to continue to be there for you."

She put one hand on his face. "You don't really know my pain. But I love that you think you do. You're a good man, Lin. A good man. But just think about it again."

Later that night, back at home, Nadine lay in bed and talked on the phone with her big sister, telling Claudette everything about the weekend. She concluded, "I mean, Lin is ready to be a family."

"Oh, I saw that coming a long time ago, girl."

"I know he's a good man, Claudette, but I just don't feel like I truly de…"

"No! Don't say it! – I am so sick of what that man did to you. And whatever you think your issues are, I'm sure Lin sees beyond them. Darn, Nadine! The man loves you!"

"I know…and I love him. But I just got the kids back and want to rebuild my relationship with them. There's just too much that's happened to me, Claudette!"

"Things do happen in life, Nadine. People make mistakes every day. You were defending yourself—and there ain't nothing wrong with that. Are you going to allow Charles to continue to control you—even from the grave!?"

Nadine remembered her conversation with Mrs. Cole and said softly, "Lin's mother said something similar a while ago."

"You see? I'm not wrong about this, Nadine. I'm your big sis. I wouldn't tell you anything wrong. And it's not just about you. Your kids deserve a happy home just as much as you do."

"Yes, you're right."

"Yes. I am. And another thing, Nadine. You are no longer a victim. You are a survivor, and for that you deserve every bit of happiness that comes your way. Does Lin make you happy? Does he make you yell it from the top of Mount Everett? Shout until your feet say *no more*?!"

Nadine lay back on the bed and closed her eyes. "Yes! Yes, I am in love, Claudette!"

"Well hallelujah, hallelujah!" And they both laughed.

Nadine's grin went wide. "He makes me feel loved. And secure." Yet right away she added, "But I'm still scared."

Claudette chuckled. "That will go away! But seriously…I know it can't be easy given all you've been through, but those are some skeletons you'll have to bury in order to be truly happy. And Lin has already proven not all men are alike. He's been nothing less than delicate and nurturing toward you. I do know a thing or two about a no-good man—and Lin ain't one of them."

Claudette soon had Nadine laughing at the tale of her crazy weekend. She spent it cleaning a house where the owners had a Saint Bernard who kept drooling and messing up everything she had just cleaned. "So, anyway, girl, I'm glad one of us enjoyed the weekend!"

"I love you, Claudette."

"I love you too. But if you don't want that man…"

"Don't even say it."

"Well, you know the rest. That man is the finest thing I've seen in a long time. And it certainly doesn't hurt he's got a great career, money, and a home. Oh, and a mother who is *nothing* like Phyllis!"

"Amen to that!" Nadine then said in a low tone, "Yet, I'm always pushing him away."

Big sister ended the conversation with, "Sis, it will all work out. You'll see!"

First thing Monday morning, Claudette decided to call Lin. She didn't waste much time with small talk – she got right to the point. "Look, man – you're good for my little sister and her kids. You should have heard her going on about the weekend you guys had."

"Yeah, we had a great time."

"She's scared, Lin. And scared people run. But I know my sister. She loves you. She needs you."

"Yeah, Claudette, I feel the same way. And I would never hurt her. I'd cut my own wrist first."

"I believe you. Besides, if you hurt my sister, I'd cut *your* wrist." They both chuckled, then Claudette got serious. "Lin, what I want to hear from you is what you really want."

"I really do want to marry Nadine. When I first met her, I saw this delicate woman walk in the attorney's room at the prison – and immediately I was taken aback. Was hard for me to believe she could ever have been capable of killing someone. But as I listened to her in that first visit, I understood why it all happened, and even then, what I wanted was to hold her and make her feel safe. Right then when I first met her – I wanted to do something special for her. But I couldn't. Not then."

As Claudette listened a thought came to her of a way to get them together – so, like her usual self, she blurted, "Let's plan a surprise proposal!"

"What?"

"You know, so you don't give her the opportunity to say no."

"Alright…but just how do we go about this?"

Later in the week Claudette met Lin at a jewelry store. They were looking in a glass case filled with shiny stones when a clerk approached and said softly, "You two make a nice couple."

Claudette giggled. "Oh, no – not me. I'm not the bride. It's my sister."

"Oh, sorry. I just assumed."

The guy started apologizing but Lin cut in. "No problem." Then he pointed and asked to see the ring.

Claudette's eyes widened. "Are you sure?"

"Why wouldn't I be?" He slipped the ring on Claudette's finger, stared at it a few seconds and with a smile said, "Perfect!"

Claudette held her hand up and whispered, "Yeah…perfect."

The clerk said, "Excellent taste, sir. I'll take it now."

Lin snapped his fingers at Claudette. She blushed and said, "Oh, yes, of course."

The next part of the plan was for Claudette to plan a family dinner for Saturday evening, so soon thereafter she was dialing her sister's number. Nadine kept insisting she would bring something, for that's how their special events were usually handled – but Claudette remained adamant. This time around *she* would be doing all the cooking.

On Friday afternoon Claudette picked the children up at school. A bit later she received a call from Nadine saying she had just got off work and was on her way over, but Claudette insisted, "Take your time, Nadine. The children are helping me prepare for tomorrow. And come to think of it, I'd really like them to stay – so why don't you just go on home and relax. You've had a busy week."

"Well, it has been a busy week. But it's no problem to swing over and pick them up."

"Nadine, take yourself home! Relax in a hot bath – sleep late in the morning – there's absolutely no reason you should come rushing over here."

"You sure you don't need my help?"

"Yes, ma'am. I have all the help I need."

"Well, if you say so. Okay then."

Claudette added, "Oh, there is one thing you can do. Pick up Mama and Daddy tomorrow. Mama always needs help with him."

"Alright then, see you tomorrow. Kiss my babies for me."

"Will do!"

Some while later Claudette and the children finished the food prep then cleaned the kitchen, and soon thereafter settled in the living room to watch television. Before long Carolyn turned toward her beloved aunt and said, "So, Aunt Claudette – what's really going on tomorrow?"

Claudette smiled ear to ear. "Well, I *guess* I *can tell you now.* Tomorrow, Lin is going to propose to your mama!"

The children's eyes went wide. They first stared at her then looked at each other. She could tell they were excited and having some trouble hiding their excitement, and then they were shouting, "Yoo hoo! Yoo hoo!!" Then uncertainty. "Are you sure? How do you know?"

And so, their beloved aunt answered with a finger to her lips. "Don't say a word. It's a surprise!"

The next day the children obviously had a difficult time containing their excitement. Dinner was scheduled for four o'clock, but Lin and his parents showed up two hours early. It was the first time Claudette had met the parents. Mrs. Cole stood back and gazed at Claudette with a big smile and said, "Why, you're just as pretty as your sister."

Her husband stood at her side. "A family of beautiful women! I'm Ernest, Lin's father."

Then Mrs. Cole was saying, "What can I help you with, dear?"

Claudette smiled big. "Oh, I like her! But Mrs. Cole, everything's just about ready." Claudette's menu included barbecued chicken, pork roast with potatoes, carrots, celery and onions, baked mac & cheese, rice, green beans, cabbage and corn on the cob. She would wait till closer to dinner to prepare the cornbread and dinner rolls. She and the children had been working hard since last night.

Mrs. Cole said softly, "Do the children know?"

Claudette grinned. "Yes. I told them last night." Then she added, "Oh, I know! There is something I need help with. Blowing up the balloons."

They all pitched in and soon had the balloons ready. Then flowers arrived—twenty dozen roses in different colors and two boxes of rose petals.

Carolyn asked in awe, "All of these are for Mama?"

Lin answered, "Yes, ma'am!" He was hanging a long red ribbon with notes from the beginning of the hallway all the way down to Claudette's bedroom door. No one knew what was on the notes and he wasn't telling. He put all the balloons and roses in Claudette's room, and soon the children began watching from the window, to see their mother arrive. As soon as they spotted her, Lin and his parents rushed to the other bedroom. The children went to the door, to greet their mom and grandmother. Martha had hold of a cake carrier. She said, "Claudette, sure smells good in here, girl. You must have outdone yourself."

Claudette was next to the couch where Sam had settled. She started toward the kitchen, calling out, "Well, Mama, I had some good little hands helping." She immediately filled a cup with coffee for her dad.

And soon they were setting the table. Claudette said, "Oh, Nadine, I did want to light these candles. Would you go look on my dresser and get the matches?"

"Sure."

As soon as her sister turned toward the hall Claudette joined the children as they stopped what they were doing too – to follow Nadine down the hall. Martha watched too as Nadine stared up at the ribbon. Then she caught sight of her name and her eyes went wide. "Claudette," she called out. "What is this?"

But already she was reaching up and pulling a small note from the ribbon. It read, *"Nadine, you may not believe in love at first sight, but I do."*

She twirled around. Her four followers were standing quietly. She held up the note and said again, "Claudette, what is this?"

Claudette's face beamed a broad smile. "What does it say?"

Nadine read it out loud.

Claudette shrugged. "So, open the next one."

"But I mean – what's going on?"

"Just play along. Open the next one."

And Nadine did. *"If you could only see yourself through my eyes, you would see why you're so special to me and why I love you."* Again, she turned to her family, and this time she grinned big. "These are from Lin."

Claudette called, "Keep going, girl!"

323

The third read, *"You are the first thing on my mind in the morning and the last before I fall to sleep at night."* And the next, *"From the first day we met, all I've wanted to do was to protect you and love your hurt away. I may not be able to solve all of your problems, but I promise you you'll never have to face them alone."*

By this time Nadine's eyes were more than misty yet those behind her encouraged her to keep going. And at last, she was facing the bedroom door. There was a note taped to it. She pulled the note off and opened it very slowly. She took a deep breath and read it silently – then clapped her hand over her mouth.

Carolyn, bouncing on her toes, said, "What does it say, Mama? What does it say?!"

Her vision clouded with tears; Nadine spoke the words aloud. *"Grow old with me. Be my best friend for life."* Misty-eyed, she stared at her family and said softly, "What are you guys up to?"

Claudette suggested, "Open the door."

William piped up. "Yeah, Mama! Open the door – it's a surprise!"

Claudette was now glancing his way with a finger over her lips. Then Nadine put a hand to the doorknob and very slowly began opening it. She spotted the abundance of colorful roses and balloons that filled the room.

Those behind her came rushing forward to see. Claudette exclaimed, "Wow! This is nice!" And just then, from the other bedroom, the Coles came on their tiptoes. They had been listening carefully for their cue, the sound of Nadine opening the door.

Nadine now turned her wide eyes toward them, not noticing the Coles, and said softly, "Did you all do this?"

William was so excited he couldn't stay quiet. "We helped blow up the balloons!"

Nadine turned back and faced the bed strewn with rose petals. At the center there was a silver tray holding a blue velvet ring box and a note. Her eyes went wide and very hesitantly she reached for the note. As soon as she opened it and glanced at it, Claudette asked softly, "What does it say?"

Nadine lifted her head, her eyes misty with tears. "It says, '*Marry me.*'"

Instantly Lin stepped out of the closet. He asked, "Will you?"

Nadine sucked in a deep breath and turned to face him. He stepped over and took the ring box in his hand, then knelt before her on one knee. She pressed her lips together, her eyes still wide and misty. He pulled the box open, and Nadine's hands went to her face. She whispered, "Oh, my God!"

Under her breath Claudette said, "He did good."

Mrs. Cole was nodding appreciatively. The ring was indeed gorgeous. White gold with three diamonds, a 1.74 carat radiantcut light yellow diamond at center, and to each side triangleshaped diamonds. Now Lin was taking Nadine's hand. As he slid the ring onto her finger he said,

"I love you, Nadine…and want to make you happy. So, in front of your family and mine…I ask, "Will you be my wife?"

Nadine moved slowly and thoughtfully and reached a hand to his cheek. Her eyes were still brimming as she whispered, "Yes – yes, I will."

He was still on his knees. Now he clasped her hand and kissed its palm, then got to his feet – and all the others cheered and clapped. Lin hugged Nadine hard, and her feet left the floor. Lin's parents moved close and soon were taking Nadine in their arms and welcoming her into the family.

Then Martha, with tears streaming down her cheeks, kissed her baby girl on the cheek and said, "Baby, I am so proud of you." She reached her arms around Nadine and Nadine hugged her in return – eyes still glistening with joy, and Martha looked into her daughter's eyes and said, "Now let's go eat." She chuckled then and added, "We can't let all that good food go to waste."

Soon after dinner, Lin and Nadine set off on a ride. They found the bar at the Hilton still open and right away spotted a bistro table. As soon as they took their seats he reached across the table and took her hands in his. She gazed at the ring and grinned. A waitress approached and offered to take their drink order.

Lin announced, "We're celebrating our engagement!" He lifted Nadine's hand.

"Wow!" the waitress said. "Now that is nice. Congratulations to you both! Have you set a date?"

Nadine said softly, "Not yet – but soon."

Lin said, "I'll have vodka and orange juice. What you want, babe?"

"A glass of chardonnay would suit me fine."

When the server walked away Lin grinned and spoke. "So – soon, huh? How soon?"

"Oh, babe, I don't know. I'm working on the new line for the charity fashion auction this coming spring. That takes up a lot of my time. I'd have to plan a wedding in between everything else." "Well, it doesn't have to be anything elaborate. Besides, I've got a feeling you'll have plenty of help… your sister, your mom, my mom and some others. You can just delegate – won't need to do everything yourself."

"You forgot you."

"Of course – sure, I'll help. I'm going to do all the handling of the honeymoon plan."

"Darn! The honeymoon. Where should we go?"

"I'll surprise you."

TWENTY-THREE

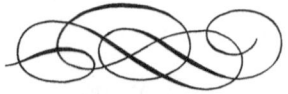

Looking To The Future

Time, it seemed to Nadine, had just kept passing her like a strong wind. Already, the charity fashion show was done, behind her. And summer had come and gone. Still the wedding had not been planned. Now the holidays were approaching. How had the time passed so quickly?

The Coles invited everyone for Christmas Eve dinner and exchanging of gifts. It was time now for her and the children to leave the house if they were to arrive on time. Just before Nadine and the children were about to head out, they heard a knock at the door. Carolyn ran to answer it. As soon as she caught sight of the woman in front of her, her mouth fell open, her eyes stretched.

The woman said, "Carolyn…oh how you've grown!"

Carolyn made no move. She felt like a stone. The woman said, "Well, are you going to let me in, child – or just stand there looking at me like you've just seen a ghost?" The woman smiled.

"Carolyn, who's at the…" Nadine froze. It was Phyllis. She drew in her breath and demanded, "Why are you here?!"

"I came to bring Christmas to my grandbabies. It's cold out here – you know?"

Nadine rolled her eyes. "Let her in, Carolyn."

"Well, I can see the joyful spirit hasn't visited you yet."

"My joyful spirit was just sabotaged by an evil one."

"Nadine, I'm not here to fight with you. This is the Lord's birthday. I came in peace."

Nadine let out a long heavy sigh and said, "Right."

Phyllis made her way to the couch, put down her bags, took off her gloves, glanced around and said, "So, where is William?"

Carolyn closed the door. "He's in his room. I'll – I'll just go get him."

Nadine folded her arms across her chest. "Why didn't you call first?"

"Oh, I figured I'd surprise the children." Phyllis noticed the overnight bags in the living room. "Well… looks like you're going somewhere?"

Just then Carolyn and William came in. Phyllis opened her arms and cooed, "William, dear, come give Nana a hug."

He approached her very slowly. Phyllis said "Now normally, I'd say wait until tomorrow, but I just want to see your faces when you open these gifts. Come on. There are three for each."

The children hesitated. Nadine also hesitated before agreeing and nodding yes. From one of the bags Phyllis pulled a small flat gift box wrapped in paper decorated with red and white candy canes and said, "I even brought something for you, Nadine." Nadine stared at the box.

"Go on. Take it. It's nothing big."

"Why did you buy me a gift?"

"Like I said, I came in peace."

Nadine sighed and took the gift. "Thank you. I didn't get you anything."

"I wasn't expecting anything from you, Nadine. Open it."

"No, I'll wait until tomorrow."

William smiled. "Open it, Mama. Let's see what it is."

Nadine settled in an upholstered chair and began the unwrapping. Her audience waited to see her reaction. As soon as she spotted what was inside, she pressed her lips together. The children immediately understood something was wrong when Nadine dropped the box on the floor and rushed out of the room.

Carolyn frowned and asked, "What happened?" She could see what was in the box. "It's just a scarf."

William raised his shoulders. "Maybe she didn't like it."

Phyllis narrowed her eyes. "No, she liked it. I let her borrow it once. I thought she might like to have it back."

The children were pleased with their gifts because money had never been an obstacle for this grandmother. Even so, neither of them had much to say to her other than the routine standby – "Thank you."

Phyllis slapped her hands on her lap and stood up. "Well, I guess I'll go. And let you two go on about your business." As she was walking out the door she spun around and said, "My phone number hasn't changed. You can still call me, you know."

As soon as the door closed behind their grandmother, the children dropped everything and ran to their mother's room where they found Nadine face down on the bed. She sat up and said, "Is she gone?"

"Yes, ma'am," Carolyn said. "What was wrong with the gift she gave you?"

"It was cruel. And she knew it."

330

"I don't understand." Still seated on the edge of the bed, Nadine blew out air and proceeded in a low voice to explain. "She let me borrow the scarf the day I married your daddy – so I would have *something borrowed*. She didn't mean it today as a gift. She meant it as a reminder."

William settled on the bed beside her. "I'm sorry, Mama."

"Baby, you didn't do anything you need to say sorry for." She glanced from boy to girl and said, "Did you get nice gifts?"

William grinned. "Yep. And I can't wait to play my games."

"That's good. What about you, Carolyn?"

"Well, I got a new Walkman, some jewelry and some clothes."

Nadine scoffed. "One thing I can say about her, she will spend money on you."

Carolyn lowered her head. "We didn't tell her you were getting married. We really didn't say much of anything."

"Good! I figured she was asking a lot of questions. She wasn't even supposed to be here, but she always has made her own rules."

At her parents' house, Nadine filled Claudette in on the news of Phyllis's unannounced visit. Claudette grinned wide. "Oh, I wish I'd been there – so I could have punched her in the face!"

"I should have told her to get out of my house, especially when she gave me that stupid scarf. But for the kids' sake, I didn't want to make a scene."

Martha, in the kitchen, overheard and stepped inside the living room. "Oh, Nadine, don't beat yourself up. You did the right thing by not making a scene in front of the children. But, sure, most people would have thrown that gift right at her. Anyway, we need to hit the road. Lin and his family are waiting. Now that's worth talking about."

As they pulled into the driveway, they spotted Lin. He had obviously been watching and waiting. Once inside, Lin gave Claudette and Martha a tour of the house while the children, as usual, busied themselves playing with the dogs. Nadine managed to pull Lin aside and inform him about Phyllis's visit, and soon they all left for his parents' home.

And once there, as soon as they stepped inside the house, they caught the scents of freshly baked gingerbread and other spices. The men gathered in front of the television in the den. The women busied themselves in the kitchen, working over each other...talking, laughing... as if they had done this before. The young Carolyn paused for a moment and watched. These were now the women in her life, and *this* her future.

The table was soon laden with many foods. They all stood around the table hand in hand, in a circle, to say grace. The sense among them all was of the future, a good future. When the grace had been said Nadine spoke to Mrs. Cole, telling how her family was looking forward to trying her German dishes.

Mr. Cole then glanced toward Nadine and his son and said, "So, when is the wedding?"

Nadine smiled wide. "Soon. It's just that everything this year has been so crazy."

Martha said, "I saw this wonderful dress, Nadine, that I thought would look great on you."

Nadine spoke softly. "I kinda wanted to make my own dress."

Claudette popped a piece of bread in her mouth and said, "Well, yuh betta get started."

Nadine grinned. "I know."

The conversation continued around the table. Mrs. Cole shared how she had always wanted a big family, and that she had two miscarriages before becoming pregnant with Lin. She went on to speak about her son, said he was quite the athlete growing up – playing basketball and soccer, and on the debate team in high school. She spoke also about the hard time that some gave him about being biracial – especially when blacks and whites started going to school together.

Nadine and Claudette glanced at each other and said aloud how they could sure relate to that. As the evening continued, Nadine was hugely aware of the joy and happiness of both families together – a blessing in the present time, and a time for looking ahead.

After breakfast on Christmas morning, Lin gave Nadine a gold heart-shaped locket. Inside was a picture of the two of them. Nadine grinned and said, "This looks like one of the pictures we took in the picture booth at the fair."

"It is. We had so much fun that day, I thought maybe you'd want to remember it."

She leaned over and kissed him on the cheek. "Thank you, baby. It's beautiful."

"Look!" William was pointing. "It's snowing! It's snowing!" And soon they were all gathered close and peeking out the window.

Nadine said, "Snow on Christmas Day! Ah, it makes it a perfect day!" She hurried to the door and said, "Let's go outside!"

The children followed, and found their mother opening her arms wide and raising her face to the sky. She stuck out her tongue to catch snowflakes, so they did the same. The others were still at the wide window. Claudette shook her head, grinned and said, "She's so silly."

Martha added, "She's finally enjoying life."

Lin patted Claudette on the shoulder. "Come on. Let's join them."

The five of them played in the snow - all acting like children. Soon though they hurried inside to warm by the fireplace, and not so long after that, the visitors were on their way home. The talk as they traveled was of the time spent with the Cole family – the house, the food, the hospitality.

Soon after Nadine arrived home her friend Candy dropped by with three gifts. Candy said, "I'm sorry to be coming by late, but you've been busy lately." They were soon settled on the couch and Nadine filled her dear friend in on everything that had happened the past few months.

When she told of the mother-in-law's 'gift,' Candy said, "Nadine, very soon that woman won't even matter, because you will be Mrs. Linfred Cole. You'll be living in a different town – and enjoying life, as you should!"

Nadine grinned wide. "Yeah, I'm really excited. It just seems like a dream though. I keep looking at this ring and thinking that tomorrow when I wake up, it won't be here – you know?"

Candy chuckled. "I just keep looking at that ring and saying 'Dang!'…But yes, it is really alright – for you two are going to be so happy together." She grinned wide and added, "Girl, you have no idea how many women have tried to catch him! Ha! Well, they'll just have to be disappointed."

They laughed big then Nadine said softly, "Well, you know none of this would have happened if it wasn't for you."

"What?!"

"Yeah, it's true. You're the one who contacted Lin and sent him to me in that god-awful prison. I owe you so much, Candy."

"Oh please, girl – we're friends. And friends look out for each other. Just like when we used to look out for each other during school integration. Remember how the black girls used to treat me when George Walker started liking me? They were so-o-o jealous. And I wasn't interested in him one bit, not because he was black, but because he was such a *geek*."

Nadine chuckled. "Those girls didn't even like him. They just didn't want to see him with a white girl."

"But he got a girlfriend that year, right?"

"Yeah. Like I said, they just didn't want a white girl to have him." They laughed big, then settled in for a long catch-up chat.

TWENTY-FOUR

Time to Say Goodbye

On New Year's Eve, Lin and Nadine hosted a small private celebration at the lake. There were eight guests – the children, and Claudette and Candy and their dates.

Claudette approached hanging on the arm of her date and in her usual not-at-all-bashful way called out, "Everyone – this is Wayne. Wayne, this is my family and good friend."

Nadine leaned toward Claudette. "I thought you weren't thinking about a man."

"Hey, nobody wants to be alone at the New Year, girl."

They all gathered around the fire with their hotdogs and marshmallows on a stick. The time together went quickly, a joyful time that seemed too brief, when all of a sudden someone noted it was close to midnight. The adults got to their feet and soon all were standing in a circle as the adults raised their glasses of champagne and began spouting their New Year resolutions.

Then the countdown to midnight – goodbye to 1982 and all the painful years behind it. The children reveled in great joy as they set off fireworks and they all loudly welcomed 1983. "Happy New Year! Happy New Year!"

Then Lin held his glass high and said, "People say how you bring the New Year in sets the foundation for the rest of the year. *If it's true*, I predict this is going to be a wonderfully fine year!"

Soon after that fine gathering, Nadine became acutely aware of a need to speed things up if she was to be ready for a wedding when the date rolled around. She wanted to alter the dress Lin bought in the auction for her wedding dress, so she began staying late at the boutique to complete her vision. One evening her boss, Ann, came in and said, "How's it coming?"

"Great!"

Ann then placed a shoebox on the table and said, "I have something for you, Nadine." "For me?

"Open it."

Underneath the tissue paper Nadine found a pair of white satin shoes with a rolled bow on the top and a clear rhinestone in the middle of the bow. The sides of the shoes were open, the heel and toes closed. She drew in her breath. "Oh…Ann…they're beautiful!"

"For your wedding day. They're from Italy."

"Oh, you always did have good taste, Ann. Thank you so-o-o much. I haven't had a lot of time to prepare for my own wedding."

"I know. But I'll make sure you have all the time you need from now on. After all, it's your big day."

"Oh, Ann, thank you! I so appreciate it!"

"So, where will the honeymoon be?"

Lin walked in – just in time to give the answer. "Europe." Nadine blinked a couple of times as she looked up. "Oh, hey baby. How did you get in here?"

"The backdoor is unlocked. You should check on that Ann."

Ann's eyes crinkled. "Yes, I should. So, Europe?"

"I want Nadine to meet some of my family in Germany. They won't be able to come to the wedding. Then I want us to spend the rest of our time in Italy."

Ann turned to her apparently unable-to-speak employee. "Oh, wow, Nadine! You're gonna love Italy."

Lin kept his eyes on his wife-to-be and said, "That is, if Ann can spare you for two weeks after the wedding?"

Ann declared, "Absolutely! You're leaving me anyway – right, Nadine?"

Nadine exhaled and pushed her hair back. "Well, I really hadn't given it much thought because…well, I guess because I hate to leave you, Ann."

"Well, it's for a good reason, right?"

Nadine smiled at Lin. "Yes, yes, that's true." Her smile faded as she thought – she could not quite believe this was all true. But of course, it was. Again, she smiled at Lin. Ann, turned to exit – wishing them a good night.

Days later Nadine completed her dress and was ready to start on the dresses for the bride's party. She set up a sewing machine on a table in her bedroom and brought in a dress mannequin. Carolyn loved watching her mom work on the dress meant for her and couldn't wait to see it finished. The fabric was a lovely lavender with flowers, and Carolyn could already see how the bodice and dropped waistline and tulip skirt were coming together.

Nadine designed the dresses for Claudette and Candy in a dark purple color with a shell bust bodice, spaghetti straps, and a full ankle-length skirt with a large floral bow at the left hipline. Soon there was only one more dress to make – for Lonette. Lonette was a fashion design student hired by Ann to assist Nadine.

The date for the wedding had been set and was fast approaching. The closer it came, the more excited the children became about moving to Louisville to live with Lin. Nadine decided to clean out the closets and start the packing process. She pulled a large box out of the living room closet packed with stuff from the old house in Clarksville. Phyllis had thrown out most of the stuff from that house, but Claudette managed to steal away some photo albums and a few other things.

The children were seated on the floor next to Nadine as she sifted through the photos. They caught each other's glance as they noted how their mom kept wiping her face with her sleeve. Finally, William slipped an arm around her and said softly, "Mama, maybe you shouldn't look at those pictures."

Carolyn spoke with a quiver. "Yeah, Mama! They bring back bad memories."

Nadine agreed and immediately began putting the pictures back in the box and taping it up. She pushed the box aside, heaved a deep sigh and said softly, "Let's go for a ride." "To where?" Carolyn asked.

Nadine murmured, "I just need a little closure."

The children were not sure what it meant but they hopped in the car without even a question. Nadine first made a quick stop where she bought some flowers, then continued down the road the children knew led to Clarksville. Both brother and sister wondered why they were going where they seemed to be going.

As they arrived, Carolyn peeped sideways at her mother and raised a brow. "Why are we here?"

Nadine sucked in her lips and proceeded forward, driving very slowly along a narrow path. She brought the car to a halt by a small family cemetery. Within sight was a tombstone with a carved name: *Charles William Hunter*. She put on the safety brake and shut down the engine, then turned to face her children, moving her gaze from one to the other. She said, "I want you two to know… that I loved him too."

The children turned and gazed at one another. Both looked perplexed. Carolyn turned back toward Nadine and asked, "Can you really love someone who hurts you?"

"Yes, Carolyn…you can."

William lowered his head. "Can you love someone – and *not* forgive them?"

"Well, William…God teaches us to forgive. At some point, we have to – so we can move on."

He raised his head and looked directly into her eyes. "Have you forgiven Daddy?"

She spoke softly. "Yes. I have." Then she turned to open the door.

Carolyn shook her head. "I don't know if I could ever forgive Nana for what she did to us."

"One day you will. Come on."

Nadine put the flowers below the tombstone and sat on the ground beside it. She was soon weeping. The children put their arms around her and soon they too wept. The moment had been a long time coming, for not ever, not once, had they had the chance to grieve together. In the weeks following, Nadine and the children would understand how that precious time together had affected healing, for they had each been like an abandoned plant in need of water. Now they could fully live. Now they finally had some closure.

~❖~

At last, the week of the wedding did finally arrive. Three days before the big day, Nadine and her family drove up to Louisville and unloaded their bags at Victoria's Bed and Breakfast, where the wedding would be held. It was an old plantation house built in the 1800s and had been renovated several times. It set far from the street on twenty-five acres secluded behind large oak trees which lined each side of the driveway. The place was pictureperfect, with trimmed shrubbery and bright flowerbeds, and the house white with black shutters and a huge wraparound porch.

They entered the foyer, a large open area with a mesmerizing chandelier above the curving staircase that led up to the second floor. Nadine admired the antique oak furniture. The historical charm of the fireplaces, the formal dining room and the décor raised the eyebrows of most of the guests. Claudette began running her fingers over the keys of the baby grand and exclaimed, "Wow! This place is straight out of a catalog!"

The old red barn had been renovated to accommodate 125 guests. The coordinator showed Nadine where the wedding and reception would be held – outside, not far from the flower garden and gazebo. Nadine chose gardenias as her floral choice, partly because the fragrance from the gardenias was intoxicating and seemed romantic.

The Bridesmaid Brunch was scheduled for Friday afternoon in the formal dining room. Friday night, the bachelorette party would be held in the parlor and the bachelor party in the barn. The bridal party consisted of Carolyn, William, Claudette, and Stanley – one of Lin's attorney friends who was also the best man, plus Candy and her boyfriend Rob, and James, another friend of Lin's. And Lonette – from the boutique.

Soon Lonette arrived at Victoria's Bed and Breakfast. She hurried to find Nadine and exclaim, "Nadine, this place *is beautiful*! Thank you so much for asking me to be a part of your special day!"

"Oh, thank you. I appreciate you accepting. Did you try on the dress? Did it fit?"

"Oh, yes. I don't know how you had time to make all these dresses."

"Well, Ann was gracious to me, allowing me the time. Has everything been okay at the boutique?"

"Yeah, but I know I can never be you."

Nadine grinned. "Just be you, Lonette – just be you!"

Everything was going smoothly, nothing to complain about. The Bridesmaid Brunch was a hit. Good food, good conversation – much laughter. Family from both sides arrived from all over. Lin's family from Germany had heard so much about Nadine – they were glad to finally meet her.

Then came the night, with music and dance at the bachelor and bachelorette parties. The staff stayed busy keeping up with serving both parties. In time to come Carolyn would think much on this night. She had never seen anything like it. She and William were permitted to attend the first couple of hours of the parties. When the children's time had ended, they left the adults to do what adults do on these occasions. The older generations also left early – Lin's parents and Martha.

As the night went on Stanley, the best man, after a few drinks, swirled his drink around and caught Lin's eye. "Man, you should have let me get some strippers in here. After all, I am the best man – and that's what we do!"

Lin grinned and said, "This close to Nadine? Man, you must be kidding!"

James chimed in. "Yeah, I don't know her, but maybe..."

"Nah nah – the only woman I'm looking forward to seeing naked *is my bride!*"

James chuckled. "Oh, okay. That good, huh?"

Stanley and James exchanged glances. Then Stanley said, "Ha! Have you seen his woman?"

David glided over. "Woo, have you even seen his future sister-in-law?" And the jive talk and teasing continued. Meanwhile, the ladies at the bachelorette party were having some fun teasing Nadine about the honeymoon night. Nadine blushed, and laughed.

At that point Claudette began a little performance, her rendition of a sexy Nadine – walking, talking. "What did you say, Lin? Bring my beautiful brown round over there? Oh, my!" And Claudette fluttered her eyelids and held her hand over her heart.

Nadine threw some pretzels at her. "You guys are crazy! And wrong!"

Claudette moved to the window and was gazing toward the barn. She said, "Shhh!" Seconds later she added, "Hmm, they're loud – and so is the music! I think maybe they're having too much fun without us."

Lonette threw her head back – licking her lips after the last drop of her drink. Wiping her mouth with the back of her hand, she said, "What you saying, girl?"

"I'm saying, let's take our party to their party!"

Candy slapped her hands together. "Now that's what I'm talking about!"

Nadine held up a hand. "Wait a minute, girls. Do we really want to crash their party?"

Claudette set her hands on her hips. "Hell, yeah!"

Candy said, "Oh, Nadine – grab those bottles of champagne. Let's go give them a real party!"

Lonette pushed her glasses up on her nose and moved toward the door. "I'm with her!"

They were just setting out when they heard a loud voice. And whoever it was cried out again. "Hey-y-y!"

When Claudette recognized who it was, she flung her arms wide – shouting, "Loretta! Oh my God! Girl, I thought you weren't coming!"

Loretta dropped her bag. Popping her gum, she said, "Well, you know I'm not much on flying, so I drove."

Nadine's eyes went wide. "Alone?!"

"Yeah. I couldn't wait for the rest of the family."

Lonette asked, "Where did you drive from?"

"Georgia." She grinned big. "I wasn't about to miss my cousin's wedding!" She reached out to hug Nadine and pulled back to look into her eyes. "I hear he's fine as wine and twice as nice. And knows how to keep his hands to himself. And judging by this place, I'd say he's got money too."

"Well, his pockets are definitely not empty. I'm Candy." She extended her hand.

"Well, we have gotten quite integrated, haven't we?"

"Ok." Nadine said. "Now Loretta, I have quite a few white guests. In fact, my future mother-in-law is white. So please, be nice."

Loretta blew a large bubble and sucked it in. "Oh, no! So, you got one of those oreo brotha? No worries, cousin. I'll be nice. Let me get a drink. And where are the men in this party? What kind of bachelorette party is this where there ain't no men?"

Claudette grinned. "Oh, the men are in the barn! And we're about to join them!"

Loretta threw her arm around Claudette's shoulder. "Ok cousin – well, lead the way!" And they all pranced together toward the barn. Some carried food, others bottles of champagne, and as soon as the guys caught sight of them, they began howling and cheering.

David said, "Aww yeah! Bring it on!" He stood at the barn door and kept saying "Hello, hello" – as the women marched in.

Lin suggested, "Hey, let's change up the music."

Stanley headed over to the stereo. "I got you, bro." *Lady's Night* by Kool and the Gang brought everyone to their feet. The partying continued till three in the morning, at which point Nadine announced, "Alright, everyone. My wedding is at one this afternoon. And I don't want anyone to miss it or show up hung over. So, let's just call it a night."

Nadine and Lin strolled the grounds holding hands. She combed her hair back with her fingers and gazed up at the sky. "It's a beautiful night."

Lin was not looking at the sky. He said softly, "I love when you do that."

"Do what?"

"Brush your hair back away from your face. You're so cute."

He pressed his lips against hers. Nadine pulled away and took his hand. "Come on, Mr. Cole. We are the guests of honor at a wedding this afternoon. And we both need our sleep."

Lin whined playfully. "I don't want tonight to end."

"I don't either. But if it doesn't, we can't get married. And if we can't get married, we can't…." She raised her eyebrows several times with a smile as wide as the moon.

Lin growled. "Coming, dear."

Hand in hand, giggling like teenagers, they ran part of the way back to the inn. When they reached it, they shared one last kiss.

Claudette was waiting up and said, "Sneaking off again?"

Shortly after the sunrise, the children awoke and hurried to Nadine's room and jumped on the bed singing, "Wake up! Wake up!"

Carolyn announced, "Today's your big day!"

Nadine roused herself very slowly, but soon her eyes twinkled, and she said, "Yes, yes, it is! And I'm so glad I get to spend this day with you two."

"There's breakfast in the dining room."

"Well, by all means, Carolyn, you two go get breakfast." "Aren't

you coming?" William asked.

"Oh no, baby. I'll have my breakfast in here – because it's tradition the groom can't see the bride before the wedding – on the wedding day."

"Why?"

Carolyn answered. "It's bad luck. So come on, little brother, let's go eat."

Soon thereafter the staff served Nadine breakfast in her room, and Claudette and Candy and Loretta carried their food up to dine with her. Candy said, "Good morning, bride to be."

"Oh! You guys came to eat with me. Thank you. I was starting to feel left out."

Loretta scoffed. "Now you know we weren't gonna let you eat by yourself!"

After breakfast, Claudette and Loretta began helping Nadine with her hair and make-up. Claudette said, "You know, having the wedding here was a good idea, because it really cuts out a lot of preparation on our part."

"Yeah. It was Ann who told me about this place. Apparently, someone she knew got married here too."

Loretta said, "Well, I bet this place ain't cheap. Though I'm sure you don't have to worry about money, girl."

Nadine smiled and agreed. "Actually, I don't."

By twelve noon, just about everyone was almost dressed. Nadine sat at the vanity in her wedding gown looking at herself. Her hair was done neatly in an up-do with dangling curls at the sides. She started putting on her lipstick.

Claudette stood behind her. "Are you ready for this?" She was holding the veil.

Just then Martha walked in. She said, "Oh Lord, let me." And took the veil from Claudette. It was a birdcage style with three silk roses and feathers with a mixture of pearls and rhinestones scattered about. The length of the veil stopped just below Nadine's nose and was held in place by an attached comb.

Martha stepped back and looked. She said softly, "Oh, it's just lovely, Nadine. I have something for you." She reached in her purse and pulled out a pair of satin fingerless gloves, elbow length with lace embroidered over the top of the hands and a loop to go over the middle finger.

Nadine took in a deep breath. "Oh, Mama."

"Something old. Put them on."

"They're beautiful. Where did you get these?"

"My mama made them for me when I married your daddy."

Claudette ran her fingers across the gloves. "She made these? The embroidery is beautiful."

"Yep."

Nadine looked her mother in the eye. "Why didn't you give them to me when I got married the first time?"

Martha smiled big and said, "This time just feels right."

Nadine stood up and reached out to hug her and said softly, "Thank you, Mama." When she stepped back, she added, "Well, I guess I'm all set. I have something borrowed, my handkerchief from Mrs. Cole. I have something new, my shoes from Ann. And something blue, my garter from Candy. And now – I have something old!"

"Yep, sounds like you're ready, baby. Now let me stand back and get a good look at you."

Nadine twirled around for her mother. Ann knocked on the door. "Wow, Nadine you look amazing." She pulled out her camera. "Ok, let me get a picture of everyone together."

Before moving into position for the photo, Nadine turned for one last look in the mirror. And almost without any sound she whispered, "Goodbye, Nadine Hunter."